WANING MOON

WANING MOON

Book #2 of *The Luna's Pack Trilogy*

L M LISSETTE

Dreams In Ink

This novel is dedicated to all the book boyfriends that have made it possible for women around the world to tolerate their husbands.

Contents

I

The soft breeze and sunlight kiss my face as I sit on a cliff over-looking the valley. The songbirds sing as if they remember me. My name is Darya, and I'm the Luna of the wolves. I sat here 15 years ago. That was two days before the love of my life, my devoted mate and my daughter's father, killed me. While my death freed the Lunar Pack from their curse, Tarq's love and a powerful spell brought me back to life. I have loved every moment since then.

I tilt my head to the side as Tarq's soft muzzle slides over my shoulder, and his nose glides along my jaw. *"My Love,"* he says, inhaling my scent. *"We have been away from the pack long enough."*

I sit up and turn toward him with a frown. "He said he would meet us here," I remind him. "We can't just give up."

"Dar, that was three days ago." Tarq sighs, lowering his head to my lap. *"I don't think he's coming."*

I slide off the rock to sit next to my Alpha. When he doesn't move, his nose ends up in my face. I lift my eyebrow. "Is there something you wanted to say?"

Tarq bumps his nose into mine. *"I miss my bed, Dar."* His eyes narrow in a weak attempt to glare at me.

Grinning, I stay nose-to-nose with him. "Is my Alpha needing some attention?"

"Yes." His response is instant and honest.

I love my Alpha.

Standing, I look over the valley and consider our companion. "I think we should send some guards out to search for Chase, just in case."

Tarq rolls down onto his side, releasing a gaping yawn as he stretches. *"He's not one to get into trouble, Dar. He knows how to take care of himself."*

I'm pretty sure he's hiding something. Tomorrow is my birthday, and he knows I hate it. My wolves keep trying to have parties, but it feels like we're celebrating the day I died. *Honestly, I'd rather die again.*

"Miles might have an idea where to find him."

A smile slowly spreads across my face. I doubt Miles will know where to find Chase, but tomorrow is the full moon. Spending time with Miles and Dax will definitely improve my birthday mood. I love the immortal Alphas, and watching Tarq play with his father is a heartwarming highlight. Not to mention my cuddle time with the laziest wolf I know.

After 15 years together, Tarq and I have mastered many necessary skills. One of the most important is the art of distraction. So, of course, now I'm distracted.

"Miles won't know where he is, but we need to be home in time to see them." I raise my eyebrow and tap my foot on Tarq's back paw until he looks at me. "Come on, My Love. I know you want to see them too. Will you ride back with me?"

Tarq twists around to nip at my boot playfully. I smirk, backing away from him. He groans and rolls to his feet. With his head low, he begins to stalk me, licking his lips as if I were a meal. I might as well be. Tarq is happiest with parts of my body in his mouth.

He's walking forward faster than I can retreat, so he quickly grabs me into his arms when he shifts. Tarq slides his hands across my back, and his lips capture my mouth in a stealthy attack. I reach up to cup his cheek with a smile.

Tarq pushes his forehead against mine. "I love being a wolf, but my arms miss you."

I wrap my arms around his neck. "I love spending time with you in any form, My Love."

Grabbing my thighs, Tarq lifts me and hooks my legs over his hips.

His hum and growl start simultaneously, and he tries to slip his hands into my shorts.

"We need to go, Tarq," I whine. "We can sleep at the cabin tonight but can't stay here."

We're half a day's ride away from the cabin. If I let him have his way, it'll be dark when we make it there. My body craves him, but traveling at night is too dangerous, even with two of my guards in the woods nearby.

Tarq sighs. He fears the dangers more than any other wolf but doesn't particularly like to hear them. "Then I should probably put clothes on, huh?"

Pushing him away from my neck, I smile. "We wouldn't want to offend Bones," I say before giving him one last kiss.

He releases my legs. "That's a stupid name for a horse."

I raise my eyebrow, pulling clothes from my saddlebags. "Your daughter was ten and wanted to name him that."

We have this conversation often. Tarq thought letting Annalisa name the horses was cute when she was five. He regrets it now.

"Dar, he's a black horse," Tarq grumbles as he jumps into his jeans. "Have you ever seen black bones?" He pulls his shirt on and cups my jaw to rub his lips against mine. "She was your daughter that day."

"You can complain if she decides to name her child 'Chair' or 'Boulder,'" I say with a sly grin.

Tarq snorts. "No," he says, chuckling as he pushes me away. "I'll renounce my throne and run away." He squints his eyes and shakes his head. "'Chair?' Really, Dar?"

Leaning against the horse's shoulder, I watch him adjust his shirt. Being my Alpha and a father hasn't slowed him down one bit. Tarq's still just as fun and unpredictable as the day I met him. It doesn't hurt that we stopped aging when we bonded, and at 41, he's still walking around in the beautiful 26-year-old body I love to watch.

Looking up, Tarq catches my grin. "I thought you said we have to go." He steps forward and pulls me against him.

I happily tuck against his chest and relax into his heartbeat. "I love you," I whisper. "You are everything in my world."

Tarq rests his chin on my head as he starts to hum. "My world only exists because you are in it." He kisses my head and throws me into Bones' saddle.

Bones, being a four-year-old colt, is not impressed. He instantly jumps away from Tarq and enthusiastically tries to buck me off his back. After a few spins and a close call with the tree branch, he's finally calm. Tarq and Annalisa trained Bones, but there was no settling him, which is how he became my horse.

"I'm sorry," Tarq says, frowning. "I keep forgetting about his shenanigans."

I pull my foot from the stirrup and point to it, reminding Tarq that he can't jump onto the colt's back. He chuckles as he swings up behind me, and I send Bones into the woods too fast for any of his usual misbehaviors.

* * *

We canter silently through the forest for a few hours. Bones knows this trail well, as I stop at that cliff often. I relax against Tarq, listening to my guards call their positions to each other. They aren't allowed to run near me. It's for my safety, but I find it lonely.

"Do you think letting Chase try to speak to his old pack was a mistake?" I ask as I slow the worn-out colt.

Tarq slides his fingers over my hip. "He offered, Dar."

"I should've said no."

He smiles at me as I turn around. "I'm sure he's fine."

When I narrow my eyes, Tarq wiggles his face, trying to straighten it. "What do you know?" I ask him accusingly. He continues to adjust his face to maintain his somber appearance. "Tell me now, or you're running to the cabin."

Tarq laughs. "Fine, I'll race you then."

My Alpha hops off the horse and throws his clothes at me before dashing toward the cabin. I take my time packing the clothes. Some-times, I feel like life is a big rush, and we are always running.

"Are we taking our time, Luna?" Ash, one of my summer guards, steps out from the brush to my left. He's quiet, reserved, and usually stays hidden, but he knows my patterns well.

I smile. *"Let's just enjoy the day, Ash."*

* * *

Edith set up a ward barrier around the cabin's grounds, so my guards stop just inside the trees as we ride up at sunset. We've built small paddocks off the side door where Dax only had hitching posts. I throw Bones' gear on the fence before heading to the house.

Exhausted, I enter through the side door, toss the saddlebags on the table, and fall onto the couch. Tarq has started a small fire, and it smells like he's been cooking venison.

"It's about time you got here," my Alpha says as he leans over the back of the couch. He holds a plate of venison biscuits out, but his lack of clothes is distracting.

"Didn't have enough time for clothes?" I lick my finger and slide it from his chest to his belly button.

"Clothes get in the way," he says, picking up a biscuit and holding it to my mouth. He stares at me as I take a bite. "So, have you had enough to eat yet?" *I'm not even sure why he cooked these.*

I toss the plate onto the coffee table. "Get over here, Alpha." Grab-bing his arm, I pull Tarq to me and hook my leg over his hip as he lies down. I push his face out of hiding and make him look me in the eye. "We're still going to talk about what you're hiding from me."

Tarq grins as he hops onto his knees and lifts me enough to get my shirt off. "Oh, absolutely." He unbuckles my belt, slides my pants down, and pulls my boots off, clearly distracted.

I frown. "Tarq, what did I just say?"

He throws my pants and pounces back down on me. Pausing to exhale over the sensitive skin inside my hip, Tarq runs his hands up my body to rest them on my ribs. "I heard something about wanting me to bite you." His mouth travels up my body. He laps his tongue over my neck and bites down on it. My Alpha's tongue rolls over the skin between his teeth.

My back arches against his attack. "Yeah," I say between breaths. "That's what it was."

Tarq slides his arms under my arched back and releases my neck, laying his body back down on mine. I love the way it feels when he lays on me. His weight makes me feel safe.

My hands slide over his back, pulling at his shoulders before gently trailing down his biceps. Tarq claims my mouth, pushing past my lips and massaging my tongue as he rolls his hips to ask for my permission. I whimper into his mouth and hook my legs over his hips, inviting him to take more.

When Tarq pulls back with a gentle kiss, he opens his eyes. Their soft tan coloring with tiny black specks are the most beautiful things I have ever seen. My Alpha's eyes never show a want or need. He always looks at me like he could never imagine loving anyone else.

I have an easier time with our physical needs, but I like giving in to them just as much. I melt into Tarq as he enjoys my body. My fingers dig into his skin, giving his nerves the attention they deserve. I have memorized his body, but a refresher occasionally doesn't hurt.

Tarq claims me until he's had his fill. He grabs my thigh and twists my hip, triggering our release. His growl intensifies with each movement until he collapses onto me with a deep sigh. Tarq's hum replaces his growl as he slides his hand under my shoulder. I rest my cheek against his when he tucks into my neck.

Twisting my body, I put my back against the couch's pillows. Typically, Tarq wants to roll over the top of me to sleep, but he's exhausted. He barely sleeps on trips. He tucks himself firmly into my neck and rubs his lips over my skin a few times before his body begins heating up.

"Sleep well, my Alpha," I whisper. "I love you." I lie quietly, listening to his hum with a smile as I run my fingers through his hair.

These quiet times allow me to reflect on the past years and plan for the pack's future. Wolves came from all over to join the Lunar Pack.

There's only the Blood Pack still outstanding. I believed Miles when he said they'd be trouble, but I have yet to find a solution. The militia was an issue, but we pushed them back when we experienced a food shortage. Now, there is plenty of hunting and farmlands to sustain all of my wolves living at the lake.

Kissing Tarq's forehead, I slide my hand around to his back. He pulls me closer, pressing his face harder against my neck. When he sleeps, his body automatically heats up. Between that and his hum, I don't stand a chance. My wolves' voices flood in, filling my dreams.

* * *

The sun shines through the wall of windows when I wake. Tarq hasn't moved from where I left him. He happily sighs as I curl my arm to slip my fingers through his hair. Smiling, I pull at his tips and listen to Ash try to recruit my cabin guards for his ball team. I stifle my giggle when they tell him he's crazy for trying to beat Tarq.

"*Luna?*" Amelia interrupts my eavesdropping.

"Amelia, I'm married to your son," I remind her, smiling. "*At some point, I hope you will feel comfortable enough to call me Darya.*"

Amelia's struggled to find her place. Dax was Tarq's father. She was pregnant already when she met Bruce, her mate. I've spent time with Bruce over the years, and I'm trying to help them reconnect. I've failed every attempt so far, but I'm not willing to give up. Her pause before responding is normal.

"*Yes, Luna,*" is her standard response. "*Annalisa was worried you wouldn't make it home for the full moon.*"

"*Is she still mad that we left her home?*"

"*Yes,*" Amelia tells me instantly.

I roll my eyes. Future Luna or not, my daughter is still a typical teenager. "*We'll be home tonight. Tarq needs a little more sleep.*"

"*How long has it been?*" Traveling with us frequently, she knows Tarq doesn't sleep on the road.

"*Five days.*"

Amelia doesn't respond right away. Tarq is the only unpredictable member of his family. Amelia is silently grumbling about how stubborn her son is. There are probably a few remarks about how he's just like his father. I can only hear them when they talk to each other or me. I can't help giggling as I think about what must be going through her mind.

"Are you telling on me?" Tarq whispers from against my neck. He takes a deep breath of my scent and shifts a little closer. "I'm fine. I just need a little more Luna. Tell Mom we'll be home once I've had my fill of you."

I lift my jaw, letting him snuggle closer to my neck. Once I feel him heat up, I know he's returned to sleep. *"Maybe you could come with us next time,"* I tell Amelia. *"He doesn't listen to me."*

"It would be my honor," she says.

"Please tell your granddaughter we'll be home once her father has rested," I say.

"Yes, Luna. We'll see you soon."

* * *

It's midday by the time Tarq is functional. Since talking to me in his sleep, he hadn't moved a muscle. He wakes me by biting my neck, scaring the shit out of me, and I promptly shove him off the couch. *I'll admit that his thud on the floor is oddly satisfying.*

Tarq laughs. "Well, I love you too."

I roll forward, looking over the edge of the couch as he stretches. He slides his arms behind his head with a grin. I watch his skin react as I trail my fingertips over his chest.

Tarq twists his face. "Did we talk to my mother this morning?"

Here we go. I arch my eyebrow. "Maybe."

His twisted face frowns. "Did I tell her I needed to have more of you?"

"No, My Love." I giggle, sliding my fingers over his jaw. "You told me, and I chose to withhold that information from her."

Tarq sighs in relief. "That was horrible last time."

I narrow my eyes. "Is that why you won't sleep on the trail?"

"No, Dar," he answers. "It's too dangerous out there. Although, admittedly, it is a concern."

"Tarq, it wasn't that bad. She got over it." I roll onto my back. "You were sleeping."

He sits up and slides his hand over my stomach. "Excuse me, Luna." He raises an eyebrow. "I told my mother how good it felt inside your body."

"Tarq, you were dreaming," I manage to choke out through my laughter, remembering Amelia's surprised yelp. "She forgave you." I love and support my Alpha in everything he does, especially since he can laugh with me when he does things like that.

Tarq flops back on the floor in a huff, and I lean over to run my fingers over his arms. He closes his eyes and starts to hum as I open my hand to feel along his ribs. Tarq begins to swell as my hand moves over his stomach, touching the top of his hips. Lost in my appreciation of his beauty, I graze my fingertips over his hips until his eyes open.

"I shouldn't have done that," I say, chewing my bottom lip. "We need to leave, my Alpha, or we'll be late."

Tarq takes a deep breath, flashing a smirk. "Then late we shall be."

I twist to jump over the back of the sofa as he lunges at me. His growl makes me giggle as I stand behind the couch, ready to run. We're going to be late. I won't be getting away with what I've done. I might as well let him hunt his prey. He twitches, and I spin around, squealing as I run to the kitchen with him right behind me.

* * *

I make it to the paddocks by midafternoon. I left Tarq dressing in the house to have this quiet time. Bones calmly chews his hay as I gently place the saddle on his back, trying to avoid his typical antics.

"Luna," Ash calls out to me. *"There's a wolf here requesting an audience."*

Tarq steps out of the cabin and lifts his eyebrow, noticing my pause. "What is it?"

I put my finger to my lips. "Ash says a wolf is asking to see me," I whisper.

"Luna?" Ash sounds nervous.

"I'm coming, Ash. Hold him by the road."

"Yes, Luna."

Tarq stares, waiting to be told what's happening. He doesn't like that he can't hear all the wolves as I can.

"Ash is going to meet us by the road," I whisper.

Tarq lifts my hips as I step into the saddle before joining me. "He didn't tell you who it was?"

"He only said a wolf wanted an audience."

"At least it's a wolf," Tarq snorts. "I've had enough of the militia's shit for now."

Rubbing my hand over his arm, I nudge Bones forward and relax into Tarq's warmth. He has a point. Most of the issues we've had recently were all militia attacks on our wolves.

"There they are now," Tarq announces, pulling me out of my head.

My cabin guards stand as we approach while Ash's tall frame looms over a tan wolf. He's one of my favorite guards outside of our companion. Ash spends so much time chasing me around in the summer that his shiny coal-black coat bleaches to brown by the end of the season. He bows and leads me away from the new wolf when I drop from my saddle.

"He says his name is Bastian, and he's only here to talk," my guard says as I kneel before him.

"Is he alone?" I reach for Ash's chin and look at the new wolf behind him. He didn't stand up when we arrived, which the guard would take as a sign of disrespect.

"Yes, Luna."

I study the young wolf for a moment. His chin rests on his front paws, and his eyes focus on me. I stand up and hold my hand out, waiting for Ash to slide his jaw into the hook I make with my fingers. As I approach the group, the cabin guards back away, and the young wolf stands.

"Luna," Bastian says, bowing.

I can only hear wolves that are loyal to me. In the beginning, many were unsure of what drew them to our pack, and it took them a while to speak directly to me. *This is different. This wolf knows who I am and isn't one of us.*

Ash stops me before I reach him. "You have your audience, Bastian," I say.

Bastian begins closing the gap between us. Ash turns, pulling his lips back and snarling at him. The young wolf keeps his eyes on mine and continues stepping forward. *"Please, just call me Bass,"* he says, slowing his steps. *"I mean you no harm, Luna."*

Raising my eyebrow, I slip my hand over Ash's head to calm him and lower to my knee. The young wolf steps up, placing his jaw in my hand. He stares into my eyes without blinking.

"I've heard you calling out to your wolves," the young wolf calmly says as I slip my hand down his neck. *"I don't understand how, as I am of the Blood Pack."*

My hand freezes on his shoulder. He seems calm. I'm not feeling any emotions emitting from him at all. I don't know if that's normal since I've never met a wolf who didn't want to join our pack.

I straighten my back and drop my hand. "Why are you here?" Tarq hits the ground behind me as he slides off Bones' back.

"I assure you, Luna, my intentions are pure. I will not harm you." The wolf's eyes leave mine when Tarq's hand rests on my shoulder.

"I will not ask you again, Bastian."

The young wolf sits down and studies Tarq. *"Is that your Alpha?"*

With a sigh, I stand up. "I only give one warning." I walk away with Tarq by my side.

"Luna, I'm sorry," he calls after me as Ash snarls a warning. *"My name is Bastian. I'm from the Blood Pack and Chase's nephew. I want to help you."*

I stop, jerking Tarq back with me. My Alpha looks down, confused, but I stand still, chewing on my cheek, considering Bastian's words. As our companion, Chase is heavily involved in our lives. Turning away his family wouldn't feel right.

"My parents are dead," Bastian continues. *"Chase is the only family I have left, Luna, and he loves you. I don't know why I can hear you and my pack, but I can."*

Turning back to him, I drop to my knees and hold my arms out. I don't know why he's here, but he's lost his family, and that's not easy. Bastian approaches me, eyeing the other wolves and Tarq. He slips into my arms and sighs, resting his jaw against my back.

"*Thank you,*" he says quietly.

"Don't thank me yet, Bastian. How can you help me?"

Bastian backs up and sits down to view Tarq and me respectfully. "*I don't know, but I want to try to end this fight.*" The young wolf looks from me to Tarq and back again. "*I could give you information or something. I want to see my family.*"

"I understand," I say, reaching for his chin. "Do you have anything for me right now?"

"*Nothing you don't already know. I've been following you for two weeks.*" He chuckles slightly. "*Your guards need training.*"

"*And your pack doesn't know you can hear me?*" I curl my hand under his jaw to feel for a hum but frown at its absence.

"*My parents and I...*" Bastian ducks his head and lowers his eyes. "*We were different. I had to learn to hide things.*"

Pulling him to me, I hold the top of his head to my forehead. "*I'm sorry you lost them.*"

Tarq doesn't like silence, and this wolf is making him nervous. He places his hand on my shoulder and squeezes. "Is everything okay, Luna?"

Taking a deep breath, I slide my hand around Bastian's jaw again before I pull away from him. "We're fine, my Alpha." I slide my hand over Tarq's. "Bastian and I were discussing what it's like when your family is different."

Tarq takes my hand and helps me to my feet. "That can be a challenge," he says, placing his hand on my hip, ready to pull me back as if Bastian now somehow poses more of a threat.

"Bastian, can you meet me back here in one week?" I ask, reaching back out for his jaw. I don't address my wolves this way. They receive the same respect they give me, and I'd prefer to be on my knee, but Tarq's hold on my hip is firm.

"I will meet with you, Luna," Bastian promises. He steps forward so I can slide my hand under his jaw and pull the fur on his throat.

"Your pack won't miss you?"

Bastian chuckles. *"I'm a little faster and stronger than them, Luna,"* he says, backing away. *"They won't notice."*

"Bass, what were your parents' names?" I ask as he bows to excuse himself.

"Misha and Arika," he says, bowing again. *"I'll see you in one week, Luna."* He jogs into the woods and drops from sight.

"Come on, we need to go, or we'll miss the full moon." I pull Tarq back to Bones. No matter how confused I am, I can't forget what is happening tonight.

<h1 style="text-align:center">2</h1>

It's past sunset when Bones slides to a stop at the back porch of Dax's old house. I jump off the horse as soon as Tarq is out of my way. My Alpha grabs my arm and pulls me to him.

"What happened back there?" he asks. "Do I need to be worried?"

Reaching to cup his cheek, I smile. "I believe a missing piece of the puzzle may have just found us, My Love," I tell him.

The back door bangs against the wall, and voices spill out from the kitchen. Among the noise is a laugh I have not heard in years. My eyes begin to water, and my breath catches in my throat. Tears drip down my cheeks when I see Dax walking toward me in human form. My head starts to shake, and I reach for Tarq but miss him, landing on my knees.

"No, no, Dar," Dax says, reaching for me and pulling me to my feet. "There's no crying on your birthday." He rests his chin on my head as I cling to him, sobbing like a child.

"Hey, Dad," Tarq says from behind me, apparently expecting this. "Sorry we're late."

Dax grabs Tarq by the neck and pulls him into our hug. "You're here now, and you're safe. That's all that matters."

"How are you even here?" I sputter through my tears. "I mean, why aren't you a wolf? Wasn't that the deal?"

Dax releases Tarq and pushes my hair from my face. He leans away, looking down at me. "A birthday present from Luna."

I tighten my grip on him. Luna's not the most giving person, and I'm pretty sure he'll disappear if I let him go. But then it dawns on me that I might have another gift. I pull away from Dax, smiling. "Miles?"

Dax chuckles and relaxes his grip. He knows how special Miles is to me. After finding out how their father died and what Miles had gone through because of his mother, I spent a significant amount of time just showing him love. We didn't find out he was bonded to me until a year after they died.

"He was in the kitchen the last time I saw him," he tells me as I cup his cheeks. "Go find him. I know he wants to see you." He pulls my hand off his face and kisses my palm.

"I love you, Dax," I whisper.

"I love you too, Dar."

Hands touch me from the moment I enter the house. My wolves have gathered to celebrate my birthday. I spot Nate playing cards at the table. Stopping beside his chair, I lean down so he can kiss my cheek.

"He's outside with little Luna," Nate whispers with a wink. *My guards know me well.*

I'll find my daughter in the front field with the younger wolves. As soon as I get near the front door, I hear him. I step through the entryway and try to acknowledge the wolves on the porch, but this damn Alpha has me wrapped around his finger.

"Y'all know the rules," Miles shouts at the teenagers as they jump around. "Get over there. Hey! Leave her alone." He throws a ball at one of the wolves. "Stop touching the little Luna!"

Miles is lazy. His wolf is tall and spindly, and I'm pretty sure it's because he'd rather lie around with me than play ball with the kids. They mess with him, and he jokes back, but no wolf in this field would ever challenge him. Miles stands in the middle of several teenage wolves, pushing them off my daughter as she holds the bow Dax had given me.

"Set up," Miles orders, holding a ball in the air. The wolves line up, standing still as statues. He launches the ball, and they take off. Miles shakes Annalisa by her shoulder. "They're all yours, Little Bit." When he looks up, his eyes land on me, hanging onto the porch banister. He reaches his arms out. "Come here, baby girl."

I run down the stairs and fall into his arms, hiding my crying as best as possible.

"Mom, it's your birthday. You can't spend the whole night crying." Annalisa is the spitting image of her father with sandy blonde hair that falls halfway down her back. She's taller than me and more goofball than emotional. She has my eyes, though. They are so dark that they look black if the light doesn't shine directly on them.

Miles covers my face with his arm. "Your mother has always been emotional about her wolves," he says, needlessly defending me. "You might learn a thing or two from her."

"Still, you'd think she'd be happy to see you." I can hear the teenager about to jump out of my daughter's mouth and cringe. "It's been, like, a hundred years." *And there it is.*

Rolling my eyes, I look up at Miles. I smile through my tears and cup his cheeks. "I've missed this face." I pull his lips to mine, listening to his hum. A kiss means more to Miles than to me, but he will not take more than I'm willing to give. We didn't realize that tasting my blood would bond an unbonded wolf to me as a Luna.

"You haven't seen Edith, have you?" Miles says, pulling away. "I need to thank her for being there, you know... when it happened."

"I haven't, but I think she'd like to hear it from you for once." I smile at him, slipping my thumb over his cheek. Miles and Chase easily made their way into my heart. I wish it were as easy with the rest of the Blood Pack. *Which reminds me of that young wolf.*

Dax and Tarq noisily exit through the front door, shoving each other. Tarq wraps his arm around me and kisses my cheek while Dax punches Miles in the arm.

"Dax, can you take over for Miles for a bit?" I ask.

Tarq lifts his eyebrow. "Everything ok?"

"Of course, my Alpha," I say, brushing my hand over his cheek. "I just want to talk to Miles for a minute."

Miles steps back as Tarq tucks into my neck. "I love you, birthday girl," he whispers.

"Go play with your father," I tell him. My eyes flick toward Dax, who's hugging his granddaughter. "Take Annalisa with you."

"Miles," Tarq says, putting his hand out to the Alpha. "Enjoy my wife."

We watch the other Alphas join the kids up the hill. Dax hands Annalisa a few rubber balls to rub over her neck and hair. When she breathes on them, I turn to Miles. "Do you still have one of those balls?"

Miles pulls one from his pocket and hands it to me. "You two are never going to grow up, are you?" He shakes his head as I rub my scent on the ball.

"Probably not, Miles," I say before whistling quietly to catch Dax's attention. The Alpha rolls his eyes as he quickly hides the ball I toss to him.

I hook arms with Miles and lead him away from everyone else. Leaning my head on his shoulder, I relax into our quiet understanding of each other. Thinking about how long he lived without truly feeling loved hurts my heart.

Taking a deep breath, I look up at him. "Miles, do you remember a kid named Bastian?"

Miles points to a spot in the field with tall grass the horses hadn't cut down yet. "Arika's kid? Sure," he says thoughtfully. "What about him?"

"He came to see me today," I tell him as we sit. "That's why we were late."

Miles raises his eyebrow. "That's charming. What did he want?" He lies back in the grass, inviting me to join him.

I turn around and lie with my head in his lap. "He can talk to me but is still Blood Pack," I say, piecing together our conversation. "He said he and his family were different."

"Well, that's true." Miles squints in thought. "It was a struggle with them. They were loyal but had a different way about them. It's hard to explain."

"That's a lot like Tarq's family." I look at the Alpha. "Miles, you're not..."

Miles chuckles. "No, Dar," he says. "That kid is not mine. I told you I couldn't have kids."

We remain silent until the wolves on the hill start to howl. I sit up to see them jumping around and holding their noses in the air. "Here we go," I say, looking down at Miles.

Dax yells at them, pretending he doesn't know why they are acting up. "Shut up," Dax growls. "What's wrong with you fools? Get over there!"

The young wolves line up as best as they can.

"Be still," Dax barks. "Why are you looking at me? We'll stand here all damn night."

Tarq is beside him, guarding Annalisa. The young wolves jump around so much that he puts himself between them and his daughter. When Dax raises his hand with the ball, Tarq figures out what's happened. As wolves, they have a heightened sense of smell. The kids smelled their Luna on the ball long before Tarq could, but now that he's next to it, they don't stand a chance.

"It amazes me that he hasn't eaten you yet," Miles says, shaking his head.

"Woman," I hear Tarq growl. "What are you doing to me?"

My Alpha shifts as Dax launches the ball, shredding his clothes and charging down the field. Tarq effortlessly passes the other wolves and rips the ball out of the air. Watching him driven crazy by my scent is one of the most exhilarating experiences I've ever had.

"*You are pure evil, woman,*" Tarq says, jogging toward me, quickly catching my scent in his current form.

I laugh. "I love you, my Alpha."

"*I'm going to play a few more rounds,*" he says, stopping beside me. "*Can you hold this for me?*" He drops the slobber-covered ball in my lap.

Frowning, I wrinkle my nose. "Why, Tarq?" I whine. "Why can't we go one day?"

As he chuckles, I remove the ball from my lap and reach for his jaw. Tarq slides his chin across my hand, continuing his advance so I can slip my fingers through his fur. My hands travel over my Alpha's shoulders and down his front legs.

"*You make me happy, My Love,*" he tells me, tickling my ear with his whiskers.

"You are my happiness, my Alpha," I whisper. "Now go play with your father. A run might do you some good."

Tarq backs up, sliding his muzzle across my cheek and pressing his nose to mine. I shake my head and shove him away. He runs up the hill and promptly jumps on Dax, knocking him over. They have one of the strangest bonds I've ever seen, but they have a fierce love for each other I may never understand.

I look down to see Miles watching me. "Do you think I should trust him?" I ask, slipping back into our conversation.

The confused Alpha raises his eyebrow. "Who, Tarq?"

I click my tongue. "No, Miles. Bastian," I scoff. "Why would I...? Just... Bastian. Should I trust him?"

Miles laughs. "I am not your husband, Dar. I can't follow your crazy conversations."

Laughing, I roll onto his shoulder. I know he's right. Tarq and I have a unique way of communicating. "I'll accept that, but can we be serious? I can't wait until next month to have this conversation."

Miles considers my question as he slides his fingers through my hair, staring at the moon. "Misha and Arika were defiant at times but solid wolves," he says slowly. "They were honorable pack members. I would assume that they taught their kid to be honest. I would give him a chance."

I sit up. "I asked him to meet me in a week."

"Bring your Alpha, just to be safe." Miles joins me in watching our family as Tarq jumps in front of Annalisa to block her shot. "Maybe bring a few of your guards, you know, in case he's... busy." His eyes squint as he watches them play.

Wrapping my arms around Miles' neck, I lean on his shoulder. "I wouldn't have my family any other way, Miles," I tell him as I smile at them. "I wouldn't change them any more than I'd change you." Kissing Miles' cheek, I glimpse Chase ducking into the house. "Miles, why don't you lend your brother a hand out there?" I suggest while keeping my eyes on Chase. "I need to talk to my companion."

"Can you send Edith my way if you see her?" Miles requests, helping me to my feet.

"Sure." I slide my hand over his shoulder as he leaves to join the game.

I watch Miles for a moment before turning to the house. Following Chase's path, I find him talking to another guard in the backyard. He nods when I approach, dismissing the guard. "Is everything ok, Luna?"

I grab his arm and pull him away from the house. "I am upset that you tricked me into staying away from the lake to plan this," I tell him. "We will talk about that later, though."

Chase frowns. "I'm sorry, Dar," he says, dropping my title now that we're alone.

Shaking my head, I put my hands on his chest. The Alpha chooses our companion. He is the wolf so heavily involved in our lives that he is closer than family. Chase naturally fell into this role. He is a lifeline for me when Tarq and I are apart.

"When's the last time you saw your nephew?" I ask.

"Bass?" He looks down at me, confused. "Years ago, probably. Why?"

My brow furrows in thought as I step into him, letting him wrap his arms around my shoulders. Chase's mate died last winter from complications with her pregnancy. I spend plenty of time allowing him to hold me as I pull the excess negative energy off him. "Stay home for me this week, please."

"Sure, Dar." Chase heats his body and rubs my back. It's a hot summer night, but he knows their heat comforts me, especially when distracted.

Smiling, I cup his cheeks. "Thank you," I say. "Can you find Edith for me? Miles wants to see her."

Chase nods and slips out of my hands. I head back through the house to find that the wolves are leaving. The full moon is normally a family gathering, so my wolves aren't used to being out all night. I slide my hands over them as they pass me until I reach the front field, where my family is bickering over their game.

Dax hurls the ball and squints at me. "What's going on, my beautiful?"

Looking up with a smile, I reach out to him. "Dax, you should spend time with your family, not worry about pack business."

"Darya, you are my family," he says with a raised eyebrow. "Why don't you lay some of that on me?"

My eyes settle on Tarq. He's back to harassing Annalisa. I nod toward the house. "Not here." I lead him back to the porch and sit on the step. "I met a wolf today. He said his family is similar to Tarq's."

"How so?"

"Miles says they were defiant but honorable. His parents are dead." I lift my eyes to his. "He's Blood Pack, Dax, and I can hear him."

Dax crosses his arms and leans against the railing. "That's new."

"There's more," I say, wincing. "The kid says he's stronger and faster than his pack. He sounds about 15 or 16 but didn't look any bigger than our kids."

Dax nods and rubs his fingers over his lips. "Tarq was thicker than an adult at 16." He looks to the field at his son. "That's about the time the aggression really showed up, though. We had a way to channel it. Sure hope that's not what that kid's dealing with."

"He said he wants to help. Tell me what to do, Dax." I frown. I'm in uncharted territory. Dax must have something useful for me after 176 years of life.

He kneels by my feet. "I can't make that decision for you." Reaching up for my cheek, Dax pulls my jaw until I look at him. "Darya, you have accomplished more than I ever imagined you would," he whispers. "You and Tarq are amazing with these wolves, and they love you. When the time comes, you'll know what to do."

I lean on his hand. "Thanks, Dax."

"You're welcome," he says, helping me off the step. "Now, let's get back to the family."

I look toward the hill and see that Edith has found Miles, and some emotions are happening up there. I narrow my eyes, noticing the scene lacks a family member. "Dax, where's Amelia?"

The Alpha winces, rubbing the back of his neck. "Yeah," he draws out the word. *I'm not going to like this answer.* "She was asleep when I left her. She wouldn't stop crying."

"I know you love her, but I need you to leave her alone," I say, pulling him around to face me. "I've always been straight with you, Dax. I'm trying to repair her relationship with Bruce, and I'd like you to please stop getting in the way."

"Darya," he says, sighing. "I sent them away together to make it impossible for her to deny him, and she still refused to bond with him. You've done some amazing things, but I don't think anyone will change her mind." Movement beside us catches his attention. "What do you suppose he wants?"

We watch Anthony march toward us. He had stood by Edith while she bawled like a baby hanging off Miles before abandoning her. He holds a sealed envelope out to me.

"This came for you," he says, handing me the envelope. He extends his hand to Dax as if they see each other daily. "The party's clearing out. I think I'll gather my wife and the mini-you—take them back to the house."

Anthony turns toward Miles as he drags Edith toward us.

"She's all yours, man," Miles huffs. With a sigh of relief, he dumps her into Anthony's arms.

On full moon evenings, Annalisa usually goes home with Edith and Anthony, so she runs up, knowing it's time for her to leave. She quickly hugs Miles and me but then spends extra time with her grandfather. As easily as I can name Miles my favorite immortal Alpha, Annalisa cannot deny that Dax is hers. Her grandfather has a special place in her heart.

My daughter leans her head against his chest. Dax hooks her hair behind her ear and holds her to him. She told me that she loves how Grandpa quietly listens to her when she needs to talk. I didn't have the heart to tell her that he's not exactly quiet about it, spending the entire time complaining about "kids these days" and telling her to grow up.

"I'll always be back, Little Bit," he whispers. "I'm only a full moon away." He gives her one final squeeze and then steps back. "You just keep practicing what I told you, and we'll talk next month." He nods toward Anthony and watches her walk away under the reformed Commander's arm.

"*What's that?*" Tarq pokes the envelope with his nose.

I hold it up and look at it. "Can't be anything good." I slide my hand over his head. "Why don't you find some clothes and meet us inside?"

Tarq jogs toward the house as Miles holds his arm out to escort me. There are only a few hours before the Alphas leave, so I rush them into the kitchen. We enter the front door just as Tarq exits the back room.

"Dad, I think I might steal this shirt," Tarq says, pulling one of Dax's tank tops over his head. "It's comfortable."

Dax sits beside me and rolls his eyes. "What the hell am I going to do with it? I'm dead."

Miles snickers as he sits across from me. He tries to take the envelope, but I pull it out of his reach.

"Miles, that does not have your name on it," I say, lifting my eyebrow.

He laughs. "I don't see your name either." He's right. There's just the militia seal in wax over the flap.

"But I'm in charge," I retort.

"I'm the oldest," Miles responds.

We could do this all night. He usually wins because I lose my ability to hold a straight face.

"Miles, you're dead."

"Whose fault is that?" He smirks at me.

Round 400 goes to Miles.

"Why don't we just open it?" Tarq says, saving me from admitting defeat. "I'd like to know why the militia is sending us mail."

Opening the envelope, I slip the letter out and scan it. "A militia General has requested a meeting with the pack leaders." I slide it in front of Tarq.

As he reads it, Miles lifts his eyebrow. "No."

"I agree," chimes Dax.

"He makes a point not to request the Luna," Tarq says, squinting in thought. "Like he's intentionally trying to undermine you or suggest we both go. I agree with them, Dar."

I touch my forehead and sigh. "Let us have a lesson in our hierarchy, gentlemen," I start. "First, there's me. Then there's Tarq. You guys aren't even on the list because... say it with me, you're dead!"

They all begin to object at once.

"You can't ignore us just because we're dead," Dax says.

"We're older and wiser." Miles, being the oldest, constantly brings up age as seniority.

Tarq puts his forehead against my temple. "For once, I agree with them. That has to count for something."

"STOP!" I yell, giving myself a moment to think in their stunned silence. "I don't want to rule the world. I just want my wolves to be safe. I have to try if this is a chance for peace."

The Alphas look at each other.

"You're going to do this no matter what we say, aren't you?" Dax asks.

"I would appreciate your assistance in devising a plan for this meeting," I plead.

Dax sighs. "Yeah, alright," he says, frowning. "Let's get to work. Tarq, get some paper."

The Alphas have a shorthand that I will never understand. I like to watch them work together on plans and projects. Usually, they would just lie in the field and talk things out with each other, but this time, in human form, there are pencils and scratch paper. They grab the items from each other, swearing they have a better idea. It's like watching children bicker, but this is their process.

Eventually, Dax looks out the window, frowning. "It's that time, guys." He turns to scoop me into his arms and kisses my head. "Happy birthday, my beautiful."

When he lets me go, Miles is behind my chair. Standing up, I slide into his arms. "I hate saying goodbye to you, Miles."

"I will always come back to you, Little One," Miles promises.

I want to be in this moment with Miles. I feel he deserves it, but I'm distracted watching Tarq and Dax cling to each other. This evening was their first time together in human form since we broke the curse, and Tarq found out Dax was his father.

The men hold onto each other with their faces buried in their necks and their muscles flexed. As I stare at them, their love for each other is obvious. Although Tarq seemed to expect his father to show up tonight as a human, he probably didn't realize this goodbye would be difficult. It's hard to enjoy Miles' embrace when I know my Alpha is struggling.

"You two take care of yourselves and stay safe," Miles whispers, calling my attention away from Tarq.

I look up and smile. Miles disappears as I reach for his cheek. I love Miles and feel his absence instantly every morning after a full moon. Today seems slightly more challenging after feeling his arms for the first time since his death, but Tarq needs me. He doesn't handle sadness and heartache well.

I pull Tarq into Dax's room and usher him onto the bed. He was too caught up celebrating my return and didn't get to mourn for his father when we broke the curse. I knew this would be hard on him. Holding Tarq in my arms, I do my best to support him without interfering as he finally feels this loss.

My mind wanders, thinking about how he grew up. Bruce told me how lonely Tarq had been. The other children didn't want to play with him because he was much stronger than them. Due to his temper, Dax removed Tarq from the schoolhouse and became his teacher. Although they fought like cats and dogs, Dax was his only friend.

Tarq begins to heat up as he falls asleep, and I think about Bastian. He had told me he was stronger and faster than the wolves in his pack. He is traveling alone, and at such a young age, that seems lonely. *I wonder if he's experiencing the same childhood.*

"Bass?" I call out to him, hoping he'll respond. As the minutes pass, the silence hits me harder with every breath. *"Bastian? Can you hear me?"*

I'm not prepared for my sadness when he doesn't respond. I've never liked giving up on things, but I can't make Bastian talk to me if he doesn't want to. Snuggling into Tarq, I settle in for a long rest. My Alpha's heat nearly lulls me to sleep when a voice appears in my head.

"Luna?"

I smile at the sound of Bastian's voice.

"Is everything ok?" he asks me.

I can't help the giggle that escapes as he responds exactly how my guards do whenever I call out to them. *I can't ever just want to talk to someone.*

"Yes, Bastian," I respond. *"I'm fine. We just had a tough evening, and I wanted to check on you."* I look down at Tarq, still sleeping against my chest. *"I wanted to make sure you were ok."*

Bastian chuckles. *"I'm used to taking care of myself, Luna."*

"That sounds lonely." I frown. I traveled alone often as a thief, but I had friends and fellow thieves that I would visit. Bastian doesn't respond. *Maybe he really is comfortable by himself.* *"Thank you for letting me check on you, Bass."*

"I'll see you in a week, Luna."

There are so many unknowns concerning this kid, but one thing seems abundantly clear—he's aged well beyond his years.

3

A few days after the full moon, we hit the trail for the basin. The General had set up a camp on the west side for the meeting. Anthony fought with us, wanting to escort me, but he is still a criminal wanted for desertion. I treat Anthony like one of my wolves and refuse to put him in danger.

"Mom doesn't seem right, Dar," Tarq says, watching her nearly run into a tree stump.

"I sent Bruce away last night," I tell him as I slow Bones. "He doesn't need to watch her mourn Dax again."

I will always love Dax, but he has turned selfish over the years regarding Amelia. He's having trouble letting her go, but Bruce is her mate. I can't give up on them yet.

"I accept how Bruce treated me because I don't think anything else would've worked." Tarq shifts his gaze up to me. *"But why didn't he tell her how he felt?"*

"She loved your father, Tarq," I tell him, frowning. "I think Bruce didn't want to force himself on her. He said they had many fun moments on their travels when Dax banished them, though."

"You'll talk to her tonight and make sure she's ok, right?"

I shake my head with a smile. "Yes, My Love."

The sun sets as we arrive at our destination. Our territory has stretched to within a mile of the basin's edge. We're spending the night at a small cabin Tarq fixed up with some guards. They call it the guard shack, but it's quite lovely, and the guards tend to argue over whose turn it is to stand watch.

When Bones is taken to the paddocks, I approach the front porch alone while Tarq sets up the perimeter. Amelia lies with her chin between the railing bars.

"Are you ok?"

Amelia lifts her head slowly. *"I'm trying to be, Luna."*

Sitting beside her, I reach for her jaw. "Amelia, I'm not the Luna tonight," I tell her. "I'm simply a daughter concerned about her mother." When Amelia only stares into my eyes, I continue. "I believe I would love Tarq just as much without our bond. I'm not sure I would survive losing him."

Amelia's head becomes heavy in my hand.

"You have every right to your feelings, Amelia," I whisper, kissing her muzzle. "I can call in some more guards to help until you're ready."

She nuzzles my cheek. *"Thank you. I'll stand guard tonight."* She lifts her eyes to Tarq when he steps behind me. *"Make sure my son sleeps."* She sighs, sliding her muzzle back into its slot.

Amelia's finished talking. *I'm not really sure she was ready to start.* Tarq helps me to my feet, and we back away from her, stepping into the one-room cabin.

"Do you think she's going to be ok?" Tarq asks. He leans on the door once it's closed.

"Maybe one day, my Alpha." Turning around, I eye the bed like an exhausted infant. "It's been a long day."

"No longer than any other day, Dar."

His hands slide over my hips, lifting my shirt over my head. Tarq's touch is soft as his hands glide over my skin to my belt. After it's unbuckled, my shorts fall to the floor. I kick them off with my boots.

"I wish we could stay home," I whisper as his arms wrap around my waist. "I feel like I could sleep for a month."

Tarq tosses me onto the bed. Crawling up to the pillows, I try to curl into a ball, but he grabs my legs and straightens them.

"Tarq," I whine. "What are you doing? I'm tired."

Stalking me on his hands and knees, Tarq crawls up my body. He glides his tongue over my skin, and his hot breath leaves a cooling sensation behind. His arm slides under my leg to pull it to him so he can sink his teeth into my flesh.

"What was that you were saying?" Tarq licks his teeth as he grins.

Scowling, I push him off the bed and wrestle with his pants until they fall. "I said I was tired, but now I have something to do first."

Tarq laughs as I give in to my nerves. I've never been interested in saying no to him, so I'm unsure if I could. Knowing that I'm tired, Tarq quickly targets all my favorite spots and sets off an enthusiastic celebration within my body.

Breathlessly, I lay my head against his chest. "Can I sleep now?"

Tarq tucks my hair behind my ear. "Yes, My Love, now you can sleep." He rolls his shoulder over me and slides his fingers through my hair a few times before his body begins to heat, lulling me to sleep.

* * *

After a quiet sunrise, we travel to the west side of the basin. Our group stops before reaching the mobile base, and Tarq nervously paces nearby while giving orders to the guards. Amelia is on the verge of tears, although I suspect it has nothing to do with today's adventure.

The plan is relatively simple. My guards are skirting the camp but will stay out while I go in alone. If this is an ambush, they will only get one of us, and Tarq will be able to finish raising our daughter to become Luna. If they are serious about meeting for peace, I should be the one to go as the head of the pack. It would be considered rude to send anyone in my stead.

I've been putting my life on the line for my wolves for 15 years. As their Luna, this is my job. I'm not a fragile doll who looks down at them from my throne. I love these wolves and will find a better future for them. Unfortunately, that means constant battles with my Alpha.

"I don't like this plan," Tarq says as he steps in my path.

I kneel before him, taking his jaw. "My Love, this is your plan," I tell him, lifting my eyebrow. "You came up with this along with your father and uncle."

"Darya, why the hell are you listening to me?" he snaps. *"You've never listened to me before. Please don't start now. This plan is stupid."*

I rub my hand over his cheek. "We have to try, Tarq," I say, frowning. "I love you." I kiss behind his whiskers before standing up.

"I love you too," he grumbles as I step into my stirrup and sling onto Bones' saddle.

* * *

The soldiers don't even look at me as I dismount and lead Bones into their camp. I weave through their tents, looking for someone with enough rank to help me find this General who invited me. Just as I consider the possibility of being invisible, a gun is cocked nearby, and someone swings a sword, resting it against my throat.

"You must be the Luna," a voice sneers behind me.

The soldier holding the sword twitches his hand to prove his blade's sharpness. I freeze as I feel blood trickle down my chest. My Alpha can see through my eyes, and he will be watching. If he sees that I'm injured, he won't be able to stop himself from charging in here, trying to save me.

The sneering man walks into my view. "My name is General Kerst," he says with a smirk. "But you probably already knew that." I'm no longer accustomed to how his eyes travel over my body. "There's not much to you, is there? Where are your wolves?"

"They're close." I may be highly regarded in my world, but humans see me as little more than an annoying pebble in their boot. No matter how hard I try, I cannot get them to take me seriously, and I have to deal with men like this.

"The invite was for all of you, not one of you," he states. "Are you trying to insult me?"

Tilting my head, I narrow my eyes. "General," I say, ready to educate him. "I fear someone may have misled you regarding the politics within our pack. We are not a democracy. It's a monarchy." His eyes widen for a moment. "Granting you an audience with the Luna is not disrespectful."

"Where's your Alpha?" The General returns to sneering.

My sigh is nearly involuntary. "General, if you aren't interested in discussing a peaceful resolution with me, we should end this meeting."

The General leans near my face. "This is a conversation for men, little girl!" he shouts.

Well, this is not going as planned. "I'm sorry that I wasted your time, General," I say, hoping I can still make a simple exit. "I'll just be leaving."

The General laughs and swipes his hand as he turns away. The blade leaves my throat, but two men step on either side of me. One twists my arm behind my back by my wrist. They shove me forward, following the General. We weave between the tents until we reach the center of the camp.

They push me into a large tent full of crates and cages with thick metal bars. As I look around, their intentions are clear. Tarq is eerily quiet as I stare at their plans for our pack. The General leads me to a chair in the middle of the cages. *He knew I would come, and this was where he planned to hold me—probably to control my wolves.*

The General grabs me by my shirt and slings me into the chair. One of his soldiers wraps a blindfold over my eyes.

"*Fuck,*" Tarq shouts. "*I'm coming!*"

"*Stop! You're who they want! He's after the whole pack,*" I call out to him. He has an advantage I lack. I can't see through his eyes as he can mine. I can only hope that he listens to me and won't endanger himself. "*Hang tight, please, my Alpha. Let me think.*"

They've tied my hands to the back of the chair, and my ankles are bound together. Someone slips a sack over my head, which I feel is pretty close to overkill but still won't stop me. The only thing keeping me here is the rope binding my hands.

"*It shouldn't take me long to get out of here,*" I tell Tarq.

The rope wrapped around my ankles is then tied to the chair's back legs, pulling my feet back. A noose is slipped over my head and tightened around my neck. It's secured in a way that forces me to strain upright to continue breathing. I've been dealing with the militia for 40 years. When I think they can't surprise me anymore, they invent new ways to be cruel.

"*Ok. Plan B.*"

"*I'm coming,*" Tarq announces.

"*Tarq, I cannot lose you,*" I plead. "*Please just stay there and let me think up plan B.*"

"*I can't lose you either, so you better come up with something quick,*" he grumbles.

My wolves are all talking at once. Tarq has passed on my orders, and they aren't interested in following them. Thankfully, my Alpha is the only one who would contest me if he thinks I'm in mortal danger. Right now, I'm just the General's bait to lure the pack. I tune out my wolves and think through my situation. The ropes binding me, the noose, blindfold, hood...

"*Shit,*" is all I can think. My thoughts are foggy.

"*Got a plan yet?*" Tarq is going to grind my nerves today.

"*If you come near this camp before I tell you, I will let them kill you,*" I growl.

Tarq chuckles. "*No, you won't.*"

"*Well,*" I grumble. "*I'll imagine it with a damn smile.*"

"*Ok, now you're just being mean.*"

I take a deep breath and sigh, trying to clear my head. "*No, Tarq. I love you very much and do not want anything to happen to you. Now, please, let me think.*"

I let my wolves filter back into my thoughts. Going over their strengths, our guard consists of some of the pack's best wolves. Some are fast, others strong, and many are cunning and quick-thinking, but none is the total package. The strong are slower. The fast wolves aren't as strong. Chase would be beneficial as he's used to fighting beside my Alpha, but not enough to count as another Tarq.

That's when the answer washes over me. "*Bass?*" I take a few deep breaths to keep myself calm, trying not to panic over his silence. "*Bass, I need your help.*"

"*What's wrong?*" Bastian finally responds.

"*How far are you from the basin?*"

"*A couple of days, maybe. Why?*" I can hear the tension in his voice.

"*Can you head in this direction?*" I ask, remaining calm with him. "*We could use your assistance.*"

"*Tell me what's wrong, Luna,*" Bastian snaps gruffly.

"*The militia has me,*" I tell him. "*They are trying to trap the pack.*"

"*I'm on my way,*" he instantly responds.

Breathing has become increasingly difficult. I try to take a few slow breaths but cough through my attempt. My heart begins pounding, and I'm lightheaded.

"*Baby, I need your help,*" I call out to my Alpha.

"*I'm coming!*" Tarq shouts in my head.

I swallow, trying to create moisture in my throat. "*Help is on the way. I need you to stay there and get him through the guard.*" Closing my eyes, I slow my breathing. "*I need a vision.*"

"*You don't sound so good,*" Tarq says sadly.

My head is spinning, causing me to feel dizzy. I lean forward against the ropes and throw up. Fresh blood runs down my chest when the noose catches the cut on my throat.

"*Please, My Love?*" I beg.

As my eyes roll, a vision of our lake appears.

"*Why don't I take you home then?*" Tarq still sounds sad, but I can tell he's trying.

"*It really is a beautiful lake.*" I relax in the chair with a deep sigh, letting the rope pull on my throat. My breathing settles into a regular rhythm as I watch the dragonflies drink from a shallow area at the edge. My heart rate slows as we sit in silence.

"*Dar, who is coming to help?*" Tarq asks quietly.

"*Bastian,*" I reply, sighing.

"*Why him?*" Tarq asks. "*You don't even know him, Dar.*" He changes the vision, showing me our meeting with Bastian from his point of view.

I watch as Bastian approaches me. Ash is beside me, snarling and a heartbeat away from attacking the young wolf. The vision begins to fade away.

"Hang on, love." I request. *"Replay that."*

Tarq starts from the beginning. I walk up to Ash and speak with him. Although I can look around in the vision, Tarq primarily focuses on Bastian. I watch the young wolf rise and bow. He moves in front of me so that I'm blocking Tarq's view. My Alpha would never accept this lack of vision, so he joined us.

When Tarq reaches for my shoulder, the young wolf looks up at him, and I gasp. Tarq's eyes are unique. I've never seen their equal. Their coloring is unusual, but how they gaze upon me is also unique... until now. Bastian's eyes are a deeper brown but display the same soft and caring expression that Tarq always has, even when mad. His mood shows on his face but never in his eyes.

Tarq continues the vision. I stand up and walk away from the wolf before stopping and turning around. I kneel and hug him after he tells me his family is gone. As I'm hugging him, he looks up at Tarq.

"Stop it right there," I tell him.

The vision stops, and I'm able to study Bastian in a still image. He looks up at Tarq as I hold onto his neck and shoulders. His gaze is the same as when looking upon me.

"Darya, what am I looking at?" Tarq asks.

I don't know what this means, so I'm unsure how to explain it to him. *"We need to learn more about him,"* I say thoughtfully. *"I need you to let him through the guards' line, my Alpha."*

"I don't understand how he can help us."

"He's strong like you, Tarq," I say, my thoughts coming out as whispers. *"We'll need him to help you get me out of here. But right now, My Love, I need sleep."* My exhaustion is getting the best of me. My entire body feels heavy. *"I'm going to take a nap. Please stay there and wait for Bastian."* Tarq's silent. *"I need you to give me your word, Tarq."*

"I don't want to, but I will do anything for you," Tarq resigns. *"I love you, Dar."*

Everything starts to spin again.

"I love you too, my Alpha."

* * *

The back of my head slams into a post, jolting me awake. My arms are pulled back, and my hands are tied together. Opening my eyes, I find myself outside in a cluster of smaller tents.

"Hey, sunshine." The General smiles as he moves before me. He slips a noose over my head and tightens it around my throat while humming merrily.

I narrow my eyes. "Just hang me if that's what you're planning." My voice is raspy, and my throat hurts.

"I'm going to rip that asshole in half!" Tarq growls.

Even his angry voice soothes me. *"Easy, My Love."*

The General clicks his tongue as he shakes his head. "No, little girl, I need you to flush out your pack." He pats my cheek. "Live bait works best when you're hunting wolves."

"How long was I out?" I ask Tarq.

"About five minutes shy of me coming in there alone." Mad and scared is not a good combination bottled inside my Alpha.

"Tarq?"

"A day, Dar," he grumbles. *"An entire day! Where is this wonder kid you think is so important?"*

Rolling my eyes, I look down at my chest and accidentally show Tarq the blood that's run down my shirt. It's all dried, so I'm not actively bleeding but still horribly weak.

"Dar?" Tarq sounds apologetic. *"That looks really bad."*

"Give me a minute to find Bastian." I'm unsure how much energy I have left, so I need to take care of this while I still can.

The General steps back in front of me, smirking. "That looks like it hurts."

"Wait until you feel teeth ripping your flesh from your bones." I return his smirk. "Nothing compares," I sneer, knowing the carnage my wolves will leave behind.

He grabs my jaw and puts his forehead against mine. "We'll see, little girl." He shoves my head back and walks away, leaving me in the middle of the tents, surrounded by his soldiers.

"*Bastian?*" I call out.

"*I'm nearly there. Where am I going?*" he responds, sounding out of breath.

"*We're on the west side of the basin,*" I tell him, breathing slowly, trying to clear my head. "*The militia camp is at the edge of the forest.*"

"*I'm on the north side,*" he says. "*It'll take too long to go around. I'm going straight through.*"

It's hot in the basin with the sun shining directly on me. I haven't had any food or water, and with this blood loss, I'm struggling. "*This just keeps getting better, doesn't it?*" My thoughts slur as I close my eyes in an attempt to alleviate the spinning. "*I need you to talk to Tarq.*"

"*I'm trying, Luna. He won't talk to me.*"

My hands ball up into fists as my jaw clenches. "*TARQ!*"

"*Yes?*" After 15 years of this man, I know his head just dipped, and his ears have tucked back.

"*I don't feel good,*" I yell at him. "*Stop being an ass!*" I take a deep breath and lean my head back. "*I'm sorry. That was mean.*" Bile begins to collect in my throat. "*Bastian is close. I need you to talk to him. Have the guard hold the perimeter while you two come in here. Work together, Tarq.*"

I take a few more breaths, trying to calm down.

"*Darya?*"

He sounds scared, or it could all just be in my head. Everything is foggy, and I've started sweating, although I'm not sure where I found that moisture in my state of dehydration. My legs shake under me. "*Kill them all.*" As my eyes roll, I fall forward on the ropes and release the bile.

* * *

I wake to a falling sensation just before my face gets mashed into Tarq's chest. My vision is blurry, but the color red dominates my view. The metallic stench of blood fills my nostrils. He's whispering, but I can only hear a swishing sound. He jolts, a crash follows, and bright lights shine in my eyes.

As he places me on something hard and cold, Tarq gently wipes my hair from my face. He turns his head and yells. It's loud, but I still can't understand what he's saying. From what I can tell, he's taken me to the pack doctor, Will.

My eyes burn in the bright lights. I close them, trying to find relief. My body violently shakes, and someone starts slapping my face. The motion doesn't set well with my stomach, so I roll my head to the side and throw up.

* * *

There's a soft mattress underneath me the next time I wake. I'm in the back room of Will's office. He only has one patient room in the small clinic we built for him. I normally yell at him whenever we're in this room because he's forever trying to make me stay when I'm injured or ill. Then Edith would show up with tea, and I'd leave. *So why am I here?*

My body protests as I turn my head to look around the room. Tarq is standing beside the window, watching the rain. He looks tired as he leans his forehead against the glass. It's dark outside, making me wonder how long I've been here. I try talking, but nothing comes out when I open my mouth.

Tears drip from my eyes, and I sniffle, shooting a burst of pain through my chest. Hearing me, Tarq turns while I feel something press down on the bed beside me. He's at my side in a flash, grabbing my hand and causing me to gasp painfully from the movement.

He holds my hand still. "Hey you," Tarq says, smiling. He brushes his hand over my face, wiping my tears. "I know it hurts, My Love. I'm so sorry. Just keep fighting, ok?"

"Luna?"

The weight on the right side of the bed moves. I slowly turn toward it and see a beautiful wolf looking over me. I try to smile but can only manage a wince.

"Bastian."

His front paws are on the bed, and there's a tube running from his leg. The fluid is red, so I assume it's blood. *"You don't look so good, Luna,"* he says sadly.

Squeezing Tarq's hand, I extend my other fingers over the bed for Bastian. He slides his muzzle into my hand. *"Why can't I talk?"*

"Doc says you hurt your trachea," Bastian tells me. *"You passed out and basically hung yourself before we could get to you. You had a tube in your throat to keep it open for a few days."*

I turn back to look at Tarq. His eyes are so soft that they make me want to cry. *"Can you tell him that I love him?"*

Bastian looks at Tarq and then back at me. *"He doesn't need me to tell him. He knows."* He watches me stare quietly into Tarq's eyes. *"You needed a lot of blood, Luna. He gave all he could, but it wasn't enough."* He pauses and follows my eyes. *"He'd never admit it, but he's pretty weak right now."*

"I'm exhausted, Bass," I admit.

Bastian carefully presses his muzzle to my cheek as my head falls. *"Sleep, Luna. You're safe here. We'll watch over you."*

* * *

"I love you," Tarq sweetly says as I wake to something cold pressing against my neck.

I lay my head to the side and land on my Alpha's muzzle. It's still raining but lighter outside, so some time has passed. Everything hurts just as much as the last time I woke up. Tarq's eyes are alive with love, and I want to smile at him, but I'm in too much pain. *"What's wrong with me?"*

Tarq steps onto the bed, causing it to creak under his weight. He gently places his muzzle against my cheek. *"Will refuses to talk to me without you,"* he grumbles. *"He should be back soon."*

There's a movement to my right, and I slowly turn my head toward the young man who walks through the door. I've never seen him before, yet somehow, he is familiar to me.

"Bastian?"

Tarq follows my eyes. *"We've been trading off so that you would have someone to talk to,"* Tarq tells me.

Opening my hand for his, I try to smile at the young man.

"Hi, Luna," Bastian whispers with a smile. "It's nice to see your eyes again."

I stare at him as my head begins to fog back up. *"Are you both ok? Is the pack safe?"*

I can't be sure I've asked my questions because Tarq doesn't answer me. *"You were right about him,"* he says thoughtfully. *"I'm not sure I could've saved you without his help."*

"Please, Tarq," I beg. *"Is everyone ok?"*

My eyes roll closed before I hear any reply.

4

Noise dominates my world, sounding like our battles against the militia. My head throbs from a loud banging as I thrash around. A beeping filters in, and then a solid buzz, but all I want is silence. When I try to tune it out, a voice pushes through clear as a bell.

"Hey, my beautiful. You're not supposed to be here."

I stop thrashing, and tears begin streaming from my eyes as I turn around. "I love you, Dax, but I'm not ready to be here yet."

He steps forward and pulls me into his arms. "It wasn't such a good plan, huh?" he asks.

I frown, letting him hold me to his chest. "They wanted the whole pack," I tell him. "There were cages. They held me as bait." I think about everything that I can recall. "Something happened. I got sick."

Dax leans down and takes a deep breath. "Poison."

"That would be my guess."

"I can smell it," Dax tells me. "It's some kind of plant. I assume they bled you? And Tarq's been giving you blood?"

I'm tired. Even in this black hell, I can't seem to feel normal. "Him and the young wolf I mentioned. He helped Tarq get me out of that camp. I saw a tube coming out of his leg."

Dax leans back and narrows his eyes at me curiously. "Darya, when you were kidnapped and bled, you would only accept Tarq's blood," he says. "You'd only take it from him as a wolf. We tried a lot of blood, including mine. You rejected it all."

I scoff at him, too tired to be mad. "Why am I just hearing about this now?"

Dax shrugs. "It didn't seem important until now."

"The more I learn about this kid, the more confused I am," I say, shaking my head.

Dax steps back and takes my hand as noise begins to filter back in. "Your story isn't over yet, Darya." He kisses my knuckles. "Go get some answers. I'll see you soon."

* * *

I fall away from Dax and wake to find myself in the cabin's main bedroom. Rolling my eyes to clear them, I look around.

"Go slow, Luna." Bastian appears to my left.

I swallow, finding my throat painfully sore. "How long?" I whisper.

Bastian sits on the edge of the bed and holds a cup of water to my lips. "It's been about two weeks since we got you."

I frown, thinking about all the time that's passed. Tarq hadn't answered my questions about our pack. They could be dead. "Safe?" One word is all I can say.

"Yes, Luna." Bastian smiles. "Your pack is safe. Your Alpha is a strong leader."

The door behind him opens, and I clutch my chest as Tarq enters the room. He's carrying a tray of steaming bowls. He smiles when he sees that I'm awake.

"Hey, Dar." He crosses the room, setting the tray on the bedside table. "I've missed you." He kneels on the bed and kisses my cheek.

"Love you," I whisper.

"I love you too." Tarq braces me as they move pillows around so I can sit upright. "Thank you, Bass. Edith needs to mark you so you can shift. We'll need more blood soon."

Bastian hands him the last of my pillows. "Yes, Alpha."

"Enough of that," Tarq grumbles. "I told you, that's not how our pack works."

Bastian bows and leaves the room.

"Help him," I whisper.

Tarq grabs the bowl and feeds me a spoonful of soup. "Help him?" he scoffs. "What help could that kid possibly need? Shit. I needed his help to get you out of there, which I'm not proud of, by the way."

Bastian got mad at me when I didn't answer him. If he's anything like young Tarq, it won't be long before he's a danger.

"Like you," I try but cough, distracting Tarq from my words. He holds the cup of water to my lips so I can drink. "Mad," I whisper.

"Darya, enough," he snaps. "They could've used magic. Edith says it's too dangerous to use tea, so you have to heal on your own. That kid can wait a few more days." He sighs deeply and feeds me some more soup. "Your heart stopped a few times, Darya."

Tarq's not afraid of many things, but his greatest fear is losing me. He's upset and staring at the food, refusing to look at me. *Bastian will have to wait.*

I squeeze his arm and put my hand over my heart. When he looks at me, I mouth the word "love."

Tarq smiles and cups my cheek. "I love you too, Dar."

* * *

A few days later, I'm allowed to go downstairs for a change of scenery. Tarq insists on carrying me, but it's worth it. Edith watches over me from the dining table while Tarq relaxes on the couch so I can rest my head on his lap.

Bastian hasn't left my side long since we've been here and lies on the floor beside me. I rub my hand over the dark patch of fur on the young wolf's hip. Tarq has one too. It's the mark that allows them to shift within the boundary.

"Where do you find these stunning wolves that fall over themselves to help you?" Edith asks as Tarq turns on a movie about a cat and some dogs traveling over the mountains.

My throat is still tender, but I can talk better daily. "I'm grateful for them both."

"If you won't loan me your husband, I could settle for the fresh meat." Edith eyes the new wolf.

Bastian chuckles but leaves his eyes closed. *"You should probably tell her I'm only 16."*

I slide my hand from his hip to his shoulder. "He is a nice piece of meat, isn't he?" I say, smirking.

Tarq chuckles, and Bastian sighs. *"Or you could've just said I'm too young for her,"* he grumbles.

I cough as I giggle, and Tarq hands me my water. "Bastian wants you to know he's only 16."

Tarq grabs the glass from me and takes a large swig.

"I've waited this long," Edith says thoughtfully. "A few more years won't kill me."

Tarq spits his water all over me, and Bastian sighs again as he rolls to put his head under the table. *"Oh, Jesus."*

* * *

After another week, Edith announces I'm healthy enough to travel back to the lake. My wolves have been quiet, giving me time to recover, but I've missed them. Annalisa is staying with her grandmother, who's still struggling. It's time to go home.

Bastian sits on the porch with me while Tarq readies our horse. I lean against his arm, holding his hands. "I owe you my life, Bass."

"Luna, before you thank me, you should know everything." The young wolf looks down nervously.

I reach for his cheek. "You're in my world, sweetheart," I whisper, smiling. "Don't you dare look down. You might not be in my pack, but you're still my wolf."

Bastian leans onto my hand, enjoying my gentle touch. His bones are more pronounced than I'm used to seeing, and his wolf lacks muscle. Something is going on with him that he's not willing to discuss.

"Why don't you tell me what this is about, Bass?"

He moves my hand from his face. "I had to call in a favor."

His frown makes me more nervous than his words. "A favor from whom?"

Bastian looks back down at our hands. "We needed to clean the camp so no one would know what happened," he says. "There was so much blood."

"Bass, what did you do?" My brow furrows, and my head shakes.

He licks his lips and swallows hard. "No one is better at hiding death than my pack, Luna," Bastian says, leaning his forehead to mine.

I close my eyes and pull my lips into my mouth. Even as a teenager, he has to know what this means. This one favor he has asked of our enemy could cost me everything. I take a deep breath and pull away from Bastian. "You had no other choice?"

"It was the only option, Luna," he says sadly. "You were dying. We couldn't get to you fast enough, and Alpha needed to shift to carry you." He stops to take a shaky breath. "You both needed me. I did what I thought would protect your pack. I'm sorry, Luna."

Releasing his hands, I open my arms to him. He falls into me, burying his face against my neck and shoulder. I lean my head against Bastian's, running my fingers through his hair.

"Bass, what did they ask for?" I whisper.

He doesn't pull away. "A meeting," he murmurs. "My Alpha wants a meeting."

"Do you trust your Alpha?"

Bastian sits up, looking me in the eye. "He will keep his word," he promises. "He wants your blood, but he's only requesting a meeting right now."

"Have you told Tarq?" I ask, slipping my hand over his neck.

Bastian turns a shade of pink. "No, Luna," he admits. "He's a bit of a hothead."

I giggle. "So are you, though."

Bastian ducks his head, but I catch him by the chin. "We don't feel shame for our feelings around here, Bass." I turn to look at Tarq. "Does he look ashamed?"

Bastian follows my eyes and watches Tarq. My Alpha's leaning over the paddock fence, staring at me. He has his foot on one of the fence rails, and a piece of straw hangs from his mouth.

"That's because he has you," he says.

Smiling, I squeeze the side of Bastian's neck. "And, now, so do you," I remind him. "I won't abandon you." I pull him back into my arms. "I need you to stall the meeting, Bastian. I can't make that trip yet."

"I'll do my best."

I look over at Tarq. "And let's keep this between us for now." I pull away from Bastian and smile. "I think my Alpha's been through enough this month."

"As you wish, Luna," Bastian says. He helps me stand and holds his arm out to escort me to the paddock. "I'll be in touch." He kisses my cheek before passing me to Tarq.

"Be safe, Bass," I say, touching his arm.

Bastian smiles as he pulls his shirt off, leaving it on the paddock rail. He steps just inside the woods and seamlessly shifts as Tarq does before running into the trees. I'm too shocked to be upset about the pants the teen had destroyed.

Tarq doesn't notice as he tightens a buckskin's cinch and leads him from the paddock. "You ready?"

"Tarq, we need to learn a lot more about that kid," I whisper with my brow furrowed.

Tarq slides his arm around my waist, guiding me to the side of the horse. "Come on. Up you go."

I let him help me onto the horse. "Where's Bones?"

Tarq jumps up behind me. "Let's get you home, My Love. We've been away long enough." He turns the horse toward the road without answering me.

* * *

My favorite place in the world is in front of the fireplace in our bedroom. Dax made the rocking chairs that cradle me as I stare at the fire, holding the cold cup of tea I never intended to drink. I'm wrapped in blankets even though it's warm because I struggle to keep my body temperature up, thanks to whatever that General did to me.

Tarq's footsteps on the stairs make me smile. "How are you feeling today?" He closes the bedroom door and brings a plate of toast to the table beside me.

"Stronger every day now that we're home," I say, smiling.

Tarq lifts me from the chair and sits down, cradling me in his arms. "I thought we might see Will this afternoon," he says. "Let him check you over."

He hands me a piece of toast and rests his head back. I'm unsure of the last time my Alpha slept. He stays awake all night watching me.

"It might be nice to get out," I tell him. "Maybe Edith and Anthony could go with me so that you can rest."

Without opening his eyes, Tarq licks his lips with a sigh. "No."

"Then I'll ask Bastian to come help. Tarq, you need sleep."

"I'm fine," he grumbles.

"Tarq?" I whisper.

"I said I'm fine," Tarq growls, still not opening his eyes.

I lean back against his arm. "Tarq, you're not fine," I say sternly. "If you growl at me again, it won't end well." Standing up, I pull him over to the bed. I crawl across the mattress, dragging him with me, and lie down. "I will call Bastian for help if you don't rest." I lift my eyebrow. "So, do you want to sleep or have an unknown wolf in the house with your daughter?"

Tarq reaches out, pulls me to him, and rolls his chest over me. It's not long before I feel his body heat up as he falls asleep. His warmth is all I need to follow suit.

* * *

When I wake, the nearly full moon glares through the windows. I'm cold, which means Tarq isn't holding me. I pat around the bed, but he's not there. Sitting up slowly, I spot Anthony reading in my chair by the fire.

"Where's Tarq?" I ask.

Anthony puts his book down and picks up a bowl of cut fruit. He smiles as he approaches the bed. "He's gone to get the Doc." Anthony sits beside me, holding an orange wedge. "He'll be back soon."

Rolling my eyes, I take the orange. "Persistent shit, isn't he?"

Anthony chuckles as he moves the pillows around and holds his arm out. "We're all worried about you, Darya," he says, pulling me to his chest. I curl against him, and he throws the thick blanket over me. "Edie says those two wolves nearly killed themselves to save you."

I accept an apple slice he offers. "Where's Annalisa?" I ask once I swallow.

"She's fine, Darya," he answers. "We just want to see you feeling better."

Anthony had just caught me again on the day I met my first wolf. I punched him and knocked him over a table, causing a very satisfying thud if I were being honest. He hated me. Today, he's comforting my sick body with his warmth and telling me how worried he is. This is the world in which I thrive. My enemy has become one of the most influential men in my life.

"It's time to start teaching her about her duties," I say. "I could have died, and Tarq wouldn't have known what to do." Lifting off Anthony's chest, I look down at him. "From what I understand, Tarq didn't leave my side. Can you imagine what would've happened if I'd died?"

Anthony sighs, patting my hand. "Your kiddo's been staying at our house," he tells me. "Tarq's been... on edge. It scares her."

I sigh with pursed lips. "The full moon is tomorrow, right?" Anthony nods as I push the fruit bowl away. "Can she stay with you until then?"

"Sure. We'll bring her," Anthony says, removing the bowl. "Edie wouldn't miss a full moon with your family."

A ruckus downstairs causes me to try to sit up. Anthony braces me but doesn't let go. The front door slams against the wall, and I grab my chest as yelling and growling erupt. When something breaks, Anthony holds me down as he gets up.

He points at me while crossing the room. "You stay here." He opens the door to slip out, closing it behind him as the shouts continue.

I claw at the blankets until I'm free. That's Tarq down there. He's the only man or wolf they fear when he gets angry, and I need to get to him. The uproar downstairs dies down as my feet touch the floor. I'm slightly unsteady, and my legs shake as I cross the room. When I reach for the door's handle, it swings open, knocking me back.

"Shit, Dar," Chase shouts, reaching out for me. "I'm sorry. Let me help." He sets a bag on the floor and pulls me to my feet. When my legs try to give out, he scoops me into his arms and carries me to the bed. "Are you ok?"

"Where's Anthony?" I watch him retrieve the bag and raise my eyebrows expectantly when he faces me. Chase knows Tarq needs me right now, and it pisses me off that he's carried me back to bed, further away from where I'm needed.

"He went to help Nate with Tarq," my companion says as if this is standard information about which I should be calm. "I have something from the Doc. He figured out what kind of poison they used."

He produces a vial of clear liquid and a syringe. I grab a paper that falls from the bag.

"Oh, hey," Chase says, trying to stop me. "I need that. It has your dosage."

I move it away from him, quickly scanning the scribbling. The dosing information doesn't make sense, but one thing here surprises me. "Hemlock?" I say, looking up to stare into Chase's eyes. "They poisoned me with hemlock?" They could only have introduced the poison through the blade and perhaps the ropes. They would've needed an outrageous level of concentrated hemlock to affect me this much.

"Can I have that back, Dar?" Chase asks with an outstretched hand.

"Chase?" I mumble slowly. "What kind of evil has the time to create a poison like that?"

Chase sighs, cupping my cheek. "Luckily, an evil we will never have to encounter again."

He sets the vial down to read the dosing instructions, allowing me to pick it up. "This is just steroids." I frown.

Putting his hand over mine, Chase gently takes the vial from me.

"Once it got in your blood…" Chase's voice fades. He slides the back of his fingers over my cheek, wiping a tear I didn't know was there. "Doc said bleeding you was helpful —" he starts.

"But the damage was already done," I finish for him in a whisper.

"I'm sorry, Dar." He pushes the needle into the vial and pulls back on the plunger.

"And Tarq knows?" I ask. "Is that what's set him off?"

Chase pulls my arm forward and sets my elbow on his knee. "He didn't take the news well," he says, frowning. Chase wraps his hand around my upper arm, making the vein stick out. He taps it with his finger before poking me with the needle. I wince as he quickly pulls back to ensure he's in the vein and empties it into me.

"Ok, Dar," Chase starts as he collects the items he brought. "Doc says you need to rest and give these meds time to work. They should help your breathing and heart."

Yeah, like that would ever happen. "No, you need to help me get to Tarq before he does something he regrets."

Although I want to object when Chase carries me down the stairs, I probably wouldn't have made it alone. It's quiet in the house. As Chase sets me down, I take in the destruction of my living room. There are some broken chairs, a hole in the wall from where the door crashed, and a spray of blood along the bookshelf.

I hold my hand out to catch Chase's arm before he moves away. "Where is he?"

Chase knows better than to test me when it comes to my Alpha, and I wear my feelings all over my face when I'm mad. He holds his arm out and helps me to the door. It creaks as it opens, almost yelling at us about its damage.

I brace against Chase as he helps me to the edge of the porch, where I can see what is happening. Tarq is crouched in front of the horse stalls. He leans against the wall and holds his head in his hands. Anthony and two of my guards aim their rifles at my struggling Alpha.

I love my wolves. I have repeatedly proven that I will do anything for them, but they will not get between my Alpha and me. He has a fierce love that will cause him to cross the depths of hell to get to me. His fight right now is internal. He is straining to stop himself from hurting those who keep him from me. *And I want to burn each one of them for this crime.*

I release Chase's arm and hold the rail as I rush to the stairs. There are just three steps, but I only manage two before I need to sit. "Let him come to me," I say through my teeth.

Tarq jumps up and shoves the men aside to fall before me. He lands on his knees, sliding his arms around my waist and hiding his face in my lap. I feel fear and anger radiating from him as I slide my fingers through his hair. I've never forcefully helped Tarq with his emotions, but I suspect I'll need to after a month of pent-up fear.

I take a breath to calm down and look at my wolves. "If you keep my Alpha from me again, you will wear your shame for all to see," I warn them. From the corner of my eye, I see Chase rubbing his wrist. His mark was an accidental wound. Before she passed, Jules spoke of a true wolf punishment that marks the human and alters the wolf. It's meant only as a severe penalty, and I've never had to use it. I hope I never will. "Leave us."

Bowing their heads, Chase and the guards disperse quickly. Anthony stays behind, watching Tarq cling to me. "Darya?"

"Anthony," I say slowly, trying to contain my anger. "You may not be one of my wolves, but I will mark you just the same. I said leave us."

I watch as he backs away before turning toward the woods. Once he's out of sight, I open my knees and allow Tarq to come closer. His arms tighten around my waist as his head rests against my hip.

"You're going to have to talk to me," I whisper, pushing his hair away from his face. "You're scaring everyone, My Love, including your daughter."

Tarq slips down onto the bottom step and looks up into my eyes. His gaze is still loving, but his face tells a different story. Holding his hair back, I run my thumbs along his cheekbones.

"Why are you so mad, my Alpha?"

Tarq tries to hang his head, but I stop him. "Darya, I..." he starts.

"This is..." He pulls my hands off his face and turns away from me. Tarq holds his head in his hands, defeated.

I move to sit behind him and attempt to pull him to my chest. Tarq is stiff and tense, fighting me, so I pull up on his shirt and wait until he raises his arms, allowing me to pull it over his head. While sliding one hand over his chest, my other slips under his arm to press against his ribs.

I kiss his shoulder and wait for him to lean back. "It's either the guards or me, My Love," I whisper into his ear. "Here we go. Are you ready?"

Tarq sighs, knowing I won't help him without his permission. He leans against me and nods. I push heat to my hands in small waves before applying steady pressure. His breathing evens out as his muscles begin to relax. What causes harm to all others gives me the ability to soothe my Alpha. It is the one thing that eases his fury and allows me some control over him.

"It was my fault," Tarq says, sighing. "I didn't want you to go in there. I shouldn't have let you." He squeezes my hands and moves them to different places on his skin. "I should've stopped you. I failed you."

Leaning my head against his, I squeeze him tightly with my arms. "It was my choice to go into that camp."

"Darya, I —"

"No," I cut him off. "It's my turn now. You don't get to take all the blame without hearing my role." Tarq's body stiffens slightly, so I adjust my grip on him and give him a moment to settle back into my touch. "I told you from the beginning that I was going. You tried to stop me, but I wouldn't listen. You did your best, along with the Alphas, to create the least dangerous plan."

Tarq turns to face me. "How can you say this is your fault?" he sputters. "I'm your guard, your Alpha, and I put you in that situation."

I place my palms over his cheeks and spread my fingers across the sides of his head. Pulling him to my lips, I push heat straight into his face, where it has the most significant effect. Tarq parts his lips and lets me slide my tongue over his as he melts into me. At this point, my Alpha would usually deepen our kiss before throwing me over his shoulder. Under the influence of my heat, he just relaxes and enjoys the tender moment.

Pulling my lips from his, I press our foreheads together. "We want a peaceful life for our wolves," I say. "We did not ask for this fight. The fault lies with those who are dead. Why don't we let the blame die with them?"

A tear falls from Tarq's eye.

"I love you and will not lose you to your anger," I tell him sternly. "Especially when it's pointed inward." He leans against me and presses his ear to my chest as I do with him. I wrap my hands around his head, pushing heat and allowing him to relax the rest of his anger away. "Can you help me to bed and stay with me this time?"

Tarq slides his arms around me and stands up, lifting me to his hips.

I wrap my legs around him and smile. "Hey there, you."

"Thank you," Tarq murmurs.

I gently press my lips to his before whispering, "Take me to bed, My Love."

Although Tarq has lifted off me when I wake, I'm still tightly wrapped in his arms. I turn and push my face into his chest, breathing him in. I've never been able to describe his scent, but it is perfectly his and never seems to change. It's a relief to see him returning to some sense of normalcy.

A soft knock on the door catches my attention. "Dar?" Chase whispers.

The hinges squeak slightly as the bedroom door swings open. When I peek around Tarq, I see our companion holding up the vial of steroids.

Chase smiles at me as he sits on the bed. "It's good to see him sleeping finally. He looks peaceful."

"And I will kill you in my sleep if you don't leave us alone," Tarq grumbles as he pulls me under his chest while pushing his face into the pillows.

I giggle at him as Chase shakes his head. He's used to Tarq's grumpiness when he's tired. I slide my hand over my Alpha's cheek until he releases me enough to roll out from under him. "Chase is here to help, My Love," I say. "Then he will leave." Rolling over, I put my arm in Chase's hand with a wink.

Tarq curls around me, watching Chase. "That's supposed to help?" he asks, eyeing the syringe.

Chase wraps his hand around my arm to create pressure. "This will help her breathing," he says. His voice is calm, but his face is nervous. He knows Tarq doesn't accept responses that don't answer his questions. Dax taught his son well.

"So, it'll make her better?" Tarq presses.

Chase focuses on my arm, pretending it requires his full concentration. Tarq continues to stare at him, wanting an answer. When he begins to growl, Chase nervously glances at me.

"It's ok, Chase," I say, smiling. "Nothing will make me better, Tarq. The damage is irreparable. These steroids will help me live with it."

My Alpha studies our companion's every move, making him nervous. Chase taps my arm and jabs me. He finishes quickly and bows to us before leaving.

Tarq rolls onto his back so I can prop myself up to look down at him. "I really missed you," he tells me, tucking my hair behind my ear.

"I'm right here, My Love," I tell him, soaking in his warmth. "I will leave this world on my terms. No one else's." Tarq continues to run his fingers through my hair, distracted by his thoughts. "Why don't we make some food, and we'll ride down to see your father? It'll do you good to spend time with him."

* * *

Later that evening, we're riding the buckskin toward Dax's house. "It's time to start teaching our daughter more than horse training," I say.

Tarq takes a deep breath, and I feel him look down at me. "She's a little young, don't you think?" He straightens his shoulders as if he's just finalized a decision. "There's plenty of time for that."

"No, it's time, Tarq," I tell him. "She can't stay a little girl, and I cannot live forever."

"Yes, you can," he states plainly.

Lifting my eyebrow, I twist around to face him. "Then I would have to live without you, and I'm not interested in that life."

Tarq scowls. "Fine," he grumbles. "But I want my objection on the record."

I giggle. "It has been noted."

We're late, but the time to think and prepare was nice. The moon is high when we arrive at the back door. It's quiet since it's only our small family gathering, minus Amelia, as I'd ordered her to stay home. She wasn't happy with my decision, but I'm tired of fighting with Dax about her.

I slide off the back of the buckskin with Tarq's help. "Are you ever going to tell me what happened to Bones?" I ask, eyeing the little horse.

Like every time I bring up the colt, Tarq winces before redirecting me. "Come on," he says. "Dad's probably waiting for us." He holds his arm out. *I'll never find out what happened to my horse.*

Tarq escorts me to the porch and into the kitchen. My eyes land on our daughter as she sits at the kitchen table with her face buried in her grandfather's shoulder. I hear her crying as Dax turns to us and nods.

"What the fuck?!" Tarq shouts, laughing. "I'd have gotten my ass kicked for days if I ever got on the table!"

I don't particularly care where Dax is lying, but he is, in fact, lying on the kitchen table to provide the shoulder for Annalisa. With a grin, I shake my head. *"What's going on?"*

"She's afraid," Dax says. *"You've been sick, and Tarq was scaring her."*

"I'm gonna shift," Tarq says, helping me sit beside our daughter. "Will you be alright?"

"We'll be fine, My Love," I respond, smiling. "You guys go on. We'll be out in a little while."

Tarq leans down to kiss me before disappearing into the back room.

"I can stay," Dax offers.

I tug the fur on his throat as he presses his muzzle against my cheek. "I think the Lunas need to handle this alone, Grandpa." I pause as Annalisa looks up at me. "Why don't you go spend time with your son? Anthony and Nate should be around here somewhere."

Tarq peeks around the corner, waiting for me to give him a way outside that avoids Annalisa. He has no idea how to handle his daughter's emotions. Dax hops off the table as I open the door, and they bump my hand with their noses as they pass.

"I'm sorry Daddy scared you," I say, rejoining my daughter.

Annalisa is nearly a corked bottle under pressure. "It wasn't just

Daddy," she practically shouts. "You almost died. I had no one because he wouldn't leave you, and I didn't know what to do." I pull her to me by her neck. "The wolves looked at me like I was supposed to take over, but all I wanted to do was cry." She huffs loudly as her forehead falls onto my shoulder. "I can't do this. I'm not you."

Rubbing her back, I let her catch her breath. "I won't always be here, Annalisa," I caution her. "You will be the Luna one day. Today is not that day, but it's coming just the same." I slide my fingers through her hair and decide on a lesson. "Why don't we start with a little relaxation?" I whisper, leaning back. "We'll work on one of Grandpa's favorite Luna gifts so you can spend time with him while you learn."

My daughter sits up, looking into my eyes. "Is Daddy ok?"

"Was he that bad?"

My question triggers more tears. "He yelled at me for chewing too loudly," Annalisa sputters. "He said I would wake you up."

I put forth great effort to frown, but the thought of Tarq yelling at Annalisa for chewing proves too much.

"Mom!" she yells. "It's not funny!"

Shaking my head, I burst out laughing. "I'm sorry, honey," I choke out. "It's hilarious. He yelled at you for chewing." Coughing interrupts my laughter, and Annalisa scowls, passing me some water. "Ok, come on," I tell her as my cough subsides. "Daddy's fine. We'll work on calming the wolves. Grandpa loves it."

Pulling her from the table, I lead her to the front porch and sit on the top step. We watch the wolves from our perch. Edith is in the field with them, manning my bow while Nate throws the ball. Tarq keeps trying to bite Anthony, who's quite annoyed with him. Miles is lying a short distance away. It won't be long before he joins us.

"When you look over this group, what do you see?" I ask Annalisa.

She studies them quizzically. "I don't know," she huffs. "A bunch of children that have too much energy?" I smile as Dax knocks Tarq's legs out from under him, and her father falls flat on his face.

"Close your eyes," I instruct. I hold Annalisa's hands in her lap as she follows my instructions. "I'm going to tell you what they're doing, and I want you to picture it in your mind, ok?"

Annalisa frowns. "Mom, I just saw them. How is this any different?"

"Have a little faith, child. Some things are just below the surface," I tell her as Miles slinks beside me, rubbing his muzzle over my cheek before settling his head in my lap. "All you have to do is look."

She scowls and slouches but keeps her eyes closed.

"Grandpa is lying on his back, and Daddy is trying to bite his feet," I say, narrating the drama in the field. "Grandpa's trying to get him off, but Daddy's nearly gotten him a few times. Oh, now he's using his back paws." Annalisa's scowl fades as I'm sure she's picturing their shenanigans. "He's pushed him off. Nate is stepping up with the ball, so everyone is lining up."

A smile spreads across her face while she quickly finds the humor in their behaviors. My family rarely functions under a serious note. Miles is the wolf who taught me that.

"They are all still," I continue. "Oh, Grandpa just knocked Daddy over. There goes the ball." Annalisa's smile broadens. "Daddy stole Edith's arrow. Well, she gave it to him, but now he's chasing Grandpa. You don't want to know what he's saying. Daddy and Grandpa get mouthy when they're together."

As her smile reaches its fullest, I call out to her grandfather. *"Dax, come here for a minute."* The black wolf slides and turns back toward us. *"Be quiet. Don't let her hear you."*

I continue narrating for a few more minutes as Dax settles before Annalisa. Miles adjusts his position when I shiver. He hums as his body heats up. For a wolf who couldn't shift for 151 years, he is skilled at positioning his body to provide me with the most heat.

"Ok, honey, I'm going to move your hands. Just keep your eyes closed and listen to my words." I reach her hands forward, laying them on Dax—one on his cheek and the other along his jaw. "Nate just threw a ball at Daddy's head. I think it's the one I put my scent on last month because your father is rolling around on it. Now Edith is threatening to shoot him if he doesn't return it." I cock my head to the side, confused. "What are they doing out there?"

"Keep going," Dax tells me. *"It's working."*

"Ok, baby," I say, releasing Annalisa's hands. "I want you to picture Grandpa. Think about his black fur. Remember how it always shines in the moonlight." Dax closes his eyes and relaxes in her hands. "Picture his blue eyes and how they look right through you." Dax begins to hum. "See him as he walks. He always has that confidence about him, as if you could never guess what he's about to do." Dax chuckles sleepily. "Ok, open your eyes."

Annalisa's eyes slowly open and rest upon her grandfather. He's barely upright, drooling in his state of relaxation. She raises her eyebrow and smirks at him while she slides her hand over his face and tugs his ear. Dax flops onto his side, leaning against her leg.

"I told you this was his favorite thing," I tell her, giggling.

Annalisa's brow furrows. "Is this how you help Daddy?"

Frowning, I look into the field. Tarq is lying down beside Edith, staring at us. "No, baby, Daddy's different," I explain. "It takes something much stronger to help him. That's a lesson for another day."

Out in the field, the game has stopped. The younger wolves have started to leave, and Tarq is lazing about, waiting for someone in his family to want to spend time with him. He is trying very hard not to move. The tall grass behind him is swaying rhythmically, making me smile. As much as I hate wrinkling my nose, it annoys Tarq that his tail wags when he tries to remain still.

"I'm gonna have Daddy sit with you," I tell Annalisa. "He's not very good at apologizing, so maybe you could let him relax with you and Grandpa."

Annalisa smiles and winks at me as she plays with Dax's lips.

"Get over here and sit with your daughter," I call out to Tarq.

He jumps up in the field. *"What am I getting out of this?"*

"We won't talk about how you yelled at her for chewing," I say with my eyebrow arched.

Miles chuckles as he sits up.

"Deal," Tarq says, jogging in our direction. He steps onto the porch and bumps my hand. *"How are you doing? Are you ok?"*

"I'm fine." I smile as I kiss his muzzle before using Miles' shoulders to push myself to my feet. *"Make nice with your daughter, My Love,"* I tell him before turning away.

Miles walks with me to the field. He's never far on the full moon. The Alpha rubs his muzzle over my hip until I catch his jaw. I look down at him as I rub my thumb over his whiskers. "I love you, Miles."

"I know, Little One," is his usual response. His hum is all I need to hear.

We approach Edith, and I let go of Miles to link my arm with hers. I point down the hill, away from everyone else. "I need your help with something," I tell her.

She arches her eyebrow but walks with me as Miles drops to my left side. "I can't heal you," she says, frowning. "Tarq already asked."

I smile and pat her arm. "I know the poison sealed my fate. I'm just hoping for a reprieve from the symptoms."

We reach a quiet area, and Edith stops me. "What's going on?" she asks, lifting her eyebrow.

"I have to meet with the Blood Pack," I tell her, looking down at Miles. "I need to make that trip and can't do it feeling like this." Miles sighs but doesn't share his opinion.

Edith looks at me in disbelief. "So you want me to make you appear healthy so you can ride to your death?"

Cupping her cheek, I smile. "No, Edith, I need help making the trip." I turn her to start walking again. "Their Alpha only wants a meeting for cleaning the militia camp. Bastian assured my safety." Edith doesn't respond, staring at the ground before us. "So, will you help me?"

She takes a few more steps before turning toward my family on the porch. "I'll do it for them," she declares. "They deserve this time with you."

Smiling broadly, I pull her to me. "Thank you."

Edith pushes me back and gives me a stern look. "You must remem-ber your limitations," she warns me. "Just because you won't feel the pain doesn't mean it won't be there."

"I'll be careful. I promise. Come on," I say, reaching for Edith's arm as Miles and I look at the sky. "We need to get up there. This is the first time Annalisa will be here when the guys leave."

Miles stays by my side as Edith helps me up the hill quickly. I'm beginning to feel those limitations. My chest is on fire, and I can't breathe enough, causing her to slow down and watch me with worried eyes. We've nearly reached them when a voice calls out, stopping me.

"Luna," Bastian says. *"We're out of time."*

My sudden stop pulls Edith back. "What's up, honey? You ok?"

Taking a slow breath, I lift my head and smile at her. "Everything is fine," I say, reaching out to my side for Miles. "How soon can you have me feeling better?"

"The potion takes a day to brew," Edith says.

"Could you start on that tonight for me, please?" I ask, maintaining my smile. "Bastian says I'm out of time." Her eyes widen. "Edith," I say sternly. "I have not shared these details with anyone, so I need you to calm down and breathe."

Edith gasps. "Darya? You haven't told Tarq?"

I look at my Alpha as he says goodbye to his father. "Look at him," I say, nodding in his direction. "He's happy. Would you want to ruin that?" I smile down at Miles and slide my hand over his muzzle. "They needed this, and I needed to let them have it."

"Luna?" Bastian calls out.

"A week, Bastian. I need a week." Bastian falls silent, but it's too late as I feel Miles disappear from under my hand. "Come on, Edith. This isn't gonna be pretty."

Edith helps me up the rest of the hill, but we stop before reaching my daughter. Annalisa is crying into her father's fur with her arms clinging to his neck. Tarq's head rests on her back, and his eyes are closed. I watch as he sighs deeply.

"Are you ok, My Love," I asked Tarq, holding my finger to my lips for Edith.

"We'll be ok," he answers.

"I'll leave you two alone," I tell him, pulling Edith back to walk around the house. *"Bring her home when you're ready."*

"Take the buckskin," Tarq commands. *"I don't want you walking that far."*

"Yes, My Love," I answer.

Edith and I quietly tiptoe around the house to avoid interrupting them. We quickly reach the back porch and stop beside the buckskin.

"Tarq is nervous about your condition," Edith cautions. "You can't blindside him with these things anymore. He'll not handle them well."

Placing my hand on her arm, I smile. "Why don't you help me with that, then?" I ask. "If I appear healthier, he'll worry less." Edith frowns as I swing into my saddle. "I'm sure everyone would feel better."

* * *

A quiet knock on the door wakes me in the afternoon. Tarq jerks from the sound. He's still asleep, but his growl begins to rumble, and he pulls me deeper under his shoulder. I place my hands on his chest and push a small blast of heat through them. It makes me smile when Tarq's growl simmers to a hum.

Peeking out from under my Alpha, I see Chase approaching us. When I smile, our companion sits on the bed. He helps me untangle my arm from Tarq, laying it across his lap. Chase has a look like he needs to say something. As my companion, I've come to know this wolf well. I need to wait until he's ready to talk to me. If I push him, he never will.

"This is the last dose for a while, Dar," Chase whispers. "After this, it'll just be a small dose once a week." He straightens my arm and taps my vein. His eyes narrow, and his mouth twists before he looks at me. "He's getting worse, isn't he?" His eyes travel over my Alpha's arms, which have an unrelenting grip on his Luna.

I frown, following his eyes. "He's scared," I whisper back. "He only does love and anger well. He doesn't know how to process fear at all."

Chase's jaw tightens. "Dar, he's not accepting your diagnosis," he hisses. "You need to make him understand what happened. What if he stops letting us treat you?"

I take a moment to compose myself before responding. "Chase," I start, trying to find the right words. "I know you mean well, and thank you for taking care of me, but you're overstepping." Tarq tenses his arms. I push more heat to him and urge Chase with my other arm. "Can you please finish? I need to let him wake up."

"Yes, Dar," Chase says, turning to his work. "I'm sorry." He finishes giving me the shot and leaves the room quietly.

Tarq groans and stretches his legs as I trail my hand over his ribs. He lifts off me with a yawn. His hand slides firmly against my skin as it travels down my body and reaches for my leg. He kisses the top of my head, then pulls my thigh over his hip. I let him pull me on top of his body as he rolls onto his back to complete his morning routine.

"Good morning to you too," I say with a crooked smirk. Tarq's lying under me with a grin and his eyes closed. I've stared at him for over 15 years, and the view never loses its beauty.

Tarq smiles as he opens his eyes. "I might have missed sleep." He slides his hand along my jaw, and his fingers caress my neck. "I definitely missed waking up to you, though."

He pulls me in for a kiss. The moment our lips meet, my heart begins to flutter. The pain from my lungs overpowers my ache for him. I push my forehead against his to take a breath or two to alleviate the discomfort. When Tarq tries to kiss me again, I know I need to distract him.

"Baby, there's something I need to tell you."

Tarq freezes underneath me. He pushes me away by my face to look me in the eye. "Nothing good ever started with you needing to tell me something."

I laugh. "That's not true," I say, lifting myself off him. "I said it when my water broke, and you got a beautiful, healthy daughter out of that."

Tarq frowns. "That's not very good odds."

* * *

A few hours later, I made it halfway downstairs. I refused to let Tarq help me, so here I sit, waiting on a damn miracle. He's in the kitchen banging pans and utensils around as he makes me something to eat. He's furious, but at least it's aimed appropriately at me.

"Tarq," I call down to him. "You're not listening to me."

A loud clang sounds as Tarq throws a pan across the kitchen. "I am listening," he growls. "You're not going." There's another crash, but whatever he threw this time breaks when it lands. "Shit!" he screams.

I slide down a few more steps on my butt. I'm still out of breath, but at least I'm already sitting if I pass out. "It's the deal Bastian made for the militia camp," I say, taking a few slow breaths. "I have to go, and I would like you to come with me, please." I reach the bottom step and lean against the railing, exhausted.

"I'm gonna kill that kid," Tarq declares. A clattering indicates he's moved on to the silverware.

Pulling up with the railing, I brace myself against some of the chairs to make it to a smaller armchair. "You will do no such thing," I say in my most forceful whisper. *Shit, it's hard to yell when you can't breathe.* "We don't even know who he is. He could be your brother or cousin."

Something large and metallic clangs in the kitchen. "Oh, don't start with that family shit," he shouts. "Dad and Miles told you there aren't any other kids."

That's true, but how could they be positive? Miles told me he was sterile, but is that an absolute certainty? I think Dax was telling the truth about not being with many women. He comfortably traveled with his wolves, and until they met Edith, they couldn't shift away from the lake.

My eyes land on the furniture in the living room. In all of our years here, we'd never replaced it. Amelia had picked these chairs when she lived here with Bruce. We built a small cottage a short walk away to help her start over, but she didn't take anything from this house. I've always hated the color.

"Why do we still have these horrid green chairs in here?" I call out to Tarq, trying to change the subject since we'll never agree.

He slaps a wooden spoon on the counter. "Because my mother fucking likes them!"

Tarq can't switch gears as fast as I can in conversations. He can talk in circles and avoid answering questions, but he cannot transfer from a screaming match to answering a simple question. My giggle starts small and almost innocent, but it doesn't take long before I'm in hysterics.

"Did you seriously just yell at me about your mother's chairs?" I laugh and cough at the same time.

Tarq comes out of the kitchen and kneels before me, taking my hands. He kisses my knuckles with a crooked grin. "What can I say? I was on a roll." He puts an elbow on each side of my legs, holding our hands to his lips. "Baby, please stop trying to kill yourself."

"Bastian said his Alpha will honor the meeting, Tarq."

"Why do you trust him?" He puts his face in my hands.

I pull on his jaw until he looks into my eyes. "He's cut from the same cloth," I whisper. "I have to believe he's as honorable as the man he resembles."

Tarq releases a sigh of defeat. "When are we leaving?"

"Tomorrow," I say, smiling.

"Quit gloating." He scowls, pulling me from the chair and wrapping his arms around me. "Just promise me you won't die. I only agreed to once, and you keep doing it, Darya."

"I told you I will not leave this world until I'm ready." I slide my hand over his neck and run my fingers through his hair. Laying my head on his shoulder allows him better access to my skin, where he can take in my scent and relax.

Tarq inhales deeply before sliding his tongue over my skin, ending just below my ear. "I may have broken some shit in the kitchen," he whispers.

I giggle at him as he finally switches gears. "May have?"

"There were circumstances beyond my control," he states, pulling away from me. I raise my eyebrow and hold him before me until he continues. "Dar, I can't be held responsible for what I do when you talk about killing yourself."

Frowning, I click my tongue. "I don't remember having that conversation with you," I say, shoving him toward the kitchen.

Tarq chuckles. "Ok, but you're still gonna help me clean it up, right?"

6

Edith had finished her potion by the next afternoon, and we immediately hit the trail. Tarq insisted that I ride Annalisa's white filly named Grease. I'm relieved to have Chase join us on the trip. Tarq is calmer when our companion is nearby.

"Are you doing ok?" my Alpha asks.

"I am exactly how I was five minutes ago," I say, narrowing my eyes at him as he jogs beside me.

Tarq chuckles and speeds up. Grease tries to follow him, but I keep her slow until he's out of sight. If he were to bolt forward, I'd be unable to hold her back. My daughter has turned into one hell of a horse trainer.

"I'm here, Luna," Bastian calls out. *"How far out are you?"*

He said his Alpha would only give me a week if Bastian escorted me. I frown, thinking about his age. Our junior guard members age out at 19. Until then, I keep them away from the militia and battles. They train, but I allow them to enjoy their childhood before facing the hate outside our boundaries. Bastian never seems to stay still and is tasked with things he should not be handling at his age.

"Half a day, maybe," I tell him. *"We just left."*

"Where are the house keys?"

I hang my head. *"Tarq broke the locks,"* I say, cringing. *"Only the scanner works."*

"So it has a code?"

A giggle mixes in with my cringe. *"No, it's a fingerprint scanner."*

"Luna, I don't understand. What am I missing?" He genuinely sounds confused.

"It's Tarq's nose print," I say, laughing out loud. *"He's the only one who can unlock the damn house."*

"Oh, Jesus." Bastian falls silent.

"We'll be up there soon," I tell him. *"Just hang tight. The guards were expecting you."*

Bastian doesn't seem to have a lot of humor in his life. He started to chime in eventually while with us at the cabin, but Tarq's goofiness puzzled him. I giggle, picturing him lying on the porch, trying to understand what Tarq did.

Tarq notices my laughter and drops back. *"What's so funny?"*

"Bastian's at the cabin," I say, smirking. "He was asking how to get inside."

Tarq stops, causing Grease to halt. *"Why do you need to tell everyone about the stupid shit I do when I'm bored?"*

"You didn't have to be at the cabin or bored." I laugh.

Tarq resumes an easy jog, taking Grease with him. *"Yes, I did,"* he says playfully. *"You were all crazy and hormonal and shit."*

"Pregnant, baby," I scoff. "I believe the word you're looking for is pregnant."

Tarq continues to jog, not looking back. *"That is not the story historians will tell."*

I shake my head. "As long as they tell the tale of our epic love, I don't care."

"I love you too."

"We should pick up the pace, though," I urge him. "I don't want that kid thinking he needs to come down the mountain."

Tarq shoots forward, and Grease darts up the trail after him.

* * *

It's nearly sunset when we arrive at the cabin. Chase appears beside me before I reach the boundary. When the three of us travel together,

Chase always runs in the back. He spends most of the time calling out my guards' positions to Tarq to alleviate some of my Alpha's stress.

"Make sure you bring your saddlebags inside, Dar," he reminds me. *"I'll need to mix up some medicine before we leave."*

"I'll get them," I promise.

He veers toward the shed I had built for them. Tarq shifts seamlessly with barely any effort. It's much harder for the rest of my wolves. It has locks they can manipulate with their paws or noses and clothes to wear once they've completed their shift. I wanted them to have a private place where they could feel protected.

There's been no sign of Bastian. *"Hey, Bass? Where are you?"* I ride to the paddocks, listening for him, but there's no response.

Anthony is already untacking his horse. "Just leave her, Darya," he tells me. "I'll take care of her."

"I'll take care of my own horse, thank you," I say, pulling the saddlebags down to throw them over the rail. Loosening the cinch strap, I allow the girth to swing freely.

"You're so damn stubborn," Anthony barks. "Edie told you to take it easy."

Ignoring him, I watch Chase approach us. I'm pulling Grease's bridle off when he reaches the paddock. Tarq steps onto the porch and nods to Chase. I'm suddenly slung onto his shoulder and hauled away from my horse. "Are you kidding me?" I shout. "Put me down!" I kick my legs and push away from his back, trying to force my way to the ground.

"It's for your own good, Dar," Chase says, grabbing the saddlebags.

I rest my chin on my hand, giving up. Chase takes a few more steps before a distinct growl erupts beside the paddocks. Bastian steps out of the brush, his head hanging low.

I slap my hand on Chase's back and kick my legs. "Chase, put me down... now," I hiss.

Chase turns to see Bastian stalking him. He gently puts me on my feet but then trips, spilling the contents of the saddlebags.

"Easy, Bass," I say gently, holding my hands out as I move between Chase and him. "It's ok, honey. Chase was just helping me." It's no use.

Just like when Tarq was younger, Bastian isn't listening. He stares at his uncle, moving to the side, trying to get a clear shot at him. "Chase, I really need you to move."

My companion scrambles to collect all the ingredients. When Chase stands, Bastian snaps and lunges at his uncle. Tarq jumps over the railing and shifts, barreling straight at us. My Alpha's snarl is deafening.

"Darya, run!" Tarq shouts.

Bastian is too close for that. Chase won't survive this attack. I swing my fist charged with heat, slamming it into the side of Bastian's head and knocking him back. He rolls over and lands right back on his feet.

Tarq reaches us before he can lunge again. He jumps in the air, grabbing Bastian by his scruff and flipping him over onto his back. *"Both of you get out of here!"*

Grabbing Chase, I rush him to the porch as the wolves attack each other. Their limbs tangle as their chests collide. Bastian's right hind leg is injured, but he refuses to back down. He rears up and lunges teeth first at Tarq's face. The snapping of their jaws sounds like lightning ripping across the sky.

I can't bring myself to leave them. Chase attempts to pull me to the door, but I stop him. "I'm going to wait for them," I tell him. "I need to make sure they're ok."

"He's got some anger issues," Chase says, lifting an eyebrow. I rub his arm before he disappears inside the cabin.

Tarq latches onto Bastian's throat and throws him onto his back as I lean over the railing. Bastian kicks at his face, but Tarq firmly holds him down. My Alpha's growl starts low but quickly escalates. As it rumbles across the yard like an earthquake, Bastian falls still, clearly submitting.

"Bass?" I call out. *"Are we good?"*

"Holy shit, he's strong," is his response.

I giggle, shaking my head. *"He is my Alpha, Bastian,"* I point out. *"Now you need to convince him to let you up."*

"You're not gonna help?" Bastian sounds surprised.

"You have an anger problem, Bastian. We can help you," I say. "Lesson one. Convince Tarq to let you up."

I leave them to walk through the cabin, looking for my companion. I find Chase in the kitchen. He has herbs and vials scattered about with cutting boards and measuring cups along the counter.

"Why did he attack us?" he asks.

Sitting on a stool, I look over his work area. "Just a misunderstanding," I tell him. "Can we talk about all this while they're busy? I'd like to keep this quiet if we can."

Chase lines up some of the bottles. "Edith did some research," he starts. "She says they would mix these daily in the old days to help with asthma symptoms." He sets a pot down. "She believes it will help to open your airways." He begins measuring some of the powders to mix. "She did warn that it reportedly tastes horrible."

I smile crookedly, remembering the first night I met Nate. "The best ones always do," I say, quoting him. "Did she tell you about the medicine she made?" I pick up one of the full vials. They are encased in rubber to protect them from breaking.

Chase picks another one up, shaking it a bit. "Edith said you'll take these once daily," he tells me. "She said morning is best and to shake it. There's two weeks' worth of them." He puts his vial back and reaches for mine.

"Did she tell you what it does?" I ask innocently, handing it to him.

"No," Chase says, frowning. "She did say that you can take them together, though. Maybe this one will taste better."

I wink at him. "Let's hope."

The side door slams open, followed by a commotion in the living room. Exchanging looks with Chase, I follow the sounds to find my Alpha holding a teenager in a headlock.

Tarq sees me and releases Bastian. "Hey, My Love," he says, smiling. "Are you ok?"

Stepping up to him, I raise my eyebrow and tug at his shorts. "Did you steal these from the shifting shed?"

"Yes, ma'am, I did," he says, slipping his arm around my waist.

"Some kid lost his damn mind and almost killed our Luna. Sadly, this destroyed my clothes."

I shake my head as I turn to Bastian. Ash and his wife, Neala, are my junior guards' caretakers. I'd told them about what I'd observed of Bastian's body. Neala advised me to get my hands on him every chance I got to check his muscles' thickness. The only injury I see is on his thigh, but she will not be pleased with my report about his body.

"How's your hand?" Tarq asks. "That was one hell of a punch."

Bastian closes his eyes and leans onto my hand when I reach for his cheek. "Are you guys ok?" I ask. "Bastian, that cut looks deep."

He opens his eyes and smiles at me. "It's just a scrape, Luna," he says. "It'll heal."

"Nonsense," I scoff. "Your uncle is in the kitchen. He'll get you fixed up." I tug the ends of his sandy hair. "I suspect there might be an apology that needs to be said."

Bastian chuckles and bows before leaving in the direction of the kitchen.

I frown, dropping onto the couch. "It was like he couldn't hear me," I say sadly.

Tarq sits and pulls me into his lap. Finding his heartbeat, I relax into his chest, more exhausted than I'd like to admit. "He couldn't," he says, twisting his face in thought. "It's hard to describe. You just get mad, and the anger takes over. Dad called it 'seeing red.'"

Deep in thought, I slide my fingers over his chest, watching his skin react. "I hit him pretty hard, right?"

"There's no mark," Tarq says slowly. "Dar, who is that kid?"

I frown. "I don't know, but we've got to get his temper under control."

Tarq rolls down onto the couch and lays me in front of him as he tightens his arms around my waist.

"How did Dax help you?"

"I love you, Dar," Tarq mumbles instead of answering me. He moves down the couch and buries his face in my neck, handing me the TV controller.

I giggle as he starts to hum. "Are you tired, my Alpha?"

Tarq groans quietly. "I just took down the strongest wolf I've ever come across, Dar," he mumbles. "I'm gonna need a nap." His breathing quickly evens out, and his body heats.

I hold my finger to my lips as Anthony and Bastian join us. Anthony carries a few plates of food but just places them on the table and flops onto the other couch. Bastian sits on the floor close enough to me that I can push his hair away from his face. He flinches a few times before settling.

"What are you, kid?" Anthony asks abruptly, glaring at the teenager.

Bastian looks confused. "I don't even know how to answer that," he says. "I'm a wolf. What else is there?"

Studying Anthony, I realize he's just concerned about his extended family. I slide my hand over Bastian's shoulder, and the teenager leans his cheek onto my hand. "It's ok, Anthony," I tell him calmly. "We'll help Bastian find his way."

"He's a danger to you."

"He can't hurt me," I remind him.

Anthony's eyes shift to me as he scowls. "Have you lost your mind?" He's angrier than he's been in years. "Tarq nearly killed you thinking you needed protection, or did you conveniently forget that?"

Bastian twists around to me. "Your Alpha was like me?"

Smiling, I trace my fingers down his jaw. "Once, yes," I say. "And sometimes he still is." Bastian tries to lower his head, but I hold him up by his chin and run my thumb under his lower lip. "That's why we want to help you. He knows how you feel because he's been there." I look at Tarq, still deep asleep, tucked against my neck.

"What makes you think I want his help?"

"Bass, you tried to attack your uncle when he was helping me," I say pointedly. "I may not have wanted his help, but that didn't mean I was in danger."

Bastian frowns, pulling away to lower his head. I reach for his chin and push it back up. He leaves his eyes cast down, proving my point.

"This is why, Bass," I say, smiling. "A wolf with your strength should never feel shame for something they do." Bastian sighs and rests his head against my hip. "You can stay in our bedroom upstairs if you'd like. I don't think Tarq will be making it up there tonight."

"Is it ok if I stay down here with you?" Bastian's cheeks turn a slight shade of pink.

Glancing up, I see Anthony passed out on the other couch. "I think we're out of chairs, sweetheart."

With a smile, Bastian grabs a pillow from behind Tarq. "I'm used to harder surfaces, anyway."

I roll to my side and push my back into Tarq. His heat quickly disperses throughout my body, soothing the day's aches. "Do you want me to turn a movie on?"

Bastian shakes his head and tucks his pillow in front of my hips. "Turns out, getting my ass kicked is pretty exhausting." He curls his arms under the pillow and lays his head down, sleepily smiling. "I've never met anyone like you."

I push his hair from his face. "That would make sense since there's only one Luna."

Bastian closes his eyes while I slide my fingers through his hair. "I didn't know anyone else was like me either."

"Even in the desert, you will find water if only you know where to look," I whisper, noticing the plates of food have been left untouched by the teenager.

Bastian pulls his right hand from under the pillow and sets it on my hip. My fingers pause in his hair, and my body tenses as I look at it. Something about his touch is off. It's not like any other wolf's touch. I spend the rest of the night drifting in and out of sleep, but Bastian never moves.

* * *

In the morning, I sit in the kitchen holding a coffee cup, watching Chase prepare my medicines. "Let's start with the nasty stuff," I tell him.

Chase shakes the bottle of brown liquid and pours it into a glass. "I made up two weeks' worth to match the number of vials Edith sent." He slides the glass to me.

Hearing him laugh when I gag from sniffing the mixture is nice. "You seem like you're doing better," I say, leaning over to grab his hand. "Is the medical training helping?"

"I'd be lying if I said I didn't miss her every day," Chase whispers sadly. He had started working with Will a few months after Bristol's passing. He seems to enjoy helping others. "Maybe I could've saved her if I had any of this training."

I reach for his cheeks and wipe his tears away with my thumbs.

"I hope my training will stop someone else from going through what I have," he whispers.

"You would have been an amazing father," I tell him.

Relaxing into my touch, Chase allows me to pull his excess emotions. We moved our companion into our house after Bristol passed. I often found myself sandwiched between him and Tarq in bed when he had tough nights. Tarq built Chase a wing off the kitchen to keep him close when he thought he was ready to move out, and I disagreed.

Chase takes a deep breath and taps the glass of medicine before moving away to look out the window. I chug the nasty brew, fighting with my stomach to keep it down. "They're just about ready out there," Chase tells me, turning away from the window. "You need to take that other stuff and grab the saddlebags. I'm gonna go shift." He slides the second vial to me and sets the saddlebags on the counter.

I grab his arm before he can make it past me. "You'll let me know if you need to talk, right?" Chase only smiles and pats my shoulder before leaving through the back door. I take deeper breaths, testing the disgusting medicine, and find I can move more air.

"Did he lose his mate?" Bastian's voice makes me jump.

I turn around to find him standing in the doorway leading to the living room.

"Hey," I say, eyeing him curiously. "How long have you been there?"

Bastian ignores my question and crosses the room, grabbing the vial from my hand. He sniffs its contents before holding it over the sink, tipping it slightly. "What is this?" he asks.

"Excuse me?" I growl, narrowing my eyes. "That's my medicine, and you do not question me."

Bastian remains still other than to raise his eyebrow. "This is not medicine," he says, tipping the bottle more. "I know a potion when I smell it. What is it?"

The back door opens, and we both jump at the sudden noise. Bastian smiles with his eyes still locked on mine.

"I sent you in for the Luna, not a break," Tarq growls.

Bastian continues to smile, placing the vial in my hand. "I was just helping Luna with her medicine," he says. He leans to kiss my cheek, nods to Tarq, and walks straight out the back door, closing it behind him.

Tarq watches him leave before turning back to me with a furrowed brow. "What the hell was that?" He sits down and runs his hand over my cheek.

I lean into his touch with my eyes closed. "I'm not sure," I admit. "I think he was testing his boundaries."

"I'm not ok with that."

Opening my eyes, I smile at him. "I wouldn't expect you to be, My Love. I will tell you if I need your help."

Tarq slides his hands down my neck as he licks his lips. He pulls me to him, kissing me gently. "I can't help wanting to protect you." He moves his lips to my forehead and breathes out, sending fiery waves across my body.

Pushing him away, I quickly drink the potion. A warming sensation washes over my body as I set the vial down. I release the pressure from Tarq's chest, allowing him to come closer. I push my fingers into his hair, and he stops with his lips barely touching mine.

Tarq's hands hold my jaw as his eyes search mine for permission. His breathing becomes strained, and his muscles shake from tension. He's been patiently waiting for this moment. I've set this in motion by inviting him into my space.

As I lightly rub my lips against Tarq's, he releases the breath he'd been holding. With his eyes closed, his fingers find the zipper holding the front of my tank top closed, pushing it down. Tarq slips the straps over my shoulders, and it falls to the floor. His hands land on my ribs. He spreads his fingers and pushes them to my back, setting off every nerve under his touch.

I move off the stool and look down at my belt with a frown when Tarq breaks it to remove my shorts. "We're gonna talk about that later."

Tarq grabs my jaw and pulls my eyes back up to his. The pressure he has on my face borders on too much. His muscles shake from the restraint he's using, and his breaths are short and shallow. "Are you sure about this?" If I overlooked his internal fight before, it is evident in his voice. "Dar, I'm a pair of shorts away from being unable to stop myself."

My Alpha will never take anything from me that I'm not willing to give. He will love and protect me with an unrivaled fierceness. Although he will honor and obey me until the day he dies, his body's need for me is powerful, and I must be careful.

I slowly breathe onto his face to help him relax and calmly slide my hands down his ribs. I can feel his body still shaking, but his breathing settles. Slipping my fingers into the waistband of his shorts, I pull them away from him and allow them to slide down his hips, removing the barrier keeping him from me.

Tarq crashes onto my lips, and I slide my tongue into his mouth. My nerves are excited to receive his attention, but if I move too suddenly or push him too quickly, his instincts will take over, and he'll hurt me. He pulls my thigh to his hip, and I step onto the stool. He's shaking as I lift my other leg. When the back door opens, neither of us turns toward it.

"Get out!" Tarq yells.

His growl vibrates the walls as he leans over me and presses the button under the counter that locks all the doors. As I hear all the locks clicking, Tarq pushes himself into me. His growl settles into a steady rumble as he relaxes, claiming me repeatedly.

My nerves enjoy every touch Tarq gives them, firing whenever he moves. His tongue tastes my mouth, and his fingers pull at my hips with every push. As his muscles' tension eases and the pressure within me builds, my deepest nerves reach out for him. I let him move a few more times before I tip my hips to him, allowing him into my furthest reaches and setting my nerves ablaze.

My back arches, and my nerves release an exploding sensation that has me yelling at a volume anyone within a mile could hear. Tarq moans through his release until he drops onto the stool with me as his growl quiets to a hum. Hanging off his neck, I take slow breaths while he tickles my shoulder blades with his fingers.

"Who came in here?" I ask once I've caught my breath.

Tarq leans away from me. "I don't know, Dar. I was busy."

Giggling as I grab his face, I pull him to me and brush my lips over his. "You have made my life much more than I ever dreamed it could be."

Tarq threads his fingers in my hair and holds me still. "I dreamed I would find someone who'd tolerate my shit," he says, smiling. "I just didn't think you existed."

I laugh at him as he pulls me in for a kiss. "Well, I love you and all your shit, crazy man."

Tarq kisses me a few times but then returns to my serious Alpha. "I want you to take it easy on this trip, Dar," he tells me, leaning back to stop me from kissing him. "I don't want you pushing yourself. We'll get there when we get there."

"As you wish, my Alpha," I whisper.

Growling, Tarq bites my neck and helps me slide off his lap. He grabs my clothes from the floor, and I put them on as he hands them to me. "That medicine is starting to help, huh?"

I swallow hard as my eyes shift to the floor. I can't lie to Tarq. He's always been a partner in every part of my life. *This is different.* His fierce need to protect me would cause him to lock me away if he knew I wasn't getting better. I pull my shirt on and decide on a truth that will satisfy his curiosity as I zip it up.

"Edith found an old remedy that has made breathing much more manageable," I say, smiling.

Tarq wraps his arms around me and stares into my eyes as he presses his lips to mine. "I love you," he whispers. He lets go of me, steps back, and shifts, bumping into the kitchen table.

I shake my head with a smirk. "I keep telling you this kitchen is too small for that."

He shakes his fur out and slides his muzzle against my hand. *"Anthony still gets pissed when he has to see me naked."*

"That's right," I say, grabbing my saddlebags. "And now there are two of you."

"Shit," Tarq grumbles. *"I didn't think about that."*

Mashing the button under the counter, I direct him through the living room. "Come on, My Love," I say, opening the side door to let Tarq out of the house. "Let's go make some new friends."

7

The first time we made this trip, I thought being the Luna would protect me. I know better this time. The Blood Pack reminds me too much of the militia. They don't play by the same rules as any other wolf and pose a threat.

After a while on the trail, Bastian falls back to walk beside me, leaving Tarq to lead our group. With nothing else happening, I focus on the teenager. I can listen to everything my wolves say to each other. They can't hide anything from me. But Bastian is not truly my wolf, so he's silent unless he chooses to speak to me.

Bastian is a beautiful wolf. His fur is slightly darker than Tarq's, and his dark roots create brown stripes in the tan. Bastian's frame is nearly as large as Tarq's but lacks density. His hips are thin, almost bony. *I should also find an excuse to get my hands on his wolf.*

I swing out of my saddle and step around the mare to walk beside the teenager. "Tell me about your Alpha, Bastian," I say, breaking the silence. I reach for Bastian's head, gasping when he jumps away. "Easy, Bass," I say softly. "What's going on?"

Bastian steps toward me. *"My Alpha wanted a report,"* he tells me. *"I can only talk to one of you at a time."*

I move to kneel before him. "And this morning in the kitchen?" I ask. "What was that?"

My wolves will typically sit and relax when I kneel to them. Bastian stands, looking down at me. *"My parents wanted another kid,"* he growls. *"Probably hoping to have a normal one. Someone gave them a potion. I was ten when I watched them die in the pool of blood they spit on our kitchen table.*" He stretches his neck to carry his head at its highest.

I reach for his jaw, but he shies away from my hand. Sighing, I sit back on my heels. "I don't know how things have been for you for the past six years, Bastian, but we support one another in my pack."

"*I didn't tell you that so you could hold me while I cry,*" Bastian says sharply. "*It was a warning. Witches are dangerous.*"

I reach out for his jaw again. "Bass?"

He looks around me at the rest of the group traveling ahead of us. "*We're falling behind.*"

Respecting Bastian's wishes to be left alone, I step into my stirrup and mount Grease. "Our witch has been with us for many years, Bass," I tell him. "We will find the witch that killed your parents."

I hiss to Grease, sending her forward. She breezes past Anthony, galloping until she finds Tarq and slows to jog behind him. I giggle as the horse stretches her neck and bites Tarq's tail.

Yelping, he jumps forward. "*Stupid horse,*" Tarq grumbles. "*Who names a white horse Grease?*"

I laugh at his outburst. "She's your daughter's horse, and you taught our child everything she knows about training horses," I remind him. "It's your fault if she's a jerk trainer."

"*Why would she teach the damn horse to bite my ass?*" He falls back to jog beside us.

"She bit your tail, Tarq. Not your ass."

"*Darya,*" he says, readying to educate me. "*My tail is attached to my ass. Therefore, it is ass-adjacent. Making it close enough to qualify.*"

"And what a great ass it is," I say, smirking.

"*I know, right?*" he announces, chuckling. "*Why don't we hurry this along so you can grab it later?*" He darts forward without waiting for my answer, and Grease takes off.

* * *

By nightfall, we reach the spot Anthony says we spent our first night the last time we made this trip. Tarq sends some of the guards to hunt, but after a while, Bastian goes out and comes back with a large buck. He drops it by Anthony and grabs some shorts before heading back to the woods.

"I warned him about shifting around Anthony," Tarq informs me.

I notice the differences between what Tarq will normally bring back versus Bastian's kill. He had gutted the buck, whereas Tarq rushes back to me and won't bother with that detail. Also, after a long day on the road, Tarq will always grab a few quick bites of the shoulder before bringing it to camp. This buck is in pristine condition. If I didn't know what I was looking for, I might not be aware a wolf had taken it down.

My brow furrows, and I look at Anthony. He doesn't seem to notice anything is off. He slices the hide along its spine and hands me the knife to continue the cut down its hind quarter.

"At least the kid cut the gut and took care of the entrails for us," Anthony says, eyeing Tarq.

"Boy, I will punch you in the throat," Tarq growls. *"Dar, get my pants!"*

Looking up, I raise my eyebrow at him. "Tarq, sit down. After all these years, he's still getting to you?"

Tarq turns his head to stick his nose in my face. *"Yes."*

Clicking my tongue, I grab his muzzle and gently blow into his nose. His head becomes heavy as his eyes roll closed.

"Damn you, woman," Tarq says whimsically. *"Forget the pants. Come with me."*

I smile and kiss his nose as Bastian comes back into camp. His expression makes me turn away from Tarq. "Bass? What's up?"

Bastian doesn't respond as he sits, tossing another log onto the fire. There's a darkness to him as he stares at the flames. Tarq shakes his head to clear it and studies the teenager with me.

"Baby, get my pants," he tells me, eyeing Bastian. *"Let me try talking to him."*

"Emergency, Anthony," I say, pulling some jeans from my saddlebags.

Anthony grumbles and ducks closer to the area he's slicing to avoid seeing Tarq naked.

"I'll call Chase and Ash in, My Love," I tell Tarq as he shifts. "Take your time."

Tarq jumps into his jeans and leans down to kiss my temple before walking around the fire to shove Bastian. "Come on, kid. Let's take a walk."

"Chase, Ash, come to me, please," I call to my wolves.

Bastian stays seated and doesn't respond.

"Go on, Bass," I plead. "Let him help."

Bastian glares at me, heaving a pine cone into the fire. He stands to follow Tarq into the woods.

Ash is the first to arrive. *"Luna? Is everything ok?"* he asks. *"Where's Tarq?"*

I reach out, and he sets his jaw in my hand as Chase approaches. "Tarq is taking care of something," I tell them. "So I thought we'd spend some time together. Nothing wrong with that, right?"

As our companion, Chase spends plenty of time in camp with us. He relaxes instantly against my leg, watching Anthony set slabs of meat in pans near the fire. *"Who got the buck?"* he asks, distracted by his stomach. *"You'll like this, Ash. Anthony's a good cook."*

Ash hasn't spent much time in camp. He stiffly sits nearby as I work at the buck's hip, cutting large steaks for when the guys return. I strip a few ribs for the guards as they drool over Anthony's cooking.

Once we finish with one side, Anthony flips the carcass, cutting the shoulder and hip loose. "I'll throw these on the spit for you guys," he says to the wolves.

I nod to Anthony and turn to my bleached brown wolf. "Ash, come here and relax," I say, holding my arm out. "Anthony is a good cook, but it'll still be a while." I lay against Chase's hip, and Ash gingerly crawls beside me. I relax into their warmth as I rub Ash's shoulders.

"How are you feeling, Dar?" Chase asks.

Smiling, I tug on his front leg. "I'm pretty tired, Chase," I confess.

Ash pokes my cheek with his nose. *"Sleep, Luna. We'll stand watch."*

"Thank you, Ash."

* * *

"Darya, I need you!" Tarq shouts, waking me up.

I bolt upright, startling my guards. They jump to attention, snarling and looking for the threat.

"Luna, what is it?"

"I don't know, Ash," I hiss, silencing him. *"Tarq, are you ok?"*

"I'm fine. You need to get on your horse," Tarq says. *"Make sure you have Edie's tea."*

Saddling Grease quickly, I dig through my saddlebags until my hands land on a vial of tea. My guards watch, waiting for my orders. "Ash, stay with Anthony," I say, sliding my hand over his muzzle. "Chase, you should come with me. I think your nephew is hurt." I jump into the saddle and pull the filly's reins off the branch. *"We're ready."*

I look at Chase as the first howl rings through the air. Grease slings her head up and begins to jump around nervously. She's trained to do this but has a habit of running off before knowing what direction to go. Chase moves out of her way as she canters in place.

When Tarq's second call sounds, she locks onto his position, and I drop her reins, letting her run to him. Chase stays beside us as I lie against her neck, trying to escape the tree limbs she isn't dodging. Grease bursts into a clearing and veers to avoid running over Tarq, nearly throwing me over her shoulder.

"Shit, Dar," Tarq shouts. *"I'm sorry. Are you ok?"* He jogs beside the filly and shifts, helping me dismount. He pulls a pair of shorts from my saddlebags and nods across the clearing. "He's hurt, Dar."

I follow his eyes, seeing Bastian near the trees. His ribs are moving fast, but they aren't lifting much. It's dark in the trees' shadows, so I grab the tea and move closer. Once I'm near enough to see the fear in his eyes, I give him a wide berth, approaching his feet first.

I stuff the vial in my pocket and drop to my knees. Bastian tries to move away, whimpering in pain. "Easy, Bass," I whisper. "Let me help."

The injured wolf just stares at me with wide, fearful eyes. I sit back on my heels, giving him a moment to relax. He pulls his lips back to snarl when I tuck my hair behind my ear.

"What did you do?" I hiss at Tarq.

He frowns. "Why is it always me? He's the one that lost his shit." He's pacing at a distance, staying out of Bastian's view.

I begin crawling toward the young wolf. Surveying his injuries, I do my best to ignore his threatening snarl. *He doesn't look like he could get up anyway.* There's blood running from his nose. A deep gash runs across his shoulder, and there are puncture wounds around his ribs.

I reach for Bastian's paw. He screams in pain when he pulls it away from me. "Chase, come here."

Chase crawls along Bastian's back, laying his head along his nephew's. *"I've been where you are, nephew,"* he tells him. *"She broke my shoulder once, and I had to shift to heal."*

"Don't tell him that," I scoff. "That was an accident."

Chase chuckles, and I try to reach for Bastian's paw again. He doesn't scream when he pulls away this time, so I hear the gurgling from the wounds. *He's punctured at least one lung.*

"We don't have time for this," I tell Chase. "He'll either bleed out or suffocate. I need you to scruff him." Chase begins to move back to position his jaws over Bastian's neck. Tears well up when I see the level of fear and panic in the teenager's eyes. "Chase, wait."

I move around Bastian's legs, and he begins to snarl as I approach his head. "Bass," I say softly. "I'm going to kiss your muzzle. If you want to bite me, you can. But I hope you'll see that I trust you not to hurt me." I drop down onto my elbows and lean close to his ear. "I will not hurt you," I whisper, kissing behind his whiskers.

Bastian's snarl stops, but his breathing becomes labored. I quickly move back into position and nod to Chase. My companion opens his jaws, grabbing a mouthful of Bastian's scruff. He continues to pull back until he triggers the right nerve.

"Alright, honey, let's get you a little calmer." Moving slowly, I reach out for his paw. As I crawl forward, I lightly rest my hand on him. "There we go. See? That doesn't hurt." Rubbing my fingers in small circles, I move up his leg and survey the damage. "Do you want to tell me what happened?"

Bastian closes his eyes, breathing rapidly. I'm unsure if it's panic, fear, or anger, but he's not talking to me. Scanning his body, I find the only uninjured location and wrinkle my nose.

"Bass, we're going to get a lot more personal," I tell him. He opens his eyes and watches me crawl between his front and back legs. "It would appear the only part of you my Alpha didn't bite is your butt."

I carefully rub my hand over his hind quarter. My wolves generally begin to relax instantly from my touch, but Bastian doesn't.

"It's not working," I hiss to Tarq.

"Dar, do something."

Tarq has stopped pacing and is now crouched, watching the young wolf slowly die from his injuries. His death would set in motion a series of events I'm not sure I'd survive. Tarq would be exiled and not allowed to reside among the pack. He would have to live alone with the painful memory of killing another wolf.

I only have one other option. Tarq's the only wolf who's benefited from my fire touch, but this kid has many of his abilities. "Bass, I'm going to try something," I whisper, leaning so he can easily see me. "I need you to tell me if this hurts. Can you do that for me? We'll call it a favor."

Bastian opens his eyes, looking at me with less fear. *So you'll owe me?*

Winking, I scratch his hip. "Don't press your luck while my hand is on your butt." I move my hand from his leg and press it between his front legs. Pushing against his fur, I keep going until I feel skin below my fingers. "Alright, honey, here we go."

I push heat to my hands, increasing it as I feel Bastian's muscles relax. The teenager's eyes are closed, but it's clear they have rolled back.

"It was about a girl," Tarq whispers. "Their pack is so small and not allowed to mingle with ours. They rarely find their mate." He chews on his finger as he drops to his knees and relaxes. "He thought he had."

I shake my head. "I don't understand, Tarq. His girlfriend broke up with him? That wouldn't be worth this."

"His girlfriend had a mate, and she bonded with him," Tarq continues. "No one told him about the color of his heart." He cringes. "I might have laughed."

"Tarq!" I scoff. "He had a broken heart, and you laughed at him?"

"Come on," Tarq whines, frowning. "You know I don't do feelings. That's your department."

"You need to shift," I grumble. "We're all having this conversation."

"Dar," Tarq continues to whine. "You're better at this than I am."

I want to laugh. Tarq's love is fierce. It's his strongest emotion, but he doesn't understand or like talking about it. However, this boy should learn what these feelings mean from a man, not a woman, even if I am the Luna. "You did this, so you're going to help me fix it," I tell him. "I'll also need you to help keep him warm while he heals."

Tarq drops his shorts with a huff and shifts.

"Bass, when you're ready, I need you to shift," I say, turning back to the young wolf. "I have something that will help you, but it only works on humans." Bastian doesn't respond, but his ear flicks in my direction. "In the meantime, my Alpha and I would like to talk to you about mates and how that feels. I'm sorry, sweetheart, but that pull is too great. Your girlfriend didn't stand a chance."

"*I still loved her,*" Bastian says, sighing. As he blows out, a clot flows from his nostril. I know very little about medical stuff, but that can't be good.

Tarq crawls closer to us. "*When you meet your mate… How do I describe it?*" Tarq pauses, putting his nose to my leg. "*Well, she'll smell amazing. You won't be able to get enough.*" He takes a deep breath and closes his eyes.

"*She'll have a bright color around her,*" I continue. "*It could be any color, but it will pulse to your heartbeat.*"

Tarq licks my leg. "*And she'll taste pretty damn great too.*"

"*Ok, that's enough out of you,*" I say, laughing. "*I don't even think that's part of it.*"

Bastian wheezes as he chuckles, and Chase nuzzles his head.

"*Above all else, you'll not be able to leave her side,*" Chase says sadly. "*She will become a part of you, and you will crave her presence.*"

I try to hide my frown as I look at Tarq. I might have underestimated Chase's pain.

Tarq stares into my eyes. *"When you meet her, you'll finally understand why you're alive,"* my Alpha says quietly. *"You'll do anything to make her happy and keep her safe."*

Sniffling, I blink back my tears and lean to kiss Tarq's nose. "I love you too, my Alpha."

"I want that," Bastian says sadly. He falls still and shifts under my hands.

"Oh, Bass," is all I can say as I take in the full extent of his injuries. I roll him back against his uncle and see that his shoulder and bicep are shredded. There are at least a dozen puncture wounds along his ribs. Letting my hand on his chest heat up, I pour the tea into the corner of Bastian's mouth. He swallows as it hits the back of his throat.

Tarq hangs his head as I move away from the teenager. *"He was coming for you."*

Standing up, I pull Grease's saddle and unfold her blanket as I twist Tarq's words in my head. *"I don't understand. Why would he want to hurt me?"* I throw the blanket over Bastian and roll him back onto his side. Chase tucks against his back while Tarq slides in against his stomach as I adjust the teenager's limbs.

"He said he would make me feel as he did," Tarq says, rubbing his muzzle against my cheek. *"He wasn't fighting me. Every time I knocked him down, he'd get back up and head for you. He wanted to kill you."* I relax against his ribs. Tarq curls around to touch his nose to mine. *"I couldn't let him hurt you."*

I rub his muzzle, kissing behind his whiskers. His fears are understandable. Wolves can't bite me, but they can still kill me. I have one weapon against them, which wouldn't work on him anyway. *"He's so damaged,"* I say, sighing. *"What have they done to him?"*

Bastian begins to shake, and Chase tells me it's from shock. My wolves heat up to help him as I push my hands under the blanket to knock him back out.

"Why isn't that burning him?" Tarq asks the same question that was on my mind.

I squint my eyes in thought. *"I think it might have something to do with his strength."*

"I can see that," Tarq replies thoughtfully. *"It'll be a while before he's healed. You should sleep, Dar."*

"I love you," I say, stretching my legs under his chin. *"Thank you for protecting me."*

"I love you too." He curls around to lay his head on my legs.

* * *

It feels like I've only slept a few minutes when I wake to Tarq sticking his nose in my face. He's curled around and bumping his nose into mine, which he knows annoys the shit out of me. I grab his muzzle and heat my hands, sending him into a euphoric daze as I gently lay his head back down. "You're lucky I love you."

"Why do your hands glow?"

Sitting up, I see Bastian has returned to being a wolf. He's back to his dry, calm self. He was different during the weeks we spent at the cabin, but since then, he almost seems to have switched off. I saw his relaxed side the other night, but once we left... *Hang on. He saw that?*

Bastian rolls upright and stands up without disturbing the other wolves. One thing I'll say for the kid is that he might be the most graceful wolf I have ever met. *"You owe me, Luna."*

I cringe, pulling away from Tarq. *"Not here."* Standing up, I nod toward Grease. *"Come with me."* I quickly saddle the horse and remove Tarq's shorts from my saddlebags. "Shift," I instruct Bastian.

The young wolf narrows his eyes. *"No."*

Shrugging, I turn back to the horse. "Then we're done." I swing into the saddle and nod to him. "I wish you a good day, Bastian." I lift my reins to turn Grease.

"Fine," he grumbles. "Give me the shorts." I smile, handing him the clothes. He puts them on and gestures to his body. "As ordered. Now what?"

Slipping my foot from the stirrup, I reach my hand out for him. He slings up behind me, and I steer Grease away from the other wolves. Tarq won't be happy, but he and my companion can easily track my scent. I want to see if I can get through to Bastian since Tarq obviously can't.

"Are your parents buried at the cathedral near the compound?" I ask, breaking the silence after a while.

"No," is his response.

"Are they somewhere you're able to visit?"

"No," he repeats.

Clearly, his parents aren't a way in with Bastian.

"What was your girlfriend's name?"

"What does it matter?" he barks. "I asked you a question." He's so angry that it's pulsing off his body in waves.

I kick Grease, sending her west at a gallop. After avoiding contact, Bastian finally reaches for my hip when the horse leaps over a log. She settles into an easy canter, and Bastian leans against my back. *I'm missing something with him. I can't put my finger on it.*

When we pop out of the woods, we emerge into a cemetery. I stop Grease and point to the ground. "Why don't we walk for a little while, Bass?" We jump down, and I walk in front of him, sliding my hands over the stones. "Why are you so angry, Bass?"

"I'm not angry," he scoffs angrily.

"You tried to attack me last night," I say, turning toward him. "You wanted to kill me."

Bastian stops a few feet from me.

"My Alpha took you down. You got back up, and instead of fighting him, you aimed that anger back at me." I take a step toward him, and he backs up. "Bastian, that is not a one-time anger. That is years or a lifetime of anger. Why are you so angry?"

Bastian continues to back up. His head lowers, but not from shame. *What is that?*

I continue moving toward him, watching as a stone caretaker shed looms in our path. "A break-up would cause heartache, Bass, not anger.

It's not that your girlfriend bonded, what is it?" Bastian's back lands against the shed, and I close the gap between us. I've never forced myself on a wolf, but I have to take this chance with him, so I push against him from our chest to our feet. "Why are you so angry, Bastian?"

The young wolf stays stiff against the wall. He turns his head to the side, staring into the distance. After a while, Bastian's body starts to relax. He flinches when I move my hands to place them on his hips but settles quickly.

"Everyone leaves me," Bastian murmurs. He leans his head against the wall, closing his eyes. "My parents wanted to replace me. They might as well have left years before that potion killed them." He opens his eyes and looks down at me. "When you're finished, you'll leave too." He slides from my grip, walking away.

"I'm here near the horse with no name," Tarq calls out. *"Are you ok?"*

I roll my eyes as I follow Bastian between the grave markers. *"Shift for me. I think I'm gonna need you,"* I tell him. *"And that horse has a name, Tarq."*

"Sure, if you call 'White Mare Number Two' a name."

Sighing, I shake my head. *I swear I love that man.*

"Do you know who's in these graves?" I ask Bastian as he stops to look at a more decorative stone.

I place my hand over one of the wooden markers and test its stability before moving to the next. Bastian turns his attention toward me. I move around him, watching how his focus targets my hands.

"Did you notice there are only dates on the markers?" I ask, making a large circle. Bastian doesn't answer me. I slip my fingers over every marker. I stop at the gravestone before him and lean over it on my elbows. I move my hands quickly to thread my fingers together, and he flinches.

"Luna had this cemetery set up for the soldiers killed while attacking us," Tarq says from behind me. "We offered their bodies to the militia so they could return them to their families, but they didn't want them. Our Luna couldn't stand leaving them just for following orders. So she had them buried here. The dates are the day they died in battle."

"I don't leave anyone," I say as Tarq steps beside me. "These people were my enemy. You are my wolf. I would never leave you." Bastian's focus has shifted to Tarq. "Will you ride with me for a while today, Bass?"

8

We returned to the trail after Bastian agreed to ride with me. I'd given Tarq a rundown of what I'd noticed about the young wolf, including his unusual obsession with my hands. He said he had some ideas but wasn't interested in sharing them. Tarq advised me to wait for Bastian to show me he was ready. *Only I don't know what that means.*

"What happened last night?" Anthony asks as he rides up beside us.

"It was just a misunderstanding, Anthony," I tell him, smiling. "We've handled it."

Anthony eyes the teenager. "Lay a finger on her, and I will end you." I know he means what he says, but I wish he'd kept that threat to himself because Bastian nervously pulls his hand off my hip.

"Oh, go on, Anthony," I say, irritated that he'd erased the little progress I'd made with the young wolf.

Anthony winks and drops back to watch over me from behind.

"Don't worry about him, Bass," I say quietly. "You're safe with me. I promise."

Bastian puts his hand on my shoulder and looks back at Anthony. "I'll keep that in mind."

"Is there anything you want to talk about?" I ask. I turn to look up at him when he remains silent, and he blushes. "What is it?"

"What was it like for you when you found Alpha?" he asks, turning a deeper red. "You told me what it would be like for me, but what about my mate?"

My face scrunches up a bit. "Well, it was a weird situation. Tarq knew I was his mate, but I didn't understand what was happening." He drops his hand to my hip, and I pat it reassuringly. "Tarq was patient and kind. He waited for me to be ready for him." I hook my leg over the saddle horn, looking up at Bastian thoughtfully. "Once I'd spent some time with him, I just knew he was mine," I say, smiling.

"You didn't see the colors?" Bastian asks, confused.

"That's not how it works for Lunas." He flinches when I raise my hand to touch his face but catches my fingers and rubs them over his cheek. "We don't see the colors as your mate will," I continue. "The bond is the same, though. You will find your mate one day and have an unconditional bond with her."

"Why didn't he do anything about it?" Bastian whispers, looking ahead of us.

I follow his eyes to see Tarq dropping back to walk beside Grease. "He was waiting for me to be ready for him," I say, squeezing Bastian's arm. "I was the one who decided to bond with him." I look down at Tarq. "Not that I stood a chance."

"I would've waited forever for you," Tarq says.

"I think you waited long enough, my Alpha," I tell him.

Bastian's eyes drop to my hands. "Why did your hands glow?"

"Dar, did you forget to tell me something?"

"Yes, I did," I respond quickly. *"Now, hush, My Love."*

"Maybe that's why he watches your hands," Tarq suggests.

"Is it only when I use them?" I ask. "Like this?" I lay my hand on his thigh as I would a normal wolf.

Bastian shakes his head. "No. It was when Alpha woke you up, and you made him sleep."

I let my hand heat up and feel his muscles relax.

"Like that," he says, sighing. "Holy shit, that feels good. What is that?"

Tarq chuckles.

"That is one of Tarq's favorite Luna gifts," I answer. "This is a fire touch. It burns all other wolves, but we think your strength protects you from it."

Bastian blushes again as his eyes focus back on my hand. "That's beautiful."

I pull my hand off his leg, shaking it. "I don't know why you're able to see that, but that is what your mate's entire body will look like when you find her."

Bastian doesn't respond, but he had become tense when he lowered his voice—*when Tarq joined us. "Baby, can you give me a minute to test something?"* I ask Tarq. He drops back, darting off the trail so the filly won't follow him. I pull back on the reins and squeeze Bastian's leg. "Why don't we give Grease a break?"

He slides off the horse and then helps me down from the saddle. Now that it's just us, he relaxes and allows me to take his arm as we walk.

"Bass, can you tell me about your Alpha?" I look up at him, but he's staring into the woods. Asking about his Alpha is how I lost him last time, and it seems I'm headed down that road again. "Miles was the Alpha of the Blood Pack when you were born," I say, hoping to change the subject fast enough. "You probably don't remember him. You were just a baby." He looks down at me. "Did you hear about the first time we met? He tried to kill me."

Bastian pauses for a moment, surprised.

"Yep," I continue. "Miles ordered one of his men to throw a spear, and Tarq took it to the chest." I pat his hand. "He didn't think much of me back then."

"Why is your horse's name Grease?" Bastian asks, changing the subject.

"My daughter," I tell him. "She's named every horse born in our fields since she was five." Bastian relaxes back into the conversation. "This one was named after her favorite movie about four years ago. She was going through a musical phase." My eyes flick up the trail, landing on Tarq and Ash further ahead. "Drove her father crazy with that one."

"I figured you had to be a parent," Bastian says thoughtfully. "But Alpha doesn't seem to know how to be an adult." He watches Tarq as he bounds beside Ash, discussing their last ball game. "He doesn't act like an Alpha."

I smile as Tarq bites at Ash's legs, and the two take off, racing each other. "He doesn't like to be called Alpha," I say, turning to Bastian. "He's found a way to release the excess energy that doesn't hurt anyone. He's loved and respected by our pack, and we wouldn't have him any other way, Bass. We wouldn't want to take away something that makes him happy."

The teenager silently stares into the distance.

"Who taught you how to ride?" I ask, trying another tactic.

"My father."

"Did you two spend a lot of time together?" I ask in my sweet voice, fearing I've lost him.

"No." *Yep, he's gone.*

I step in front of him, placing my hand on his chest. I've been tip-toeing since the beginning, so I try to just go directly at him. "Bass, I don't know how to get to you."

Bastian looks down, pulling my hand off him. "Then stop trying." He pulls Tarq's shirt over his head. "Why bother? You're just using me to get your peace." He pulls the shorts down and hands them to me. "I'm just a wolf." He shifts and runs up the trail.

I lean against Grease's shoulder. *"Baby, this isn't working."*

Tarq charges back at full speed, shifting into my arms. "I'm sorry, My Love," he whispers. "Let's give him some time to figure us out."

* * *

After that, Tarq rode with me for the next few days. He explained his plan to me. *If I'm being honest, it terrifies me.* Tarq has trained horses most of his life and has extensive experience with abuse victims. His idea is to work with Bastian as he does with those horses. He wants me to ignore the young wolf, leaving him alone. He believes that Bastian will slowly enter our space once he decides that we are safe and wants to spend time with us. *I don't want this to work. I don't want to think about what would cause that beautiful wolf to need this.*

We lie near the fire three nights later, relaxing. Tarq hands me his front paw for a rub, and I spot Bastian watching us from inside the trees.

"He's almost ready, My Love," he says, catching me glancing in the teenager's direction. *"He hasn't taken his eyes off us all day."* He bumps his nose into mine.

"If you don't stop doing that, I'm gonna pull your whiskers out."

"No, you won't," Tarq teases. *"You love my whiskers."*

I wrinkle my nose. "I really do," I say, giggling.

I relax back into our nightly routine of quiet humming and pad rubs. Looking around the camp, I watch Chase and Ash finish dinner. I've mentioned to Tarq a few times that I can't remember seeing Bastian eat, but he assured me he has to be eating something if he's still alive. *That's not comforting, but it is true.*

"Tarq, I don't want this to work," I whisper, catching the young wolf watching us again.

My Alpha knows me better than any other person in my life. He slides his muzzle over my arm. *"You can't erase the past, My Love,"* he reminds me. *"We will figure out what that kid needs from us so that we can help him find a brighter future."*

"Thank you," I whisper.

Taking a deep breath, I stand and begin the routine Neala recommended. Chase and Ash initially protested, but they both get good night kisses every night now. Neala told us that I needed to show tremendous love for everyone. She said that it would create a desire. Chase is used to my affection, but Ash gets noisy, exaggerated kisses because they embarrass him.

Once I'm finished with my guards, I turn to my Alpha. "How about some cuddle time, My Love?" Sliding into my arms, Tarq hooks his front leg over my shoulder and pulls me down. He lays his leg over my arm while I tuck into his chest and curl my legs against his gut. His back paws brace my lower back to keep me securely against him all night.

"I miss this when we're home," I confess.

"I prefer you naked in my arms," Tarq chimes.

I reach up and feel around for his face above my head.

"Woman, what are you doing?" Tarq chuckles. *"You're gonna poke my eye out."*

I giggle, tugging his ear when I find it. *"Go to sleep, My Love. We have a teenage boy to win over tomorrow."*

"He's nearly there. Have faith."

* * *

When I wake, Tarq has his leg hooked over my shoulder, holding me against him. I adjust my arm, and he presses down on it as something quickly moves away from my back.

"Don't move, Dar," Tarq says.

I tuck my arm against my chest and snuggle back into him, pretending to still be asleep. *"How long do I have to stay like this?"*

"Until he thinks we don't know he was here," he instructs.

I'm thankful my face is in his chest as my brow furrows. *"What?"*

Tarq sighs, tucking his nose against my back. *"The kid came and laid with us a few hours ago,"* he says. *"He jumped up when you moved."*

The fact that Tarq's plan is working is not a blessing. As wolves, they take on many traits from the canine animal. They have strong instincts that make them powerful hunters. When someone has physically betrayed their trust, they take shelter in their wolf instincts. The fact that Bastian doesn't even feel safe as a wolf means that someone has betrayed him as a human and broken his wolf.

"What have they done to him?" I manage to ask as I fight my tears.

"Whatever it was, they will regret it," Tarq promises.

We only lie still for a short time before Anthony crouches beside us. "I have no idea what you two are playing at, but I know you're awake," he whispers. "Let's go." Anthony hates being away from Edith almost as much as being left out of a plan.

Pushing Tarq's leg off my shoulder, I sit up and look down at him. He rolls onto his back, stretching his legs and sticking a paw in my face. I grab it and pull it into my lap to rub his pads. "I don't want to leave him behind, Tarq," I whisper. "I want to get him out of there."

"*Dar, we don't know anything about his situation,*" Tarq warns me. "*He could be the damn Alpha for all we know.*"

"He was different at the cabin, right?" I narrow my eyes, trying to remember when I was sick. "He seemed calm."

"*He was a little weird, but I was distracted,*" Tarq says thoughtfully. "*He only slept when you were touching him. If I didn't need him, he'd shift and jump on the bed with you to sleep. I thought you were pulling emotions off him, but he's too strong for that.*"

"He's my wolf, Tarq," I say, frowning.

"*Let's give him today. We'll see if he'll come around tonight.*"

* * *

We spend another day jogging through the woods. Chase runs quietly beside me, allowing Tarq to stay out of Bastian's sight. I look for the teenager and fight my smile whenever I catch him watching me from behind a tree. It's hard to keep my mind from wondering what he might have endured.

"*It's a good thing, My Love,*" Tarq tells me after the fifth time I excitedly report that I've seen Bastian watching me. "*He's trying to decide if he should trust you or not. Let him figure this out on his own.*"

"I feel like he's our kid," I admit. "*Is that weird?*"

"*They are all our wolves, Dar,*" Tarq says, chuckling. "*He just happens to be a young, damaged wolf.*"

"It makes me want to hug our daughter."

"*Then let's get this over with so I can take you home to her,*" he suggests. "*We'll be at the boundary lake soon.*"

* * *

Tarq's right, of course, and we drop onto the lake's beach within an hour. It's a beautiful sunny day at the mountain lake, and the heat radiating from the sandy beach is calling me. I pull Grease's saddle off before she walks into the water. Dropping her gear, I flop down and sprawl in the sun.

It's not long before Tarq's nose begins to push against my head, lifting me so he can lie under my shoulders. "You almost died last time we were here," I murmur.

"That wasn't here, Dar," Tarq reminds me as if it changes the situation. *"It was over there in the woods."* Tarq rolls onto his side and stretches his legs.

"We don't have to go that way, do we?"

"For you, My Love, we will go around," Tarq says sweetly.

We spend the rest of the day lounging around in the sun. Anthony builds a fire and makes camp with the help of some guards. *Sometimes, it's nice being in charge.* I glanced around a few times, looking for Bastian, but Tarq told me to leave him alone. He said I needed to ignore the kid so that he would want my attention. I don't like it, but Tarq's been right so far.

By nightfall, the camp had cleared out to just Tarq and me, with Anthony standing watch by the trees. I lie against Tarq's shoulder with his paw in my hand. I'm humming to him with my eyes closed as I rub his pads when I feel something brush against my leg. I fight the urge to jump and simply open my eyes to see Bastian lying by my feet. His whiskers touch my calf as he studies us, his eyes nervously flicking side to side.

Tarq rolls slightly, ignoring him, and gives me his other front paw. Bastian flinches when I move to accept the new foot, so I close my eyes and return to humming. Tarq quietly groans as I push forward on his toe pads, and I feel Bastian moving up my leg. I open my eyes to see him slowly crawling on his belly.

I move to Tarq's ribs, freeing his shoulder, and open my arm to Bastian. He crawls further up my body until his neck lies over my arm. Tarq moves his legs forward to make room for him, and the young wolf rests his jaw on my Alpha's shoulder. I remain as still as possible until Bastian relaxes and finally rolls onto his side, putting his back against me.

Tarq curls around and pokes Bastian's face a few times. They both sneeze and sigh as they settle into each other. I take the opportunity to slide my fingers through Bastian's fur. I'm paying attention this time and feel his ribs aren't filled like my wolves'. His spine is missing the layer of muscle that should be covering it.

Tarq's wolf is much bulkier than his human form. Bastian made a point of wearing a shirt whenever he was around me to cover his leanness. I curl my arm under his neck, rub that hand over his head, and try to remember how he felt after they saved me, but I can't recall specifics. One thing I clearly remember is that I have never heard Bastian hum. I fear what I might have missed while this young wolf saved my life.

When his body starts to heat, Tarq rolls over a little more and calls the guards closer to the beach so he can sleep. I curl up to the two sleeping wolves and count this a huge success. Tonight, this beautiful young wolf will feel loved. When he wakes, he'll know it wasn't a dream.

* * *

Tarq is the first to wake in the morning and rolls from underneath Bastian and me. I hear the young wolf lick his lips, and he slides his head so that it's against my face as I wrap my other arm around him. The only warmth coming from him is from the sun, so I know the teenager is awake, but he's letting me hold him and not panicking or nervous. Even though I want to hear him hum, I'll accept this small victory for now.

A shadow crosses over us, causing me to open my eyes. Tarq squats next to us and tugs Bastian's fur. "Come on, kid," he says. "Get dressed." He holds out a pair of shorts.

I latch onto Bastian and frown at Tarq. "What are you doing?" I whine. "Let us sleep."

Tarq lifts his eyebrow. "You, my Luna, are going for a swim."

Bastian jumps out of my arms and shifts, grabbing the shorts.

I roll onto my back and stretch before turning to Tarq with a frown. "Baby," I continue my whining. "It's early, and that water is probably cold."

Tarq laughs. "And that has never stopped me before." He leans down, grabs my arms, and hauls me off the ground.

I find myself thrown over his shoulder, and Tarq swings me around a few times before heading to the water. I scowl at Bastian. "I suppose this is fun for you too?"

Bastian blushes as he smiles. "I miss swimming."

"Then let's go swimming," I say with a wink.

We pass Anthony on our way to the lake, and he shakes his head. "Are you two ever going to grow up?"

"Not today, Anthony!" Tarq shouts, entering the water. He stops once he's waist-deep and turns to Bastian. "I'm not exactly sure why, but I have this burning need to throw our lovely Luna in every body of water we come near." I push off his back so he'll cradle me in his arms and allow me to participate in the conversation. Tarq looks down at me and winks. "What do you say, Bass? Wanna help?"

I shake my head and turn to Bastian. The kid's smile is contagious. I've seen his stern face and frown so much that he looks like a completely different kid. I hate that I'm about to be thrown into a lake that's probably freezing, but the excitement in this beautiful boy's eyes makes me want to let them.

I reach my hand out to Bastian and let him take my arms. They countdown together as they swing me before hurling me over the water. As I suspected, it's freezing and knocks the wind out of me. When I surface, I face away from them as I struggle to pull air back into my lungs. I haven't taken my medicine yet, and I'd forgotten how much this hurts.

When I have some air movement, I swim back to Tarq, shivering. I need his heat. There is no way I can completely catch my breath while I'm this cold. I wrap my arms and legs around him as he pulls me back into the deeper water.

Tarq heats his body while I move to press as much of my skin against him as possible. It's a relief when the water around him begins to warm up. "It's a big lake, Bass," Tarq says. "Why don't you help me?"

Understanding that this is a teaching moment for the wolves, I reach out to Bastian to encourage him to join us. He steps toward me until my hand lands on his chest.

"Instead of simply letting it happen, you're going to tense your muscles," Tarq instructs. "So flex and release your muscles to create the friction around them."

Tarq turns so I can watch, pulling my hand off the young wolf. Bastian closes his eyes, and steam begins to rise from his skin. He smiles and puts his hands out to his sides, skimming the top of the water. Soon enough, warm water starts to come from his direction too.

When he opens his eyes, they're bright and alive. "I didn't even know we could do this."

Now that they've warmed me enough, I turn back to Bastian, placing my hand on his chest. "There is good inside you, Bass," I tell him, smiling. "There are a lot of things you can do. You just have to change how you view yourself."

Bastian reaches out, sliding his fingers under my arm.

"You are so much more than just a wolf, Bass. Your strength does not define you," Tarq tells him. "You don't have to be how others see you." Tarq shifts me around so that he's cradling me. He steps toward Bastian and sandwiches me between their bodies.

Setting me in Bastian's arms, Tarq dives into the water and swims away. Whatever he's doing, he's given me a moment to run my hands over the young wolf. I rest my cheek against Bastian's collarbone as he leans against my forehead. He's watching the water, looking for Tarq as I slip my hand over his ribs and back. I feel his shoulder blades and then slide down to his hips.

My Alpha resurfaces as I press on Bastian's chest. The teenager calmly allowed me to inspect him. He's still not humming, but I suspect he knew what I was doing. My wolves don't have any fat in their bodies. A muscle layer lies just under their skin, and Bastian's is severely depleted. Fueling their bodies takes a lot of food, and he's not getting enough.

I trail my finger along his jaw. "Bass," I whisper. "I want you to stay with us."

Bastian lifts his head. "Luna..." he sighs, turning away.

"Hey, Bass," Tarq calls out from the deeper water. "Our Luna loves to eat fish. Why don't you help me get her some?"

Smiling, he looks back down at me. "Is that ok?" Bastian asks. "Will you be alright?"

That damn smile. I put my hand on the teenager's chest. "Go," I tell him. "You should have some fun while we're here. I'll be fine." I lift my legs off his arm, and he sets me down before diving into the water to join Tarq.

Quickly walking out of the water, I grab my boots and head straight to the fire Anthony had relit. He holds my saddlebags out to me as I approach him. He looks angry but waits until I'm taking my medicine to unleash it on me.

"You are taking unnecessary risks to hide this from everyone," Anthony barks. There's a bite to his words, but he means well. He snatches the potion vial from me while I'm chugging the nasty herbs. "This one can be heated. It would probably help after that cold water."

"We all need this right now, Anthony," I say, sighing. "Try not to judge me too harshly." I watch him swirl the potion around in the vial as he holds it over the heat. He hands it back to me before the rubber encasing begins to melt.

I drink the warm potion slowly. Anthony was right about the warmth helping after enduring the colder water. I stretch out next to the small fire and let the sun dry my clothes while the guys spend time together. As the pain in my chest subsides, I listen to my wolves. I'm looking for one voice, and she's rarely in her wolf form because of her work with the junior guards. I smile when I find her.

"Neala?" I call out. *"Do you have a minute?"*

"For you, Luna, always," she responds.

I smile. Neala is my child whisperer. *"I need you to meet us at the cabin,"* I say apologetically. I don't want to take her away from the kids in the bunkhouse, but I can't deny that I need her. *"I'm bringing that kid back there with us, and I need your help with him."*

The smaller packs had a harder time with the militias and rebel groups before we became one pack. Their children were stolen. When we got them back, they would stay with Neala and Ash. We didn't find any as old as Bastian, but if I want to get through to the boy and his wolf, I'll need Neala's help.

"I'll need to set up the schedule for Nate," she says. *"I can meet you at the cabin in three days."*

"Thank you."

9

The guys return with half a dozen small fish. They're pushing each other and laughing about something Tarq thought looked weird. Bastian says it's a fish, but Tarq swears he saw a miniature monster. I'm almost mad when Anthony interrupts them.

"Do you want me to cook your tiny fish?" he asks.

I giggle at Tarq's growl. "You did sort of fail at fishing, My Love."

Tarq lifts his eyebrow. "Bass, take care of that," he says, flicking his hand toward me.

Shaking my head, I put my arms out in a worthless attempt to stop Bastian. He grabs me by my hips, throwing me over his shoulder. Laughing, he spins a few times as he walks toward the water.

"No, Bass," I whine. "I just dried off!"

Bastian walks into the water and pulls me off his shoulder. I'm still begging him not to, but I can't stop these wolves once they have something planned that entertains them.

Bastian looks down, smiling. *I'd let him throw me into a fire as long as he smiled.* "Here we go, Luna. One," he counts, swinging me. "Two." Bastian moves me away from his body to make room for a bigger swing, laughing the whole time.

"Well, look at this happy little family," a woman sneers from the beach.

I want to look toward the voice, but I can't peel my eyes off Bastian. His smile faded instantly as his body tensed. His jaw clenches, and his eyes focus on the water. He'd nearly dropped me but now holds me tightly against his chest.

"Alpha was wondering why he couldn't reach you," the hateful voice says. "Now I see why."

"Dar?" Tarq's stronger as a wolf and would shift if he sensed danger.

"Stay there," I answer.

Bastian breathes deeply as he lowers my feet to the ground. He's staring at the water but whispers, "I'm sorry."

He backs up, holding his arms out to stop me from following him. I push past his arms and grab his hip. My hand rests on his chest, and I wait for him to look into my eyes.

"Please, Bass," I beg. "You don't have to go with them. We want you to stay with us."

The woman laughs. "Yeah, baby Beta," she bellows. "Go play house with the Luna. I could do your job so much better. Wait 'til Alpha hears this shit!"

I'm not surprised often, but I didn't see any version of this coming. I'd heard the term Beta over the years. It's what some packs called their second in command. Dax didn't use the title, and there's no need for it now since Tarq is second to me.

Tarq's growl pulls me out of my head. "Bass?" I can't hide my shock.

When Bastian looks down at me, the happy kid is gone. "I didn't know how to tell you," he says. The teenager spins around, catching the woman by the neck. He drags her up the beach and slams her against a tree.

Tarq runs to me as my knees buckle. *"What the hell just happened?"* he asks.

I look up the beach and see Anthony just inside the trees with his rifle pointed at Bastian. "I don't know," I confess.

Tarq moves to sit beside me. I turn to face him and put my forehead on his shoulder.

"How strict are you feeling about the 'don't kill wolves' rule today, Dar?" Tarq is serious but won't break pack law. He's mad.

I wrap my arms around his front legs. "I trusted him," I whisper. "I feel so stupid."

I look over the water when Tarq begins to growl. I can tell by the intensity that someone is coming near us, but my heart is broken enough.

"We need to go," Bastian says. "More will come."

Tarq's snarl deepens so much that I feel it in my bones. This is the snarl that will clear battlefields. *"Get the fuck away from her."*

The unmistakable sound of a rifle's hammer clicking comes next. "I'm pretty sure that wolf is telling you to back up, mate," Anthony warns.

"Luna?" Bastian begs.

Tarq pulls his legs out of my arms as he curls around me. *"You will not touch her."*

Needing a moment, I stand up and walk away. I just need to think. He's second in command to the man that wants me dead. He probably ordered some of the attempted attacks on us. I want to hate that kid for playing me, but I can't.

I kick at the water. *Why the hell is he a Beta? He's just a kid.* Tarq's screaming at Bastian and hurting my head. Whistling for Grease, I ball up my fist and put it to my heart. When she stops beside me, I jump onto her back and kick her until she's galloping through the woods.

I let her run freely, just getting the distance and not caring where she goes. Ash soon falls in beside me. He's the wolf who always accompanies me when I need a calm, level head. He runs silently beside us until I finally stop Grease in a moss-covered grove.

Ash lies near some logs as I slide off the filly's back. I reach for his jaw when I sit beside him. Ash might not be used to spending the night in camp with me, but he's used to this. My wolves can sometimes be overwhelming, and it's hard to get quiet time to think. Distance helps, and Ash is normally the wolf that comes with me. He's a man of few words, and I appreciate that quality.

"I feel like I should've known, Ash," I tell him, scratching his shoulder blades. "You knew, though, didn't you?"

Ash stretches his neck to give me better access. *"I'm not that good."*

My hand stops as I focus on an earlier question. *"What's on your mind, Luna?"*

I turn and lay my head on his shoulder. I do this whenever we end up in this position, and Ash always stiffens nervously. I've accepted that he'll never fully embrace my friendly side. "There's something I can't wrap my head around, Ash," I say, turning to him. "Why would a 16-year-old be a Beta?"

Ash rolls to his side so that his shoulder cradles me. *"That might be the best question of them all, Luna,"* he says. *"There must be wolves with much more experience."*

"Would you want him on 'Team Ash?'" I ask, mainly teasing, but he knows what I mean.

Ash pushes me slightly with his paw as he chuckles. *"That's just ball. I'm not sure I'd want a loose cannon on my team for the game of life, though."*

"You've been watching him for a while now," I say, rolling toward his head. "Do you have any idea why he's so different?"

Ash bends to look me in the eye. *"It's not that he's different, Luna,"* he starts. *"It's that he's like Tarq. Have you considered that he might be Tarq's son?"* His ear twitches nervously when I frown. *"His age would put him born about a year before you met our Alpha."*

"Let's pretend that could never be possible," I say, cringing. "I'm not ready to even consider that." Thinking Tarq could have other children makes me want to throw up. *I know I'm being childish, but I couldn't handle it.*

Ash chuckles but then tucks his chin. *"Apologies, Luna,"* he says.

Smiling, I tug his fur. "Ash, there's no need to stand on ceremony. I need to hear your thoughts, even if I might not like them." I wink at him and relax back against his shoulder. Ash follows me by lifting his head to continue looking into my eyes. I reach for his chin. "What is it?"

"Luna, by chance, could he be Annalisa's mate?"

His question catches me off guard. *She's still a little girl.* I shake my head. "She's too young for a mate, Ash."

"The appearance of a mate could happen at any time, Luna," Ash reminds

me. *"Mates are generally about the same age. If you remember, we asked you to assist with Brock and Rachel."*

I nod, cringing. I don't like it, but he has a point. Tarq and I are just one year apart. And I had to issue an order to ensure 17-year-old Brock would wait since his mate was only 13 years old. *Luna had also mentioned that Cathal was powerful.*

Sighing, I take a break from my thoughts to listen to my Alpha and shake my head. I'm not sure Tarq could have picked a better wolf as our companion. He and Chase are having an analytical pros and cons conversation about whether they should kill Bastian. They won't, but they need something to fill the time while they wait. I tune them out when Chase decides that killing his nephew "requires exercise" should be listed as a con.

"Ash, what do I smell like?"

Ash dips his chin again, looking confused. *"Luna?"*

"I'm serious, Ash," I say, laughing. "Go with me here." I sit up and look down at him. "What do I smell like to you?"

Ash curls around to my thigh and sniffs. *"Well, Luna, you smell like flowers."*

"So, I smell the same to all wolves?" I ask. Tarq and Dax both said I smelled like flowers, and I remember smelling the scent when I relived Tarq rescuing me, but I never bothered to see if it was the same for everyone.

Ash pokes me to take another deep breath but tucks his nose in shame.

I reach for his chin with a smile. "We'll have none of that, Ash." I pull his muzzle to my lips as he places it in my hand. "Besides, you've seen Tarq stick his nose to me for hours. I'm used to it."

Ash chuckles, laying back. *"That wolf loves his flowers,"* he says, still laughing. *"Don't get me wrong, you smell good, but Tarq loves flowers. My Grandma said she'd always catch him in her garden when he was little. He'd shift and lay there smelling the blooms. She said she'd chase him out with a broom before she knew he could shift inside the boundary."*

"Really?" I manage to say through my laughter.

"You might smell good to us, Luna, but your scent is perfect for Tarq."

"And what does Annalisa smell like?" I'm pretty sure I know this answer. Dax mentioned it before he died.

"She smells like fruit," Ash says, twisting his head. He doesn't spend much time near her since he's usually on the road with me or training the junior guards with his wife. *"I believe it's peaches. Why?"*

I narrow my eyes, looking around the forest. *It's perfect fruit harvesting time if we can find some.* My nose must be wrinkled because Ash bumps his nose to mine, making me swat at him.

He chuckles. *"Now I understand why Tarq does that."* He laughs some more but then taps my knee with his paw. *"Seriously though, I haven't seen that look in a while, Luna. What are you thinking?"*

Smiling, I lift my eyebrow. "How's your sense of smell today?"

"My sense of smell, Luna?"

"I think we should test your theory," I tell him. "It would be nice to have some fruit with our fish for lunch. Do you think you could help me find some?"

Ash jumps up, bowing. *"I am at your service. I suppose peaches are on the menu?"*

I pull myself up with the hook he creates with his leg. "Always the clever one, Ash," I tell him, winking. "We'll need my saddlebags. Tarq and Chase are goofing off. I'll talk to Tarq while you have Chase bring my bags."

Ash nods and calls out to Chase. I turn to the filly, calling out to Tarq.

"My Love, I need you to have that kid pass a message to his Alpha."

"Are you ok?" Tarq asks, sounding worried.

"Yes, My Love," I answer. *"We are getting fruit to go with the fish. Have that kid tell his Alpha to meet us at the beach. We'll not be traveling into their territory."*

"What kind of fruit are you getting?" Tarq asks, distracted by his stomach.

"Tarq?"

"Yeah, you're right. I'm not really hungry anyway." His voice trails off. *"Where's Chase going with your saddlebags?"*

Sometimes, I wonder how we get anything done with how Tarq's mind works. *"My Love, I cannot carry food in my pockets."*

Tarq chuckles but doesn't respond. Ash guides Chase until he's able to pick up my scent. I'm leading Grease to a rotted stump when he finds us.

"Dar, something is off about Bastian's situation," Chase says, stopping me. *"I think he needs help."*

Kneeling, I catch his muzzle and hold it to my cheek. "Chase, I will not abandon my wolves but cannot endanger the pack. I promise you that we'll figure this out." I kiss him behind his whiskers. "I need you to trust me and not make a move unless I tell you to."

Chase pulls back from me with his head tilted. *"What are we doing?"*

Winking at him, I step onto the stump. "We're going hunting."

* * *

My life is worth a lot of gold in some circles. As guards, their lives are strict. They don't protect me because they have to or because it's their job. They love me as much as I love them. We have this type of bond because we do things like hunt fruit, and my wolves get to laugh and have fun competing to be the best "hunter."

Grease follows my guards as they dart around the forest. They find strawberries, blueberries, oranges, and apples. Chase found a grapevine, but Ash was the one who found the peach trees.

Chase jogs to me after he shakes a limb on the peach tree and pelts Ash with loose fruit. "You know he's bigger than you, right?" I ask, smirking.

"I'm prettier, so it's ok," Chase responds. *"How are you feeling?"*

"I'm doing alright, Chase," I tell him, packing the last fruits. "Edith told Anthony to annoy me into taking it easy."

"We love you, Dar," he tells me calmly. *"We only want to take care of you."*

"I don't think I've thanked you for your overprotective ways, but I do appreciate you, Chase," I say, smiling. "Trust me as I trust you, and we'll get through this."

Chase puts his muzzle to my face and gently licks my cheek. *I love you.*

"I love you too," I say, kissing the tip of his nose. "Let's get back and see if we can't solve some of this mystery." I throw the saddlebags over the filly's withers before hopping onto her back. "After you," I say, nodding to my wolves. They dart toward the beach with Grease on their heels.

* * *

Dropping onto the beach, we find Tarq glaring at Bastian while Anthony sits on a stump with his rifle trained on him. Bastian stands and tries to approach me, but Tarq blocks him, snarling.

"Did he talk to his Alpha?" I ask Tarq.

"I would've had to shift to tell him," Tarq says. *"Every time I twitch, the kid moves."*

I roll my eyes. "Anthony, Tarq's got this," I say, eyeing the ex-Commander. "Can you see to the fire?"

Anthony lowers his rifle as he backs away from Bastian.

"Luna, please —" Bastian starts.

I snap my eyes toward the teenager. "Stop!" I shout. "I've heard enough of your lies. I'll be the one talking, and you will listen."

He lowers his head. I have so many thoughts and questions circling that I can't keep anything straight. Wolves in power don't show shame. They don't show fear either, and he's watched my hands as if they would hurt him if they got too close.

"I no longer trust anything you've told me, so you will tell that Alpha of yours to meet us here," I say.

Bastian's eyes dart up to me. There's something in them that I don't recognize. He opens his mouth to speak, but I stop him.

"Don't talk to me! He'll be here by nightfall, or we'll be leaving." I turn away from him as he pulls his shorts down and shifts.

"*Don't turn around,*" Bastian says. I drop to my knees, grabbing my saddlebags. "*Just listen, please.*"

I pull the bags to my chest and feel a tear roll down my cheek as I freeze.

"*He's already on his way,*" he rushes to say. "*He knows what he wants. That's what Vera was here to tell me. This isn't a negotiation.*"

I look up to see Anthony staring at me curiously. I shake my head at him.

"*Once Tynan sets his terms, the clock will start. You'll run out of time,*" Bastian warns. "*You need to leave, Luna. Please.*"

Hearing what that asshole wants doesn't sound so bad. I place my saddlebags before me, setting the fruit on a plate. Tarq's snarl grows too loud to ignore. "*I do not run!*" I snap at Bastian. "*Now shift before Tarq reaches his limit.*"

"*Please, Luna.*"

"Kill him," I say, turning to face Bastian.

My Alpha launches at the teenager as he slides down on his shoulder, instantly submitting. Tarq latches onto his throat and steps on his chest. Bastian shifts under him, his eyes on me. This boy who smiled so infectiously just a few hours ago is now breaking my heart. I want to run to him.

"Let him up," I whisper.

Tarq releases Bastian's neck but pushes off his chest, causing him to double over, coughing and gasping.

"*Baby, I need you to shift. His Alpha is on his way.*" Tarq's head snaps in my direction. "*I don't want him to know you're stronger than his weapon.*"

Tarq shifts and dresses while Ash and Chase take his place guarding Bastian. He sits by the fire with me, leaving them on the beach a short distance away. Tarq rubs my back, watching me work on the fruit. When a tear drops onto the orange I'm peeling, my Alpha pulls me to his chest.

"I asked Neala to come to the cabin," I whisper. "We had him."

Tarq gently rocks me. "And now he's the enemy," he replies. "Was he talking to you?"

"His Alpha's name is Tynan," I start. "He's on his way here now. Bastian said that a clock will start once he sets his terms." Tarq sighs, laying his cheek on my head. "He told me to run," I whisper.

"Why's a 16-year-old a Beta?" Tarq mumbles sadly.

I squeeze his arms and look up at him. "I think it's time we find out." I move away from Tarq, wiping my face. *Chase, Ash, let him come to me.*

The wolves stand and back toward me. Bastian jumps up and walks forward as they let him. His eyes stay on me.

"That's far enough." I stop them once he's close enough to talk. Bastian frowns but stays quiet and sits. "Has Tynan been the Alpha since Miles?" I look up at him between pulling strawberry stems. His eyes shift nervously. "Do I need to repeat the question?"

Bastian sighs. "Luna, things aren't the same for us..."

"Then tell me!" I bark.

"Alpha gives orders, and you just do them," he mumbles. "He told me to find you. I thought you could stop him."

"Bastian, you're his Beta," I sneer. "You don't just follow orders."

The young wolf falls back onto the sand. "Killing me would be a mercy," he says quietly. "I think he had my parents killed. He ordered the house to be burned with their bodies in it."

Covering my gasp, I glance at Chase and shake my head. He lays his chin back on his paws. The fact that they were his family does not escape me.

"He locked me up until I'd do anything to get out of those chains," Bastian whispers.

My eyes shift from Tarq to Bastian. I'm not sure I want him to continue. Suddenly, I'm not at the beach but in a cellar. There's a dirt floor, and I look down, finding metal shackles around legs attached to chains. I'm following the chains to the wall when the vision fades.

Bastian rubs his eyes as if trying to erase something. "He chained me to that wall for four years. Every day, I prayed for help. I thought the Luna my mother spoke of would come for me."

Tarq braces me as I lean on him. My mouth opens to heave air as tears stream down my face.

"You never came. I did what I had to."

Tarq is just as paralyzed as I am. He puts his hand over mine and stares at me. I catch a tear on his cheek with my thumb. There's no sense in trying to wipe mine away.

"He will honor the meeting, Luna," Bastian says dryly. "He will give you his terms, and, in the end, you will give him what he wants, or he'll kill anyone in his way to take it."

"I would've come for you if I'd known," I whisper.

Bastian turns his head toward me. "It only took me six years to forgive you for that."

I wipe my face quickly when Anthony slides a plate of fish over, rubbing my shoulder. Tarq helps me split the fruit, but I take more peaches for one dish. "You should eat," I whisper, crouching before Bastian.

"Thank you," he whispers back, taking the plate. The teenager slides his fingers under my arm as he had in the water.

My breath catches as I back away. I nod to Ash and settle next to Tarq. Rubbing my hand over where Bastian had touched, a smile threatens to creep across my face. *I haven't lost him. I just need to take him from that man.*

Anthony hands me the rest of the plates. "The master fisherman didn't get enough for your wolves."

Tarq growls at him.

"Stow it, wolf," Anthony barks. "That wasn't your finest catch, and you know it."

"Yeah, it really wasn't," Tarq replies, chuckling.

I shake my head, but they're distracted, so I can't complain. With glances toward Bastian, I pick at my food. I'm not hungry, so there's not much on my plate. Bastian tosses chunks of fish to Ash and his uncle, not eating any himself.

"I don't suppose you boys like fruit too?" he asks them. I sigh in relief as he throws some berries to each one, but my chest tightens when he grabs the peaches. He puts the fruit to his nose, taking a deep breath. "I haven't had peaches since my parents died." I watch as he slowly bites into the fruit and groans, rolling his eyes.

Ash raises his head.

"Not a word, Ash," I say quickly.

He lays his chin back down on his paws. *"Yes, Luna."*

Bastian licks his lips. "That's better than I remember."

Tarq isn't paying attention to Bastian's enjoyment of his peaches. My Alpha hasn't eaten any of his food. His head is against my shoulder, and I know he's having trouble stomaching Bastian's childhood. His wasn't easy, but he was cared for and loved.

I can't focus on anything other than the peaches and my daughter. I'm about to share what I know when a strange voice booms over the quiet camp.

"Well, would you look at my wolf," the voice sneers. "You got him all tame and shit."

Tarq and I stand up, knowing exactly who this must be. My wolves tense but stay where they are. Bastian instantly cowers, and Anthony reaches for his rifle, setting it across his lap.

The man who approaches us is only slightly taller than me. His black hair flops down his neck, looking greasy and unclean. He's wearing a leather coat and pants, and I can't help wondering why in this heat. He doesn't appear to have any weapons but strides like he's the biggest wolf here.

He hasn't even looked at us. He's glaring at Bastian. As he steps closer to him, the teenager scrambles to his knees. "I told you I never wanted to see your ugly ass face again! Shift!" He's yelling as if they're across the beach from each other. Every enunciated word makes Bastian flinch. By the time Tynan stops talking, my hands are shaking.

When Bastian looks at me one last time, he's as broken as an aged-out stallion. The sweet boy closes his eyes slowly and shifts. I swallow hard and step forward, my hands fired and ready to go, but Tarq reaches out, stopping me.

"Get behind me, now," I call out to Ash and Chase. They both stand tall as they back away from Tynan. I hear Chase's growl, but I've never silenced him. I won't be starting now. Not when I'm questioning the wolf-killing law myself.

As my wolves give Tynan the room he needs to move freely, he walks up to Bastian and punches his muzzle. The teenager's yelp rings through my body, clenching every muscle it touches. I open my hands and try to step forward again. Tarq's fingers dig into my skin until I release my fire into him.

"Don't you ever ignore me again!" Tynan turns from scowling red-faced at Bastian to smiling pleasantly at me. "You must be the Alpha killer."

"You're Tynan?" My tone lets him know he does not impress me.

The short, leather-clad man runs his eyes over my body. "You would be correct." He kicks some logs around before picking one to sit on. "You try to steal my soldier, drag me out here 'cause you're slow as fuck, and you don't even offer me food? That's rude." The man looks as though we're conversing over tea and biscuits.

"I don't want you to stay, so no, I'm not feeding you," I tell him.

"Yet you'll feed my wolf?" Bastian ducks as Tynan swats at him, hiding his head in shame. "Whatever," Tynan continues, oblivious to his surroundings. "I cleaned up your mess even after you killed our Alpha, so here are my terms. The Blood Pack will join the Lunar Pack when you give me what I want. You will accept a death sentence or bless my marriage to your daughter, naming me Alpha of all wolves."

I'm not sure where I am getting all this fire from, but this man would've died a hundred times by now. My hands are out to my side, ready to kill him again.

"I'm feeling generous," Tynan says, nodding. "Your daughter will be 15 in six months. She'd be ready for me then, so you have until her birthday to decide." He stands up, straightening his jacket. "I await your decision." He kicks sand at Bastian. "Let's go, shit bag."

I'm frozen as he turns and disappears into the trees, with Bastian slinking behind him at a safe distance. I stare after them. *What the hell just happened?!*

10

The five of us stood stunned while reflecting on what we'd seen. We've experienced hate over the years from humans. It was mostly militia, but there would be a hateful civilian every once in a while. Never has a wolf acted in this way. That man is a horrible disgrace to the name "Wolf."

"What the fuck just happened?!" Anthony yells.

I slowly turn in his direction. I have no idea how to answer him. My only thoughts revolve around Bastian. *That man took my wolf. He chained him, beat him, and took him from me.*

"I'm going to kill that man!" Tarq shouts. His growl vibrates the ground under my feet. He storms over to the log Tynan had sat on and heaves it into the fire, throwing embers all around.

"Darya, what the hell was that?" Anthony steps beside me.

I crash onto the sand when he touches my shoulder.

"He's so much stronger than them," Tarq continues ranting. "Why doesn't he just take him out? Get away from them. Leave. Why doesn't he choose us?"

Chase slides his muzzle under my arm to brace me and touches his nose to my cheek. *"I trust you,"* he tells me. *I'm not sure I trust myself.*

"It's worse," I whisper.

"How can someone so strong be controlled by someone so weak that he beats children?" Tarq paces across the beach.

"We can't kill a wolf," I remind him.

Tarq lifts an eyebrow. "Oh, I'll find a way."

Taking a deep breath, I straighten my back. "Baby, there's something I need to tell you."

Tarq stops, staring at me with a frown. "Aw, not with this again," he finally says.

"He's her mate," I whisper.

Chase turns so suddenly that he hits me with his muzzle. I grab his face and pull all his emotions, draining him because I'm positive I'll need them for Tarq in a few minutes.

"What?" Tarq says, confused. "Who's whose mate?"

"Bastian is Annalisa's mate."

Tarq's hands curl into fists. His jaw clenches, and his lips pull tightly across his teeth. Chase steps back as I lift my hands off him and let them fire. Ash appears at my other side in case I need his help. Tarq is generally unpredictable, but when he's angry, he can be dangerous. I've never seen him this mad.

When he finally moves, he jams his fist to his forehead and screams at the top of his lungs, "FUCK!" He drops his hands and stares at me.

I grab my chest. I'm fairly certain my heart is breaking. I close my eyes, taking a deep breath as I feel Tarq's hands slide over my face. I think I needed his touch more than he needed mine. My fire might calm his emotions, but his love soothes my soul.

"What are we gonna do?" he asks as I open my eyes.

"We can't stay here," Anthony barks.

I think for a moment. *We had him. He slept peacefully and played with us. Bastian wanted to be with us, and I finally heard his laughter.* "The cabin," I say. "He was always comfortable there. We need to go back to the cabin." I climb to my feet and look around for my boots. "If he gets away, that's where he'll go."

"Who?" Tarq is still mad and unsure where to point his anger. "Dar, no. I wanna kill that kid or save him. Maybe just kick his ass."

Tarq stands beside me and cups my cheeks again. This time, his face matches his eyes. He's ready for me now and wants a decision. From the corner of my eye, I can see Anthony and my wolves staring at me too. *It's time to be their Luna. I need to make a decision.*

I close my eyes, going over the facts one more time. *Bastian saved my life. We earned his trust, and he played in the lake with us. His beautiful smile and infectious laugh made everything seem brighter somehow.* I sigh as Tarq wipes a tear from my cheek. *He's Annalisa's mate. There is only one option.*

"He's not ours to forsake," I say, opening my eyes. "He's hers. We need to find a way to help him."

Anthony is the first to move, throwing the dirty dishes into his bags. Tarq is the second, collapsing and dragging me into his lap. He cradles me against his chest, and I'm fine with letting him. I watch Anthony move around the camp as if the rest of the world were moving in slow motion. Finally, he kicks sand over the fire and grabs my boots.

"We need to get you out of here," he whispers, crouching beside us. Anthony's time in the militia makes him invaluable in these situations. He leaves emotion out of his tactical decisions. "I think you're right. If he comes back to you, it'll be at the cabin. You need to lock down little Luna too."

Anthony leaves my boots, and Tarq looks into my eyes as I slide my hand over his face. Of course, he's right. That horrible man that beats on children wants my little girl. I need to put a team of guards on her.

"I suddenly want to hug Bruce," Tarq says sadly. "Like, hug him a lot, Dar."

With a small, understanding smile, I kiss his lips gently. "And I want to talk to the Alphas, but for now, My Love, let's get out of here."

* * *

As soon as we hit the trail, I began working with Nate to ensure wolves surrounded Annalisa. She was under Edith's care, but the witch is meeting us at the cabin, so my daughter will stay in our house with Amelia.

The sun is setting as we pull up next to a creek. I swing my leg over Grease's neck to drop out of my saddle, but Anthony slides his horse to a halt in my way.

"It's not safe to stop," he tells me. "We need to get you to the cabin. We'll be riding straight through."

"That's another day and a half, Anthony," I say, shaking my head. "My wolves can't do that."

"*He's right,*" Tarq says, stopping beside Anthony. "*We'll do what is necessary to ensure your safety.*"

"My Alpha," I plead. "Our companion got hurt the last time I let someone push you. I don't want anything to happen to any of you."

"*Do you know how we would feel if anything were to happen to you?*" Chase asks, walking up behind me. "*We would never forgive ourselves. We could not live with the knowledge that we failed you.*"

Sighing, I look from one wolf to the other. *How do you argue with that?*

* * *

We're not doing well when we reach the cabin in the early morning, a day and a half later. I'm having trouble keeping my thoughts straight. Tarq started singing to me just before it got dark and kept going all night. It pissed the other wolves off because he was too tired to focus it on just me. He used this technique to help me when I first woke up as Luna and all the wolves' voices came flooding in at once.

As Grease stumbles up to the cabin, Edith rushes to me. I try to dismount, practically falling into her arms. "Alright, Darya," Edith says soothingly. "Let's get you to bed." She helps me to the bedroom. I'm so tired I don't remember climbing the stairs.

After dressing me in night clothes, Edith rubs a cool rag over my face. As she lies me down in the bed, I can feel tears wanting to come out, but just like my words, they won't. I lift my arm to reach for Tarq, but he's not there.

* * *

The sun shines through the window when I open my eyes. I blissfully sigh as I feel Tarq's weight and nuzzle his chest. His weight has always provided my greatest comfort. I want to leave him sleeping, but his stomach growls, reminding me that he hasn't eaten in days.

I remember Edith painstakingly covering me in night clothes, but Tarq probably wandered through the house as a wolf and wouldn't have bothered to shift until he flopped onto the bed. That would explain why I find him naked as I slide my hand down his body.

My Alpha groans and starts his morning stretch routine with an exaggerated yawn. He pulls me onto his chest, leaving his eyes closed.

"Good morning, My Love," I say, smiling.

"I'm hungry," he says, putting the underside of my wrist to his lips.

"So, did you want some breakfast?" I ask as my eyes roll closed.

His mouth continues to travel up my arm, waking my entire body.

"I could be convinced," Tarq whispers, still against my skin. He slides out from underneath me and straddles my legs. His hands slip under my shirt as they travel up my back, pushing it up until I let him take it off.

Tarq tangles his fingers in my hair, pulling it aside to expose the back of my neck. He leans down to whisper in my ear. "Then again, there seems to be plenty to eat right here." He wraps his teeth around the nape of my neck, pushing his tongue against the skin. I inhale as deeply as possible and whimper as I mash my face into the pillows.

Sliding his lips and hands over my skin, Tarq enjoys my body. My nerves reach out to his touch, relishing his attention and missing him when he leaves. Lying with Tarq transports me to a different world where only he and I exist, giving us a reprieve from our stresses.

As he sends me over the edge, I bite a pillow to muffle my moans, and my body clamps down on him. I rock my hips, causing Tarq's release. Fighting every tense muscle, I push him into me until he collapses onto my back.

Catching his breath, he lifts off me enough to let me roll over underneath him. Tarq buries his face in my neck. "I am actually kinda hungry," he mumbles.

"I would expect nothing else from my bottomless pit." I slide my fingers through his hair and enjoy this quiet moment with my Alpha since we don't get many.

I close my eyes, and suddenly, I'm somewhere else. A putrid scent hits my nose. I look down, seeing blood and vomit on the dirt floor.

The shackles on my wrists are heavy. I'm looking through Bastian's eyes, and he's in the cellar.

I'm about to be sick, but Tarq is still on me. I shove him off me and pull at the edge of the bed. I look closely and see blood trickling down Bastian's leg. My eyes roll, and the vision fades.

Running to the bathroom, I throw up in the sink. Tarq follows me and pulls me into his lap as he sits on the bathtub's edge. He rubs his hand over my forehead and cheeks.

"Are you getting sick?" Tarq asks, looking worried.

"He's back in that room. He's chained to the wall again." I close my eyes with a sigh, leaning against his chest.

Tarq pulls my face back to where he can see it. "Who?" he asks. "What room?"

Shit. I forgot to tell him about that.

"With everything that happened... I'm sorry, I forgot," I stammer. "When Bastian told us about being chained, he showed me a vision of the cellar. I don't think he knew he did it."

Tarq shakes his head. "Dar? I don't understand."

"I saw the chains just for a second on the beach," I tell him, thinking through all I saw. "He's back there; only it's worse. That man put him back in the cellar and hurt him."

My Alpha carries me back to the bedroom. Setting me on the bed, Tarq paces across the room. He clenches and releases his fist several times before picking up a vase and throwing it against the wall.

"Dar, I want to run in there and rip all their throats out," he yells. "I will end them all. How could they do that? They are a disgrace!"

My chest is aching, and I need my medicine. I rummage around in the drawers, looking for clothes. "Tarq, the law is clear about killing wolves," I remind him. "It's an ancient law that I'm not interested in testing. You can't justify one killing and not another." My hands land on some lounge clothes from when I was sick. "Tarq, get dressed. We'll get some food and talk to the others. We need to go see Byron."

Tarq grabs his pants, throwing them across the room. "What's an elder gonna do? Tell you a bedtime story?"

I put my clothes down, raising my eyebrow. "Feel better now?"

Tarq rolls his eyes as he leans over to retrieve his pants. He slips them on and sits down beside me. "My little girl deserves what we have," he says sadly. "That boy is broken glass, and it's that asshole's fault."

Sliding my hand over his neck, I pull him to me. "We need a plan," I whisper. "We can't just run in there, hoping for the best. We don't even know where he is."

"Can you talk to him?"

"I wish I could, My Love. He's not a wolf chained to that wall. He'd have to shift." I run my fingers through his hair until he relaxes slightly. "I promise we will do what is best for everyone, including our daughter."

Once Tarq has helped me dress, he seems calm enough to discuss a plan. We wander downstairs to find Edith and Anthony in the kitchen. Anthony busies himself at the stove. He fries eggs and ham, making sure I notice his disapproving looks.

"Here, Darya," Edith says, sliding my medicine across the counter. "And don't worry about him," she adds, looking at Anthony from the corner of her eye. "He's just jealous. It sounded like fun, though." Edith winks at me while Anthony rolls his eyes.

Tarq leans forward with a groan and puts his forehead on the counter.

"This is why you're not allowed to stay with us at the lake anymore," I scoff.

Edith giggles and walks around the counter. "Pish tosh, Dar," she says, stopping to rub my shoulder. "Look at him." She moves on to slide her fingers up Tarq's back. "This man is downright beautiful. The whole world wants what you have." Her fingers slip into his hair, and she tugs at it as her lip draws into her mouth. "Hmm. The things I do to you in my dreams. Baby, I make you scream."

Tarq leaves his head on the counter but turns to me with pleading eyes. "I'm gonna go out for a run."

"You are not," I say, running my fingers over his cheek. I turn to

Edith, glaring at her. "Leave him alone. You have a husband. Go play with him."

"Oh, I do," Edith laughs, walking around the counter to Anthony. She slides her hand up his shirt. "Anthony would never admit it, but he appreciates your yummy husband just as much as I do."

I openly gawk at Edith. She is a highly trusted advisor, but it takes four to five times longer to get anything done with her when Tarq is around. This is normal for her. Looking at my Alpha, I honestly can't blame her. *He is beautiful.*

I slide my hand over Tarq's neck. "Edith, please focus," I say, turning back to the witch. "Anthony, you too. We need to talk. Bastian's been chained back to the wall he told us about."

Sliding a plate before me, Anthony leans on the counter. "And you derived this information from your morning activities?"

I throw a slice of ham at him. "You two are perfect for each other."

Anthony smiles. "I know, right?"

Edith smacks his hip before passing two steaming mugs to Tarq and me. "Seriously," she says. "How do you know?"

"I assume Anthony's already told you that I figured out who Bastian is," I say, handing a slice of ham to Tarq. "I would like that to stay between us. My wolves know better, but you two like to share things." I point my finger at Edith and Anthony. "He has many of the same abilities as Tarq. One of which is that he can show me images. He showed me where he is."

Anthony's eyes narrow as he pushes away from us. "How do you know he's not playing you, Darya?" he asks. "Your heart is in the right place, but that psycho has cracked that kid." He's right, and I want to be cautious, but I can't. *It's Bastian. The kid I finally saw was so happy to experience the love we showed him.*

I look over at Tarq and see his jaw tense. Quickly rolling up some ham, I jam it into his mouth as soon as he opens it, knowing he's about to say something he'll regret later. "I don't think he knows he's doing it," I say, turning away from Tarq. "From what I saw, he's not in good shape."

Tarq swallows the ham and joins in on my line of thinking. "The first time I did it, I didn't know she was there," he tells them. "I was... emotional. I was thinking about something I saw and wanted her to be there." He turns to me with a small smile, sliding his thumb over my cheek as he grabs my neck. "And then she called my name and scared the hell out of me."

I slide my hand over Tarq's arm. "Using that information, as long as I don't tell him I'm there, he shouldn't know I can see his images."

"So what do you want to do?" Edith asks.

"She wants to go see Byron," Tarq answers.

Anthony throws his hands up. "Because story time is gonna save the fucking day?" He turns back to the food cooking on the stove.

Tarq spits his coffee across the counter, spraying Edith.

"Honestly," she says, stepping back and grabbing a towel to clean herself off. "We can't take you two anywhere."

"I can't believe you, of all people, just said that!" Tarq laughs heartily.

"The next Alpha of our pack is chained to a wall while a weak little man beats the shit out of him," I growl through my teeth at them. "That man is hurting that beautiful boy!" I'm yelling, but it's justified. I understand that they didn't see what I saw. They should still be taking this seriously. "You can put whatever word you want on it. Call Bastian damaged, cracked, or broken, but we **are** saving him!"

I relax back onto my stool, trying to catch my breath. Byron broke an ancient magical law a decade ago, and I had to banish him from the pack for endangering us. He's still an elder, but he lost his historian abilities, and I can't talk to him as I can with the wolves in my pack. My only choice is face-to-face.

"I don't know how to save Bastian from that man without killing wolves or getting him killed," I say slowly. "There might be something in our history that could help, so I would like to speak to Byron."

As Edith pats my hand, Anthony grabs my plate and pulls the pans from the stove. "Alright, let's get packed," he says.

Tarq steals some ham off Edith's plate, causing her to scowl at him.

"Your husband just took my wife's plate," Tarq complains to justify his actions.

I try to look through Bastian's vision, but I still can't find anything to help me locate him. Rolling my eyes, I retreat to the silence of the living room. Away from their bickering, I sit in the calming peace so I can hear my thoughts.

"Bass? Can you hear me, sweetheart?" I call out, hoping for an answer. I find myself in the same situation I was in 15 years ago, trying to will a young wolf's voice into my head. My eyes are closed, but I feel Tarq sit beside me, sliding his hand over my back. *"Please hear me."* But there's no response. I look up at Tarq, and he wipes the tears from my cheeks. "I had to try," I tell him.

"You wouldn't be you if you didn't," he responds gently.

Taking a deep breath, I blow out my lips. "Ok, here's the plan," I start, switching gears and channeling the Luna within. "We're leaving Chase here, just in case. There should be a familiar face if Bastian makes it back here before we do. We'll take Ash, Neala, and the dynamic duo." I pat my legs as I think. "I want Matthew on Annalisa's guard team."

Tarq's eyebrows furrow. "That kid that follows her around like a puppy dog?" he asks, shaking his head. "Dar, he isn't even trained. Why?"

Tarq began training at a very young age. His strength made him dangerous. Dax taught him everything he knew to keep him active and drain off the excess energy.

Since taking over the pack, we required the kids to be at least 19 to begin full training. I wanted them to be able to enjoy their childhood. Surprisingly, Anthony was my strongest supporter.

"I don't need him trained," I tell him, touching his chest. "He is in love with your little girl, and a boy in love will do anything to protect the object of his affection."

Tarq frowns. "That's mean."

"Do you want your daughter safe or protect a teenager from a broken heart?" I ask, lifting my eyebrow.

Tarq's frown doesn't fade. "Fine," he grumbles. "But you're helping him with his broken heart. I screwed that up once already."

Giggling, I grab his cheeks. "Yes, baby," I say. "Why don't we get going? The sooner we find answers, the sooner we can get him out of there."

* * *

Within a few hours, we're back on the trail. We sent Byron to live at Edith's ranch after his exile from the pack. His two daughters belong with us, so I wouldn't let him leave the area. Unfortunately, his 11-year-old daughter went crazy when he passed his abilities on to her. The other rarely shifts, as her gift is the ability to see other wolves' mates, and I haven't figured out how to get my wolves to stop bothering her.

Neala is running beside Grease. She has traveled with Ash and me before on shorter trips. I enjoy her calming presence, but the fact that she works with the junior guards makes her necessary on this excursion.

"Luna," she calls out. *"We can stop by the creek for the night."* She looks up at me as we thunder down the trail.

"We are still four days away, Neala," I shout to her. "I want to keep going a little longer."

"Luna, you've not been getting enough rest," Neala responds sternly. *"And these horses are tired."*

As I look down at Neala, Grease stumbles, barely catching herself before she falls. "Of course," I say, slowing the filly. "You're right."

Tarq leads us into a quiet area by the creek for the night. I hate stopping after only traveling for a few hours, but I knew it would happen, and we're all still tired from riding straight to the cabin. Grease walks to the creek and lies down. She goes on runs with Tarq to keep fit, but she's never handled the workload Bones had.

I sit with my back against a tree, reaching for Tarq. "Come here, baby."

He gently rubs his muzzle against my cheek. *"How are you holding up, My Love?"*

Sighing, I hold him to my face. "Oh, I'm tired, my Alpha," I say. "I have this horrible feeling that we shouldn't have left."

Tarq hooks his leg over my shoulder, pulling me down with him. I curl against his underside as he rubs his muzzle over my ear to wipe my hair from my face.

"He'll be ok, right?" I mumble into his fur. "We can fix this?"

Tarq curls his leg over my arm and brushes his nose over my face. *"Go to sleep, Dar,"* he tells me. *"Things always seem brighter in the sunlight."*

A full day later, I've not seen or heard anything new from Bastian. In my panic, I'm not allowing my group to stop for the night. We're tired, so the pace has slowed to a walk, but at least it's not a stop. Tarq's not happy with me, and Anthony is openly bitching at the back of the pack, but I don't care. I see Bastian's blood running down his leg whenever I close my eyes.

Neala is still by my side. She sticks to my hip as I lead Grease, ready to provide support should I need it.

"Have you ever worked with a kid that's been through something this bad, Neala?" I ask, looking down at her.

"I'm not sure anyone would survive what you've described," she responds.

"How would you build trust?" She didn't answer me, but I think she would have told me if any of my wolves had experienced this treatment so I could rectify it.

She narrows her eyes in thought. *"Luna,"* she starts, slowly putting her words together. *"It seems his tormentor has broken him down so much that he no longer feels whole as a boy or a wolf. You will need to build him back up from scratch. He will need a place where nothing hurts."*

"What do you think I should do?"

"You are wise beyond your years, Luna." I can hear her pride. *"You have generations of Luna blood flowing through your veins."* She bumps my hand with her nose and slides her head under it. *"You will know what to do when the time comes. You just have to trust yourself."*

I run my fingers through her coat a few times while I think about her words. Finally, I tug the fur on her throat and look down at her, smiling weakly. "Thank you, Neala."

II

We reach the flower fields at sunset three and a half days later. We're all cranky, and my wolves haven't slept since the first night, but the flower fields have a way of wiping everything away. I smile as I take in the blended colors from the swaying blooms.

"This sight never gets old, does it?" Edith says, sighing.

I hold my hands to my sides, running them over the flowers. "Dax asked Luna to bring us here the night we died," I whisper.

Tarq slides his head under my hand. *"I miss him."*

"My favorite memory here is watching Tarq fall on his face while he was chasing butterflies," Anthony says, laughing.

"That seems so long ago," Edith says thoughtfully.

I pull my nails against the fur on Tarq's neck. "I love Dax, but that is not my favorite memory of this field," I say, looking down at my Alpha. "Annalisa made that memory. She had just started walking. I set her down, and she took off. The flowers swallowed her up, so I couldn't find her."

Tarq chuckles. *"I had to shift to track her."*

"Yep," I say, giggling. "That was the first time Annalisa noticed Daddy was a wolf."

"Now I think she prefers it," Tarq grumbles.

Over the years, balancing the pack with my family has been challenging. Between them and my wolves, the wolves have won more times than I care to admit. Tarq picked up my slack with our daughter. He is the one who raised Annalisa and taught her everything she knows. I was a visitor in their lives more than a wife and mother. Of course, they bicker. They are always together.

"That's not true, my Alpha," I tell him. "You fought with Dax every chance you got. I thought you two hated each other, but that's not how you felt, right?"

Tarq ducks his head and turns away from the group. *"I don't think I need to answer that."*

I grab his chin, pulling his eyes to mine. "You don't because, in reality, you love each other." He turns his eyes to the side, sighing. "Dax loves you. All our wolves and your daughter love you. Don't you ever doubt that." I kneel to him and plant a noisy, dramatic kiss on the tip of his nose.

"Stop," he says, chuckling. *"You're gonna make me blush."*

Ash and Neala hook their necks around Tarq's in support. I smile at them as they touch their noses to my cheeks.

"See, my Alpha? You are loved." Giving him one last hug, I stand and turn to resume our slow journey to Edith's ranch.

"I do love our very extended family," Tarq says happily.

As I look down to smile at him, my surroundings change. I stick my hands out as I fall to my knees. I can feel the stems of flowers, but I'm looking at boulders and mud. I'm moving slowly, hopping forward. I look down as I stop before a puddle and gasp as I recognize Bastian. I can only see his muzzle, covered in blood.

Tarq's head slides under my outstretched hand. *"What's wrong?"* he asks.

I put my finger to my lips. The image jumps again, and I crash face-first into the mud. The image fades in and out as Bastian blinks but then blacks out completely. I grab my chest, taking a deep breath.

"Luna? Please? Can you hear me?"

I hold my breath as Bastian pauses.

"I'm sorry."

I push myself back to sit on my heels in the field. "He's out," I say. "He got out somehow. We need to go back."

The entire group begins talking at once. I have wolves in my head while Anthony and Edith are talking over each other. I don't care what any of them have to say right now.

"*Bass?*" I call out to the young wolf.

I hear him, but the others are so loud that I can't understand him. "SHUT UP!" I scream.

"*He said he wanted the next Luna,*" Bastian's telling me. "*I didn't know she was your daughter. I should've never come to you. This is my fault.*"

"*Bass, where are you?*" I ask while he's quiet.

"*I don't know, Luna,*" Bastian tells me. "*The witch helped me. I've been trying to get as far away as possible.*"

Recalling the vision, I notice everything is blurry. *He's dehydrated.*

"*Bass, can you drink water from those puddles for me?*" I ask.

"*It's a nice enough place to die, Luna,*" Bastian says, his thoughts nearly a whisper. "*It's quiet here. I just wanted you to know that I was sorry.*" Bastian's voice fades with every word in his exhaustion. "*Luna?*"

"*Yeah, baby?*"

"*How did you know there were puddles?*" he asks, confused.

I giggle quietly. "*That's an excellent question, sweetheart,*" I tell him. "*I'm gonna get back to you on that, but can you drink some water for me?*" Letting my eyes focus, I realize everyone is staring at me. They obviously want answers. "Edith and Anthony, I need you to bring Byron to the lake," I tell them. "I'll meet with him there."

Anthony looks surprised. "You want me to bring him back to the pack?"

Sighing, I nod. "I'll need him under guard." Tarq rubs his muzzle along my cheek, and I pull the fur on his throat. "Neala? Ash? I hate to ask this, but can I split you up?" I ask my wolves. "I don't want to leave them without a wolf, but I need Neala for Bastian."

They look at each other before answering me. "*We will help in any way you need us to, Luna,*" Neala responds.

I pull Tarq away from my cheek, looking into his eyes. "Baby, I need you to help me find that kid," I tell him. "He doesn't know where he is."

"*I'll do my best, My Love,*" he says, trying to snuggle back up to me.

"I need you to teach him how to show me what he's seeing," I quickly add. "If you can see what I'm looking at, you should be able to see what he's showing me, right?"

Tarq pauses and sticks his nose in my face instead. *"So that doesn't sound like a good plan, Dar,"* he tells me. *"What if he uses it against you?"*

I rest my nose against his and push on him as my hands pull down on his neck, shifting his chin forward against my lips. When I exhale, all he can smell is my scent, and his hum kicks on instantly.

Tarq takes a deep breath of me before pulling away. *"Alright, just promise me you won't die."*

Grinning, I kiss his nose. "No one ever died from a vision, my Alpha."

"You'd find a way," he grumbles, shaking his head.

Everyone is sitting closely. Edith and Anthony are used to only being able to hear part of our conversations, so they know what we're about to try to do. Neala nods, letting me know she's ready to help.

"Alright, see if you can reach him." Tarq settles in front of me.

"*Bass?*" I call out and wait for a response. I look at Tarq, shaking my head. He nudges his nose toward me, urging me to try again. "*Hey, kid, I need you to talk to me.*"

"*I'm tired, Luna,*" is Bastian's response.

My eyes widen as a grin creeps across my face.

"Hey, kiddo, I heard you're not doing so good." Tarq tries to connect with Bastian, but the young wolf doesn't respond. He puts his nose against my cheek.

"*Bass? Can you hear Tarq?*" I ask. Tarq puts his paw in my lap. I grab it and rub his pads absentmindedly. "*Have you ever played ball, Bass?*" I continue. "*Our immortal Alpha taught the pack to play in a pretty fun way.*" Bastian hums quietly, so I keep going. "*Someone throws a ball across the field, and then I shoot an arrow at it for the wolves to race.*"

"*That sounds fun,*" Bastian responds.

"It started as a way for my father and me to spend time together," Tarq explains. *"But then it turned into a way to run the aggression out of me. I miss my father every day."*

The young wolf speaks up after a moment. "*Your father taught you to control it?*"

"*Not really,*" Tarq tells the teenager. "*He tried to exercise it out of me. He didn't know it would be helpful later in life.*" When Bastian doesn't respond, I roll my hand, encouraging Tarq to keep going. "*I want to teach you something,*" he continues. "*Do you think you could give it a try?*"

Bastian still isn't responding.

Neala nudges my shoulder with her nose. "*Ash told me about the beach. He said you treated the kid like family when you got through to him. He was happy, right?*"

I start to understand where she's going. "So we should act more like ourselves with him?"

"*Yes,*" she says. "*You two have a unique way of communicating. He liked that. He was comfortable with the real Luna and Alpha.*"

Smiling, I tug her fur. "Thank you, Neala."

As she steps back, I start humming to give Bastian a chance to reset. It's the same nonsense tune I hummed that night on the beach when the teenager crawled into my arms. He let me rub one of his paws before I fell asleep. I feel a tear slide down my cheek.

"*So, My Love,*" Tarq says. "*I need you to close your eyes. We're gonna give this a whirl.*"

I close my eyes, smiling at how easily he turns into a goofball.

"*Thank you, Luna,*" Tarq tells me. I hear him lick his lips. "*I will try very hard not to lick your face. I promise.*"

"*I would appreciate that, thank you,*" I reply, giggling.

Bastian chuckles, and Tarq puts his paw back in my lap.

"*Alright, kiddo, I need you to find a memory of Luna. Can you do that for me?*" He pauses for Bastian to respond, but he doesn't. "*You have to pick a strong one. It can be good or bad.*"

"*I prefer a good one,*" I vote.

"*Hush, Luna,*" Tarq says, bumping his nose against mine. "*Let the menfolk talk.*" I swat at him and rub my nose. "*Do you have a memory for me?*"

"*I do,*" Bastian immediately responds, making me sit up and smile. "*It's when we —*"

"*Wait, wait, wait,*" Tarq cuts him off. "*I don't want you to tell me. I just want you to focus on that memory. I want you to see Luna so clearly that you could touch her.*" Tarq nuzzles my cheek and then lies down with his head in my lap. I slide my hands over his face as he continues. "*See her dark brown eyes—her hair tucked behind her ear. Watch it shine as it falls down her back.*"

Tarq rolls over and sticks his paws under my jaw, wanting his pads rubbed.

"*The smooth way her hands rub our legs and pads after a long day,*" Tarq continues, humming.

"*Tarq!*" I scoff.

Bastian chuckles. "*No, Luna, he has a point. That did feel good.*"

"*Mm-hmm, it definitely does,*" Tarq agrees.

I squeeze the paw I'm rubbing and giggle at him, but then gasp when I'm suddenly at the beach looking at myself.

"*There you go,*" Tarq says, letting me know it had worked like I'd hoped. "*Just let that play through, ok?*"

Bastian keeps his eyes on me as Tarq carries me into the water. I watch myself protest as they swing me through the air and throw me over the water. Tarq talks to him while I catch my breath, but I can't understand him. Bastian's focus was entirely on me.

He only looks away when Tarq's hand swings across his line of sight. Bastian quickly steps away from Tarq before returning his eyes to me as I swim toward them. I cling to Tarq, and he walks into the deeper water, leaving the young wolf.

"*The old 'toss the Luna in the water,*'" Tarq says, pulling my concentration away from Bastian. "*Good times. Good times.*"

"*Why is that even a thing?*" I ask.

Bastian sounds weak as he chuckles with Tarq.

"*Alright, kiddo,*" my Alpha says. "*We're gonna try something else. Ready?*"

The scene fades, leaving me in the dark again. When Bastian speaks, his thoughts are barely a whisper. "*I think I'm just gonna get some rest.*"

"*No, no, baby,*" I plead, nearly panicking. "*You can't sleep yet. I need one more thing from you, and then you can rest.*"

"*For you...*" Bastian whispers.

"*She needs you to open your eyes and see her there with you,*" Tarq rushes to say. *"See her sweet smile. Feel her hand slide over your jaw."* Bastian is silent, and Tarq places his chin on my knee. *"Come on, kiddo. You gotta try for me. Smell her scent. That beautiful, amazing bouquet."*

"Have you noticed there's a hint of peaches? I love peaches," Bastian whispers as he opens his eyes, showing us his surroundings again.

"Can you look around a little bit for me?" Tarq asks.

Bastian moves his eyes slightly.

"Good job, kiddo," Tarq says calmly. *"You are one lucky wolf. You'll recognize the help I'm sending. Don't eat him."*

The young wolf's eyelids close. I can feel Tarq's breath, so it's no surprise we're nearly nose-to-nose when I open my eyes. However, I didn't expect the slobbery lick he was waiting to give me.

"Come on!" Tarq shouts, jumping back. *"He's about ten miles from Will's office. We have some guards out that way. I'll send them for Doc. Let's go get our kid, Dar!"*

I'm so happy I'm not even mad at Tarq for licking my face.

* * *

Three days later, I crash through Doc Will's office, running straight to the back room.

"Luna!" Will exclaims, surprised.

I push past him, stopping beside the tan wolf's bed.

"Sit, Luna," Will insists, pulling a chair over. "You look like shit."

Tarq steps behind him, making him jump. "Tell her she looks like shit again," he growls.

"Tarq, you know where the clothes are," Will says, watching my Alpha walk around the bed. "The kid is stable for now. I can't fix him. He'll have to shift to take the tea."

Tarq ignores him and helps me move Bastian's paws as I climb onto the bed. His ribs are rising at a speed close to panting. A tube runs from his nose, and something is clamped to his tongue.

"Don't take that off," Will says as I reach for the clamp. "It's holding a monitor." Will points to the beeping machine next to the bed.

"Can you bring us the tea?" I ask.

Will sighs with a frown. "Luna, that kid hasn't woken up since we found him. I don't think he can hear you."

"We argue about my health, not the care of my wolves. The tea, please."

Will shakes his head, retreating to his office as Tarq circles the bed to stand behind me. He puts his hand on my hip and leans over us. "How are we going to do this, Dar?"

Bastian's heart rate jumps, and his body jerks.

I reach back to my hip and rub Tarq's hand. "Can you give us a minute, My Love?" I ask, realizing that Bastian is reacting to Tarq's voice. "Why don't you find some clothes?"

Tarq kisses my cheek before leaving.

"It's just you and me now, sweetheart," I whisper. Sliding my arm under Bastian's neck, I drape his head over my shoulder with his muzzle on my chest. As I slide my hand over his side, it's clear that his shoulder is damaged. Shifting must have been extremely painful.

Carefully, I move his leg over my stomach and rub his pads. "Did you know that I died on my 25th birthday?" When he doesn't respond, I continue. "Tarq says I've died more times than he agreed to. He gets pretty mad at me when I die." I sigh, shifting my hips to snuggle a little closer to Bastian. "I understand why that is now."

Allowing him to relax, I run my fingers over the bridge of his nose and between his eyes. As I rub his ears between my fingers, I feel him release a deep sigh.

"You're important to us, Bastian," I whisper. "We won't let anyone hurt you ever again. All you have to do is want us, too." I lie back on the bed, closing my eyes as I slide my fingers under his jaw. "When you're ready, I'll be right here waiting."

I spent hours humming to the young wolf before I finally fell asleep. My fingers were sore from rubbing the pads on his toes. I had turned my head toward him and adjusted his muzzle to lie over my cheek, ensuring I wouldn't block his nose if I moved.

Tarq leans down to kiss my cheek to wake me. I jump slightly when I realize Bastian's muzzle has moved, but Tarq puts his hand on my forehead, shaking his head. He sweeps his hand over my eyes and shows me what he's seeing.

Bastian's nose is jammed into my neck like Tarq does when he's sleeping. He sweeps his eyes along my body to show that the young wolf has stretched his back legs out over my lap. They are covered in blood, but it's dried. Tarq points to the door and quietly exits.

"Hey, sweetheart, are you with me?" I whisper. I try to shift my hips against their stiffness, but the weight of Bastian's legs pins them to the bed. "I'm pretty stiff here, honey. If you could pull your back legs in, I could shift my hips and stretch out my back."

Giving up after a minute or two, I extend the one arm that isn't pinned down. As I roll my neck and wiggle my shoulders, I feel Bastian sigh onto my neck. A moment later, his back legs begin to move. His breathing speeds up, and he whines but doesn't stop until his back paws are neatly tucked under my hip.

"Hi, sweetheart," I whisper. Sliding my hand up the bedrail, I push the button that sets an alarm off in Doc's office.

Will crashes through the door moments later. "What's wrong?" he hisses. He checks all his machines and monitors and then looks at me.

"I need you to take his tubes out, please," I tell him calmly.

Will frowns. "Luna, that alarm is for emergencies," he complains. "This is not an emergency." He still begins removing the tubes and the clamp from Bastian's tongue. He pauses before removing the needle from Bastian's leg. "Are you sure about this?" he asks. "These painkillers are pretty strong. They'll wear off quickly."

"He'll be fine," I tell him. "Can you leave us?"

"He's right," Bastian says weakly as Will closes the door. *"This really hurts."*

Smiling, I turn to lay my cheek against him again. "I know, sweetheart," I whisper. "I'm going to help you with that. I promise." I push my arm further under his neck, forcing his head and muzzle onto my chest. I wrap my arm around him so my hand is over his shoulder blades. "Ok, baby, same deal as before. You tell me if it hurts, ok?"

I push heat through my hand as Bastian shakes from his pain. His body slowly relaxes, and his breathing settles into a steady rhythm. After a while, Tarq sticks his head in to check our progress.

"Come here, baby," I say. "Let's try something." Tarq puts his finger to his lips, scowling at me. "No, My Love," I say, giggling. "He needs to hear both our voices. He is safe with us, and we need to remind him of that."

Tarq sighs, giving me a confused look as he closes the door and walks toward us. "How can I help?"

"I need you to try to coax his back legs out from where he has them tucked," I tell him. "His shoulder is crushed, so I'm a little trapped."

Tarq frowns. "So, you want me to rub the kid's legs?" He lifts his eyebrow.

I grab his shirt, pulling him to my lips. "You beautiful man, if you receive, you should be willing to give," I say. "You need to teach your daughter how to do this, so it's time for you to learn too."

Bastian stiffens when Tarq growls playfully as he kneels beside the bed. He pulls his legs away with a yelp when he feels Tarq's touch. My Alpha holds his hands up in surrender.

"Give him a chance, Bastian." I slide my hand over his muzzle, careful not to cover his eyes. I can't see them, but I assume he's watching Tarq. "You're safe with me. My Alpha has been alive for 41 years and has never rubbed another wolf's legs." I pause to scratch his whiskers. "You're about to be quite elite, sweetheart."

It takes a bit, but his back half finally begins to relax, and I nod to Tarq. "Go ahead, My Love," I whisper, rubbing my thumb over Bastian's chin. "Let's see if we can teach you to soothe some tired legs."

After a few pointers, my Alpha works on the young wolf's hind legs. Although I can tell from his stiffness that he's not giving Tarq his limbs, Bastian's at least not trying to get away. Tarq continues to work as I quietly hum my nonsense tune that's been calming the teenager so far. I'm nearly asleep when I feel his back legs relax against me.

"You're going to roll his toes, cupping his claws so that he won't cut me," I tell Tarq. "Support his thigh as you extend the leg."

Tarq slowly extends Bastian's back legs and throws a blanket over his hind end. He tucks it underneath me so that it'll stay between us.

"Thank you, My Love," I say as Tarq leans over to kiss me. "Now that this is slightly less inappropriate, we can start working toward a shift."

Tarq snickers, walking around the bed to stand behind Bastian. "I figured it out when I straightened his legs."

"You guys are weird," Bastian says.

I giggle, bumping my finger on his nose. "Yes, but all our weirdness loves all of you, so get used to it."

Bastian pulls his head back to rest his nose against my collarbone and gently licks my neck.

"Ok, sweetheart," I start apologetically. "I'm going to reach up for your shoulder. This will hurt quite a bit until I can get my hand against your skin. We need to start getting you relaxed enough to shift. Are you ready?"

Bastian doesn't answer right away. I look up at Tarq, who shrugs and shakes his head. He places a hand on Bastian's back and the other on his head.

"Ok, I'm ready," Bastian tells me.

There is no way for me to roll my body toward him without moving his leg. Although I try to move gently, Bastian yelps and screams as I roll and slide my hand against the fur on his crushed shoulder. Once I push heat through to him, he relaxes back into me. His rapid panting settles into even breathing, and he licks his lips when his jaw relaxes.

As I snuggle into him for the long wait until he shifts, Tarq pulls a chair up to sit opposite me. I watch him gently slide his hands over Bastian's head and neck. He rubs the young wolf's ears between his fingers, which I do when distracted. Tarq must enjoy it if he's doing it for Bastian.

"I love you," I whisper.

Tarq stands to kiss my temple. "I love you too."

* * *

I drift in and out of sleep for hours. Neala told us that it was important for both of us to be here when Bastian shifts. She had warned me that it might take a while. I'm unsure if Bastian still trusts me as much as he did in the vision he showed us, but it was clear that he didn't trust Tarq even then. Neala had mentioned a fear of men since his abuser was a man.

The sun shines through the windows when I wake up with a teenage boy in my arms. He's shaking, so I hit him with a blast of heat. I slide my hand over Tarq's head to wake him. Moving quickly, we tip Bastian's head to pour the tea into his mouth.

Tarq shakes with rage as he helps untangle me from Bastian's grip. I take my first complete look at his injuries. His face displays various degrees of bruising, and his shoulder is pulverized. I understand why Will said he couldn't fix him.

"How the hell would someone even do that?" I hiss.

Tarq shrugs, shaking his head as I move down the teenager's body. There's more bruising and some deep gashes along his torso. I lift the blanket and gasp.

"You should've warned me."

Tarq takes the blanket from me, covering Bastian back up. "He'll heal," he tells me. "Tynan cut his tendons so he couldn't run away. It's known as hobbling."

"How is he ever going to trust anyone again?" I wrap my arms around myself, regretting walking away from Bastian the day we met him.

Sighing, Tarq pulls me into his arms and rubs my back. "If anyone can help him, it's you."

I smile, appreciating his faith. "You get the wagon hitched, and I'll call the guards back," I tell him. "Let's get him to the cabin before he heals. Neala says he needs to wake in a safe place."

When Tarq leaves, I turn back to Bastian. He groans as I cup his cheeks. Moving close, I kiss his forehead and whisper, "Sleep well, sweet boy. We'll see you soon." I push all of my heat through my hands into his face. Bastian's eyes roll back as he releases a blissful sigh.

12

After a lack of progress over the first few days at the cabin, Neala suggested that Tarq leave. My Alpha wasn't happy, but we saw the teenager improve once he left. Bastian fell into a routine that required me to stay beside him continuously, but he's moving forward and talking, so I'm proud of him.

After a week of steady progress, we begin the day in the kitchen as he helps Neala cook.

"Grease could use a run today," I say casually. "She doesn't handle boredom well."

Bastian walks around the counter, sitting beside me. "You'll be going?"

"I wouldn't miss it for the world." I smile, sliding my hand over his cheek. "Neala? You'll join us, right?"

Neala turns to us with a smile. "Of course, Luna. I would love the chance to see Ash." She winks as Bastian ignores the statement. He'd panicked the first few days when we mentioned including the men in anything.

Sliding a plate in front of Bastian, Neala joins us at the counter. The teenager eyes the plate nervously. He seems hesitant any time we give him food. After just a week, though, his ribs are starting to fill in, and his cheeks aren't sunken. He's a skilled hunter who could shame most of my wolves but wasn't allowed to eat his kills.

I rub Bastian's back with a smile. "Aren't you hungry, sweetheart?" He picks up his fork, stabbing it into the eggs. "There's a ridgeline a few

141

hours from here. It's one of my favorite views. I thought I might share it with you." Bastian ignores me and continues eating, so I turn back to Neala. "How are the junior guards handling your absence?"

"Nate has been working with them," Neala says, shaking her head. "You know he's old and set in his ways. He'll have them guarding you before they're 15."

Nate grew up under Dax's rule. He's fair with the kids but doesn't believe in change. He'll have them ready to fight in a war within five days. I giggle at the thought.

"The kids report that he's teaching them tracking," she continues. "He has them hunting Tarq when he goes out on runs."

Bastian drops his fork on his empty plate.

"Did you have enough, sweetheart?" I ask.

Neala dumps the rest of the eggs onto his plate before he can answer. His ribs annoy her. "Before you lie to us, child, I told you that you would get food and have a full stomach around here." She clangs the pan back onto the stove.

Bastian ignores her, turning to me. "Your Alpha goes for runs?"

Smiling, I bite my toast and gesture toward his plate. "He does when we're apart," I tell him. "He gets anxious when he's away from me, and it helps to release some of that energy." I watch as Bastian grabs his fork and begins eating again. "I'm going to get Grease ready."

Bastian snaps his head up, pushing his plate away. "I'll come with you."

I smile as I push his plate back in front of him. "I need you to eat, beautiful boy," I tell him, sliding my hand over his face. "You need to recover your strength. I'll be just outside that window there." I point to the window over the sink as if Bastian didn't know where the paddocks were. "So you eat and come out once you're both finished."

Bastian's expression never changes. His fear won't allow him to stay in the kitchen for long. I stand up and kiss his cheek before retreating through the living room.

Quickly slipping out the side door, I approach the paddocks. The bored filly eagerly greets me as I open the gate. "Hey, Grease," I say, patting her neck. "Let's hope today's the day." I grab her brushes as I call out to Tarq. *"My Love, you busy?"*

"I'm never too busy for you, Dar. How are things going?" Tarq answers. He normally needs a run first thing in the morning.

I brush Grease, considering his question. *"Slow,"* I finally answer. *"I'm hoping today is the day I get him to shift."*

"It's only been a week, My Love," Tarq reminds me. *"Granted, a very long week for me, but still just a short week for him."* Tarq doesn't handle being away from me well. The longest was two weeks, and it ended in disaster. *"So, I'm going to head back up there tomorrow."*

I'm not sure Bastian is ready, but Tarq knows his limits and when he needs to return to me. I've learned to overcome my body's need for him, but I'm not a powerful and destructive wolf.

Grease turns toward the cabin as Bastian sneaks out the side door. *"I've got to go, my Alpha,"* I tell Tarq. *"This boy's limit is four minutes. I'll see you tomorrow. I love you."*

"I love you too, Dar."

I turn my attention to the teenager. "Did you finish eating, Bass?"

He climbs over the fence and grabs a brush. "I had enough," is his response.

"Sweetheart," I say, sighing. "That's not what I asked."

Bastian ignores me and continues brushing Grease. The filly understands his need, standing patiently while he works through whatever thoughts attack him. The paddocks have been one of his happy places. Bastian spends hours listening to me tell him stories as he grooms Grease. I don't think he hears my stories but just listens to my voice.

I step beside him when it seems he might slip back into his head. "Why don't we take her for some grass?"

Bastian frowns and hands me the brush before opening the gait.

Hooking my arm with his, we walk beyond the cabin and past the gazebo where I married my Alpha. Grease follows us to the cattle pens Tarq had built a few years ago. I stop to look over the few dairy cows we have.

"Tarq will be coming back tomorrow," I say. "Will you be ok with that?"

Bastian's jaw clenches and releases as he looks down at me.

Turning around, I walk with him to the lush grass across the trail and sit down. "Come here, baby. I could use a break."

"Are you ok, Luna?" Bastian asks, looking worried. "Should we go back inside?"

Neala says it's cheating, but Bastian always responds if I feel ill or need his help. I believe he trusts Neala, but he's especially attached to me. I smile and cup his cheek. "No, sweet boy," I tell him. "I just want to relax a bit." I lie in the grass with my arm out for him. Bastian flops down onto my shoulder, staring at the clouds. "You weren't gonna go today, were you?"

Bastian rolls toward me and puts his hand under his chin. "I don't think I'm ready, Luna."

I pull him into my arms. "How about if I always wrap you up in my arms? You'll be safe and sound with your very own Luna bodyguard." I squeeze him tightly before leaning down to kiss his head.

He's mashed against me with his hands in his face. I'd hate to see how he would react if anyone else tried this, but he stays relaxed in my arms. He chuckles and tries to say something, but it's just a garbled mess.

"Bastian, my sweet boy, I love you," I tell him. "You are my family now, and I won't let anyone hurt you." I open my arms slightly so he can look up at me. "You're a wolf, sweetheart. That wolf does not define you, but it is part of you. You should embrace every part of yourself. What's holding you back?"

Bastian turns and puts his ear to my heart, listening to it momentarily before responding. "What if he's there?" he whispers. "What if they're there?"

Remembering how much time I spent listening to Tarq's heart, I give him a moment before I respond. "Do you love me, Bass?"

"You know I do," he mumbles.

"And are you loyal to me?"

"I will die for you," Bastian proclaims.

I slide my fingers through his hair and tug it a little. "Then I'd like you to trust me. Will you try something for me?" I ask. Bastian doesn't respond, but I can feel his eyelashes rubbing against my chest. "Put your arms around me, Bass."

He pulls away and looks up at me, confused.

"I would like a hug from you, sweet boy," I say, raising my eyebrow. I lift my ribs to allow him to slide his arm under me as I wiggle down to lay my head over his. "I've got you. I won't let anything happen to you."

Bastian tightens his grip on me and sighs. He's comfortable like this. This is how he laid the first time he slept through the night. Tarq gave me the idea. It has something to do with my scent. As he relaxes, I twist my lower body and lay my legs over his hip.

The young wolf tenses.

"It's ok, baby," I whisper. "When you're ready, I want you to shift. I've got you. You're in my arms and safe with me. I won't let anyone hurt you."

Closing my eyes, I continue to repeat my phrases. My arms stay tightly latched onto Bastian, helping him feel their security. His tension slowly eases away. I feel him tugging at the ends of my hair until he releases a deep sigh and shifts.

"Hey baby," I say, smiling. *"How are we doing? Are you ok?"*

Bastian adjusts his head underneath mine so his nose is against my skin and takes a deep breath. *"It's quiet, Luna,"* he says, sounding shy. *"How did you make it quiet?"*

Giggling, I kiss his head. *"That's all you, sweetheart,"* I tell him. *"This wolf is a part of you, so you control it—no one else. I had nothing to do with it."*

"I love you, Luna," Bastian whispers.

"Aw, I know, baby. I love you too."

I slip my hands through his fur, letting him enjoy the silence. I slide my hand over his neck and shoulder, reaching for his ribs. Feeling that they are filling out nicely makes me smile, and the muscle that encases his bones is beginning to thicken. I roll onto my back to give the young wolf more room and run my hand over his front leg.

Licking his lips, Bastian rolls forward to lay his head on my chest, turning it to put his ear to my heart. *"Luna, I think I'd like to shift back now,"* he says, asking permission.

There's an innocence to him that makes me smile. "Sure, baby," I say. "Why don't we head to the house to get you some shorts." Rolling away, I give him room to stand up.

Bastian rises slowly, testing his legs. Before I can stand, he steps up, slides his jaw over my shoulder, and drops it down my back. Smiling, I wrap my arms around his neck and bury my face in his fur. His eyes are calm, beautiful, and filled with love when he pulls back.

I cup his chin. "Come on, sweetheart," I say, grinning.

We walk back to the cabin, and Bastian stays downstairs while I retrieve a pair of shorts from the bedroom. Neala enters the living room from the kitchen as I walk down the steps.

"Look at you," she gushes. "I'm so proud of you." She kneels to the young wolf, and he steps into her arms. Neala smiles at me as I reach the bottom step. "A beautiful boy makes a beautiful wolf."

"Here we go, Bass," I say, laying the shorts over the back of the couch. "We'll give you a minute."

"Please don't go," he says, stopping me.

"Ok, baby. I'm right here." I nod to Neala as I cup Bastian's jaw.

Once Neala leaves, Bastian shifts and takes the shorts. "I don't understand," he says curiously. "How did I silence the Blood Pack?"

There's a mirror hanging by the kitchen door. I ignore Bastian's arm as I lead him to it and let him absorb what has happened. His new pack marking is winding down his arm from the center of his shoulder blade. He twists his arm, studying every inch of it down to his pinky knuckle. His eyes flick back to me.

"You're one of us now, baby," I say, rubbing his back. "You no longer belong to them. You're part of our family, and we are so happy you're here."

Bastian turns to his reflection, straightening his back and squaring his shoulders to stand taller. His new Lunar Pack marking shines on his arm like a beacon of hope for a better future. "They can't hurt me anymore," he whispers, smiling.

* * *

We work together on various chores around the yard for the rest of the afternoon. Bastian seems calmer but unwilling to leave the cabin's safety. Tarq told me he was coming back early. He's reached his limit and can't wait. I might handle it better, but I miss him just as much.

As we finish the day, I sit on a stool in the kitchen, watching Neala teach Bastian how to cook a stir-fry with rabbit and vegetables. He's refused to wear a shirt and repeatedly checks his arm as if he's afraid his pack marking will disappear. He glances at mine occasionally, and I figure he'll eventually ask why I have a mark on both arms.

"But why are you putting oil on them?" Bastian asks. "They taste good on their own." It's been a long week, but he's finally smiling and laughing. It probably doesn't hurt that rabbit is his favorite meat.

Neala laughs. "It's just for extra flavor, Bass. You'll like it. I promise." She narrows her eyes as Bastian pulls some bell pepper from the pan and pops it into his mouth. "There's gonna be nothing left to put on the plate, child." She wags her spoon at him but still grins.

Bastian laughs and leans over the counter to grab my hands. "You look happy, Luna."

Pulling my hand free, I cup his cheek. "You make me happy, sweetheart," I whisper. "Your smile brings me joy."

* * *

I've convinced Bastian to lie in the spare room at bedtime. He made me leave the lights on, but he's still progressing. I quickly change into night clothes and exhaustedly crawl under my covers. As I reach for the lamp, movement in the doorway catches my eye. Wearing a sheepish look and his thick blanket, Bastian casts his eyes to the floor.

So maybe he's not ready yet.

"Come here, sweetheart," I urge him. "It's ok."

The young wolf smiles as he bounds toward the bed, curling up in his blanket with his head on my stomach.

"I'm going to turn the light by the bed off, ok?" I ask. Bastian doesn't respond, so I pull the switch. Settling back into the bed, I pull my fingers through his hair as we snuggle in for the night. "Tarq will be here by morning. How do you feel about that?"

Bastian turns to look up at me, frowning. "You've been missing him. I can tell," he admits. "He should be here with you. He makes you happy."

Smiling, I slide my hand down his arm. "I love you, sweet boy."

Bastian moves my hand to his shoulder and leans his cheek onto it. "I love you too, Luna."

* * *

I feel Tarq's heat alongside my body under the blankets when I wake. Hot waves of his breath tickle my neck. Looking down, I see Bastian still curled up with his head on my stomach. He's only started sleeping through the night the past few evenings. He would wake up screaming or jumping away from the door if he heard Neala's footsteps in the hall.

I wrap my arm around Tarq and drag my fingers through his hair. He takes a deep breath before gently kissing my neck.

"Good morning, My Love," Tarq whispers.

I giggle quietly. "Please tell me shorts are covering your beautiful behind under this blanket."

Tarq snickers into my neck. "There wasn't gonna be," he starts. "But then I noticed the teenage boy in our bed and figured clothes would be appropriate."

Tugging on his hair, I giggle again. "How incredibly perceptive of you."

"I missed you," Tarq whispers, snuggling back into my neck.

"I missed you too, my Alpha." I rub my cheek against his as I reach down for Bastian.

After I slip my fingers through the teenager's hair a few times, he takes a deep breath and rubs his face against my stomach. His back cracks as he stretches it out, and he snuggles back in. "Good morning, Luna," he mumbles sleepily.

"Good morning, sweet boy."

Tarq slides his hand over the blankets and rests it on Bastian's shoulder. The teenager's eyes open wide in fear, and his entire body tenses against me.

"Easy, sweetheart," I whisper calmly, sliding my fingers over his cheek. "Remember I told you Tarq was coming back. You're safe with me. It's ok." He doesn't seem to relax much but pulls my hand off his cheek and tucks it under his chin. Curling around it, the young wolf closes his eyes with a sigh.

Tarq lifts his head to watch Bastian curiously. Turning to him, I grab a quick kiss before he tucks back into my neck. "I heard you were interested in going to the cliffs," he mumbles as he disappears in my hair. "I thought we might pack a lunch and make a day of it."

"That actually sounds really good," I say, smiling.

Tarq moves his hand to gently cup Bastian's head. "We'd love it if you came with us, kiddo."

Bastian doesn't respond. He curls further around my hand and buries his face in the blankets.

* * *

A few hours later, Bastian joins me in the paddocks to tack Grease. I'd left him in the kitchen with Tarq and Neala as they packed our lunch but didn't expect him to stay there. Neala told me I must let Bastian connect with Tarq and can't force it.

He hasn't told me he won't go with us, but I can see the signs. "I'd like you to try to come with us, Bass," I say, stopping by Grease's shoulder to watch him.

Bastian tightens the cinch strap and lowers the stirrup. "I'd like you to stay here with me, Luna."

I reach for his neck and pull him to me. "Can you tell me how you're feeling?" I ask. "What do you think is stopping you from leaving the cabin?"

Wrapping his arms around my back, Bastian hangs onto me dearly. "I don't know," he says. "I can't. It's just..." He sighs, leaning a bit more weight on me.

Neala said that knowing the answer and admitting it are two different things. She warned me that the most challenging part about putting Bastian back together would be the waiting. *She was right.* I know he's come a long way in a short time. I just wish I could do more for him.

Laughter filters over from the cabin as Tarq and Neala head toward us. Bastian releases me and turns back to Grease.

"Ok, then, sweetheart," I say, rubbing his arm. "Neala will be here with you, and your uncle is just a yell away on watch." I turn Bastian to me and place my hands on his chest. "You can shift if you want to talk to me. You know you're safe if you do that."

His chest tightens, but he nods. "I'll be ok, Luna."

Tarq throws the saddlebags over Grease's back and ties them to her saddle. He drops his hand onto Bastian's shoulder, rubbing his new pack marking. "That looks good on you." Bastian lowers his eyes, and Tarq pushes his chin up just as I would. "Our wolves don't look down, Bass. We are proud of you, and you should be proud of yourself."

Bastian's eyes dart to me uncomfortably before Tarq releases him.

"I'll meet you by the pens, My Love," Tarq says, kissing my cheek. He checks Grease's gear quickly before leaving to shift.

I turn to Bastian, who's moved to stand next to Neala. "We should be back by sunset," I tell them. Reaching for Bastian's cheek, I whisper, "I love you, sweet boy. I'll see you tonight."

Stepping into my stirrup, I swing into Grease's saddle. Neala nods as I steer the filly through the gate. We meet Tarq by the cattle pens, and he takes off, leading Grease into the woods.

* * *

Grease canters throughout the morning. I'm distracted most of the ride, listening to my wolves, trying to search for Bastian's voice. Tarq talks with Chase and Ash about something in their weird guard code that will never make sense.

It's past midday when we reach the cliff. I step out of my saddle and watch Tarq shift. "Do you think we'll ever get him to leave the cabin?" I ask.

He begins pulling his clothes from my saddlebag. "It hurts my soul how little faith you have in me." He smiles as he pulls up his jeans.

"What did you do?" I ask, frowning.

"Ash said that kid lasted an hour, Dar," he says, grinning. "Love always outweighs fear."

I pull Grease's bridle off, hanging it on the saddle horn. "You should've told me."

"That wouldn't have helped him, My Love," he says, arching his eyebrow. "You would have turned around."

I run my hand over the filly's neck, thinking about his words. My nose wrinkles.

"See? You know I'm right," Tarq announces triumphantly.

I scowl at him and turn toward the ledge. I step forward and close my eyes as the soft breeze hits my face. A moment later, a furry head slides under my hand. Slipping my fingers along its jaw, I tug at the fur under its throat.

"Hi, sweetheart," I say, smiling. *"Decided to join us after all?"*

"I'm sorry," Bastian says sadly.

"For what, honey?"

"Ruining your picnic with Alph... Tarq," he responds.

"We've been waiting for you," I say, opening my eyes and turning his head toward Grease.

Tarq holds some pants up.

"You knew I would follow you?" Bastian asks, surprised.

I kneel and cup his chin. *"He did,"* I tell him. *"Tarq knows how hard it is to be away from me. He figured the need would outweigh the fear."*

Tarq winks at me as he starts to pull food from the bags. Bastian shifts and takes the pants from me as I stand up. He quietly turns and looks over the valley, closing his eyes when the breeze hits his face.

"This really is amazing," he whispers. "I can understand why you like it." He opens his eyes and walks toward the edge.

Tarq slides his arms around me from behind. He curls over me as I lean back against his warmth. "Tarq brought me here for the first time the day before our wedding," I tell Bastian. "He packed a picnic, and we spent the day escaping everything."

Turning around to find us both standing behind him, Bastian's eyes travel over us, taking us in. This time, he's seeing us as one unit—his family. His jaw clenches, and his arms twitch, but then he approaches us for an embrace. Tarq and Bastian pull at each other, and I smile as I wrap my arms around Bastian's waist. Sandwiched between them, I create a safe barrier for Bastian as he learns he doesn't have to fear my Alpha.

"We've got you, Bass," Tarq whispers. I'm mushy about my wolves, but Tarq's compassion always makes me cry. "You ok in there, Luna?" my Alpha asks, chuckling. Bastian tries to pull away, but Tarq holds him against me. "Wait for it, Bass."

I scowl. "I'm a big blubbery mess, and you know it, so hush," I sob.

Tarq chuckles, letting us go. He kisses my head and puts Bastian's hand on my cheek. "Our Luna is very emotional about her wolves," he says, squeezing my hip and leaving us to unpack the food.

Bastian looks concerned as he wipes the tears from my cheeks. "I'm ok, sweetheart," I tell him, smiling. "You must've worked up an appetite on the run, though. Are you ready to eat?" Taking his hand, I pull him toward the blanket covered in food. "Tarq always says he only packs enough for himself, but I've convinced him to share a few times."

Tarq winks as I lie back on the blanket. "I heard the ladies were having trouble convincing you to eat enough," he says, turning to Bastian. "I brought you some peaches. I thought they'd convince you to eat."

Bastian's eyes brighten, and he chooses a spot on the blanket that puts me between Tarq and himself. Taking the peaches from Tarq, he rolls down onto my shoulder. He doesn't react when Tarq leans to kiss me before feeding me a chicken strip.

We talk about different views and lakes we can visit throughout the afternoon. Bastian doesn't say much but instead listens to our voices. I catch him lying with his eyes closed a few times as we discuss routes and times of day to see things. On the trip back, Tarq runs ahead, but Bastian stays close to me, running beside Grease.

The sun sets as we arrive back at the cabin. I leave Bastian with Tarq and Grease in the paddocks at Tarq's request. I still watch them through the kitchen window, though.

Neala rubs my back. "You're making progress, Luna," she tells me. "Not a week ago, he feared men and wouldn't leave your side. Now he's outside alone with Tarq."

"The full moon is less than two weeks away, Neala," I remind her, frowning. "I need to talk to Miles, and I can't take him with me."

She nudges my tea. "We'll just have to keep trying, Luna," she says. "We are fortunate that he trusts you as much as he does."

Looking back out the window at Bastian, I feel anger and sadness. "I knew there was cruelty in the world..." I trail off, turning to Neala. "He's just a child."

Neala cups my cheek. "Children are easy prey for the weak, Luna."

13

We gather for a movie night on the eve of the full moon. Bastian comfortably stayed behind with Neala for the past few days while Tarq and I visited some of our favorite spots. We've invited Ash to move into the house, and Bastian has handled that well. After talking with Tarq, I've decided to call Bruce back to the lake. If anyone can convince the boy to trust his wolf, it'll be Bruce.

Relaxing on the couch, I prop my feet on the table, and Tarq lies with his head on my lap. Bastian sits on the floor with his arm draped across my legs, but his head rests comfortably against Tarq's arm. Neala and Ash lie together on the couch opposite us. Watching my wolves enjoy themselves is when I'm truly at my happiest.

"So, Bass, what are we watching tonight?" Tarq asks, interrupting a conversation about the best spice for venison steaks. Bastian chuckles, ducking his head as Tarq turns the TV on. "You have got to be shitting me."

The movie my daughter named her horse after begins playing on the TV, and I join Bastian's laughter. Tarq smacks himself in the forehead with the controller. Neala and Ash look confused, but I remember being in their shoes years ago.

I slide my hand over Tarq's chest, grabbing the controller. "I'm excited that you get to experience this side of your antics," I tell him, still giggling.

"You are gonna be the death of me, kiddo." Tarq wraps his arm around Bastian, shaking him.

Bastian chuckles and relaxes against us to watch the movie, leaving Tarq's hand on his chest. Neala smiles proudly at him. He's come along so far that he finally spends his first night in his own bed, and according to Neala's report from her hourly checks, he slept through the night.

* * *

Bastian and I sit on the porch the next day, watching Tarq prepare Grease. "We'll be headed back in the morning, ok?" I say reassuringly. "Neala and Ash will be here. They'll stay in my room tonight if you need them." I hold his hands in his lap, unsure if his expression is fear or concern. "Bass, talk to me. What's on your mind?"

Bastian leans his forehead on my shoulder. "I can do this," he says. "For you, I will try."

"You'll have your chores to work on," I whisper. "Ash says he needs help in the garden, and then he'll help you clean the paddocks. After their conversation last night, Neala said she'll show you how to grill venison steaks today. That sounds like fun."

Bastian sighs, unimpressed.

"I'll leave right at dawn," I continue. "I'll be here by the afternoon." Bastian's fingers tighten around mine. "It's just one day, sweetheart. You can do this."

Neala and Tarq approach us from opposite directions.

"Come here, kiddo," Tarq says, holding his arms out. "I'm gonna miss you."

Bastian steps willingly into his arms. They hold each other tightly, and Tarq rubs his hands over the teenager's back.

"I'll take care of her, Bass," he promises. "I'll bring her back to you safe and sound, ok?" Tarq winks at me over Bastian's shoulder.

Neala slides her hand over Bastian's head. "He will be ok, Tarq," she says. "We have so much planned that he won't even notice you're gone."

Bastian steps back with Neala as Tarq releases him. "You can shift if you need to talk to me," I say, sliding my hand down his arm to remind him of his pack mark. "I love you, Bass."

"I love you too, Luna," Bastian says sadly.

I leave the porch and take Grease's reins from Tarq. He steps behind her, pulling down his shorts to shift. Swinging into the saddle, I look back at Bastian. *I can do this, right?*

"Come on, baby," Tarq urges. *"You'll both be fine."*

Grease takes off after Tarq, leaving Bastian behind.

* * *

Tarq leads us down the most direct route, but it still takes a few hours to get to the lake. He conditions our horses intentionally for this trip because we make it often and usually need to do it quickly. Tarq runs straight into the tack room when we arrive at the house.

I'm just beginning to work on Grease's gear when needy arms slip around me, and Tarq digs his fingers into my skin. Turning around, I grin at his sly smile.

"Oh, the things I want to do to you while we're here," Tarq whispers.

My body heats up instantly from his words, and my breath catches as my nerves reach for him. Tarq leans down to rub his hands along my body. They slide over my hips and wrap around to grip my backside firmly. His teeth scrape over my neck.

"Well, if it isn't Mister Beautiful and the woman that gets to sleep with him!" Anthony announces from the porch, making me jump.

Tarq's hands pull on me, and his lips brush against my ear. "Say the word," he whispers. "I will tear your clothes off and let him watch me make you scream."

He slides his tongue over the edge of my ear, making me consider his proposal.

"Mom! You're home!" Annalisa shouts.

Tarq whimpers as I close my eyes. "I just wanna have sex," he complains pitifully.

Giggling at him, I lean back and cup his cheeks. I would frown, but his pouting makes me smile. "I love you so much," I tell him. "You will have what you need. I promise."

"Dar, it's been a year," Tarq whines.

All seriousness has left this conversation. "Baby, it has not," I remind him. "A little longer won't kill you."

"Have you met me?" he asks earnestly.

Fifteen years of this man have left me well prepared for these moments. "You look familiar," I tell him, squinting and looking him over. "Turn around. Let me see your backside."

Tarq sighs loudly. "You have one hour, Dar," he warns me. "After that, you will be naked, having sex in front of whoever you are around."

"Yes, My Love," I say, kissing his cheek. I leave him to care for Grease and join my daughter at the house.

Stepping onto our porch, I slide my arm around Annalisa's shoulders and guide her inside. She's going on about pack gossip. She's bored staying home under guard, so her friends have been visiting to tell her what she missed. She rambles on about boys and dating and mates.

"You better not be messing around with the boys in the pack, Annalisa," I say, stopping her. "You will be their Luna one day. You are not a conquest."

She scoffs. "Ew, Mom," she says, wrinkling her nose.

I grab her shoulders, looking into her eyes. "I'm serious," I tell her. "You can't rule over someone who looks down upon you, Annalisa. Please remember that."

"You and Dad gross me out, but I want that. I want a love that makes the rest of the world jealous." She grins.

"Then that is what you will have, Sweets," I tell her, pulling her to me and saying a silent prayer for Bastian. "So, was Daddy ok while he was here?" I ask, letting her go. "I talked to him every day while he was on his runs. It seemed like things went alright."

Annalisa rolls her eyes. "He's not the same when you're not here," she complains. "And he wouldn't stop yelling at Matthew." She throws her sandy hair over her shoulder. "Why is Matthew even here?" Her eyes widen, and she latches onto my arm, pulling me close. "He's not my mate, is he?" She looks horrified.

I throw my arm around her shoulders and direct her to the kitchen, where Edith is cooking at the stove. "No, daughter," I grumble, sitting at the counter. "Matthew is not your mate, but don't you be mean to him. He is part of your protection guard."

"Oh, thank God," she says, sighing as she sits beside me. "Sometimes he looks at me like he wants to eat me." She puts her forehead on the counter.

"Edith, where's Byron?" I ask.

She slides a coffee cup to me. "I didn't feel comfortable letting him stay here with everything going on," she tells me. "I put him up in my cottage."

Holding the cup to my nose, I take in its scent. Neala has a rule about coffee around the kids, and it nearly killed me, but we honored her request at the cabin. After taking a sip, I look back up at Edith. "But where is he now?" I press. "We don't have much time."

"Anthony went to get him," Edith says, turning to the stove.

I take Annalisa's hand. "I know Daddy can be difficult when I'm not around," I tell her. "You will face the same issue with your mate. Did he teach you anything while he was here?"

She wrinkles her nose and frowns.

"I taught her how to rub my pads," Tarq announces as he walks through the living room. "It was fabulous." He wraps his arms around me from behind and growls as he slides his tongue up my neck.

"Daddy's weird," Annalisa says, returning her forehead to the counter.

Scowling, I look at him from the corner of my eye. "Your father's gonna find something to occupy himself while I handle some business."

"You're mean," he grumbles. "I'll be down at Dad's."

Smiling, I kiss his cheek. "I promise I'll come down there once I've spoken with Byron." I watch him walk across the house, turning back to Annalisa after he closes the door. "I know Daddy's weird," I tell her. "It's how he keeps himself sane. But your mate will appreciate a good pad rub too."

My daughter turns to me and gives me her signature disgusted nose wrinkle. "Daddy and Grandpa are the only wolves that like that," she whines. "Can't you just do it?"

"Is there any chance you could stop whining?" I ask.

She sighs and turns back to the counter. "Probably not."

"Great." Rolling my eyes, I reach out to check on Bastian. I call out to Neala and Ash first, but when they don't answer, I try Chase.

"Dar? Are you ok?"

I sigh at the standard response to my calls. *"Yes, Chase. I'm just checking on your nephew."*

He takes a moment to respond as he looks for Bastian. *"He's with Ash in the garden,"* he tells me. *"Dar, do you think he's gonna be ok?"*

Sighing in relief, I run my hand over Annalisa's back. The front door opens, and I see Byron step through.

"As long as he has people who love him, he'll be just fine," I tell Chase before kissing Annalisa's head and leaving her with Edith.

Joining Byron in the living room, I extend my hand. "Thank you for coming here to meet with me, Byron," I whisper. "I tried to avoid this, but there were circumstances."

He takes my hand with both of his, smiling. "I appreciate that, but I'm happy to help," he says. "Your lovely Edith has told me what's been happening."

I gesture toward the couch and lead Byron to the other side of the room. "Is there anything in the written history that can help? I'm sort of out of my league here."

Byron pats my hand with a grimace. "I've looked through the archives and haven't found a single time that a wolf has defied the Luna."

"How about the abuse?" I ask.

"I'm sorry to report that it was commonplace in the old Luna days," he tells me. "You have redefined the title of 'Wolf' and brought great honor upon it. The rules have changed under your leadership."

"Byron, what do I do?" I ask, pretty sure he doesn't have an answer.

"The wolf in me says to kill him, but I'm an elder, so I must abstain," he says apologetically. "Since there is no past to guide you, you must create one worth repeating."

He attempts to stand up, but I stop him, glancing back to ensure Annalisa is still in the kitchen. "Byron, can I have your word that what we discuss will stay between us?"

Byron furrows his brow. "Of course, Luna."

"Did you come across anything where someone abused the Alpha? Either before or after he took his vow?" I hiss quietly.

Byron gasps. I hold my finger to my lips, looking into the kitchen again.

"That's who you're working with?" he whispers. "You've found your daughter's mate?"

"He found me," I hiss back. "Now, please, have you seen anything?"

"No, Luna," he tells me, shaking his head. "They wouldn't dare. When the Luna line of succession was in place, they knew how to spot the next Alpha."

My eyes narrow. "So you knew what I should be looking for and didn't tell me?"

Byron leans back, putting his hands up. "It only states they knew what to look for, not what it was," he admits. "They would use it to keep them apart. That way, they couldn't stop aging prematurely, rendering them unable to breed."

I cringe. "I get that." I take a moment to think before inhaling deeply and standing. I put my hand out to Byron. "I'll have the guards escort you home tomorrow. Thank you for waiting."

Byron stands, bowing as he takes my hand. "Always a pleasure, Luna."

The door quietly clicks shut when I escort him from the house. Leaning against it, I close my eyes and think about the past. *They kept the kids away from each other. How?* I tap my fingers against my forehead. *Neither of these kids would forgive me.*

"Mom? Are you ok?" Annalisa crosses the living room, looking concerned as I open my eyes.

I let my hand fall to my side, forcing a smile. "Yes, Sweets," I lie. "I think I'm just tired. Maybe I'll take some food to your father and nap at Grandpa's before tonight."

She lifts her eyebrow. "That is not why Daddy wants you to go down there."

My jaw drops. "I can't believe you just said that," I mutter.

"I am my father's daughter," she announces. "And you keep leaving me with Edith, so it's your fault too."

I wrinkle my nose. "You're probably right," I say. "I haven't been around much. I'm sorry."

She puts her arm around my shoulders to guide me toward the kitchen. "Daddy has shown me everything you've done for our wolves, Mom," she says knowingly. "I know you're doing important things. Daddy says you are doing it all for me, but I think he just wants me to feel important. Our wolves deserve all you give them."

I lean my head on her shoulder. "When did you get so smart?"

Annalisa shrugs. "I'm pretty sure I was born this way. You just never listened to me."

* * *

Once I have Edith's food packages in hand, it takes me an hour to walk to Dax's house. Typically, I would ride, but I needed to think things through, and the time alone was a nice change. I step through the open doorway and set the bag of containers on the table.

"Baby? You here?" I call out.

Tarq storms through the front door, slamming it closed and clicking the lock.

"Hey," I say, frowning. "What's going on?"

He marches right past me to the back door and slams it closed too. He leans against it long enough to lock it before raising his gaze. My body instantly fires up as his mouth curls into a playful smirk. I pull my shirt off as he marches forward.

Tarq claims his fill of me throughout the late afternoon. I miss and need him just as much, but I'm the Luna, and showing my needs would reveal a weakness. Although my mind should be elsewhere, my body demands that I be in Tarq's arms, letting my nerves enjoy his attention for however long he gives it.

Eventually, I'm braced between the hallway wall and his hips, draped from his shoulders and out of breath. "I have something for you," Tarq whispers. He carries me to the bathroom.

I smile at the tub of steaming water. "I haven't soaked in a tub since we found Bastian."

Tarq smiles, setting me down. He steps into the tub and helps me follow to lean against him. "What did Byron have to say?"

Rolling my eyes, I poke my fingers at the water, annoyed. "Nothing good or helpful," I announce. "According to what he found, abusive behavior was common in the past."

"Has any pack corrected it since then?" Tarq asks.

"Well, since Luna, it wasn't common in every pack," I say thoughtfully. "Dax would've never allowed it, but at least some did." I lean my head against his jaw. "I didn't ask about the packs since Luna's rule. I'm sorry. He did say there's no record of a wolf contesting a Luna, though."

"So, no help on all fronts," Tarq huffs.

"It would've been helpful had he not disobeyed me and broken a magical law," I grumble. "Losing his ability has repeatedly been an issue."

"Edith's been working with his daughter," Tarq reminds me. "She's been able to ease off the suppression and says she's doing good with the small amount of history coming through. Maybe we'll have a historian soon." He picks up a rag and begins rubbing it gently over my skin.

I close my eyes, sighing happily. "I love when you do this," I confess.

Tarq pulls my hair aside and slides his tongue up my neck. "I prefer to clean you with my tongue."

Giggling, I let him move me around to clean me. His washing lulls me to sleep, and it's dark outside the window when I wake. I turn my head to rub my face against Tarq's. His hum starts, making me smile.

Tarq slides his hand over my hair, kissing my cheek. "Everyone will be here soon," he whispers.

"I should check on Bastian," I say.

Tarq sighs. "Baby, they will tell you if there's a problem," he assures me. "I love that kid, but we need a break, and our family needs us too."

Standing up, I reach down for his hands. "You're right," I admit. "I don't spend enough time with Annalisa. I need to focus on her."

Tarq lifts me by my thighs, and I wrap my legs around him as he heats up to dry us. Leaning back, I grab his face, pulling him to my lips as someone bangs on the back door.

"I forgot I locked the doors," Tarq says, laughing.

"I hope one of them grabbed my bow," I say, dropping my feet to the floor and leading him to the kitchen. He helps me collect my clothes as the banging continues. "This is a small house. They could just walk around." I frown as I finish dressing.

"But then they couldn't interrupt me getting laid, My Love," Tarq says, chuckling as he nuzzles my cheek. *"I'm pretty sure it's become a sport for our pack."*

With a smile, I slide my hand over his jaw and bump my finger to his nose. "Not everything is about your sex life, my Alpha."

"It should be. Everyone would be much happier."

I tilt my head and grin. "I can't deny that." Reaching for the knob, I pull the door open.

* * *

An hour later, Annalisa sits beside me on the porch steps, running her hands over Dax's face. I've tried talking to him, but he's a useless puddle of mush in my daughter's hands. Tarq is in the field running around with Miles and some junior guards who like to play ball with the Alphas. I giggle when Miles rams Tarq, knocking him over so the young wolves can pile on him.

"He acts so differently with them," Annalisa says, pulling me out of my head.

I turn my eyes back to Dax. "I know he seems goofy with them," I start, unsure how I'll explain their relationship. "Grandpa and Uncle Miles lived for over 175 years and are incredibly powerful. He may never respect another wolf as much as he respects them."

Annalisa slides her fingers between Dax's eyes. He licks his lips to catch his drool.

"They fought like cats and dogs when they were alive," I tell her. "Daddy drove them both nuts."

"I believe it," she says, laughing.

I rub my hand over her shoulders. "You need to learn each of the wolves," I remind her. "They will all be yours one day, including Daddy." I watch the wolves in the field for a little longer before sitting up and taking a deep breath. "I need to spend some time with Miles. Stay here with Grandpa, ok?"

Annalisa giggles. "I don't think he'd let me leave anyway."

Lifting my eyebrow, I pinch the tip of Dax's nose, blocking his airway. *"Woman, what?"* he snaps.

"Knock it off, Dax," I scold him. "Stay here with her. Maybe you could share and let her practice with some other wolves."

"Yeah, alright," Dax grumbles, sighing.

I shake my head and walk to the side of the field. *"Miles,"* I call out. *"Can we talk?"*

His head pops up over the tall grass, and I smile as he begins to bound toward me. I sit, and Miles slides behind me so I can lie against him.

"What's up, Little One?" Miles asks, laying his head on his paws.

"What can you tell me about Tynan?" I ask as I tickle his whiskers with my finger.

Miles groans and rolls onto his side. His lanky frame allows him to curl around and rest his muzzle over my hip. This is his preferred cuddling method if I don't ball him up against my body. *"I can tell you I spent the first three full moons after we died trying to kill him,"* he says as an answer and closes his eyes.

Miles knows everything. Of course, he knows about Tynan. "What's his deal?"

"He's the worst of the worst, Dar," he warns me. *"He was an up-and-comer I had to squash a few times. Violent, that one."*

"He had Bastian." I frown.

"You ever find out what that kid's deal was?" He opens his eyes as I look down at him. Lifting his head, he taps me with his paw. *"What?"*

"He's Annalisa's mate," I tell him.

"Oh shit! Really?"

"Tynan nearly killed him," I say, pushing his head back to my hip. "I'm trying to piece him back together." Rolling to my side, I stare at

Miles as he relaxes. "He wants my life or Annalisa's hand. What do I do, Miles?"

Miles sighs. *"Are you still opposed to a one-day pass on killing wolves?"*

"Miles!"

"Darya!" he returns, matching my tone.

"Alright," I say, giggling. "I deserved that."

Miles chuckles. *"Yeah, ya did."* He slides me further down his rib cage, rolling upright to poke my cheek. *"Sweetheart, I know you want your pack to be safe. They won't be while that psychopath is alive."* Miles flops completely onto his side. *"As much as I'm looking forward to being able to see you every day, I'm not wishing for your death."*

I tug the fur on his throat, watching Tarq approach us. My Alpha lies down on Miles' front legs and throws his head over my lap.

"Any good advice on how to take care of the asshole?" he asks, poking Miles in the face with his paws.

Miles grumbles, pulling his legs out from under Tarq. *"Baby Alpha, I will end you."*

"Tarq, leave him alone," I scold. "He only gets me a few hours once a month. You have me all the time." I scratch Tarq's whiskers, distracting him. "Miles, you spend time with Luna, don't you?"

Miles blows his lips out. *"Not if I can help it."*

"Dax said she's really calmed down," I say, frowning.

"Little One," Miles says, about to educate me. *"You look at people differently when sleeping with them. I am not sleeping with her."*

Tarq rubs his ears against my hip as I giggle at Miles.

"You could've excluded me from that," Tarq whines. *"My ears feel violated."*

"I could've," Miles says, winking at me. *"But what would be the fun in that?"*

Smiling, I shake my head. If it weren't for our bond, Miles would've given Tarq a run for his money. I slide my thumbs in their mouths and rub their gums. Thankfully, it's easy to pacify both of them so I can think without them bickering.

After going through everything, I have just one more question. I remove my finger from Miles' mouth. "The kid said a witch helped him escape, Miles," I say, waiting for him to focus. "Any chance that could be Jaxson?"

"*Probably is,*" Miles says. "*No other witch would come near us, but I protected him.*" He looks over at Tarq. "*I don't look that stupid when you rub my gums, do I?*"

I roll toward Miles' head, pulling my finger from Tarq's mouth and dumping him on the ground. "Miles, it's your own damn fault if you look stupid," I scowl. "Who licked the Luna's blood?"

Miles chuckles. "*Yeah, that was me.*"

"If you protected him and he helped Bastian, do you think I could have an ally on the inside?" I ask, bringing him back to what I need to know.

"*Dar, don't do that,*" Miles cautions me, moving around Tarq to rub his whiskers on my cheek. "*He was loyal to me because I protected him, but Jaxson is a weasel at best.*"

Tarq gives his head a hard shake and rolls upright. "*Come on, My Love,*" he urges. "*We'll have to leave in the morning. Let's go be a family while we're here.*"

I reach for the hook Tarq made with his leg and stand up, kissing him behind his whiskers. "Alright, we'll play a few rounds. Let's go, Miles." I tug the lazy wolf's ear. "You happen to be family too. You can at least keep me company."

14

We gather for a few hours on the hill to play ball. Matthew offered to throw, and Tarq and Dax's rivalry chased off everyone but our guards. Miles lies behind me, trying to convince me to cuddle with him after every arrow. Annalisa keeps putting Miles between her and Matthew. I'm unsure why she thinks Miles would bother to stop the teenager.

The wolves line up—sort of. "Y'all be still!" I yell. Matthew stands next to me, but he would never scold the Alphas. "Stop touching Dax! Tarq! Why are you touching him?"

Dax bites Tarq's ear and sneezes in his face.

"Serves you right!" I laugh. "You talk about missing him all month, and then you pester him the whole time he's here!"

"I'd rather be pestering you," Tarq says, licking my leg.

"Ok," I say, pushing Tarq away. "Matthew, if you would please?"

The young wolf launches the ball, and the pack takes off, spraying us with clumps of dirt. I approach the line once the dirt shower ends, nocking my arrow.

"Luna?" Ash's voice stops me.

Lowering my bow, I step back. *"Yes, Ash?"* I respond. *"How's Bastian?"*

"We might have a problem, Luna," Ash cautions.

I step closer to Annalisa, my arrow still loaded. *"What's going on?"*

"The kid said he was going to bed. He went upstairs. I watched him myself."

"I don't understand, Ash," I say. *"Where's Bastian?"*

"I don't know," he says, making my eyes dart around the field's edge.

"I was in the living room. He never came down the stairs, but Neala says he's not in the house."

"Did you check the paddocks? He likes spending time with the buckskin." I already know the answer. *I shouldn't have left him.* "TARQ!" I scream for my Alpha as my back bumps into my daughter. Miles curls around me.

"I don't know where he is, Luna," Ash admits as Tarq rolls back toward me. *"With that kid's speed, he could be there soon. You should take precautions."*

Tarq and Dax stop beside me as I wrap my arm around Annalisa. My eyes spot the movement they were looking for near the house. The shadows move slowly, and a set of eyes shine. I blow a shrill whistle, hoping a horse is nearby.

"I think it's a little late for that, Ash," I say sadly.

Bastian lifts his head as high as possible, pricking his ears forward. *"Who is that?"*

I lower my bow and move to stand between Bastian and Annalisa. *"Easy, Bass. Stay right there, sweetheart."* One of our geldings charges through the field toward us. "Matthew, get her out of here!"

Matthew throws a confused Annalisa on the horse, jumping up behind her as Tarq leads it away with the rest of the guards in tow. As Bastian steps toward us, Miles and Dax begin snarling.

"Luna? She was beautiful," Bastian says. *"Where is she going?"* The young wolf lifts his nose and takes deep breaths, stepping toward where the horse had gone.

The Alphas move in front of Bastian with me. *"Back up, mate,"* Miles snarls.

Bastian ignores him, stepping forward. He noisily heaves air as he pulls in her scent.

"Who the hell is this, Dar?" Dax asks, annoyed. *"He's about to meet his end."*

Stepping between the Alphas, I stand in front of Bastian.

"Luna? Is she mine?"

"What the fuck did you just say?!" Dax snarls. I've never seen him this mad.

"Why don't we talk in the house, Bass?" I ask.

The young wolf looks behind me before meeting my eyes. *"Where did she go?"*

Kneeling before him, I slide my hands along his muzzle. "Hey, baby," I say gently. "Can you focus on me?" His eyes dart between me and the area where Annalisa had gone. "I will talk to you about all of this, but I need you to come in the house before these guys stop playing by the rules."

The Alphas' snarls are deafening, but Bastian hasn't noticed.

"She saw me, Luna," Bastian says sadly. *"She knows I'm hers. Why did she run?"* He sits, hanging his head.

"Darya, who the hell is this kid?" Dax's growl deepens enough to vibrate the air.

Bastian lies down, placing his nose against my knee. *"My mate doesn't want me."*

Rolling back to sit, I lift Bastian's head and set it on my knees. "Dax, Miles, this is Bastian, and he'll need some help understanding what's happening right now," I say, rubbing the teenager's chin.

Bastian's eyes widen. *"Luna? They're dead."*

I rest my cheek against his muzzle and scratch his neck. "Let's talk, honey," I say, smiling. "I promise I'll answer your questions."

Bastian steps back, allowing me to stand up. I turn to lead him toward the house, and the Alphas show the young wolf their teeth. He jogs ahead of them, sliding his head into my hand.

"Baby, take her to Anthony's," I call out to Tarq. *"Tell him she's to stay there until we say. We'll be at Dax's when you're done."*

"See you there," Tarq replies.

I lead the three wolves into the house and close the doors. Miles stays at my hip while Bastian turns to face me as I pull a chair out. Dax jumps onto the table.

"Now you know I'm gonna have to hear your son go on about how he's not allowed on the table," I complain.

Dax calmly turns his head to me. *"It's my table."*

"Dax, you're dead," I grumble.

"Semantics." Dax lays his head down, turning to Bastian to resume growling at him.

"Come here, sweetheart." I coax Bastian to rest his jaw on my lap. "What color was she?"

Bastian closes his eyes. *"Orange,"* he says whimsically. *"She was like sunshine in the darkness. I smelled peaches."* His lips fluff out in a sigh. *"What color do you think I was?"*

Sliding off my chair, I sit before him. He nervously eyes Miles, who steps over to lay his chin on my shoulder. "You don't have a color, sweetheart," I whisper. "That's not part of your story."

Bastian tries to hang his head, but I hold him up.

"It's time to stop feeling sorry for yourself, sweet boy," I tell him, pushing his chin up to look at me. "That was my daughter. She won't see those colors."

Bastian stands up and stretches to his fullest height. He's mad when he looks down at me. *"You knew!"* he growls.

Shifting to sit on my heels, I reach for Bastian as Dax digs his claws into the table. "Oh, Bass," I say slowly. "That is not where I wanted this to go. Don't be angry. There is a lot we need to discuss."

Bastian's lips pull back to show his teeth. Miles slowly steps around me, straddling my lap with his front legs. The back door opens, and Tarq shifts, jumping in front of Bastian.

"Get it together, Bass," Tarq warns. *"You can't act like this near my daughter."*

Bastian licks his lips as he backs up and sits down. I cover my mouth with my fingers as my eyes begin to blur. Tarq doesn't even have to turn around to know what is happening.

"Baby, this isn't about you," he says. *"Can we put the tears on hold?"* He leans forward and slides his muzzle against Bastian's. *"You deserve the love of a good woman, as I have, but my daughter is just a girl. She is not ready for you, Bastian."*

I swat Tarq's tail. "Look at you, being all mushy."

"Woman, hit my tail again," Tarq growls. *"I dare you."*

Giggling, I wipe away my tears.

"Why don't we discuss this and form a plan that works for all of us?" Tarq suggests.

Bastian moves so he can see me behind Tarq and Miles. *"Can I meet her?"*

Dax stands up and looks out the window. *"It's time, son."* Jumping down from the table, Dax slides his head along Tarq's, hooking necks with him and looking at me. *"Will you be alright? You know, with... this?"*

Smiling, I scratch Dax's whiskers as Miles steps in for his hug. "We will find a way," I assure Dax. I squeeze Miles' neck as I bury my face in his fur. "I love you both very much."

Miles turns to Bastian, pulling his lips back. *"Hurt the people I love, and I will end you."*

Bastian steps back and watches as the Alphas fade. *"Where did they go?"*

Giggling, I reach around Tarq for Bastian's muzzle. He's so muddled up from seeing Annalisa that I doubt he could return to the cabin without some rest. "You're handling this very well, Bastian," I say, rubbing his jaw. "If you think you can keep it together, I'd like to take you home. I believe we all need sleep."

Tarq instantly perks up. *"Oh, please,"* he begs, jumping around. *"I miss my bed."*

Bastian ignores Tarq's antics. His ears droop, and his head ducks. *"Luna?"*

"She won't be there, baby," I tell him. "I have some things to teach her before she can meet you." I stretch my arms out as Tarq moves toward the door. "Come here, sweetheart."

Bastian steps into my arms. *"She really is beautiful,"* he says, sighing.

Smiling, I let my hands trail down his front legs. "I know, honey," I whisper. "And she is gonna love you... when she's ready."

* * *

It's past sunrise when we finally arrive at our house. I stop at the door, pausing with my hand on the handle. Tarq flashes me a look of desperation.

"I hate that I need to ask this of you, Bastian, but do you give me your word that you won't shift?" I ask, frowning.

Bastian looks confused. *"Why can't I shift?"*

"If my daughter were to see you, the pull would be too great," Tarq explains. *"She's too young, and, you know... Dar? A little help?"*

Giggling, I tug the fur on his throat. "Just promise me and keep your word, Bastian," I say. "She's not here but does as she pleases more than I'd like."

Bastian chuckles. *"You have my word, Luna."*

Tarq barges past us when I open the door and bounds up the stairs. "You too," I yell after him. "Be supportive, Tarq!"

I shake my head and let Bastian in before locking the door. I attempt to lead him to the stairs, but the young wolf gets distracted immediately, picking up Annalisa's scent in the living room. He moves around the room, mashing his nose into each cushion and dragging it across the fabric. I pull her riding coat off its hook when he notices Annalisa's hammock in the corner.

"Come on, baby, I'm tired," I say, shaking the jacket. "We'll take this with us. You can get high while you sleep."

Bastian hangs his head and lets his ears droop, looking embarrassed again. *Poor kid is so overwhelmed.*

"There's no need for that here, sweetheart," I tell him, climbing the stairs. "You just watched Tarq stick his nose to my hip for two and a half miles."

Bastian snickers. *"Except when he tripped over that log."*

"Yes," I say, giggling. "Because he was too busy smelling me to pay attention. So you are not alone, honey."

I nearly lose Bastian when we pass Annalisa's room, but he's as easily distracted as Tarq, so rubbing her jacket over his nose pulls his focus back. We enter my room to find Tarq sprawling across our mattress. Leading the young wolf to the bed, I stare at my Alpha. Bastian's neck is curled around my hip, trying to get to the jacket in my other hand.

Tarq rubs his face on the pillows. *"I don't know that I'm interested in sharing my bed with you heathens."*

Raising an eyebrow, I throw Annalisa's jacket on the bed, and Bastian jumps on him. Tarq grumbles and moves away from Bastian as he begins rolling on the coat.

"You don't play fair," Tarq pouts.

"That is my bed that you fools have the pleasure of sleeping on, so suck it up and move the hell over."

After crawling up the bed, I roll onto my back, and Tarq lies against my right side. He flops his head over my chest, letting me rub his shoulder while Bastian settles in on my left side. The young wolf pulls Annalisa's coat up to my shoulder and lies beside me. He jams his nose into it and takes a deep, noisy breath.

Yawning, I tug at his ear. "Remember, that's my daughter you're getting high off, Bass."

He lifts his nose from the coat and rubs his muzzle over my cheek. *"Thank you."*

"For what, sweetheart?" I ask sleepily.

Bastian nuzzles me once more. *"For protecting her when I couldn't."* He lays his head down with his nose against my arm and gently licks my skin with the tip of his tongue. *"I really do want her, Luna."*

These wolves know nothing of fierce love until they meet their mate. The pull is unmatched and quite overwhelming for them. He sounds so sweet and timid that I can see the boy blushing in my mind. I know he will kill anyone who dares to threaten my daughter.

Bastian uses his paws to wrap the coat around his nose and groans.

Well, she'll be safe as long as he doesn't eat her.

* * *

After sleeping through the day, we lounge in the kitchen while Tarq cooks. Bastian is searching boxes of Annalisa's old belongings to find things containing enough of her scent to take with him. I pull a few shirts she's outgrown and one of the rubber balls that somehow ended up in the box with them.

"This is weird, right?" Tarq says as he clangs his spoon on a pan.

Laughing, I throw the ball at him. "Bastian has to get used to her scent's effect on him," I tell him, shaking my head. "And you can't tell me you didn't enjoy smelling my scent back then."

He covers the pan and leans over the counter. "I still remember my thoughts," he says, licking his lower lip. "All the things I wanted to put my tongue on." Tarq takes a deep breath, and his eyes lose their shine. "And it bothers me that some teenage boy is thinking those things about my little girl."

I smile and rub his cheek but stop when I notice Bastian hiding behind me. "Alright, we'll have none of that," I say, reaching behind me to pull the young wolf into the open. "Honey, you're a teenage boy," I say, grinning. "I'd be worried if you didn't have those thoughts. Just please don't share them with us."

"I promise," Bastian says bashfully.

"And there's no acting on it," I add, raising my eyebrow. "We talked about what would happen. You have to be careful, right?"

"Yes, Luna," he responds, returning to the boxes.

We had woken up before Tarq and discussed what it meant to be a Luna and some things that would happen as they age. We discussed our scent, where it comes from, and how careful we are with it. Bastian figured out on his own that we can only accept blood from the destined Alphas.

"Luna, I'm going to need context here," Bastian says, chuckling as he produces a horrible-looking doll.

Smiling, I reach for the doll. It is sporting a bright red mohawk and fangs. I've refused to tell Bastian anything about Annalisa so they can learn about each other together. "This story I can tell you," I say. The young wolf sniffs the clothes on the counter and sits beside me. "When Annalisa was about six years old, Anthony told her a story about the tooth fairy that scared her."

Tarq growls. "That asshat told her the tooth fairy stole her teeth from her mouth at night."

"I don't like him," Bastian states.

I click my tongue as I fold his chosen items. "He'll grow on you,"

I tell him. "Anyway, Tarq made this disaster from one of Anthony's daughter's dolls and told her it killed fairies."

Tarq scoffs, pretending to be hurt. "You told me it looked good."

"And you know damn well I was lying," I say, shaking my head. "But she slept with it every night for five years, so who cares what I think?"

Tarq chuckles and turns back to the stove.

Bastian slides his muzzle along my arm, resting his jaw in my hand. *"I wish you were my parents."*

Sliding off the stool, I kneel before him. As I kiss him behind his whiskers, I pull a shirt out of a box. "If we were, sweetheart, this wouldn't smell as good."

Bastian follows the shirt as I wave it in front of his nose. He grabs it when I stop, taking it across the room.

Shaking my head, I watch him rub his face on it. "I'll never understand that."

Tarq pulls me to my feet. His arms slide around me, and he licks my neck. "We don't understand it either," he says, rubbing his lips over my skin. "But damn, you smell good."

"Do you ever get used to it?" Bastian asks, watching us.

"He wants to know if he'll ever get used to it," I translate.

Tarq leans me back, rubbing his lips over me, inhaling deeply, and sliding his teeth over my jaw. "No," he growls. He sets me back upright and turns to Bastian with a smile. "You just learn to control it so you can be functional most of the time."

* * *

We return to our room after eating, not wanting to travel at night. My plan is to relax in the one room where Annalisa's scent isn't present since she doesn't spend time there. Tarq obviously has different plans since he stole one of her pillows behind my back, and Bastian is now lying with his nose jammed into its case.

"I'm glad he gets it," the young wolf says, pulling his nose from the pillowcase. *"I feel like I'm going insane."* He folds his front legs into his chest to watch me rub his back pads.

"I know, sweetheart. That's why I'm sending you away," I tell him. *"While you're gone, I'll teach her how to help you with your feelings."*

Bastian closes his eyes, rubbing his muzzle on the pillow. As he relaxes, his hum kicks on. Tarq chuckles, and I stare at him in disbelief. It's my first time hearing it, and it's loud.

"We're gonna have to get that under control," I say, giggling.

Bastian opens his eyes and tucks his chin to his chest. *"How long do I have to be gone?"*

"I think I'd like you to work with Neala and Ash for at least a month," I tell him as I think it over. Tarq is sliding his fingertips over my legs, making concentrating difficult. *"I have one more instructor coming to help you, and if they think you're ready, you can come back during a full moon."*

Bastian's ears droop. *"The Alphas don't like me."*

"They don't like anyone, honey," I say. *"However, you can't kill them if something goes wrong."*

With a groan, he flops back onto the pillow. *"That's fair."* The young wolf's hum settles into a quiet background noise as I move to rub his front pads.

"Back in the old days, they would keep the Luna and Alpha apart until the Luna was old enough to breed." I wrinkle my nose at the words, disgusted by their implications. *"Even the words feel gross in my mind."*

"I don't want anyone to talk about my mate like that, Luna," Bastian says sadly.

"Maybe you could stop referring to my daughter as 'my mate' then, sweetheart," I tell him, lifting my eyebrow. *"It would be cruel to keep you apart. It's untested, but I want to try to do this safely."*

"Luna?" Bastian rubs his muzzle over my face. Smiling, I stay still, letting him butter me up for whatever he's about to ask. *"Can you show me how you lay with Tarq?"*

"I can," I say, scratching his chin. *"It's safer if Tarq helps us. Is that ok?"*

Bastian's ears droop nervously. *"He won't get mad?"*

"No, baby." Laying back, I roll toward Tarq. *"My Alpha? This young wolf would like to learn how to tuck me into his stomach."*

Tarq sighs as he sits up. He kisses my head, tugging at Annalisa's pillow. "Come on, kiddo," he says. "Give it up. You need to concentrate when working with the Luna."

We start by teaching Bastian how to hold me against him. Tarq shows him where to move his paws so his claws are always tucked away from my skin. He adjusts his limbs and tucks me in so Bastian can feel where I should fit against him.

"So your back paws will stay under her legs," Tarq tells him, hooking Bastian's hocks to hold his back legs still as my legs swing over them before folding against his gut. "Once her legs are tucked in, you'll slide your paws to her lower back to keep her against you." He guides Bastian to finish with his back legs.

"Luna, isn't my leg crushing you?" Bastian curls his neck to poke his nose between his front legs. Tarq takes the limb, laying it over my arm to distribute its weight evenly. *"Oh."*

Tarq coaches him through a few more attempts and then teaches him to pull me down with him. Bastian's heat begins to get to me, and Tarq's had enough when he notices my yawning.

"Alright, I'm done teaching you how to sleep with my wife," Tarq says, grabbing Bastian's muzzle and shaking it. "I wanna sleep with her now." Tarq grabs me around my waist and pulls me toward the pillows. "Come on, you two," he tells us. "We could all use some more rest."

Bastian brings Annalisa's pillow beside me and sits down. Tarq pulls me under his chest, curling down to put his face against my head. As his shoulder closes over me, I notice Bastian eyeing us. *Who knew we'd find this beautiful, shy boy under that hard shell?*

Stopping Tarq, I reach my hand out. "It's ok, baby. Come lie down." I smile as he slides his muzzle over my hand. "We'll miss you."

Bastian nudges the pillow until it's beside me so he can lie on it and put his nose against my shoulder. I giggle as his hum starts again.

Tarq finishes rolling over me and puts his hand over Bastian's shoulder. "You know you can't take the pillow with you, right?"

Bastian sighs. *"I know."*

* * *

We took our time traveling to the cabin. Grease trudged, laden with heavy packs filled with my medicine and Bastian's chosen items. Tarq convinced Bastian to goof off with him, and they zigzagged through the woods, keeping a watchful eye on me but still letting out their excess energy. My Alpha has always been himself, and I've embraced everything about him, but Bastian seems to have an inner child that never got to play.

As I stand in the paddock brushing Grease, I remember them playing. I realize I'm smiling when I see Bastian leaning on the fence, watching me.

"You look happy, Luna," he tells me, climbing over the rails.

"I'm proud of you, Bastian." I cup his cheek and hand him a brush. "You've overcome many obstacles."

"That's because you didn't give up on me," he says. "You're an amazing Luna."

I slide my hand over his arm. "With our help, Annalisa will be too, and you will be a wonderful Alpha."

Bastian stiffens. "No, Luna," he says, shaking his head. "Tarq is Alpha. I only want my mate. I don't want to take his place."

"I felt the same way." Bastian and I jump as Tarq responds to him from behind us. He takes the brush from my hand, kissing my temple. "I wanted her, but Dax was Alpha. It didn't seem right to take his place."

"It's natural to have that fear, Bastian," I say, smiling at him. "When you marry our daughter, you will marry the pack. With one vow comes the other. When it's time, you'll be ready."

"When did Ash say you were leaving?" Tarq asks.

"First thing in the morning." Bastian sighs and stops brushing Grease. "Neala told me I couldn't shift until Annalisa's old enough."

I had discussed this with her. I wanted to be the one to tell him, but Neala felt that he would take the news better from her. Watching him now, I don't think he would've taken it well from anyone.

"Sweetheart," I say, waiting for him to look at me. "I felt the effect you'll have on her and only lasted a week. I loved Tarq with all my heart, but the bond's pull was too strong in his human form. Do you understand?"

Bastian frowns, leaning on my hand. "Yes, Luna."

"Ash, Neala, and Bruce will teach you the old ways. You will learn how to support your Luna." I know I'm asking a lot of Bastian, but reminding him that he is working toward being near my daughter seems to help.

We spend the rest of the daylight hours grooming Grease while discussing the future and the different things Bastian will learn. We explain how difficult it has been with the militia because they don't respect women and how young I look. Tarq describes how he felt any time my life was in danger to help Bastian understand why he needs to be strong and allow Annalisa to age before bonding with her.

Grease has never been as white as she is by the time the sun sets. "I love you," Bastian says sadly, looking at both of us.

"We love you too, kiddo," Tarq says, scooping us into his arms. I'm no good at goodbyes, so I let Tarq talk for us. "Why don't you sleep with us tonight?"

"Can I?" Bastian asks.

He's not asking me. He knows I'd never say no.

"Tonight is your last night as my kiddo," Tarq says, pulling away and holding Bastian's neck. "You'll come back to us a proper guard. We're very proud of you."

15

"*I'll meet Bruce at Doc Will's, and we'll leave from there,*" Amelia tells Tarq a week later.

Bruce was already leaving to join the training group. It was Tarq's idea to send his mother with him. They'll bring Annalisa's blood to help Bastian overcome its effect on him. Tarq agreed that Bruce would be better prepared to help the young wolf if he knew Bastian was our daughter's mate. He may be the most qualified to teach Bastian how to work around her aura.

"*Dad's been dead for a long time, Mom,*" Tarq tells Amelia. "*Give Bruce a chance this time. Talk to him. It's time for our family to heal.*"

I rub my fingers over the soft fuzz of Tarq's chin. "Maybe Bastian will have more luck," I say when Amelia doesn't respond. "Let them work together on a kid instead of against each other. I'm out of ideas."

Tarq hums and hands me a paw. After 15 years, pad rubs are still one of his favorite pastimes. I like that he rubs the front of his muzzle over my cheek when I work on his front paws. The fur is soft, and the whiskers are short and fine. We've perfected subtle ways to profess our love for each other because saying it doesn't seem to cover it anymore.

"*Luna?*" Bastian calls out, reminding me we're never truly alone.

"*Hi, baby,*" I respond, smiling. "*How was your day?*"

Bastian struggled the first few days. It was heartbreaking. He begged to come home, and Tarq dealt with my crying. He's settled in now and seems to enjoy himself.

"We found a river and a lake," Bastian tells us. "Neala said it's the Ozark. There are so many fish that even you could catch some, Tarq."

"I had one day of bad fishing," Tarq grumbles.

Giggling, I snuggle up to Tarq, abandoning his paws. "Bass, Neala tells me you are doing well with your training."

"She's a good teacher, Luna," he says, letting me hear his smile. "Ash has been patient with me. This is hard, but I want to come back."

"I know, baby. I want you to come home too," I confess. "I'm sending someone to you. They'll bring a new challenge."

"Sending someone?" Bastian sounds hopeful.

I shake my head at the teenager. He might be dying to meet Annalisa but should know I wouldn't send her to him.

Tarq pulls his muzzle from under my neck and lays it across my cheek. "We're sending my mother," he announces, chuckling.

"Your task is to hide who you are from her while she trains you to guard your Luna actively," I tell him.

"She doesn't know who I am?" Bastian sounds confused.

"Our pack is large, kiddo," Tarq starts. "If we are to stop my daughter from making poor decisions before she fully understands the consequences, the fewer people that know, the better."

"She will be coming with your other instructor, Bruce," I continue. "He knows who you are. He'll be helping you control yourself around her blood. Bruce and Amelia are unbonded mates, so he will also be helping you learn to mute Annalisa's aura."

Bastian falls silent.

"Bass?" I say after a while.

"Luna?" he starts quietly. "If I pass their test, can I come home?"

Tarq sighs, letting his lips fluff as I grab my chest. Bastian's teachers plan to take him into the mountains to some areas they visited when Dax banished them. He will be traveling far away, but the journey will be worth teaching him to protect my little girl. Maybe it's just that he wants to come back or that he's calling it home, but he has my chest aching and my eyes blurring.

"Yes, sweet boy," I tell him. "I'll allow you to come home when they say *you're ready. I'm going home tomorrow to start teaching Annalisa what she'll need to help you.*"

"*Ash says dinner is ready,*" Bastian says. They hunt as wolves but eat dinner in their human forms. Neala said connecting Bastian to both sides of his existence was essential. "*I love you, Luna.*"

"*I love you too, sweetheart,*" I say. "*We'll talk tomorrow night.*"

Tarq tucks his legs against his chest so I can roll closer to him. After all these years, I'm used to leaving Annalisa behind. Saying goodbye to Bastian is like starting over with another child.

Being the true master of distraction, Tarq switches gears. "*Do you know how you're going to teach my daughter to create her fire touch?*" he asks.

"I thought I would have you scare the shit out of her," I say, raising my eyebrow. "Since she's your daughter, and you're the only one our fire doesn't hurt."

Tarq shifts and rolls me onto his chest. Judging by his frown, he's not impressed with my plan. "Can you try something that doesn't involve me scaring my kid?" he whines. "I think she's had enough of my anger for now."

"She's my kid too, Tarq," I grumble. "But we will try something else since you look so pitiful." I glide my fingertips over his forehead and down his cheek. "I love you, my Alpha."

Tarq closes his eyes and hums as he lets me slide my hand over his body. Heating it, I allow him to relax as his skin reacts to my touch. His chest swells as he takes a deep breath, and his jaw relaxes to release a throaty sigh.

"You make me feel like I'm about to fall asleep, but I'm excited about it," he mumbles.

I giggle as Tarq rolls over me, growling. He pulls my T-shirt over my head and slides his hand up my thigh to pull my leg over his hip. My Alpha allows his fingers to feel every part of me they can reach. He knows my body better than Doc Will ever could.

He pushes a beach image when he kisses my eyelids, making my eyes close. The sand borders on hot as it touches my back, and the sun is so bright that I have to keep my eyes closed. There's a strong breeze, and the waves quietly break before sliding up the beach to touch my skin like cold kisses.

Tarq ensures that my entire body receives his attention as we lie on that beach. My nerves enjoy his affection, even if my chest complains about the work. My touch urges him on, and my nails trail over his skin, asking for more. Once my lungs have had enough, I tip my hips to him and set off our release. We call out to each other until we're completely spent.

The beach fades away as Tarq slides off me. He's tired and tries to pull me under his chest for the night, but I can't breathe. I slide my hand down his body to push him off my ribs, giving them room. It was easy to disguise while we enjoyed each other, but I have no excuse for my labored breathing now.

"Are you ok?" Tarq asks, looking concerned.

"I just need to catch my breath, My Love," I say, smiling as I rub my fingers along his jaw. "Maybe I'll visit Will while we're at the lake."

Tarq rolls onto his side and tucks me against his chest. In my happy place with his heartbeat, my heart rate slows as my breathing settles into an easy rhythm. "I think that's a good idea," he whispers.

* * *

Once we travel down the mountain, I collect our daughter and take her to the lake. At 14, Annalisa is struggling to come into her gifts. As I walk around the lake pretending to listen to the pack gossip, Tarq is gathering some junior guards so she can practice on wolves with real emotions. She's doing well with the relaxation skill but has only practiced on Dax. Since he generally lacks emotion, I'm not sure she's adequately acquired the skill.

"Matthew keeps bringing me flowers," Annalisa rambles as I point to the grassy hill I was bringing her to. "Some of the girls already know who their mate is. How will I know?"

I hook my arm around hers and pull her toward the knoll. "Sweetheart, you don't need to worry about that," I tell her, slowly climbing the hill with her in tow. "You're young and have things to learn before you could even handle that."

As we sit, Tarq approaches with five junior guards. They have come to the house, lake, and full moon parties to play with Annalisa but rarely interact with me. I am a bit of a mystery to many younger wolves, and they are unsure how to act around me.

Tarq flops beside me, rolling his head into my lap and jamming his nose against my hip. My Alpha's behavior is something that everyone is used to and actually helps to relax the kids. I hold my hand out, indicating that I'd like them to sit before us.

"I believe you know these young wolves and, of course, Daddy," I say, sliding my hand over Tarq's face. "You spend time with them in their human form, but do you recognize any of them?"

Tarq's brought us three boys and two girls. In this bunch are Brock and his mate, Rachel. They are both quite emotional, but Brock struggles the most and spends more time in Neala's care.

Annalisa shakes her head. "I'm sorry," she says, frowning. "Please don't hate me, but I don't know who you are."

The young wolves chuckle, bringing the Alpha out of Tarq. *"Down,"* he orders, making them all fall silent and lie down.

"Sight recognition will come in time," I tell her. "However, touch recognition is something you already have, and we will practice that today while you pull their excess emotion."

Lifting my hand again, I signal the first wolf to approach us. Trish might be Annalisa's oldest friend, but her brown coat makes her blend in with the rest of the pack.

Annalisa reaches out with a smile. Trish steps forward and places her jaw in her friend's hand. My daughter automatically handles her head just as she does with her grandfather, and Trish pulls away when her hand brushes over the young wolf's eye.

"Grandpa and Uncle Miles don't mind you covering their eyes," I tell her. "No one would ever dare to attack them. However, our wolves have instincts that cause them to panic if you obstruct their sight."

I slide my hands under Annalisa's, guiding her back toward Trish.

"You have a built-in desire to love and protect them," I say as I smile and nod to Trish. "Wolves are fierce predators that rely on their senses." Trish places her jaw back in her friend's hand. "You have to remember that the wolf is the dominant trait, and they will always revert to the instincts of their wolf."

I guide Annalisa's hands along Trish's jaw and lips, avoiding her eyes and ears. Her fingers hook along the back of the wolf's jaw, and her hand lightly trails over her jowls. As Trish relaxes, I take my hands away and let Annalisa get to know her friend's canine side.

"As you absorb any extra or overpowering emotion, they will begin to relax," I murmur so I won't disturb Trish. "At that point, they may close their eyes."

"Trish?" Annalisa whispers.

The young wolf starts to pull back, but I smile and shake my head.

"Through their emotions, you will be able to recognize them," I say softly.

The next few wolves take their turn with Annalisa. She smiles as she recognizes each one of her friends. By the third wolf, she's pulling the fur on their throat, which I started doing automatically, but she's doing it for the first time. Byron had told me it is a type of familial bonding, and the wolves interpret it as a loving touch.

"*Those two are pretty mad at us, My Love,*" Tarq says. I see he's turned his head to the last two wolves, and he's right.

"*Their anger is good, my Alpha,*" I say sadly. "*It means they're still obeying me. She's too young.*"

When Annalisa finishes with them, I hold both muzzles to my cheeks. "What I have asked of you is not easy," I whisper. "You have risen to the challenge, and I am proud of you. When you are old enough, your bond will be so much stronger for it."

Tarq excuses the young wolves and moves in front of his daughter. When she reaches out for him, I stop her.

"Not yet, daughter. Remember, I told you Daddy is different," I remind her. "You won't be able to pull any emotions off him." I sit cross-legged, facing the space between them. "Life is about balance," I say, smiling. "There's good and evil, happy and sad, but there is also give and take."

Annalisa slides her hand over Tarq's whiskers. "So, what I take from them, I give to him?"

"You have a way to defend yourself, and your wolves provide you with the ammunition," I tell her. "What hurts all others will help your guard. Your guard will also provide a way to discharge your heat should it build up at an inappropriate time." Resting my fingers on Tarq's chin, I guide his muzzle to my lips for a kiss. "They depend on you as much as you depend on them. Are you ready to try?"

I let my words sit with her and think about the past. *Luna confessed that she didn't have these skills. How did they teach this back then?*

When Annalisa holds her hands out for her father's jaw, I give up on my thoughts. "You can concentrate on the negative emotions for this," I tell her. "Daddy doesn't need any of the happy feelings. He can't feel what they are, just their strength."

"*I'm always happy,*" Tarq grumbles.

"You hush," I scold him.

He chuckles, setting his jaw in her hands.

"When are you gonna teach me how to hear them?" Annalisa asks, frowning. "Grandpa tried, but it's not working."

I lift my eyebrow. "Was that what he was doing?" I ask, remembering him telling her to practice something on my birthday. "I will teach you when you're ready."

In true teenage fashion, she huffs and slouches with a frown.

"For this, child, you should visualize the emotions running through your arms," I tell her. "Feel them flow from you to your father."

Annalisa tries for the rest of the day with no success. The gentle approach isn't working, but Tarq is unwilling to let me do it my way. He thinks she is too upset about not being able to hear the wolves. He can talk to her but chooses not to.

* * *

Two weeks later, we're lying in bed waiting for Bastian's nightly chat.

We've worked daily with Annalisa, and it's clear that Tarq's preferred method isn't working. I talk with Bastian every night and his teachers every morning. They've run out of things to teach him and begun to head back in this direction. He's earned his reward and learned everything they can teach him without Annalisa or myself present.

"My Love, we're running out of time," I say. "Bastian is determined to come home. He's excelling at everything we throw at him."

Tarq stretches his leg over me and taps my hand with his paw, wanting it rubbed. *"You still need to talk to Will,"* he reminds me. *"Why don't you take Chase with you tomorrow and let me work with my daughter alone?"*

I roll my eyes. Tarq has always called Annalisa "his kid." He knows it annoys me, but leaving him here while I visit Will is ideal. Chase has cared for me since I came home from the cabin and should be involved. *I'll just let that little annoyance slide this time.*

"You get one day," I warn him. "Then we're doing it my way."

"Luna?"

Smiling, I push Tarq's leg out of my way so I can snuggle into his neck. *"Hi, baby,"* I respond to Bastian. *"How was your day?"*

"Luna, have you ever had buffalo?" he asks excitedly. *"It was huge and delicious!"*

"I'm impressed. You got Mom and Bruce to help in a hunt." Tarq chuckles at Bastian's excitement. Buffalo is a large animal, and it would've taken all five wolves working together to cut it from the herd and take it down. The young wolf doesn't have to tell us that the older, more refined wolves got involved.

"Are you sure they're mates?" he asks. *"I can't stop thinking about Annalisa, and they don't even sit together."*

I pull Tarq's muzzle down and kiss him behind his whiskers. "I told you he'd figure out something was off with them."

Tarq licks my face, making me scowl. *"They've fought it for so long that I don't think they know any other way,"* Tarq tells him sadly.

"Amelia told me that you used to walk around with Luna's fingers in your mouth," Bastian says, laughing.

"Yeah," Tarq responds dreamily. *"I still do sometimes."* He wiggles

around, banging into me until I stick my hand in his mouth. *"She tastes amazing. It's like chewing on a Luna candy."*

"Tarq!" I shout, reminding him who he's talking to.

"I mean, not for you," Tarq tries to recover. *"You don't do that. I better not catch any part of my daughter in your mouth."*

Pulling my hand away, I try to scowl through my laughter. "No more Luna candy for you, sir." Tarq tucks his chin and droops his ears. I fall for his pitiful routine every damn time. "Alright, but only if you promise not to think."

He opens his mouth and waits silently for me to slip my hand inside. *"Luna?"*

"I'm here, baby," I say, shaking my head at Tarq. *"He's right, though. It's an easy way to distract you when you're struggling, but inappropriate."*

"Yes, Luna." Bastian sounds disappointed.

"So, where are you now?" I ask, hoping to distract him.

"We left the Rockies a few days ago," he says. I can hear his smile. *"Bruce told me this morning you said I could come home. Thank you."*

Having no children of his own, Bruce has developed a strong connection with Bastian. They have been good for each other, and I don't regret sending him to the teenager. He had begged me to let him tell Bastian for the past few days.

"You earned this, sweetheart," I tell him. *"You worked hard to face all the challenges we could give you, and I'm very proud of you."*

"I should get to sleep," Bastian says, still excited. *"I want to get everyone up early."*

"Remember, baby, you can't come home before the full moon," I remind him as Tarq rolls onto his back, pulling my hand with him. *"So just enjoy the trip. Bruce will make sure you're home on time."*

"I will," he promises. *"I miss you, Luna."*

"I miss you too, sweetheart," I reply, tearing up.

"Good night, Luna. Good night, Tarq."

Tarq mumbles something incoherent, which shouldn't be possible with thoughts, but he somehow manages to do it.

"Good night, sweet boy," I say, laughing.

* * *

"Darya, how long will we be keeping this from Tarq?" Chase asks, offering me his arm. He was quiet for most of the ride to Will's office. "He's gonna be furious." Chase has been preparing my medicines and even learned how to make Edith's potion in case more was needed. He knows I'm masking my symptoms.

I step onto the porch, taking his offered arm. "Chase, if Tarq knew how sick I am, he'd lock me away in the house," I say. I stop and place my hand on his chest. "That won't help our pack or make me any better."

Chase reaches for the door handle. "I suppose you're right, but you're not doing yourself any favors by pushing your limits." He escorts me inside, helps me onto the exam table, and then leaves to find Will.

He's not wrong. Edith's potion stops me from feeling pain, but I lose my breath faster now than I did a month ago. The tightness in my chest is getting worse. I'm not even sure the horrible-tasting asthma treatment is helping anymore.

I close my eyes and focus on my guards as they patrol the nearby grounds. They are talking about playing ball. It's funny that when I took on the pack, this was just a simple game that Dax played with Amelia and Tarq. Now, it's grown into an entire sport for the pack. They even travel to play with wolves who live away from the lake. It's a nice distraction from our struggles against the many enemies we wish we didn't have.

"Hey, Luna," Will says, pulling me out of my thoughts. "I heard we need to take another look at your lungs." He squeezes my hand. "Can you tell me what's going on?"

"I've been losing my breath faster lately. It was worse at the cabin, but it's become a problem overall," I say, frowning.

"Ok, let's listen and see if we can figure out what's going on," Will says as Chase rejoins us.

My companion passes Will his stethoscope. I pull my shirt off, handing it to Chase as Will listens to different areas of my chest. When he moves to my back, I notice he's sighed several times throughout the silence.

"Lie down, Luna," Will tells me. "We'll listen to a few more things."

There's more sighing and a frown as he listens to the same areas on my chest before counting my heartbeats.

"Chase, can you give us a moment?"

I catch my companion's arm before he can leave. "I'd like him to stay," I say sternly. "Chase has been handling all my care. He'll need to know what's going on."

Chase helps me sit up before turning to Will. "I'm here to help her in any way."

"Then you need to help her straight to bed and tie her to it," Will grumbles.

Chase chuckles as I roll my eyes, knowing that will never happen.

"Ok, Doc, let's take a big step back into reality," I say, annoyed. "Why don't you give me some real answers?"

"Luna... Darya, if you keep pushing yourself as you are, you won't make it through the winter," Will cautions me. "Your lungs are too scarred to handle the stress."

"That's not an answer, Will," I grumble.

"She's looking for something she can actively do, Doc," Chase says. "She's willing to do something that will help."

"I cannot just lie down and wait for my death," I say, narrowing my eyes. "I have a daughter to train and a pack that needs me. If you can't give me any real answers, I'll continue as I have and make my timeline that much shorter." I snatch my shirt from Chase and pull it on.

Will sighs, rubbing his fingers over his lips before scratching the scruff on his neck. "Go south, Luna," he says finally. "You won't fare well in this cold, dry air. Be a bird and fly south for the winter."

Leaning back, I look away for a moment and consider his suggestion. On the one hand, leaving the bulk of the pack would not be ideal. However, on the other hand, we do have southern wolves who could use our attention, and Annalisa does need to learn diplomacy.

Will looks nervous when I turn back to him. "So the warmer, humid air will help?"

"It can't hurt, Luna," Will says. "There have been no changes to how your body sounds. The only real change is the season. It would've been worse up the mountain."

"Bristol was from the southern coast," Chase announces, perking up. "Their storm season is just ending. We might find some stray wolves from her pack down there."

Smiling, I rub Chase's back. His mate had traveled north after a bad storm in the bayou. "Can you make sure Chase has everything he needs for my care?" I ask Will.

"Luna, you need to take it easy," the doctor cautions. "No amount of warmth or humidity will heal you." He holds his hand out and helps me off the table.

"Time is all I need, Will," I say, smiling politely. "Thank you for the suggestion."

Chase holds his arm out and escorts me to the door. As we step outside, I think through the general idea. We have about a week until Bastian will be here for the full moon. Of course, we wouldn't leave without him. I sit on the step and pull Chase down with me.

"How can I help?" he asks.

I turn toward him. Sometimes, it's hard to believe Chase was the goofy blonde that made me shake my head whenever he spoke. "Your nephew would benefit from time with Annalisa away from the lake," I say, slowly reviewing the facts. "Bruce and Amelia could come with us to continue coaching him. Nate could care for the pack at the lake, and Matthew has done well under him for the past month."

"I'm a little excited about getting you and Annalisa away from Tynan," Chase admits.

"That is also a good point," I say, smiling. "Ok, let's head home and see if Tarq has accomplished anything with his daughter."

Chase chuckles and leaves me on the step to retrieve our horses.

16

I stand on our porch that night, waiting for Tarq to return from a run. He'd failed to teach our daughter how to produce her fire touch, and I've arranged to do it my way. *"Where are you, crazy man?"* I ask. *"You're not getting out of this."*

I jump as his arms grab me from behind. "Right here," Tarq whispers. "You're overdressed." He takes a deep breath of my scent.

I lean against him. "Tempting, My Love, but your way didn't work," I say. "It's time to do it my way."

Tarq sighs with a pout as I turn around to cup his cheeks. "Fine," he grumbles. "Let's do everything you want to do." In the way of the most upstanding Alphas, Tarq backs up, sticks his tongue out, and shifts.

"Why do you have to steal all my best lines?" I ask, smirking.

"You can have that one back," he says, chuckling. *"I liked it more when you said it."*

I can't help giggling. Every day with him is a blessing. "Charming, My Love." As I lead him inside, he opens his mouth so I'll slip my fingers in. *"Matthew, Trish, and Brock are upstairs,"* I tell him as we tiptoe into the living room. *"When I signal, they'll start a pillow fight. There'll be squealing, and you charge in all crazy."*

Tarq releases my fingers, turning to face me. *"This is a terrible plan."* He pushes my shirt up with his nose and slides his tongue over my stomach. *"But you're delicious, so I'm gonna do it. You're responsible if anyone dies, though."*

"I'll accept that," I say, giggling. *"Are you ready?"*

He gives me one more slow lick. *"Yeah, alright."*

I kick the coffee table firmly, and a ruckus erupts upstairs. There are a few shrieks and a scream. With a loud snarl, Tarq bounds up the stairs.

"Tarq, wait!" I shout in my best panicking-mom voice.

Annalisa's bedroom door crashes. "Daddy, stop!" she yells. "Mom, help!"

Tarq is bigger and stronger than anyone the junior guards will ever encounter. They've never seen anything like an Alpha attack. There is a reason why Tarq and Bastian were able to take out an entire militia camp on their own. The terrified screams are heartbreaking enough, but the loud crashes and the glass breaking have me hanging onto the banister with white knuckles.

My breath catches when it's suddenly silent. I listen carefully, not even detecting a footstep. I climb the stairs slowly. *"Baby?"* I call out to Tarq. *"Is everything ok?"* I reach the top of the stairs and push the bedroom door open.

"Ok, maybe your plan wasn't so bad," Tarq says sleepily, lying under Annalisa's hands.

* * *

It took me a few days, but I finally convinced Annalisa's friends to meet with us. I underestimated how much Tarq would scare them. I invited them to join their Alpha for a ball game to help them reconnect with who he truly is and not fear him because of what he becomes when necessary.

The junior guards gather before us, watching Tarq laid out under my daughter's hands. "This was an important lesson for her," I tell them, reaching out for Brock's jaw. "I'm sorry that I didn't thoroughly prepare you. That was my fault."

"This would hurt them?" Annalisa asks.

"Our fire touch will harm all but the Luna's guard," I answer. She slides her fingers between Tarq's eyes, smoothing his fur, while her friends poke his back with their noses. "Why don't you let him wake up? He was pretty excited about playing ball today."

Annalisa kisses him behind his whiskers. "He seems so peaceful." She places his head on my lap.

"This is what happens when your guard is calm," I tell her. "Their reaction is less extreme if you need to settle them."

Chase and Nate approach us from the house as they discuss our plans for departure. I reach out for Chase's arm. He crouches beside me as I move his sleeve to expose his wrist.

"Our touch can do this to our wolves if we're not careful," I tell her, sliding my fingers over his scar. "This happened before I knew about it."

Annalisa takes Chase's wrist, studying his skin. She kisses her lips on his scar and looks up, cupping his cheek. "I'm sorry this happened to you."

Smiling, I touch her cheek, knowing she's ready for tomorrow night. I wink at Chase as he gives her another moment to study his scar.

Tarq licks his lips. *"Are you two done knocking me out yet?"* he asks, sounding pitiful. *"Can I go play ball? Please?"*

Giggling, I tug his ear. Annalisa has been practicing all week. I can understand why he's tired of it. "Why don't you guys go play?" I tell the kids. "Take your Alpha with you." Tarq sits up to rub his muzzle over my cheek and then does the same to his daughter. "Go on, My Love. You have a few hours before you have to leave."

Chase and Nate lead the wolves to the field and begin setting up for their game. Although they're talking trash, I enjoy hearing the kids talking to their Alpha again.

"Why do I have to stay with Cass tonight?" Annalisa pouts.

Cass had returned to the lake to help me in the beginning. I was overwhelmed, trying to be a mother and a Luna. When Rosalee passed, she moved into her house and took over the café. Her house is the perfect place to stash Annalisa on the eve of the full moon.

"We are leaving for the winter," I remind her. "I'd like you to spend time with her before we do."

"So you were serious?" Annalisa asks. "You really are taking me with you this time?"

I stand up, pulling her with me. "Yes, child," I grumble. "Now I'm guessing you need help figuring out how to pack lightly for a long trip."

Annalisa snickers as I direct her toward the trail leading back to our house.

* * *

When I wake in the morning, Tarq is tightly wrapped around me. He'd come in late after dropping off our daughter. I slide my fingers along his side and roll away as he lifts off me. I open my eyes when I bump into a nose.

"Good morning, Luna," Bastian says excitedly.

I smile broadly. *"Hi, baby. Couldn't wait until tonight, huh?"*

Relief washes over me as I slide my hands over the wolf. In just a month, his body has changed dramatically. His shoulders are well-defined, and his neck is thicker. He moves closer so I can feel his spine and ribs. They are smooth, with muscle filling all the gaps and protecting his bones from injury.

"When did you get here?" I ask, sliding my hands over his legs.

"A few hours ago," he answers, giving me his paw. *"Tarq said I could wait here."*

I press on his main pad so that he'll spread his toes. Before he left, he was too stiff to do this, but now they extend and allow a thorough inspection. *"Did Bruce tell you we'll be leaving in a few days?"* I ask, pulling at his claws.

Bastian mashes his face into the pillows. *"I wish we could stay home,"* he admits. *"I'm tired, Luna, and I miss beds."*

"Thank you for being honest."

"I'm not sure I could survive just being a guard," he continues. *"No one ever wants to rub a guard's pads."*

I giggle. *"Oh, Bastian, I have spoiled you."*

My laughter catches Tarq's attention. He leans over me, tugging Bastian's ear. "I locked the house up last night," he tells the teenager.

"Why don't you shift? We'll cook Luna some breakfast and talk about tonight."

* * *

Bastian spends a few hours asking questions. Tarq continues loading the teenager's plate, and I smile as he repeatedly empties it. Bastian's frame nearly matches my Alpha's after his month away, and I know that took a lot of food.

"Do you have any questions about tonight?" I ask.

Bastian frowns. "What if she doesn't like me?"

"Sometimes I forget you're still just a teenager," I tell him, reaching for his face. "I want you to focus on yourself and your duties, ok, baby? Don't worry about how she feels. Worry about her safety."

"Yes, Luna," Bastian says sadly. He pushes his plate away, and Tarq puts it in the sink.

"Why don't we go practice at the lake?" Tarq suggests, sliding my medicine vials to me.

"Luna?" Bastian asks bashfully. "Can I talk to Tarq alone?"

Accepting that I can't help him with everything, I kiss the teenager's cheek and head upstairs to change clothes. It's not long before I hear them horsing around in the living room. *I'm convinced my Alpha will forever be a kid at heart.*

Once I'm finished dressing, I find them standing outside Annalisa's bedroom. Bastian rests his head on the door while his hands hold its frame. Tarq is leaning against the wall beside him.

"I was ordered to stay out," Tarq whispers, crossing his arms over his chest. "I stood just like that for days, wanting to be closer to her. That ache you feel in your chest is your body calling to her."

I lean against our bedroom door, watching them. Tarq hides these struggles from me. I could never have taught Bastian about them because I didn't know.

"She will ache for you, too, but she's the Luna. She's stronger than you. You will have to push past your needs." Tarq sighs, his eyes settling on the large painting over the fireplace.

"I'm so afraid she won't want me," Bastian admits.

I step forward as his nails dig into the wood. Tarq takes a deep breath when he sees me approach. Bastian blushes as I slide my hand down his arm.

"You will be the most beautiful thing she has ever seen," I tell him. "She will be drawn to you but won't know why." I wink at Tarq. "Your job is to be strong, but not for her or yourself. You will do it for the pack, for they will be yours one day."

Bastian takes a deep breath, turning toward me. He slides his arms around my shoulders, and I hang onto him, allowing him the time he needs. "Thank you," he whispers.

I grab his cheeks as he backs away. "We will support you in any way we can."

* * *

After reminding Bastian that he wouldn't be able to shift once we left the house, he required many more hugs. When he's had his fill, we travel to the lake. While lying in the grass with us, Bruce talks about his final lesson with the teenager. My Alpha has his head against the older wolf's hip. I lean against Tarq's shoulder and marvel at his ease with Bruce.

"This lesson may be your hardest, Bastian," Bruce tells him. *"You must learn to see past Annalisa's colors."*

I reach for Bastian's chin. "You have the unique ability to see color when my hands fire," I tell him. "I think it's because you haven't bonded yet." Holding my hand out, I fire it for him.

The young wolf sniffs my hand. *"It is beautiful, but I prefer orange,"* he says playfully.

"Bastian, that is the Luna," Bruce scolds. *"You will respect her as such."* The teenager lowers his head, but Bruce catches it with his muzzle, pushing it back up. *"No. We say we're sorry and move on. There is no need to look down."*

I smile at Bruce and turn to his young student. "We only have the afternoon, so we'll focus on this lesson until you're comfortable, ok?" I ask, sitting up.

"*Yes, Luna,*" Bastian responds.

Standing up, I cup my hand for him to set his chin on my fingertips. "Come on, sweetheart," I say. "I need you to get mad so I don't knock you out. I have more control than your Luna, but you're still too calm."

"*Get mad, Luna?*" Bastian asks.

Smiling, I decide on the easiest way to anger him. "Yes, sweetheart," I say. "Why don't you think about how Tynan wants what's yours?" Bastian's anger instantly flares. "There we go. Ok, honey, let's get uncomfortable." I let my hand heat up.

Bastian tries to pull away. "*Luna, I can't see!*" he sputters, panicked.

Bruce takes over the lesson in a smooth, calm voice. "*You need to learn to see around the colors,*" he says, nodding to me. "*You will fail to protect your Luna if you cannot see beyond her color.*" I hook my fingers under Bastian's chin, urging him forward.

Bruce walks with his shoulder against Bastian's to help guide him. The teenager's steps start small as he gingerly moves forward.

"We're just going to walk around the lake, sweetheart," I say calmly. "This is our home. Tarq and Bruce are here, so I'm safe. I want you to concentrate on allowing your eyes to focus on what is beyond that red coloring."

Bruce continues to coach Bastian. His voice stays calm and even, easing Bastian's fears.

"*I wish I'd grown up with this version of him,*" Tarq says sadly.

"*I know, My Love,*" I tell him, reaching for his head. "*But I'm proud of you for forgiving him and allowing him to become this version of himself. Without your growth, he would not have his. You are a remarkable Alpha.*"

"*That's just part of my charm,*" he responds.

Tarq curls around my hip and attempts to lick my stomach, but Bastian pulls me to the right, making him miss his target. The teenager snickers as Tarq pouts.

"*Suddenly, I feel bad for everything I did to Dad,*" Tarq grumbles.

The remainder of the day is spent walking around the lake. Neala calls the junior guards to the bunkhouse to keep them away, and Tarq handles the rest. A few of my guards stay hidden, but we aren't interrupted until Amelia announces she's returned.

Looking up, I notice that the sun has begun its descent, and Amelia has retrieved my daughter from Cass's. Bastian is quietly working on his lesson. His irritation at himself has replaced his anger at Tynan. Although I'd prefer he wasn't angry at himself, it's helping him stay awake, so I let him and Bruce work without interrupting them.

"I'll make sure she stays in the field," Tarq tells me, nervously glancing at Bastian. *"Are you sure about this?"*

"I'm sure we won't be able to keep him away from her," I say. *"We have to try something."* Stopping Bastian, I kneel to Tarq. *"I love you, my Alpha."*

"I love you too, Dar." Tarq rubs his muzzle over my cheek before jogging toward Dax's house.

I fill the silence by talking with Bruce while Bastian continues practicing. *"From what Bastian says, things aren't going well with Amelia,"* I say.

Bruce nudges Bastian's jaw so that he's not leaning on me. *"We talked a little, Luna."*

"Is there anything I can do to help?" I offer.

"I love her, Luna," Bruce confesses. *"But she's still in love with him."* He looks away from me.

"It's been 15 years, Bruce," I say. *"I don't think that's it."*

Bruce corrects Bastian again before lifting his eyes back to mine.

"I think she's afraid to love you," I tell him thoughtfully. *"You were the man that seemingly tormented her son."*

Bruce sighs, hanging his head. I stop Bastian and shove him aside, kneeling to Bruce. Grabbing the older wolf's head, I force him to look into my eyes. Bastian rests his chin on his mentor's shoulders.

"Your actions were to help Tarq and the rest of the pack," I tell him sharply. "Do not hang your head. Tarq and I understand and have forgiven you. We are very proud of the work you have done with Bastian. I promise to keep trying to help you get through to Amelia."

Bruce steps forward and puts his chin on my shoulder. *"Perhaps we're just two old dogs, destined to be alone."*

I kiss the side of his muzzle and stand as my eyes roll. "This is the one thing Dax did that I can't forgive."

"I believe we have more important matters at hand, Luna," Bruce says, nudging my hand. *"My love life has sucked for years. It can wait another day."*

With a smile, I shake my head. "Of course, Bruce," I say, reaching out to Bastian. "You ready to keep practicing?"

We return to our trip around the lake. Bastian slowly takes over entirely without any help from Bruce. I stop paying attention to where I'm going, letting the young wolf direct me around obstacles and foliage.

After sunset, Tarq tells me the Alphas have arrived and that it's time to bring Bastian to the field. I kneel to the teenager, pulling his muzzle down and resting my forehead against his head.

"Are you ready, sweetheart?" I ask.

"I'm scared," he admits.

I rub his jaw. "Do you want to do this?"

"She's mine, Luna," Bastian says with more confidence. *"I want her."*

"Ok, I will stay with you until you feel comfortable." I smile, rising to my feet.

Wrapping my hand around his nose, I allow Bastian to resume his practice as he guides me to the cabin. Bruce leads the way, intentionally walking over things that Bastian must direct me around. He's doing so well that he allows me to focus on the wolves in the field. Some junior guards are playing ball, but Nate ensured Matthew would be too busy to attend the full moon game.

As we approach the back door, I call out for Miles.

"I'm in the house, Little One," he says. *"Baby Alpha said you were bringing the kid."*

Sliding my hand around Bastian's jaw, I open the door. "Miles, get off the table," I say as we walk into the kitchen. There is no way they would tolerate this behavior from any of their wolves, so I can't understand why I have to say these things.

Miles lifts his head. *"You sure this kid's got his shit together?"* he asks, ignoring my request.

Bastian raises his nose, inhaling a deep, shaky breath.

Miles jumps down, landing in front of the teenager. *"He doesn't look like he's got his shit together."*

Bastian ducks his head, pulling his muzzle out of my hand.

"Miles, get over here and quit being mean." I kneel to him and push Bastian's nose against my shoulder. Miles steps into my arms and slides his jaw over my other shoulder. "I love you, Miles."

"I love you too, Dar," he tells me. *"How are we doing this?"*

"One paw at a time, Miles." Standing up, I pull Bastian's muzzle until he looks me in the eye. "Are you ready?"

When Bastian nods, I open the door, and we step onto the porch. We slowly walk down the stairs, and I slide my hand away from the front of Bastian's nose, letting him see where we're going.

Annalisa aims her arrow as we move forward and laughs at something one of the wolves has done further down the field. Bastian slows his steps and then stops. He begins to back up and yanks his head out of my hand.

"I can't do this, Luna." He sounds terrified. *"She's not gonna want me."*

Miles stays behind the young wolf as I kneel. *"Bass, come here, sweetheart."*

Bastian's eyes shift between Annalisa and me. His lips fluff a few times as he takes deep breaths. I'm unsure if he's trying to calm down or pull her scent, and I don't care as long as he finds a way to relax. He steps forward into my arms.

"I know this is hard after everything you've been through, but you want to protect her, don't you?" I run my hands over his shoulders as his jaw slides down my back. *"Would you like me to have her brought to you?"*

"No, Luna. I can do this," Bastian says, taking a deep breath and backing away.

Standing up, I hook my fingers under his jaw again. *"Ok, here we go— round two."*

We stand still, watching the game progress on the hill. Bastian is frozen, but with his nervousness, I fear pushing him will not end well. His eyes are soft and kind as he studies Annalisa. Bruce has remained silent beside him, letting the young wolf make his own decisions. So far, he's not needed to correct any behavior, so he's let me handle his student.

"Shit, this is gonna take all night," Miles grumbles, moving to sit on my other side.

"Miles, hush," I scold him.

Nate hurls the ball down the field for the wolves. Annalisa lifts her bow, and Tarq tries to steal it. When Dax headbutts Tarq, Annalisa laughs, and Bastian raises his head.

"Easy, Bass," I say as he steps forward. "Are we ok?"

"I'm ok, Luna," the young wolf tells me.

Annalisa looks down at her grandfather and follows his eyes. He happens to be watching our approach. The moment their eyes meet, I lose Bastian. His steps speed up, and he tries to pull me forward. When I dig my fingers into his jaw, he's supposed to slow or stop, but he yanks his head and tries to twist away.

"Baby, he's not listening," I call out to Tarq.

Dax curls around Annalisa as Tarq moves to stand between Bastian and her. *"Let him go,"* Tarq tells me. *"I'll catch him. It'll be alright."*

I let my fingers slip from Bastian's jaw, and he takes off up the hill. Bruce stays with him, but I don't think Bastian's hearing anyone right now. He quickly makes it up the slope and slides to a stop before Tarq. Miles stays with me, helping me climb the hill as I fight with my chest for air.

"Easy, Bass," Tarq says calmly. *"We're gonna go slow and let Luna intro-duce you, ok?"*

"Who's this, Mom?" Annalisa asks, causing Bastian's head to rise again.

Bastian tries to step around Tarq, but I catch his nose. *"Easy, baby,"* I say soothingly. *"You're almost there."*

I tighten my grip on his nose and nod to Dax. As he moves out of her way, Annalisa steps forward until she reaches her father, who blocks her again.

"Annalisa, this is Bastian," I tell her. "He's a little nervous, so I want you to wait right there with Daddy, ok?"

Tarq waits for her to kneel behind him before he curls around Bastian to take Bruce's place above his neck. The young wolf tries to step forward but allows me to stop him.

"Are you ready for me to move my hand?" I ask him.

"I need a minute, Luna."

"Sure, sweetheart," I say. *"Why don't you lie down, and we'll take this slow?"*

Bastian lies down as I kneel next to him, and Tarq leans over his neck, prepared to scruff him if necessary. I reach my hand out for Annalisa's.

"Bastian is your guard," I tell my daughter, slowly guiding her hand toward his muzzle. "Grandpa Bruce has been training him to protect you."

"Mom, he's gorgeous," Annalisa hisses to me as if Bastian couldn't hear her.

That was all the young wolf needed to hear. *"I'm ready, Luna."*

"I'm going to let him up, Sweets," I say as Miles moves to my left side to watch. "You'll just be still and let him come to you. Are you ready?"

Annalisa pulls her hand back from Bastian's chin, straightening up.

Miles sets his jaw on my shoulder. *"So far, so good."*

"Yeah, let's just hope he doesn't try to eat her," I respond, sighing.

Bastian stands up when I release the pressure on his nose. Keeping his head low, he steps toward Annalisa. His nose slides up her arm, but when he reaches her cheek, he pushes against her. Miles snarls as Annalisa's eyes widen.

I put my hand on Bastian's hip, and he instantly sits down, pulling his muzzle off her cheek. "Ok, let's try something else," I say, sliding my nails through Bastian's fur. "Sit back for me, Annalisa, and make a lap." She rolls back over her heels and sits down. "Bastian, if you'll lay your head in your Luna's lap, we'll teach her how to ease that ache for you."

Tarq stands over Bastian as he lies down, and Miles slides into my lap, happy to demonstrate.

"Your guard will have a physical need to be with you, protecting you," I tell Annalisa. "They feel it in their chest as an ache." I grab Miles' muzzle. "Just being near you and touching you will ease it, but we'll take this one step further and reward him."

Dax flops his head over Miles' back, chuckling at him as he acts like a dead weight.

"Fuck you, little brother," Miles somehow grumbles whimsically. *"You don't know what you're missing."*

"At least I don't look stupid," Dax retorts.

"Knock it off, you two," I scold them. When I look back at Annalisa, she's holding her hands over Bastian, trying to figure out where she can touch him. He's lying with his eyes closed, mashing his nose into her calf. I put Miles' head down. "You'll notice that your guard will close his eyes for you much more than any other wolf. You can just slide your hands over his face. Be gentle, but he won't mind what you touch."

I demonstrate on Miles by running my hands gently over his whiskers and moving back to his ears. Annalisa copies my movements and giggles when Bastian begins to hum.

"He'll do that a lot," I say, trying to explain his deep-seated need to express his love. "Bastian hasn't experienced much kindness in his life. It turns out that he really likes it."

Bastian rolls onto his side with a groan. *"I love you, Luna."*

"I know, baby," I tell him. *"I love you too."*

17

The midday sun shines on my face when Tarq lifts off me the following day. As I turn my head, my eyes land on three wolves and my teenage daughter. My eyes narrow on Bruce and Amelia, who are cuddled at the foot of the bed. Bastian and his mentor were the only wolves in my bed when I fell asleep.

When I shift my eyes to the wolf beside me, he pokes my cheek with his nose. *"She rubbed my pads, Luna,"* he tells me with bashful excitement.

"Bastian? Why is there a family reunion happening in my bed?" I ask.

"I don't know," he responds happily, looking at the other wolves. *"Don't they look adorable, though? Old people are cute."*

"Bass?"

"She snuck in here, Luna," Bastian whines. *"You can't expect me to turn down a pad rub."*

Sighing, I give in. *"I suppose not. And they do kind of look cute."* Amelia's face is tucked into Bruce's chest. His chocolate coat tangles with her blonde at their legs. He nuzzles his nose into her shoulder blades as his neck curls over her head.

"What happened to them?" Bastian asks, turning back to me.

I slide my hand over his cheek with a frown. *"Amelia was in love with Dax when they met,"* I tell him. *"She refused to bond with Bruce, and things spiraled out of control."*

Bastian curls around to check on Annalisa. She rubs her face in his fur, and he adjusts his legs to cover her back up. When he lays back down, he licks his lips and sighs comfortably.

Smiling, I scratch his chin. *"I'm proud of you,"* I tell him. *"You've done very well."*

"Luna, what if she refuses to bond with me?" Bastian asks, ruining the moment.

"First of all, Bastian, you seem to keep forgetting that I am her mother," I say, raising my eyebrow. Bastian is a sweet kid, but he is staring at me, genuinely wanting to know the answer to his question. *"Second, how old are you?"*

"Sixteen," he answers bashfully.

"And how old is she?"

"Fourteen."

"Correct. Therefore, you will not be bonding today," I remind the teenager. *"Why don't we focus on today and leave the future where it belongs?"*

"Yes, Luna," Bastian says, nuzzling his nose to my cheek.

* * *

Our journey begins two days later. To go south, we must first travel west to the river. Being this close to the Blood Pack and the militia units that know us well, Tarq has mobilized most of our guards, including the older junior guards. Neala and Ash have requested that we take Brock with us. Rachel's behavior has been causing them concern.

"Mom," Annalisa says, breaking the silence. "Can you teach me how to hear him?" She doesn't even bother to say Bastian's name anymore. He's all she talks about. Bastian is just as distracted. He works hard to learn what Tarq is teaching him but often gravitates back to Annalisa, trying to alleviate the pressure in his chest.

"I will, honey," I promise her. "Right now, Bastian needs to focus on his training." She pouts, rubbing her chest. I drop from my saddle and step in front of the buckskin. "Let's walk and give the horses a break."

She swings off Grease, joining me.

"Come here, guys," I call to our Alphas.

Bastian rounds the corner first, sprinting as if responding to an emergency. Tarq approaches at a relaxed jog behind him.

"Luna, what's wrong? Is Annalisa ok? What happened?!" Bastian slides to a stop and circles Annalisa several times before checking me over.

"Fond memories of quail calls," Tarq says, chuckling.

I roll my eyes. "Bastian, we do not hide injuries behind our backs," I point out the same thing I had to tell Tarq many years ago. "I asked you to join us, not save our lives from peril."

Tarq continues chuckling, and Bastian tucks his ears back.

"But I do feel so much safer now," Annalisa gushes.

"Don't encourage him," I grumble, setting Tarq's laughter off again. "And now I sound like Dax."

Annalisa kneels and reaches for Bastian's jaw. "Don't listen to them," she tells him. "I appreciate that you want to save me."

"How do I make her hear me, Luna?" Bastian asks bashfully.

"Neither of you is ready for that, Bastian," I tell him. *"We need to reach the river tonight. Please set up with your Luna so we can get moving."*

Bastian steps back and slides his head into Annalisa's hand once she stands. I gesture forward, and we start walking together.

"Your chest will feel tight when your guard is away," I tell her. "The longer he's away, the greater the pressure. Your body will call out to the safety he provides just as much as his body needs to know you're safe by being near you."

Annalisa rubs her hand over her chest. "So that's why my chest felt tight?"

"Yes," I say, nodding. "It's scary at first, but it won't hurt you, and you'll learn to overcome it in time." Tarq opens his jaws, slipping my fingers into his mouth. His eyes roll closed as he starts to hum. *"My Alpha, can you please be present,"* I ask, looking down at him. *"I need your help teaching these children."*

"I will do whatever you ask as long as you continue to put parts of your body in my mouth," Tarq answers, his eyes still closed while he sucks on my fingers.

"Tarq?"

"Fine," he grumbles, giving me back my fingers. *"But I'm having a Luna feast later."*

I turn to our daughter and her curious wolf. "You both have instincts that have you setting up correctly," I tell them. "Bastian will want to travel in your hand, and you'll automatically latch onto his jaw. You're telling Bass everything he needs to know through your grip, and you can direct him if needed."

"It's easier to direct you too," Tarq says. *"If you were at our shoulder, we'd trip you."*

"Daddy says it's easier to direct us too," I tell our daughter.

Bastian moves Annalisa away from us and back again. As they settle beside us, Bastian jerks his head out of Annalisa's hand and rubs his ear roughly against her hip.

"We need to teach him the thing," Tarq tells me.

Tarq used to sneak sniffs of me. I'd thought it was an act of defiance, but he'd explained that it helps him remain calm. Now that he has constant access to me, he doesn't hide it.

"One last thing," I say, waiting for Bastian to settle. "Learning your wolves is important, but this wolf," I nod toward Bastian, "is the most important." I lift Tarq's muzzle and let him slip out of my hand. He slides his nose from my hip to my ankle, inhaling my scent. "He's going to need to do that periodically so he doesn't get fidgety on you."

Annalisa watches her father take in my scent again, but Bastian tucks his nose in as much as he can without pulling out of her hand. *"Luna?"*

"It's ok, Bastian," I assure him. "You need to be able to do your job. This will alleviate the jitters."

Although Bastian will charge blindly into a military camp and kill anyone within his reach, my daughter terrifies him.

Annalisa tips his chin, rubbing her hand over his jaw. "We have a lot to learn, Bass," she tells him. "I would rather have you focused than afraid of offending me."

Bastian curls around her to watch Tarq one more time. Tarq moves slowly to show the young wolf precisely what he's doing. He barely touches me as he slides his nose down my leg. Bastian lifts his jaw from Annalisa's hand and mimics Tarq's movements. I roll my eyes as my daughter shivers and giggles from Bastian tickling her skin.

"Oh... Um," Bastian stammers, moving away from her.

Sighing, I move around the kids and point to the ground. Bastian eyes Annalisa nervously as I reach for his jaw and reposition him to sit facing the space between us.

"Bastian did not grow up with a Luna," I tell Annalisa. "Your job, daughter, is to help him feel comfortable with you." I rub the young wolf's chin. "Inside this powerful wolf is a sweet, shy boy." I wink at Bastian.

"How can I do that if I can't hear him?" she pouts.

"Bastian has ways of communicating with you." I pull the young wolf's eyes to mine. "Are you ready to teach my daughter how to listen to you?"

Bastian pokes his nose in my face and nods.

"It would appear that he's ready," I say, giggling. "So, Bastian, would you like a pad rub?"

Bastian puts his paw on Annalisa's lap.

My daughter shakes her head, laughing. "Well, that will always be a yes."

"True," I agree. "Let's try something hard. Bastian, will you die to protect my daughter?"

Bastian pulls his paw back and leans to rub his muzzle gently against her cheek. As he pulls away, he tucks into his chest, showing his shyness. I'm about to stop him when Annalisa reaches out to catch his chin, pulling him back to her.

"Perhaps you could safely protect me," she suggests. "I kind of like having you around. I wouldn't want anything to happen to you either." She kisses him behind his whiskers, triggering his hum, before letting him go.

"*Thank you, Luna,*" Bastian says.

"You're welcome, sweetheart," I say, kissing his nose. "Now, why don't you take my daughter and practice listening to each other while I spend time with her father."

* * *

We reach the river docks by nightfall. Anthony builds a fire while Tarq and I work with the different groups of guards, and Bastian settles in camp with Annalisa. It's nice to see him relaxing when we join them.

After a quick dinner, Tarq drags all the wolves out to hunt so we'll have meat to offer the boat when it arrives in the morning. Amelia returns first with four rabbits. She reminds me that they are Bastian's favorite and announces that she has done her part.

"I'm sure Bastian will appreciate your contribution," I tell her as she jogs away to lie down with Bruce, who'd stayed behind as our guard.

Hearing that the rabbits were for Bastian, Annalisa joins me in skinning them. She's been handling meat since she could walk. She's nearly as skilled with a knife as I am. My daughter's never enjoyed it, but she's smiling while working on this meal for Bastian. She's starting on her second carcass when I see her rub her chest.

"Come here, kid," I say, holding my arm out. Annalisa leans over, letting my arms wrap around her.

"My chest hurts, Mom," she whispers.

"I know, honey," I tell her, shifting her back flat against my chest. "I used to think I panicked whenever Daddy wasn't near me." I press my hand firmly to the center of her chest. "I want you to take a deep breath and push your chest into my hand. It's like you're forcing my hand away from you. You'll keep your chest lifted when you let it out."

Annalisa takes a few deep breaths, smiling as her body relaxes. "Am I going crazy?"

Remembering that I thought the same thing, I can't help laughing. "It certainly does feel like it, doesn't it?" I wrap my arms back around her and squeeze. "Your body will crave the protection your guard provides just as much as he wants to provide it. You're not crazy."

Annalisa frowns. "You didn't have anyone to help you with this?"

"Grandpa tried," I tell her. "He'd never met a Luna, though, so he didn't know what I was going through."

She sits up and rubs her hand over her chest with a smile. "I'm glad I have you, then."

"Me too, Sweets," I say, smiling back at her.

As Annalisa returns to skinning Bastian's rabbit, the slight grin on her face tells me she's already smitten with him. She's never really cared about how much of the meat she cut as long as the fur was gone, but for Bastian, she is careful to only cut the skin loose and save all of the muscle and fat below it for him.

"Anthony said that there used to be a massive arch a day and a half north of here," Edith tells us as she pokes at the fire, distracting us. "His parents took him there when he was a boy. How it fell made it resemble a fork, so now they call it the Sippi Fork."

"Rosalee liked history," I say, joining the lesson. "She told me the arch was in remembrance of the pioneers who first traveled west of the river."

"Dax said that they tore it down to discourage westward travel," Tarq adds. *"According to him, the mountains made it harder to control people."*

Tarq slides his nose along my jaw, taking a deep breath of my scent. I want to enjoy the attention but catch Bastian doing the same to Annalisa. When I turn to glare at him, he tucks his chin to his chest and curls around her, laying his head on her lap.

"He told me that he thought about taking the pack west a few times," Tarq continues.

"Why didn't he?" I ask. Apart from the wolves having to stay wolves, they would be safe from the militia and the old pack feuds.

"I'm not sure I ever asked," he admits, flopping beside me. *"I couldn't imagine living anywhere other than the lake."*

Tarq rolls onto his shoulder and taps me with his paw until I grab it. I notice Bastian mimicking my Alpha as I begin rubbing his pads. *"My Alpha,"* I say, raising my eyebrow. *"Why is that teenage boy copying you?"*

"Dar, everyone wants to be like me," Tarq says frankly, as if educating me.

I turn to lie against his ribs, bending his leg so that his paw rests on my stomach as I rub his pads. My eyes drift over to the kids. Annalisa is focused on her wolf, but Bastian is staring at me.

"Luna?" he asks. *"Can you tell us a story?"*

Neala had mentioned that Bastian continued to ask for stories while they were away. I enjoyed our long hours telling him tales about the pack and past adventures while we stayed at the cabin. Tarq got involved in them and told some of his versions. Bastian shook his head often as he'd already heard the truth.

"Bastian has requested a story," I announce. "Does anyone have a particular story they'd like to hear?"

The group begins to buzz. I'd like to hear Bruce and Amelia's stories from their time away from the pack. Anthony and Edith start arguing about whether one Anthony wants to hear is child-appropriate. Tarq begins listing the stories he alters to show him as a blameless victim.

When he catches me staring at him, he stops. *"What?"*

"Tarq, that boy did not ask for a fairy story," I inform him.

"Fine," he grumbles. *"You pick one."*

I quickly decide on one that will entertain everyone but be short enough to get the kids to bed soon. "How about the time Annalisa made me shoot her grandpa in the ass?"

"I don't see how you blame me for that," Annalisa whines. "I wasn't even born yet."

"You shot Dax?" Bastian lifts his head, surprised.

"Oh, I like this story," Tarq chimes in.

I grab Tarq's other paw when he sticks it in my face. "It's not much of a story, but it is one of Tarq's favorites."

"It's my all-time favorite," Bruce adds from over by the river.

"I bet it is," I tell him, grinning. *"But you seem happy, Bruce."*

Amelia lies beside Bruce with her nose cuddled into his chest. He closes his eyes and sighs loud enough that I can hear him.

"We were playing ball one full moon," I start, turning back to the fire. "I was eight months pregnant with my little bundle of joy." I slide my fingers through Annalisa's hair and catch her eyes drooping in the firelight. Cupping Bastian's chin, I smile. "Sweet guard, why don't you let our young Luna lie down?"

Bastian nods and moves to lie behind Annalisa. He nudges her a few times before she rolls onto him and curls up against his shoulder. He pokes her arms, making her fold them between her body and his to keep them warm. The young wolf sticks his nose in her face, causing a sleepy giggle before turning back to me, his ears pricked, ready for more of the story.

"We'd played for a few hours," I continue. "It was an awful night for Tarq as he hadn't caught a single ball."

"You try running across a field, beating a dozen wolves, and catching a ball after your father headbutts your gut," Tarq grumbles.

"Dax was indeed in a mood that night," I agree. "He wasn't even bothering with the ball. He was only aiming at Tarq all evening."

"I wish I could hear Grandpa," Annalisa mumbles.

"No, you don't, honey," I tell her, smiling. "At 191, Grandpa's got a mouth on him."

Bastian rolls onto his side as Annalisa giggles, curling his leg over her hip. *"Why do they fight so much?"* he asks.

Sliding my hand over his face, I tug his ear. "It's not fighting, sweetheart," I tell him. "They spent a lot of time together while Dax was alive. Although he was immortal, Tarq was stronger. However, as wolves, the immortal Alphas are unmatched in strength. They aren't as fast, but you will not win a battle against them."

Anthony snickers across the fire. He enjoys watching Tarq try every full moon.

"It would seem that Annalisa has always had a soft spot for her father," I continue, smiling down at Tarq. "After twelve rounds, she punched me in the bladder. I had my arrow loaded and was aiming at the ball. I looked down as I wet my pants and let go of the string."

"Forever known as the day the Luna shot Dax in the ass!" Tarq laughs heartily, kicking his legs.

"At least it's not known as the day the Luna peed her pants," I say, frowning.

"He was so mad at you," Edith says, giggling.

"He deserved it," I grumble. "It's still unclear how many times he shot Tarq."

Edith wags her eyebrows. "But he is beautiful. Scars and all." Anthony scoffs, pulling her head to his chest.

"Why don't you help me put the kids to bed, and then we'll take a walk, My Love?" I slide my hands over Tarq's head and watch the kids. Annalisa is asleep, and Bastian seems to be fading fast.

Tarq coaches Bastian as I roll Annalisa into the teenager's stomach. The young wolf moves his legs as directed, and I'm not sure my daughter even woke up throughout the process.

Moving Annalisa's hair from her face, I lift the young wolf's leg to lay it over her arm. "I expect guard behavior, Bastian."

"Yes, Luna," he promises. *"Good night."*

I nod to Bruce and lead Tarq along the river bank into the woods. There aren't trails, so we walk until we reach a small area without underbrush.

"Nate's sent a few reports that the pack is doing ok," Tarq tells me. He knows I allow most of my wolves to filter into the background. It was hard at first, but now, unless I listen for them or they talk directly to me, their voices are just a hum in my head.

"I know this is needed, and Will said it might help my lungs, but I hate leaving them all behind," I say, frowning.

I turn just as Tarq shifts. He slides his arm around my lower back and cups my cheek. My lips lose their frown as I rub them against his. I can't see his eyes, but I still melt in his gaze.

"My Love, our pack is large, and many live far away," Tarq reminds me, letting his lips stay against mine. "They will work together as we've taught them to stay safe." As I sigh, Tarq straightens to pull his mouth away from me. "Dax says good leadership is being able to step back and allow those you taught to take the reins."

"Thank you."

"For what, Dar?" Tarq ducks into my neck, taking a deep breath before opening his mouth and allowing his teeth to slide against my skin.

My fingers dig into his hips, and air rushes from my lungs as my body shivers. "For being the smartest man I know."

Tarq leans his head against mine. "That's only because you don't know that many men." He exhales and slides his lips up my neck.

"Whatever you say, my Alpha," I say, giving up and pulling him away from my neck.

Tarq nips my lip. "What should I say to get you out of these clothes?"

My hands were already pulling my jacket off. Tarq helps me remove the rest of my clothes between kisses and props me against a tree. I'm enveloped in his arms as he pushes into me and heats his body more than usual to combat the lowering temperatures. Every nerve in my body is alive, reaching out to him, wanting to feel his love.

Tarq claims all I give until my hips tip to him. I bite his shoulder as he stops and grinds his hips into mine, triggering our release. He pushes through my muscles until I fall limply against his body.

Tarq lets me tuck my face into his chest as I catch my breath. *This cold air hurts. Will was definitely onto something.*

"You're sicker than you told me, aren't you?" Tarq asks, trying to heat up more without hurting me.

It's getting harder to hide my symptoms from him. He is not the cause of my struggles, but he will surely blame himself. *It's time to deploy the only strategy that works on Tarq.*

"It's just the cold air, My Love," I tell him, masking that I still haven't caught my breath. "We'll be warmer tomorrow. I've arranged a surprise for all you have tolerated as my Alpha."

Tarq ducks toward his chest, rubbing his lips against my forehead. "I haven't done anything special to earn a surprise, my Luna, but I will still take it."

I take a deep breath to ensure I'm ready to leave his heat now that Tarq is sufficiently distracted. Leaning back, I slide my fingers over his jaw and look into his eyes. "Tarq, I would not be the Luna I am without your support," I whisper. "I could not have mended that broken boy without your blessing." I cup his cheek and rub my thumb over his lips. "You aren't the man beside me. You are the mountain that lifts me, the roof that shelters me, and the map that guides me."

Tarq kisses my thumb and tucks me back under his chin. "I will always be here for you."

"Can you be here for me in camp, though?" I ask, wincing. "Bruce is too old to be standing watch all night." He laughs but knows it's true. Cuddled up to Amelia, the aging wolf won't last long. "I promise that you'll get sleep on the boat, but you'll have to stand watch tonight, My Love."

Tarq helps me slip back into my clothes and zips my jacket. He gently rubs his lips over my face before giving me one final kiss and stepping back to shift.

"I love you, my Alpha," I whisper, sliding my fingers under his jaw.

Tarq just hums as he leads me back to camp. As we pass the wood pile, I grab an armful of logs. I throw a few into the flames and set the rest next to Anthony for him to add if they get cold. Next, I stop to check on the kids.

"Luna, I think she's cold," Bastian says. *"I'm not doing this right."*

I run my hand over Annalisa's bare leg, feeling her cold skin. Touching Bastian's stomach, I lift my eyebrow. *"Bastian,"* I say, scolding him. *"The whole point of this is to keep her warm. You need to let your body heat up."*

He pokes her cheek with his nose as I sit down beside them. *"It won't hurt her?"*

"Bastian, do as you're told, or she'll be sleeping against her father," I warn him. *"You need your rest. My daughter gets seasick on a row boat. This is going to be a hard journey for both of you."*

Tarq sits beside me, looking down at them. *"You should probably tell her he doesn't need bare skin to take in her scent."*

Frowning, I lean against his shoulder. *"I guess we have a lot to learn too."* After a few minutes, I place my hand against Bastian's stomach and feel his heat radiating. Annalisa snuggles into him with a sigh. *"There you go, sweetheart. Thank you."*

Tarq checks on his daughter and rolls down onto his side once satisfied, holding his front leg up for me. I nod to Bruce and watch as he curls against the sleeping Amelia, covering her face with his neck.

I snuggle into Tarq's chest. *"Sometimes I think about how Dax's Annalisa became the Luna at such a young age,"* I admit sadly. *"She failed in every way."*

"We've taught her how to calm the wolves and create her fire touch," he reminds me. *"Those are two things that Luna never learned."* Tarq has never been able to call her anything but Luna. Naming our child after her was all he could handle.

"Just don't leave her, ok?" I beg. *"If anything happens to me, don't leave her alone."*

"I promise, My Love," he whispers. *"Now rest."*

He nudges my head into his chest and heats his body, sending me to sleep.

18

Tarq's hum fills my ears when I wake. He's talking with Nate and some senior guards, so I eavesdrop and snuggle into him. I hear Ash talking with Brock about how he'll be continuing the trip with us. The teenager is understandably upset.

"*Good morning, My Love,*" Tarq says when his conversation ends.

"*Good morning, my Alpha,*" I say, tugging his fur.

His tail thumps on the ground. "*My surprise is here.*"

I push away from his chest and look toward the river. "I have no idea what you're talking about," I tell him, curling back into his chest. "I see boats."

"*Dar, don't play with my emotions,*" he says, chuckling. "*You convinced Will to let us use his houseboat, didn't you?*"

"Yes, I did," I say playfully. "But Chase and Brock will be with us, so tone down your usual level of crazy."

Tarq rubs his whiskers over my cheek. "*I will remind you to scream quietly.*"

I kiss his muzzle before sitting up. "How gentlemanly of you." I run my fingers through Annalisa's hair, waking her up. Bastian rubs his nose over the loosened hair. "How did you sleep, Bass?"

The young wolf lifts his leg off Annalisa. She throws her legs over him, starting his hum. Bastian licks his lips as his eyes close. "*I sleep so well when she's with me, Luna.*"

I scratch behind his whiskers. "As her guard, your body will relax knowing she is safe."

Annalisa rakes her fingers through Bastian's fur a few times before she looks up at me.

"She will also sleep more soundly with you against her," I tell Bastian, rubbing my fingers over my daughter's forehead. "She knows she's safe with you."

"He's like my personal heater," Annalisa says.

"Pretty much," I say, touching her cheek. "We have some time before we leave, Sweets. I'm sending the junior guards home. If you want to say goodbye, now's your chance."

Tarq and I walk to the boat dock. We're both preoccupied with listening to the guards, but Tarq stops when we reach Brock. I kiss his muzzle, leaving him to talk to the disgruntled junior guard.

Bruce is lying further down the dock and lifts his head as I approach him. "Where's Amelia?"

"Neala is giving her a few more lessons to work on with Bastian," he says.

Sitting cross-legged in front of him, I reach for his jaw. "Things seem to be going well. Have you talked?"

Bruce is the only wolf besides Tarq that I've always been able to cover his eyes and ears. He remains still, allowing my hands to slide over his face, tugging his ears and pulling at the fur on his neck. Bruce steps into my arms and slides his jaw down my back. The lack of hum means he's found something he likes much more than my touch. *I suspect that's Amelia's cuddles.*

"I'm doing all the talking, but I think she's actually listening to me this time," Bruce says, relaxing on my back.

"I think you might be right," I say, sliding my hands down his legs. "Amelia seems to be enjoying her time with you too, but I'd still like to check with her. Would that be ok?"

Bruce backs up, rubbing his muzzle over my cheek. *"I want her to be happy, Luna."*

"You two will be with Edith and Anthony on the big barge," I tell him. "You should have plenty of time to talk while you watch Bastian."

Bruce steps back as Tarq slides his jaw over my shoulder from behind me. *"It's obvious that those kids are falling in love."*

Tarq and I sigh in unison.

"I know," I say. "We just need Bastian to keep his promise to me."

"I will talk to him," Bruce assures us.

Smiling, I tug the fur on his throat. "Thank you."

Bruce bows as he jogs off to spend time with Amelia when she calls to him. Tarq circles me to take his place.

"So, My Love, how is Brock?" I ask.

"That kid's pissed, but I remember when my Alpha wouldn't let me have my mate. It wasn't easy." Tarq hums, sliding his muzzle over my cheek.

Leaning against him, I run my fingers through his fur. "Do you agree with Neala about separating them?" My eyes roll closed as Tarq pushes his nose under my hair and slips his tongue over my neck. "My Alpha? You cannot check out right now."

Tarq groans as he steps back. *"Imagine my needs in a teenage boy,"* he says, licking his lips. *"Yes, My Love, I agree with her."*

I frown. "If we can't convince regular wolves to resist, how will we ever stop Bastian?"

"He's been handling everything well, Dar," Tarq reminds me. *"Let's not prepare for the worst unless it's necessary."*

Tilting my head to the side, I look over my Alpha. "With everything going on and all the work we've been doing, I've missed just talking to you."

Tarq puts his paw in my lap. *"I have too, My Love."*

* * *

We're floating down the river an hour later on the houseboat. Chase and I watch Brock pout on the bow from the wheelhouse. What I feel when I'm near him is not anger. Brock's heartbroken.

"Chase," I say, breaking the silence. "What do you think is an ok age to bond?"

Chase raises his eyebrow. He didn't meet his mate until a few years ago, but he knows what I mean. "I was 16 the first time I was with someone, Dar."

"I was 17," I tell him.

"Girls statistically mature faster than boys," Chase thinks aloud. "Maybe in a year or two, Rachel can talk some sense into him."

"Until then?"

"I'll talk to him," Chase promises. "Maybe telling him what could happen if she were to get pregnant too young will help him." He holds his arm out as I finish the last of my medicine.

Wrapping my arms around his waist, I squeeze him. "Thank you, Chase."

When Tarq opens the wheelhouse door, cold air rushes in. "Sorry, Dar," he says, closing it quickly. He wraps around me from behind, giving me warmth from both directions. "What do you think we should do about him?" Tarq asks.

"I was thinking he would make a good companion for the kids," I say, narrowing my eyes in thought. "They are in similar situations, and Brock is nearly the opposite of Bastian."

The guys look down at me. I step out of their arms and lean against the back wall as they both begin to object.

"Dar, that's not for you to decide," Chase says.

"Yeah, I agree," Tarq chimes. "You don't get to pick their companion."

"Do you feel like you had a choice?" I ask, looking at Tarq. "You two were thrown together in the beginning, and when I came back, Chase was the only wolf with a full grasp of what was going on. You're the same age..."

Tarq looks at Chase, lifting his eyebrow. "Things did get easier when I had you to help me with the new pack members."

"And Chase, you are the calmest person I know, while Tarq is extremely emotional," I add.

Chase continues shaking his head. "Look, Dar, I agree that he would make a good companion, but you can't force that," he tells me. "It's Bastian's decision, not yours." He corrects the boat's course and leans against the window to lift his eyebrow at me.

Tarq reaches around my back to tug my hair. I notice that my nerves aren't reacting to him. Tarq's emotional state controls this aspect of our life. Jules told me a few weeks before she passed that for my safety, his body will turn off our nerves' reaction when he is feeling an extreme emotion. I laughed when she said angry sex with Tarq would probably kill me, but I'm sure she was right.

When I look into my Alpha's eyes, I see that his emotions are not quieting his need this time. Tarq is tired, and his eyes droop as he stands before us. He stood watch last night, and while we were at the house, he constantly checked on and watched the kids, letting me sleep. *This Luna needs to take care of her Alpha and forget about the future leaders for now.*

"Come on, My Love," I whisper. "Let's get some sleep."

"We'll be tying up to the barge at sundown," Chase tells us. "I've got this until then. You two should rest."

Chase turns his attention back to piloting the boat as I guide my Alpha to the door.

"I almost didn't leave the room," Tarq snickers. "You need to feel this bed."

"That good, huh?" I giggle.

Tarq is a simple man but is used to the finer things. Initially, his family had money, property, and access to extensive goods to trade, but now that he's my Alpha, people just give him stuff. He doesn't want or ask for it and usually tries to return it, but he likes nice things. So, if he says the bed is exceptional, I'm in for a real treat.

Will's houseboat is long but only consists of the wheelhouse and bedroom. When Tarq opens the door, it's clear that Will was used to luxury before coming to work for me. I recognize the wood of the bed frame as mahogany. The mattress looks as big as ours at home. Tarq calls it 'extra-large,' but I only know it's bigger than a king-size bed. The front of the room housed all his medical equipment, which is now at the clinic.

Tarq crawls onto the bed and pulls me until I climb beside him. Whatever this mattress is stuffed with feels like a cloud. Tarq lays his head on the pillows, and I lie against him with my head on his shoulder.

"Why would he leave this to live in the woods with us?" I ask.

"I have no idea," Tarq says. "I'm considering leaving you for this bed."

"Ok," I say, laughing. "There's no need to be dramatic."

Tarq rolls over, trapping me under his chest. "Fine," he grumbles. "I'll let you visit sometimes." His body heats as it begins to shut down.

Giggling, I slide my hand along his ribs. "Sleep, my Alpha."

* * *

I'm woken sometime later by a soft knock on the door. Tarq has lifted off me slightly but is still asleep. Knowing it's Chase, and he will come in after the second knock, I lie still and appreciate my peaceful Alpha. Even asleep, his presence assures me of my safety.

As predicted, the door creaks open after the second knock. "Dar?" Chase whispers.

Tarq will wake if I talk, so I wait for Chase to stick his head in to wave him over.

"We've tied off to the barge," he whispers, sitting on the bed. "They'll start the engines as soon as it's dark enough." He holds up his stethoscope. "I need to listen. Doc told me to memorize your lungs."

Sliding my fingers over Tarq's ribs, I urge him to lift off my chest for Chase. He silently checks the different areas while I listen to my wolves. I notice Amelia and Bruce talking loudly but not to each other, and Bastian repeatedly says, "No."

Knowing I'll wake my Alpha, I raise my eyebrow. "What's going on with Bastian?"

Chase frowns as Tarq opens his eyes. They regard each other for a moment, but then Chase sighs. "Bruce told him not to bother you, but there have been... issues."

Tarq licks his lips as he tries to wake up. "What happened?"

Glancing at me, Chase cringes. "You know Annalisa gets seasick," he starts. "Apparently, Bastian won't let anyone near enough to treat her."

Tarq heaves an angry sigh, rolling out of bed. He storms straight to the door and shifts as he yanks it open. When he launches onto the tall barge, the houseboat rocks dramatically from side to side.

"Move, Chase," I say, shoving our stunned companion. I love Chase, but I'm unsure why Tarq's anger still shocks him. I pull my jacket on as we follow him out the door. "Tarq, stop!" I shout against the wind.

Tarq is reared on his hind legs when I reach the fishing barge. He crashes into Bastian with teeth bared. Shoving Chase as he tries to hold me back, I march straight toward the fighting wolves. Tarq's snarls are so loud that I don't hear Bastian's until I'm beside them.

"Luna, look out!" Bruce shouts.

Tarq slings his head into Bastian's neck, knocking him off balance. Bastian's body falls in my direction. I dive out of his way, but my head bangs into a cleat on the deck.

Tarq jumps on Bastian before he can recover, latching onto his throat. Chase slides up beside me with a rag. He holds it to my head and pulls it away, showing me the blood. He tries to talk to me, but the wolves are so loud that I can't understand him.

I shake my head and shove it away. "Go," I yell in his ear. "Annalisa."

He nods and leaves through the doorway to the ship's hold.

As I slide my hand over Tarq's back, his snarl quiets but doesn't stop. *"Bastian, my Alpha gave an order before we boarded the boats. Do you remember that?"*

Bastian twists and kicks his back legs at Tarq, missing him. *"You didn't tell me your witch would be treating her!"* he shouts in my throbbing head. *"I may not have any say about you, but she is my Luna, and I forbid it!"*

The barge jolts as the engines start. Tarq swings his body around, giving me his hip to lean against. His heat is appreciated as the boat begins to steam down the river.

"You're bleeding," Tarq says sadly. *"I can smell it."*

I tug the hair on the tip of his tail. *"It's not that bad, my Alpha,"* I tell him. *"You can fix it when he remembers his place."*

My least favorite part about being the Luna is teaching my wolves their place. We rarely need to. It's usually the children learning that it's not a contest. There is a place for everyone, and I love them all. Tarq sighs, knowing we'll be here a while.

Bastian's growl continues for hours. He's not yielding but doesn't push on Tarq again. My Alpha stands still, only rocking with the boat, as he silently holds the young wolf down.

"The militia outlawed the use of steam engines on the river," I start quietly, trying a different approach with Bastian. Both wolves shift their gaze in my direction. "They don't allow any southbound boats to use an engine. You need a license to use one while traveling north."

Bastian's growl isn't gone, but it's beginning to quiet.

"Both of these boats have a flat bottom, so we'll be able to get into the smaller channels where you guys can hunt," I say, allowing the story to calm him. "They have paddlewheels underneath them to propel them forward, and the smokestacks are built to look like fireplace chimneys. That's pretty neat, isn't it?"

"*Luna, you're bleeding,*" Bastian says.

Ignoring him, I continue. "This barge has one in the front and the other in the back," I say, rubbing my hands over Tarq's back legs. "That way, if the river ever gets too shallow, they can act like wheels." I see Bastian has fixed his eyes on me, and his growl has stopped. "Are you done, Bastian?"

"*Yes,*" the young wolf answers, sighing.

"Let him up, my Alpha."

Tarq slowly steps back, stiff from the hours of holding Bastian down. His jaw won't open, so he rakes his teeth over the teenager's skin to release him. Tarq stretches his limbs and works his jaw a few times as he moves around me to find my wound.

"Bastian, lie down while we talk," I say, pulling my hair out of Tarq's way. "That is our little girl. Those people you threatened have cared for her since birth."

The young wolf lifts his head and pricks his ears, but I point to the deck, telling him to lay it back down.

"You fought the standing Alpha and allowed me to remain injured, but your head should be elsewhere on more important matters," I say, raising my eyebrow. "Would you care to guess what that would be?"

"*Annalisa!*" Bastian shouts, making me wince.

"That's correct," I tell him. "While you were out here fighting with people who care about her, she's been without her guard."

"*Can I go check on her?*"

"In a minute, sweetheart," I tell him as Tarq leaves us to check our group, including our daughter. "We worked hard to help you overcome your life's pain, but we cannot erase your past. I need you to start looking at the bigger picture, or you will fail to protect your Luna and her pack."

"*I understand, Luna,*" Bastian says softly. "*I'm sorry.*"

I slide my hand over Bastian's muzzle as he holds it to my cheek. "I know, sweet boy," I say. "You have some apologies to make, and then you can check on your Luna. She should be sleeping by now."

As Tarq steps out of the ship's hold, Bastian leaves me to apologize. He crossed an uncrossable line in Tarq's book. Leaning against the door, I watch them as they talk but listen to the wolves back at the lake to give them privacy. Although I realize Bastian's issue, my Alpha will never understand why someone would cause his family harm.

Once they hook necks, I open the door and let them both slip through before closing us away from the wind. Tarq steps into me as I drop to the floor against the wall and heats up.

"That might have been a little overboard, My Love," I whisper, threading my fingers through his fur.

"*That's my little girl.*"

His response is firm. He's highly protective of us, and I'll not be winning this battle. I hope Bastian learned a valuable lesson tonight that never needs to be repeated.

As Tarq calms down, I look around the back room. The barge is owned by a wolf originally from Chase's mate's pack. He's a coyote that runs wolves up and down the river. Although he's fashioned everything to look legit, his boat is often searched, so hidden compartments are everywhere.

Once Tarq has settled down, we head to the front of the barge, where the hidden room is located. Chase is waiting for us with a report about Annalisa. "She's lying down, Tarq," he says. "She's had her medicine and should sleep through the night."

Chase lifts a board and pulls a door that is fashioned to look like part of the wall of stacked wine barrels. Tarq enters the room, but Chase puts his hand on my arm to stop me.

"Are they alright?" he whispers.

I watch Tarq check his daughter and poke at Bastian's stomach, ensuring he's warming her. "They'll find their way," I answer. I cup his cheek and step past him.

Chase closes the door and steps around the bedding. He sits beside Bastian, leaning against the wall where he can monitor my daughter throughout the night. Anthony and Edith are in one corner with the lantern, while Bruce and Amelia are cuddled across the room. There are four large mattresses sewn together that cover nearly the entire floor. Brock lies squarely in the middle of them.

Getting on all fours, I crawl toward him. He's staring at Bastian, and his heartache is overwhelming. I slowly move into his eyeline so I don't startle him.

"My Love," I call to Tarq. *"Would you mind sharing me with this boy tonight?"*

I slide my hand over the heartbroken teenager's head, and he closes his eyes, letting a tear fall. Tarq appears beside me to rub his nose over Brock's muzzle.

"He needs us tonight," he agrees.

With my nose nearly touching his, I lie down facing Brock. My hands slowly glide over his fur, pulling some of his pain to make it easier to talk with him. *"Will you help me stay warm tonight, sweet boy?"*

In response, Brock bumps his nose to mine and rolls onto his side to let me lie against his gut. Tarq tucks in behind me, and the wolves tangle their legs. My Alpha slides his head under the teenager's neck. Brock sighs as he rests his head on Tarq's shoulder.

"You'll get through this, sweetheart," I promise Brock. *"You will have a beautiful life full of joy with the woman she will become."*

"I love you, Luna," Brock says, nuzzling my cheek.

I knead my fingers in his fur, still pulling the extra emotions. *"I love you too, baby. Get some sleep. Tomorrow, we'll go on an adventure."*

* * *

In the morning, the captain docks next to a small village inhabited by some of our distant wolves. After introducing the kids to a few, I bring them to a fishing lake further inland so they can stretch their legs. Tarq takes Bastian and Annalisa to circle the lake while Brock stays with me. He watches the other kids as they leave, and I can tell he's torn. The kids enjoy playing with Tarq because he's fun, but accompanying the Luna is a treat.

"How are you feeling today?" I ask, leading Brock to a sunny area in the sand.

"He's her mate, isn't he?" Brock asks instead of answering my question.

I sit down and follow his eyes. "What makes you think that?"

Brock lies next to me, setting his jaw on my leg. *"The way he looks at her,"* he tells me. *"I love Rachel, but I'm not sure I'll ever be that devoted to her."*

My fingers slide through his fur as I watch my daughter. "When you look at Rachel, can you see she loves you?"

"Yes," he answers, letting me hear his smile for the first time.

"Do you think that she sees that you love her?"

"I hope so." His frown has returned.

Lifting his head by his chin, I make him look into my eyes. "I can see it. So if she can't, it's only because she's too young." I pull his nose to my lips for a kiss. Brock pulls back, tucking his chin into his chest. "There is none of that, sweet boy. If you hang with the Luna, you're gonna get love!"

Grabbing his muzzle with both hands, I plant noisy kisses behind his whiskers until he's chuckling. I let him slide from my hands, smiling.

"Your mate is not a defining part of you, Brock," I continue. "She will complement your life in a way you never dreamed possible. This time apart will allow you to determine how you want to be defined."

Brock nuzzles my cheek before moving to lie behind me so I can lean back on him.

"You've been watching your Alpha," I say, lifting my eyebrow.

"He's a good man and a strong wolf," he says, turning to watch them again.

Smiling, I tug the fur on his throat. "He's a good role model for you boys," I say. "Hopefully, Bass will be too."

"He's almost as strong as Tarq."

Brock is not a fearful wolf but has never seen a real fight like Tarq and Bastian. I saw his tail as he ran into the ship's hold last night. Bruce had told him to go outside while Bastian acted out, but they scared him once Tarq dragged the wayward wolf outside.

"Maybe you could learn to like him if you give him a chance," I tell him.

We both look up the beach at the approaching trio. Annalisa tries to walk with Bastian in her hand, but her father keeps curling around her to poke her guard's face. After a few times, they try to put the other's muzzle in their mouth. She throws her hands in the air, frustrated with their playing.

Annalisa plops on the sand beside us, reaching for Brock's chin. "I don't know what they're doing," she grumbles. "They're all yours."

I listen as they try to nip each other's front legs. They are talking about playing ball, which Bastian has never done, so it's a worthless conversation. I shake my head. "Daddy's just being Daddy."

Brock looks back at me. *"Do you think we'll get to play soon?"*

"I'm sure we'll find some time to play," I tell him, sitting up to welcome Tarq and Bastian to the group.

Annalisa scratches Brock behind his whiskers and pulls his muzzle to her cheek.

Bastian lifts his lips to snarl at Brock.

"Knock it off," I snap at him. *"Come here and sit by me."*

Annalisa watches Bastian curl around me. Once he sits down, she turns her attention to the wolf in her hand.

"Brock's mate is too young to bond," I tell Bastian. *"Sound familiar? As Lunas, we gravitate toward those wolves that need us."* I slide my hand over the side of his muzzle. *"Look at her face, Bastian. Do you see how she's looking at him?"*

"She looks heartbroken," he says sadly.

We watch as Tarq sits down beside his daughter.

"She is pulling his excess emotion. He will still feel it, but it won't crush him anymore." I pull Bastian's muzzle to my lips and smile at him. *"She will learn to pull these emotions without feeling them, but until then, she will need your support. You don't need to protect her from her friends."*

"His mate is too young?" he asks, sounding like he finally understands.

"Yes, sweet boy. Why don't you comfort your Luna, and I will take that wolf off her hands."

I pull Brock to me, wrapping my arms around him. My daughter flings her arms around Bastian and sobs into his fur.

Tarq nuzzles Annalisa's cheek before resting his jaw over Bastian's shoulders. *"A Luna's job is never done, is it?"*

I sigh into Brock's neck. *"These kids are the future of our pack. It's our job to build them up so they will be strong enough to carry our wolves."*

19

"*D*ar! Get off the road!" Tarq yells. "*Soldiers, Dar! Get the kids off the road!*"

We'd just left the lake, and Tarq patrolled out front while the kids walked with me in the setting sunlight. I pull Brock off the road, diving behind a thick bush. Bastian pulls Annalisa to me, and I press my finger to my lips as she lies down on her stomach. Bastian crouches over Annalisa. Brock tries to copy him but ends up between us.

When the clopping of hooves draws near, Bastian growls. "*Easy, Bass,*" I say. "*Just let them pass. We don't need the attention.*"

"*They're almost gone,*" Bastian reports.

I'm listening to the hoofbeats when Bruce calls out. "*Luna, the captain said there were soldiers here.*"

"*We're dealing with them now, Bruce,*" I tell him, rubbing the boys' chests to keep them calm. "*Go wake Chase for me.*"

I can feel Brock's fear, but he rubs his nose over my daughter's cheek, trying to comfort her. I turn to see tears streaming down Annalisa's face. Giving her a small smile, I quietly hush her.

"*Coming up behind you,*" Tarq warns us as the hooves clop further away. He climbs over me, covering what Brock had missed. He pokes his nose against my face, sniffing me like a newcomer. "*God, you smell good.*"

"*Careful,*" I warn him, giggling. "*My husband's around here somewhere.*" I pull his muzzle, kissing him behind his whiskers. "*I love you, my Alpha. Is it safe to get out of here?*"

"Yeah, come on," he answers. *"Chase is coming, but I need you to get the kids moving."*

It's past sunset by the time we arrive at the boat. Bastian pulls Annalisa straight into the hold, not allowing her to see me clutching my chest and gasping for air. Brock helps me lower to the deck and sits with his chest against me. I feel his body heating up and bury my face in his fur, breathing in the warmer air.

"You don't look so good, Luna," Brock says, worried.

"I'll be alright, sweetheart," I assure him. *"The cold air just hurts my lungs."*

Tarq shifts and helps to push the boat off the dock before jumping on board. He scoops me into his arms, carrying me into the hold. Brock slips by as Tarq cradles me in his warmth and waits for Chase to finish dressing.

Chase pulls his shirt over his head and grabs me from Tarq, carrying me toward the front of the hold where Tarq won't hear him. "You're pushing yourself too hard," he warns me. "Tarq's noticed you're having trouble, and he'll figure this out."

I lift my legs from his arm and force him to put me down. Rubbing my chest, I stretch it and grimace. "I'll admit that I'm struggling, Chase, but these kids need me," I say. "They need to be ready to take this pack when it's time."

Chase catches my neck and turns me toward him when I try to pass. He holds both sides of my neck, trapping my jaw with his thumbs. "Dar," he hisses. "I've been caring for you since you returned to the lake. I don't care what Doc says. You're getting worse."

Sighing, I roll my eyes. "Later, Chase," I whisper, watching Tarq quickly approach us.

Chase has been my guard for nearly as long as Tarq, and he's our devoted companion, but none of that will matter if my Alpha thinks I'm being threatened. I pull Chase's hands from my neck, and Tarq steps beside me.

"Let's get the kids settled for the night," I say, placing a hand on each chest. "We'll stay on board tomorrow and put some distance between the soldiers and us. That scared Annalisa."

The kids are piled together in the center of the mattresses. Bastian's is the only face I can see. *"Why didn't the captain warn us, Luna?"* Bastian asks.

Brock's face is buried under his neck, and Annalisa quietly cries, cuddled against his underside. The ferocity within Bastian's stare makes me proud. I know he won't attack me, but he looks as though he's ready to defend them at a moment's notice.

I slide my hands over all three kids. *"We'll talk about that another time,"* I tell him. *"Are you ok?"*

Bastian curls his neck and pokes Annalisa with his nose. Brock pushes his face further under his neck, trying to stay hidden. *"Neither of them has seen soldiers, have they?"*

Sighing, I sit back and run my fingers through Brock's fur. *"No, baby,"* I admit. *"We let our children be kids while they can. They grew up more sheltered than you."* Feeling Brock's fear, I nearly regret that. *"Brock's strong. He'd make a good partner with some training. Maybe you could help me teach him to protect Annalisa with you."*

I stay with the kids until Tarq lifts Annalisa away from Bastian. I quickly take her place, leaning against the tense wolf and explaining what they are doing. We watch as Tarq gives her the medicine for her seasickness before sitting with her cradled in his arms. She continues crying, but she's cuddled against him, looking up at him as he whispers.

Annalisa rubs Tarq's face just below his bottom lip as she giggles. He has a thin fuzz that always covers where a man would generally have a beard. The hair below his lip is the softest, and she's always found it comforting to rub her fingers over it. He smiles as he continues whispering to her, and she's nearly asleep when he brings her back, tucking her against Bastian.

I move away from the kids as Tarq tugs Bastian's fur. "I helped her to understand how safe she is with you," he whispers. "Don't ever make me regret that." Bastian touches his nose to my Alpha's cheek in response. Tarq then pulls Brock from under Bastian. "Come on, kiddo," he says softly. "Annalisa can't handle you tonight. Why don't you help me protect our Luna?"

Brock sighs as he sits up. He slides his muzzle along Bastian's, and the two wolves pause with their eyes closed. Blinking back tears, I watch Brock accept the companion position.

"Can you tell me what scared you, sweet boy?" I whisper to Brock when he slips into my arms. Tarq lies against me, heating up and resting his hand on Brock's back.

"*I'm a guard, Luna,*" he grumbles. "*I'm not supposed to be scared of anything.*"

"Baby, everyone has fears," I assure him. "I'm afraid of snakes. If we ask my Alpha nicely, he'll tell us his greatest fear."

"*I was afraid they'd see us,*" Brock admits. "*What if I couldn't protect you?*"

"I can understand that, sweetheart, but I want you to listen to your Alpha." I rub my hand up the back of Tarq's arm. "My Alpha, would you please tell this young wolf your greatest fear?"

Tarq answers instantly. "I fear losing you, My Love."

Snapping his head up, Brock stares at our Alpha. "*He's so strong,*" he says, confused. "*Why would he fear losing you? Who could ever defeat him?*"

"Brock, if an arrow were shot at my chest and back simultaneously, how would you save me if you couldn't get to me in time?"

Tarq breathes a quiet laugh beside me. He'd used this example to explain his fear to me, and it's hard to dispute. As strong as he is, he can't be in two places at once.

"I want to believe that I could save her from anything," he explains to Brock. "But even I can't protect her from everything." Tarq slides his hand so that it rests over my heart. "I almost lost her a few times. We do our best, Brock, and we love and honor her while she's here."

Sighing, Brock lays his jaw on Tarq's hand. I turn to Tarq and smile as he kisses my lips.

"I'll work with you over the next few days while we distance ourselves from the patrols," Tarq promises. "I'm sure Bastian will help."

I'd never spent time with Brock until Neala asked for my help. With such a large pack, I know my wolves but can't give one-on-one attention to many of them. Most wolves will hum in my presence, but Brock never has. He's not interested in my touch.

My breath catches, and my eyebrow lifts when he hums against my chest. It could be anything that's set it off—Tarq's words, our family-style support, or even Bastian's chin resting on his hip. *I think it's time I find out more about this kid.*

* * *

"Sometimes I wonder what it would be like to be a normal girl," Annalisa grumbles a few days later.

We're lying on the bed in the houseboat, watching Tarq train the boys. Bastian has finished his part and sleeps beside Annalisa while she rubs his back pads. The lesson today is how to break a man in half. I'm sure ordinary girls have never seen a wolf slam their jaw on the floor to crush bones with their teeth.

"You'd be bored," I tell her.

Brock loudly crushes their last bone, and since Tarq, Chase, and Bruce work together at night to teach the boys to fight as a team, it's nap time for my wolves. Tarq steps on the bed and looks around at the lack of space. Being a massive wolf, Bastian is taking up most of it.

"*Get small, kid,*" Tarq says, chuckling. "*I'm gonna sit on your head.*" He starts curling to sit on Bastian.

Annalisa clicks her tongue. "Daddy, stop," she scoffs, giggling. My daughter doesn't need to hear her father to know what he's doing. She's used to his antics and tugs Bastian's tail. "Come here, Bass. You're not the only one who needs a nap. I don't sleep well while you guys train."

Bastian groans as he stands. He slides his head along Tarq's before crawling beside Annalisa and laying his jaw on her shoulder. I hear him lick his lips and giggle, knowing he's sneaking a taste of her. Tarq nips his tail in reprimand before snuggling between our daughter and me. Brock steps onto the bed and crawls to my left side. He nuzzles my cheek before yawning and resting his jaw on my shoulder.

"Luna, can you tell us why the captain didn't warn us now?" Bastian asks.

Tarq jams his nose under my neck, determined to sleep.

The boys stare at me. Annalisa lifts her head to look over, knowing one of the boys asked for a story. It turns out that Bastian isn't the only one who likes them.

"You know that Davis is a coyote," I start. "He runs wolves up and down the river, and what he does is dangerous. He has to be careful, not just for himself, but for our wolves too."

Bastian lays his head across Annalisa's chest, staring at me and relaxing into the story. They have become incredibly comfortable with each other, and neither pays much attention to where he lies. I found it weird, but Tarq told me that wolves don't think the same way, and our chest is simply a place that holds our heartbeat.

I rub Bastian's cheek. "Davis tried to cover his pack marking many ways, but they all failed. He came to me for help so he could continue his work. We found a way, but it was probably the hardest decision he will ever make, and we will not discuss it again after this."

I take a deep breath, wincing at my chest's tightness. Brock lays his head over my chest and heats up. He's an intelligent boy. He has figured out something is wrong but has kept it to himself.

"He asked me to exile him from the pack," I continue. "It's a punishment reserved for wolves who commit an inexcusable crime against the pack."

"So he can't talk to us?" Bastian asks. *"Even if he were to shift?"*

"Did you kick him out of the pack?" Annalisa exclaims.

I've been whispering, but Annalisa's outburst disturbs Tarq. He groans and shifts around, pushing his nose further under me.

"Sorry, Daddy," Annalisa whispers, tugging her father's ear. "Mom, why would you kick him out?"

I shake my head. "Yes, Bastian, even if he were to shift, we could not hear him. He is a lone wolf. And daughter, it was his decision, not mine. As I said, it was a difficult one that we will not discuss again."

Both boys sigh. They've spent their entire life with their pack. Bastian had a difficult time with his, but as wolves, they are never truly alone. The thought of being unable to hear or talk with their pack would be unimaginable, if not terrifying.

"I heard Anthony talking to Edith about Byron. Was he exiled too?" Annalisa asks.

"Yes," I answer. "Byron is the only other wolf to be banished. He knowingly broke a magical law that endangered the pack."

"But he's an elder!" Brock shouts in our heads.

Tarq grumbles, losing his patience with the kids.

"Let's let our Alpha sleep, Brock," I whisper. "Byron is still an elder. He is no longer a historian, which we needed him to be."

Bastian sighs deeply and shifts his hips around before moving his jaw to Annalisa's shoulder. Her eyes droop closed as Bastian tucks his nose under her neck and heats his body.

Once they're asleep, I turn to Brock. He is calmly resting his head on my chest. He snores, so I know he's awake. *"Brock,"* I say, rubbing his ear between my fingers. *"Can we talk about how things are for you at home?"*

Brock sighs and rolls his body, putting his back against me. *"I'm tired, Luna."*

I roll toward him and wrap my arms around his neck. *I've missed something with this young wolf.*

* * *

After three days on board, the captain pulls the boats into a shallow channel and docks. Tarq said he smelled some big game on the island, so almost everyone was excited about the day trip. My Alpha shoves a disgruntled Bastian up the bank, leaving me with the other kids.

I link my arm with Annalisa's and hook my fingers around Brock's jaw as we watch Tarq and Bastian leave to go hunting. "So, what do you two want to do today?" I ask the kids.

Brock hangs his head, putting weight on my hand. *"I wanted to go hunting,"* he grumbles.

Trying not to giggle, I turn to Annalisa. She's frowning in the direction Tarq had pushed Bastian.

"I want to learn to talk to him," she says sadly.

I grab her hand as she reaches for her chest. "Brock, would you be interested in helping me teach Annalisa how to hear wolves?"

The young wolf looks up at his friend as she flashes a bright smile. "Really?" Annalisa squeals.

Brock sighs, letting his lips fluff, unable to say no.

"Alright, then," I say merrily. "Let's find a spot to sit down." Leading them to a large tree, I choose a spot to sit and have them lie on either side of me with their heads on my lap. "Ok, child, you know Brock's voice. You're going to search for it among the noise around us."

Brock is relaxing with his eyes closed, waiting for the lesson to begin. To get him to loosen up, I scratch between his shoulder blades and giggle as he groans, arching his back into my nails.

"Brock, where are your sisters?" I ask, getting right to the point.

"They're probably at home, Luna. Why?"

"I haven't seen them in a while," I say, trying to keep my tone light. I don't want Brock to know I'm prying. "I haven't seen your parents either."

More anger comes off Brock than I'd like when I mentioned his parents. *"I don't know where they are."*

Working with my wolves is a balancing act. They are very emotional regarding their family and those they love, including when they are mad at them. Slipping my fingers through Brock's fur, I pull some of his anger.

"Did they go somewhere, Brock?" I ask, hoping to get something out of him before he shuts down. He lies with his eyes closed and doesn't answer, so I use the tactic that works on Bastian. "My father used to leave for extended periods when I was little to search for information about our family. My aunt Rosalee would care for me." I slide my hand over Brock's face. "Have you been taking care of your sisters?"

"Somebody had to," he answers.

Annalisa stirs in my lap. When I look down, her eyes are open, and tears drip from them.

"Would it be alright with you if I sent Neala to get them?" I ask Brock.

"You'd do that?"

Before I can stop her, Annalisa rolls over and grabs Brock's head, holding him to her. "I should've noticed," she says, sniffling. "I'm sorry."

While they have their moment, I listen for Neala and ask her to retrieve Brock's younger sisters. They are only a few years younger than him but shouldn't be alone long. Neala tells me that his parents had been moonshining for the past few years but have never been gone longer than three days. It's not against pack or militia law, but it is dangerous.

"I get the feeling they've been gone for a while this time," I tell Neala.

"I'll see what I can find out and get back to you, Luna," she says.

I pull my fingers through Annalisa's hair, moving it away from her face. Fresh tears are still leaking from her eyes. "I think we're going to change today's lesson," I say, frowning.

Annalisa sits up. "Mom, no!" she shouts. "I want to talk to Bastian!"

"Some things are more important, Annalisa," I say, cupping her cheek. "These negative emotions will crush you if you don't learn to control them."

With a scoff, Annalisa stomps back to the boat, clutching her chest. I remember this. I shouted at Dax and collapsed in the field near Edith's ranch. My Alpha's voice was the only sound I wanted to hear.

"Should I go after her?" Brock asks.

"No, Brock," I say. "She's going to need to hear a calm voice. I suspect she'll end up sitting with Chase." Winking at him, I tug his ear. "Besides, now I get you all to myself."

Brock chuckles and lifts his front leg to allow me to rest my head on his ribs. He pushes me until he can lean his head against my hip.

"Neala says your parents typically aren't gone more than a few days. Is that right?" When Brock doesn't answer, I tug the fur on his throat. "How long have they been gone, baby?"

"Two weeks," he answers, sighing.

"I'll send some guards to look for them," I promise the young wolf.

When Brock doesn't respond, I glance to find him studying me.

"You're sick, aren't you?"

"It'll be fine, sweet boy," I reassure him. "That's why we're on this trip."

"Do you remember about ten years ago when chicken pox went through the pack?" Brock lifts his head to look down at me. *"When he caught it, my grandfather said, 'It'll be fine.' He wasn't talking about himself."*

His grandfather didn't survive the illness, but I grin, knowing he will be the perfect companion for the kids. "But it is still why we're on this trip," I say, lifting my eyebrow.

Brock curls around to nip at my cheek. *"I'm not sure we're ready to lose you, Luna,"* he says.

"Then I will have to stay with you for a little longer, huh?" I smile at him.

With a sigh, Brock relaxes back down to my hip. His body heats up, and his hum starts again as he falls asleep.

Dax and Tarq were right. I've taken too much on alone and failed this boy and his sisters. *How many more have I missed?*

"Take one teenage boy away, and you end up cuddling with the other," Tarq says, making me giggle.

I look up to see him approaching from the beach. *"We'll be stopping in the old wildlife refuge tomorrow,"* I tell him. *"I'd like to send the kids out hunting together. Would that be ok?"*

Tarq lies down behind Brock, putting his chin on the teenager's shoulder. He turns his head so that his nose touches mine. *"I think that's a good idea. Bastian's taken to this one. They should make a good team."*

I kiss the tip of Tarq's nose and slide my hand down Brock's leg. *"I've been preaching to Bastian about the big picture, but we've missed something with this one."* I frown, looking up at Tarq. *"We need to do better. I'm supposed to protect them, not just rule over them."*

"We're going to make mistakes, Dar," Tarq reminds me. *"It's how we fix them that counts."*

I relax into Brock and rub my finger over the bridge of Tarq's nose. *"My Alpha?"* I say slowly. *"We seem to be missing a teenage boy."*

Tarq stretches his legs with a groan. *"We took down a bear. He's bringing it back."*

"Tarq?"

"What?" he whines. *"Dax made me bring the big game back by myself. It builds character."*

He opens his eyes to find me scowling.

"He's fine, Dar."

My scowl turns to a frown, and Tarq rolls to his feet.

"I'll go help him," he grumbles and jogs away.

My giggle wakes Brock. "Come on, sweetheart, help me find our young Luna."

I spot Bruce and Amelia in their human form together on the houseboat when Brock and I reach the barge, so I send him ahead. I hadn't found Amelia alone to speak with her, and I feel my support might not be needed now. She's comfortably leaning against Bruce's chest with his arms loosely draped over her hips.

"Bruce, I thought you might like to know that Bastian is on his way back," I say, stepping onto the deck. Bruce has made a point of shifting whenever Bastian is around to support him. "Could I have a word with Amelia?"

Bruce smiles as I wink at him. He cups Amelia's jaw, pulling her lips to his as Brock calls out to me.

"She's with Edith," he tells me. *"She wants to try to hear me. Is that ok?"*

"Yes, honey," I respond. *"Just don't let her out of your sight."*

Amelia watches as Bruce steps into my arms. I don't see him like this often, so hugging is required. "Happy looks good on you, Bruce," I whisper.

"Thank you for not giving up on us," he replies.

As Bruce pulls away, I can't help appreciating him. He has aged beautifully. His tan skin is smooth, his brown eyes radiate so much life, his chocolate-colored hair holds no hint of gray, and his muscles are so well-defined they flex when he thinks about moving.

I slide my hand down his abs and tug at the waistband of Tarq's shorts. "I wouldn't let Tarq catch you in these." Smirking, I lift my eyebrow. "He might be my Alpha, but he's still Amelia's son and wouldn't want this image."

Bruce chuckles as he kisses my cheek and leaves me with Amelia. She smiles broadly as I reach out to her.

"I wanted to check in with you to see how you were doing," I say as she wraps her arms around me.

"Oh, Luna!" Amelia gushes, relaxing against my shoulder. "I will never regret my time with Dax. We loved each other, and he gave me Tarq, but I have really missed out."

I giggle, knowing precisely what she means. "Dax means the world to me, but I had a difficult moment when I realized he knew I was Tarq's mate." I take a deep breath and rub Amelia's back. "I think what got me through everything in the end was remembering that Dax was happy and deserved that too."

Amelia sighs, pulling me over to the bench. "He's happy now, though, right?"

I shrug. "He seems to be, but I'm not worried about Dax. I'd like to know how you're doing."

Amelia squints her eyes in thought. With how gracefully wolves age, there's only the tiniest hint of a wrinkle. "It's a lot to take in, Luna. I understand why he did what he did, but I can't help thinking there was a better way."

"I don't know how Bruce felt about Tarq as a kid, but he respects him now." I run my hand down her arm. "I don't doubt that he has always loved you."

"I never felt it," she says, frowning. "I thought Bruce was there because he had to be."

"In the beginning, I thought so too," I tell her. "Once we started talking, I saw a different side of Bruce."

"He is different, isn't he?"

"Amelia, Bruce loved you enough to give you the freedom to be with the man you chose without guilt."

Amelia blushes, ducking her head. "I'm lucky he stuck around and came back for me."

"I doubt he sees it that way," I tell her.

"*I don't,*" Bruce says quietly. He jumps from the barge and steps onto the bench to hold his muzzle against Amelia's cheek. *"I would've waited forever for her to choose me."*

With a smile, I take a deep breath and squeeze Amelia's hand. "I'm gonna let you tell her that, Bruce." I kiss the side of his muzzle and leave them alone.

I find the rest of my group in the ship's hold. Bastian is sprawled out in the middle of the mattresses, nose-to-nose with Annalisa. She's staring at him as if looking into his soul.

"Bass, explain."

"She wants to try to hear me," he says, licking his lips.

I walk around the room to see my daughter's face. *"She looks... uncomfortable."*

Bastian chuckles. *"Luna, I feel like we've crossed many lines,"* he tells me. *"We don't need to pretend we have boundaries. She looks constipated, but I still love her."*

20

"When Davis said it was safe to use the houseboat, I thought it would be just us," Tarq pouts.

We're standing on the back deck just before dawn. I know he needs time with me, but the kids are used to sleeping with us. All three bounced happily beside us as we snuck off the barge last night.

"So did I, My Love," I tell him, giggling. "We took them away from everything they know, Tarq. They'll settle in eventually."

Relaxing into his heat, I watch the crew tie the barge in a small alcove and swing the back end to tuck the houseboat against the beach. Davis's men are all humans he's saved and helped over the years. They know what we are and respect us as such. They each bow their heads and address me as they pass.

"Dar, we can baby them or teach them to be strong," Tarq grumbles once we're alone. "We can't do both."

Turning to Tarq, I rest my hands on his chest. "I beg to differ, my Alpha," I say, frowning. "There is strength in love. Bastian's love for Annalisa brought him back from the depths of hell. Brock's love of being part of our family saved him from crippling depression, and my love for you brought me back from death more than once. Showing these kids love has built their confidence and trust."

Tarq scrunches his face and sticks his lower lip out. This is his "I agree with you, but I'm not happy about it" look, and I'm nearly required to giggle at it. "Ok, but we're still sending them all hunting today, right?" he asks, grinning.

"Yes, my Alpha."

Tarq pulls my jaw, pressing his lips to mine. My hands slide to his waist, and my fingers dig into his hips as his tongue tastes my top lip. My Alpha steps into me, causing my nerves to reach for him.

"Let's wake them up and kick them out," he whispers over my lips.

Giggling, I move my mouth away. "I am proud of this nurturing Alpha you've become."

Tarq slides his arms around my waist and tucks into my neck. "I'd rather be nurturing you right now."

Pulling his face from my neck, I guide him back to my lips for a deep kiss. "The sun will be up soon," I remind him, rubbing my nose against his. "We left our daughter in bed with two boys. We should probably get back in there."

Tarq laughs. "Well, aren't we just model parents?" Sliding his arm around my waist, he guides me back into the bedroom, where our daughter is still asleep, surrounded by her wolves.

I climb onto the bed and pull Bastian's nose from under Annalisa's neck. *"Hey, baby, come talk to me for a minute."*

Bastian releases a gaping yawn and slowly rolls over to face me, tucking his back paws under my legs. He rubs his face on the pillows and then opens his eyes to look at me.

"I know you're tired, honey, but I wanted to see how you are feeling about things," I say, rubbing my finger over the soft fuzz under his nose as Tarq lays down behind me.

"Luna, I'm thankful every day for the life you've introduced me to. I love you for the chance you've given me." Bastian looks at Tarq's hand on his shoulder. *"I love Tarq for all that he's taught me, and I am in love with your daughter, but I fear the things you hide from me."*

I hold Bastian's muzzle to my cheek. *"What could I possibly hide from you?"*

"I've been distracted, Luna, but I remember you're taking potions daily. Your witch was making a salve yesterday."

Sighing, I slide my hand over his jaw. *"Tarq and I will stay behind while you kids go hunting with Chase today,"* I tell him. *"It's the perfect time to medicate my lungs, sweetheart."*

Bastian pulls his nose away and bumps my cheek. *"Luna?"* His tone clearly tells me he doesn't believe me.

Lifting my eyebrow, I bop his nose with my finger. *"Sweet boy, this is not about me. I'm asking about you. You are the wolf in charge of keeping my daughter safe."*

Bastian sighs and flops back down onto the pillows. He starts to hum as Annalisa rolls over, sliding her arm around him. *"I think I'm the only one in danger when she's around me, Luna."*

I giggle as he tucks his face against mine and drifts to sleep. *"I think you might be right about that, sweetheart."* Relaxing back into Tarq's heat, I join the kids.

* * *

It's nearly midday when I kick the kids out. I know they're tired, but a greater need demands my attention. Chase walks past me with a large pot of water as I stand on the deck, watching the kids. There's a glob of something waxy bobbing around in it.

"Just put that pot on the stove and let the wax melt," Edith says, putting her arm around my shoulders. "Deep breaths, Dar. The deeper that gets into your lungs, the better."

Anthony had decided to join the kids, and Edith didn't want to be alone. As she steps down from the houseboat to join them, the kids line up along a small stream they'll follow to find game. They're goofing off, which makes Edith laugh.

I lean on the railing, watching the boys. "You guys listen to Anthony and Chase." They nod and return to playfully nipping at each other's legs. They've settled into the easy companionship I was hoping for, but I raise my eyebrow when my daughter ends up between them in their horseplay. "If anything happens to Annalisa, you'll answer to me."

Chase jumps from the boat and nods up the stream, telling the kids to get moving. "They'll be fine, Dar. Please get some rest." Chase knows my Alpha well and points at him with his eyebrow arched before following the rest of the hunting party.

Smirking, I turn to Tarq. "He's talking to you, My Love."

Tarq is leaning over the railing. He's been quiet this entire time. His muscles are tight, and he only moves his eyes toward me.

The moment the kids drop from sight, Tarq stiffly turns to me. "I heard you need to take deep breaths," he says, a devilish grin creeping across his lips. His head lowers as I take a step back. "Those were the doctor's orders, right?"

My nerves call out to my Alpha, but I still step back as he begins to stalk me. "No, the doctor told me to get rest."

Tarq quickly catches me, sliding his hand across my lower back. Holding me tightly to his body, he cups my cheek and rubs his lips against mine, stealing my breath. "When I've had enough, you'll need it."

Nipping at my lips, Tarq pushes me back into the bedroom and kicks the door closed as he shoves my coat over my shoulders. He's pulled my shirt off and broken my belt by the time we've crossed the room.

Finally having this time behind closed doors without children anywhere near us, we spend hours enjoying each other. My nerves never stop firing as they reach out for Tarq's attention. I slide my hands over his skin, getting reacquainted with how he feels under my fingers. The air fills with Edith's medicine, and my lungs pull it in as I repeatedly call out to my Alpha until we finally collapse.

Tarq rolls onto his side. "Now you can rest."

I giggle as I stuff a pillow under my head. "What is this stuff we're breathing?"

"Eucalyptus," Tarq tells me, moving closer and laying his leg over mine. "The healer used to crush the leaves and have us boil them when we were sick."

He closes his eyes and hums as I slide my finger over his jaw. "I'm proud of your work with the boys," I tell him. "They've become a solid team."

Tarq opens his eyes, sighing. "You were right about them. They're well-matched and naturally trust each other. Brock is quite protective."

Adjusting to remove pressure from my chest, I rest with my forehead against Tarq's. "It's more than that. He seems to have the desire to help others. He's been caring for his sisters."

"Annalisa told me that," he says. "Something about his parents not being around."

I pull away from Tarq. "I was trying to teach her to hear the wolves. She only heard my part of the conversation. His parents are missing."

"They're what?"

"We've been preoccupied, My Love," I say, touching his cheek. "I'm listening to Dax's advice, and Neala is checking on all the kids as we speak."

Tarq frowns. "Is anyone else missing? What else did we miss, Dar?"

I know my proud Alpha. Any failure is a sign of weakness, and I'm about to tell him how weak our leadership has been. "The senior guard is checking on everyone and looking for Brock's parents. So far, only two others have been reported missing."

Tarq sits up and looks down at me. "Who else is missing?"

"Ash says Gaine has been gone for four days, and no one can remember the last time they saw Darius." Rolling onto my back, I reach for Tarq's cheeks. "They're doing their jobs, My Love. We taught them well."

"Byron's Gaine?" Tarq asks, confused. "The mate-maker?"

I sigh, urging him to lie down. "You know she doesn't like to be called that. She only sees mates. She doesn't make them."

"She was part of the team that I sent to the basin. They watched over the Blood Pack and made sure they did what they said they would." Tarq rubs his forehead. "Where is she?"

"Her sister said she was meeting with a boy but wouldn't tell her who."

Tarq squints his eyes. "The crazy sister?"

"Tarq, can you please focus on the important facts?"

He lowers himself on top of me, enveloping my body in his arms with a sigh. "I'm tired, Dar. I just rode the hell out of you. You do this on purpose."

Loving Tarq has never been a problem. On the other hand, getting him to focus when he's tired or distracted has always been an issue.

"The guard is doing their job," I whisper. "It might be time for us to follow the doctor's orders, My Love." I hear Tarq mumble incoherently as I run my fingers through his hair. I kiss his neck as he heats up. "I love you, my Alpha."

* * *

Later that evening, the hunting party gathers in the hidden room as the captain starts the engines. Bruce and Amelia cuddle in the corner alone. Since they bonded, I've let them distance themselves from the group to enjoy each other's company. The rest of the group sits in the center of the room, discussing the different roles of our pack members.

"Luna, shouldn't I be with them? I would need to know that too." I can hear Brock's frown. He likes to spend time with me but is very interested in learning new things. I have him sitting in a corner with me.

I'm lying on his shoulder, watching the group with him. "Normally, yes, sweetheart, but we're waiting for Neala. She's brought your sisters to her house."

Brock lays his head down and stretches out his legs. *"I taught them to care for themselves while I went to the lake. I'm sure they were fine,"* he grumbles.

I tug his fur. "You did a good job, but they'll stay with Neala and Ash until we find your parents." I roll to face his head. "Neala just has a few questions for you."

Brock stays quiet, and I can feel his body heating. I half expect him to start snoring when he speaks up. *"Anthony's a good tracker."*

"He is," I say, smiling. "Did I ever tell you how Anthony and I met?"

The young wolf curls around to look at me. *"I didn't realize there was a story about it."*

Their love of stories will always make me smile. I tuck my arms into his chest, trying to find some warmth.

"Luna, you should get a blanket. It's cold in here tonight."

"I'll just tuck into you, and we can talk. I promise to make sure I'm warm enough, though."

Brock lifts his front leg, allowing me to tuck into his gut. I settle into his heat and tell him about Anthony hunting me over the years. He and Bastian have mixed feelings about Anthony. He's strict with them, and since he can't hear them, their actions are all he has to go by. The closer the boys get, the more they play, which pisses Anthony off.

"I always managed to escape, but I couldn't shake him," I say, slipping my fingers through his fur. "He always found me. Still does when I find myself in trouble." I look over my shoulder at Anthony. He taps the side of his eye and winks. "Did he teach you any of his tricks?"

"He said he'd take them to his grave."

"So, you know what you have to do, right?" I ask, turning back to him.

Brock sighs. *"No. I dug him a grave. He didn't think that was funny."*

Laughing, I pull his muzzle toward his chest and lean back. "You did not!"

Brock bumps his nose into mine and nuzzles my cheek, chuckling. *"I nearly pushed him into it. He said he would tell us."*

I giggle, shaking my head. "You are brave, my young wolf."

"Do you think he'll ever teach us?" Brock asks.

"If you prove yourself to him, baby, he will," I tell him. "Maybe you should avoid trying to put him in a grave, though."

Brock sighs. *"I'll try."*

I tuck back into his chest, settling into his heat. We lie still, listening to the conversation from the center of the room. They are discussing the guards and trainers. Nate is the head of the senior guard, and Tarq and Anthony work closely with him. They'll keep the kids busy for a while.

"You seem to be comfortable working with Bastian," I say, changing our subject. "How is that coming along?"

"He knows a lot about fighting," Brock says, almost confused. *"Tarq has to remind him to work with me like he's never fought in a pack before."*

"He did spend a lot of his time alone, but he seems to like us," I say, smiling.

"He doesn't talk about himself." Brock lifts his head to study Bastian. *"Where did he come from?"*

"I'm sorry, honey, that's not my story. When Bastian is ready, he'll tell you."

Brock sighs, curling his neck around the top of my head. *"I think she knows."*

Bastian and Brock have developed a shorthand that they think everyone should understand. I went through this with Tarq and Chase. "Who knows what, baby?"

"Annalisa," Brock answers. *"I think she knows he's her mate."*

I groan unintentionally. "She's young and smitten. You boys are quite adorable." I pull at Brock's fur playfully.

Brock lifts his head. *"Luna?"*

Frowning, I tuck my face further into his fur. On the one hand, I could not be prouder of the kids I am readying to take over our pack. On the other hand, however, I wish they'd stop noticing the things I'm trying to hide from them.

"As their companion, it'll be your job to remind Bastian of his oath to me if it's ever needed."

Brock moves, trying to see my face. *"Luna, why would I need —"*

"I'm sorry for the delay, Luna," Neala interrupts. *"I'm ready now, though."* I included Brock in the conversation when she started speaking to stop his inquisition.

"Neala, I haven't heard from my sisters," Brock announces, nestling in for the conversation.

"They're ok, Brock," she assures him. *"They're asleep in the bunkhouse right now after that long trip to the lake."*

I lie with Brock, slipping my fingers through his fur as he talks with Neala. He remains calm as she promises to keep them safe, and he lists their individual strengths for her. Strangely, he hasn't asked about his parents.

"Brock, do you remember your parents mentioning a location or area?" Neala asks. *"Perhaps a name?"*

"They packed warmer clothes, so I assumed they were going to the

mountain." Brock discusses how long his parents would be gone and the direction they often headed with Neala. "*I think they talked in code. My mother would tell my father the rooster crowed, but we don't have chickens.*"

"*Your sisters said that too,*" Neala says thoughtfully. "*That certainly is an odd thing to say. Is there anything else you can think of that might help?*"

"*Did your parents ever mention Darius or Gaine?*" I ask, interrupting them.

Brock twitches a little. "*The mate-maker? No.*"

That poor girl. Gaine's gift is to see wolves' mates. The image comes to her in a vision. It's designed to help wolves find their mates even if they are far apart. Her father's indiscretions triggered her gift to be transferred to her from her aunt. At age 23, Gaine is known far and wide. She refuses to shift and give all the wolves access to her at once. *And I can't say I blame her.*

"*I am pleased you all get along and work together,*" I say, sighing. "*However, I would appreciate you not calling Gaine that anymore. You should set an example for your pack, not fall in with them.*"

Brock hooks his front leg over my shoulder and presses his paw to my back. It's his version of a hug, and he's the only wolf I've cuddled with who's small enough to do it. "*Yes, Luna. I'm sorry.*"

As Neala continues asking Brock about his parents, I roll over to watch the rest of the group and let their voices drown in the background. Anthony moves his hands around as he describes something, and Bastian is doing his best to pay attention as Annalisa rubs his back pads. After a few minutes, I realize I haven't heard Brock's voice. I look up to find him also staring at the group.

"*Neala, I think he's had enough for now,*" I tell her, rubbing his chin. "*Keep me posted.*"

Bastian lifts his head as I sit up. His eyes shine, and his ears prick forward. "*Luna,*" he starts excitedly. "*Will you tell us a story?*"

Like the Alpha he's modeled after, Bastian gets bored quickly. In the true form of a companion, Brock lifts his head, intrigued by the idea of a story versus joining the lesson. Tarq continues to talk, moving on to watch rotations, unaware that he's lost Bastian's attention.

Approaching the group, I kiss Tarq's cheek. "My Love, I believe you have taught these children all they can learn for one night. Bastian has requested a story." Edith hands me a teacup and sits beside Anthony. She enjoys the stories too. I suspect it's because she's in half of them.

Tarq pulls me to his lap. "Fine," he grumbles. "What kind of story do you guys want?"

All three kids perk up. Annalisa is the future Luna, Bastian is her Alpha, and Brock is their companion. With all their power and the future before them, it's easy to forget that they are still children. The boys look at me, knowing I have the better stories, whereas Annalisa shrugs and looks to Edith for ideas.

"How about the time Dax shot me in the ass?" Tarq suggests.

The kids groan.

"What?" Tarq has perfected his offended look over the years.

I lean back and look up at him. "My Alpha, your father shot you every chance he got. No one believes you were innocent anymore."

"But I was," Tarq whines. He grabs Brock's jaw, pulling him so they face each other. "You believe me, don't you?"

Brock stands frozen, unsure how to handle the situation. He doesn't want to lie, but the truth could insult our Alpha.

Giggling, I pull Tarq's hand off Brock. "He's just playing with you, sweetheart. Go sit down." Brock nuzzles my cheek and lies down beside Annalisa.

"Luna, you always tell stories about the past and other people. Can you tell us a story from when you were young?"

Bastian's request catches me off guard. I don't often think about my life before I became their Luna. "I don't know, Bass," I say. "I'm not sure there's much of a story there. I was just a girl trying to survive before becoming the Luna."

Anthony begins to chuckle, making us all turn in his direction. By the time he sits up, he has our undivided attention. "If any of you believes your Luna was an angel, I will squash that right now." He lifts his brow and scans the room.

Tarq takes a deep breath. "Alright, Anthony, I'll bite. What do you have for us?"

I've always relaxed with my wolves but never considered telling them about my thieving days. The Alphas, Tarq included, would prefer the pack see me as their untouchable Luna.

Tarq leans back, allowing me to recline against his chest as the kids move around us to face Anthony. "I will remind you that you are talking to the kids about their Luna," Tarq says.

I slide my hands over the boys' heads as they lay them on my lap. "Nonsense, Tarq. I make mistakes, as will my daughter. You can't hold us to an image of perfection." I slide the back of my fingers over Annalisa's cheek, making Bastian curl around to check on her.

"I'll probably only get to tell one story before Tarq threatens to kill me, so I'll try to make it a good one." Anthony is being serious, and I know he's probably right. If Tarq is the man who lifts me, he is also the man who will kill anyone who knocks me down.

I glance up at Anthony and see the devilish smile that spreads across his face. Most of his stories about me would have a moment where I bested him, probably making him bleed. However, there was one where he got the jump on me because I had no idea who he was. Taking a deep breath, I settle into Tarq and wait for Anthony to begin the story of how we met.

"Your Luna was about 13 when she started stealing from the militia," Anthony says. "She started small, stealing cloth and furs at first. Annoying really. This puny kid had several regiments pissed off, chasing their tails. Then she stole a captain's horse."

"I didn't know it belonged to anyone important," I say, scowling. "She was pretty. I thought she'd fetch a good price."

"Oh, she fetched you something," Anthony howls. "That captain had my orders changed, and I was told to stop her by any means."

I look down as Bastian lifts his head. "It's ok, baby," I tell him, sliding my hand down his neck. "Enjoy the story." He lays his head back down, and I reach for Brock's shoulder. He's lying behind Bastian and has stretched his neck to claim a spot on my lap. Tarq can only lean back on one arm because of the boys, but his other hand rests on Brock's ribs. He's learned that these kids view me as another mother and want to sit on Mom's lap.

Anthony stretches out and lies down with his head on Edith's lap. "It didn't take me long to pick up her trail once I got to the basin," he continues. "First time I caught her was easy. We set up a silk shipment, and a week later, I had my hands around her neck. What were you? About 15, then?"

"Yep," I say, nodding. "It was a week after my birthday."

"I thought I had her wrapped up quickly and was headed home in record time until she tried to sneak out a window." He stops to grin at me as I roll my eyes. "She fell out the window and busted a rain barrel. Some poor skunk didn't appreciate having the shit scared out of it and sprayed the hell out of her."

The room erupts in chuckles and giggles. Even Tarq has trouble hiding his laughter from me. "That spray got in my eyes," I pout. "It was all I could smell for weeks."

"You were smelling yourself!" Anthony yells as he continues laughing loudly. "I was so damn pissed I had to smell that shit that I threw her in the pond."

Tarq laughs. "That doesn't get the smell off!"

"That's not what I was trying to do," Anthony continues, chuckling. "I didn't know she could swim. I figured I'd just pull her body out in the morning."

The boys lift their heads, confused. Brock begins a low growl, but I slide my hands over the top of their heads.

"She was fine, wolf," Anthony grumbles. "She swam to the other side of the pond. I even gave her a few weeks to air out before I went back after her."

"It's ok, boys," I say. "Anthony and I have a past. I did some pretty horrible things to him over the next ten years."

The boys still don't settle. They both nuzzle my cheeks, and Brock sits up, resting his chin on my shoulder. There are clearly some mixed feelings about this story.

Brock eyes Anthony. *"I like your stories better, Luna."*

"I don't think we should let him tell stories anymore," Bastian says sadly.

"I agree," Brock says, nudging my cheek.

Giggling, I rub my thumbs behind their whiskers. "Ok, we'll limit Anthony's stories."

Tarq rubs my thigh and shifts forward, moving the wolves with me. "At least you got rid of the smell." Pushing Brock off my shoulder, he tucks his face near my neck. "I wouldn't enjoy that as much." He lifts me off his lap so he can stand up.

Smiling, I tug the boys' ears and trace my fingers over Annalisa's forehead, finding her asleep. "I think it's time for you boys to get some rest," I whisper. I roll Annalisa into Bastian as he stretches out and help him tuck his back paws behind her.

"Luna, can I sleep with you tonight?"

I turn to see Brock sitting behind me. I stand up and slide my hand over his head. *"I would love for you to lie with us tonight."*

21

Frowning, I close the door to the hidden room and lean against it. We've been stuck on the boat for a week now, and Davis just told me that today is the same as the rest. Militia has been spotted patrolling the towns nearby, and it's too dangerous.

"*Luna,*" Brock says, stepping toward me. "*You frown every day when he leaves. What's wrong?*"

I kneel before him. "The captain said we won't be able to visit with the wolves who live near here."

Brock steps into my arms, sliding his jaw down my back. "*Do you think we could fish today?*" Brock asks.

"You know? That's a good idea," I say, smiling. I rub my hands over his shoulders and down his legs. "You'd have to shift, but fresh air would do you good."

Brock steps back and sits. "*Then Bastian couldn't join us.*" His voice is firm. Their bond has strengthened, and he won't leave his companion behind.

My eyes wander over his head, focusing on Bastian as he comforts Annalisa after she's taken her sea sickness medicine. "I think I have something else for him to work on that he'll need some privacy for anyway," I say, winking at Brock. "Come on. Let's see if we can get you some time topside."

After working with the captain, everyone prepares to spend some time fishing for the day in the sunshine. It's cool enough that they can wear long sleeves to cover their pack markings. As everyone prepares

257

excitedly, Bastian's ears prick forward. He sits up with bright eyes as I approach.

"Not you, sweetheart," I tell him, watching his ears droop. "You're going to stay down here with my daughter and me—all this Luna love just for you." I smile and rub his jaw.

Tarq slides his arm around my lower back, scooping me toward his chest. "The captain said the river is too busy around Memphis to be searched," he whispers. "He said we could use the houseboat."

With an apologetic smile, I cup his cheek. "That will be perfect, My Love. I'll take the kids there to work with me while you watch over the rest of our wolves."

"No, Dar," Tarq whines, frowning. "I meant for us to spend time together."

"I'm sorry, Tarq," I whisper. "It's time for your daughter's next lesson."

Pulling my jaw, he presses his lips to mine. "You should probably warn Bastian about how much he'll miss his Luna while she's being the Luna."

As I slide my arms around Tarq's back, I let my hands heat up in small, unnoticeable bursts. These won't calm him, but it'll make it easier for him to leave me for the day. "I hear you, My Love," I whisper. "You go do Alpha things, I'll go do Luna things, and we'll meet in the middle when we're done."

Tarq slides his hands down my body, pushing me against him. "I love you," he whispers.

"I love you more than I can ever say in my lifetime," I say, smiling. "Will you join us when you're done fishing?"

"Sure." Tarq kisses my cheek and leaves to plan with the rest of our group.

I'm sneaking Bastian across the deck when Chase stops me. "Dar, hold up a minute," he yells, approaching with the boiling pot. "This helped you last time, so we should do it again."

I step onto the houseboat and reach for the pot. "Thank you," I say, pausing as I think about Tarq. "Watch him. He's a bit on edge."

As our companion, Chase spends more time with me than Tarq, but he knows my Alpha well. He knows exactly what to look for and will distract Tarq while I'm working with the kids. Chase nods, leaving as I join the kids in the bedroom.

"What's that, Luna?" Bastian asks.

Setting the pot on the cast iron stove, I light the dried leaves to start the fire. "Tarq says it's eucalyptus," I tell him. "Edith mixes it into the boiling salve. Let's talk about you two, though. How are you?"

Annalisa sits cross-legged on the bed, running her fingers through Bastian's fur with a frown. Bastian is staring at me, but it's obvious that I have very little of his attention.

Hopping on the bed with them, I grab his chin. "Talk to me, guys."

Annalisa takes a deep breath, lifting her eyes to me. "I'm fine, Mom," she says plainly.

"She's not ok, Luna," Bastian says sadly, nuzzling her cheek. *"I want to help her."*

I slide my hand over his back. "I agree, sweetheart. Why don't we teach her how to hear you?"

My daughter instantly perks up. "You mean it this time?"

"The only way you will be able to find his voice is if you know what it sounds like." Leaning over, I open the bedside table's drawer and pull out some bandages Will left behind. "I'm going to have to blindfold you." I pause as Annalisa frowns. "And bind you so you can't take it off," I add, cringing.

"What? Why?" she shouts.

"I don't want to do it then," Bastian adds.

I hold both of their cheeks. "Listen to me, both of you," I command. "Bastian is not allowed to shift in your presence. This is the only way."

"Please don't tie her," he begs.

"I know you don't like this, sweetheart, but I don't believe she'll leave the blindfold on."

Bastian pulls his head from my hand. *"I don't need to talk to her that badly, Luna."* He lays his head down, looking away from us.

Sighing, I turn to Annalisa. "Baby, do you want to do this?"

Her eyes drift to Bastian. "More than anything," my daughter whispers.

The wolf's head pops up to look back at her.

"Bastian has issues with restraining you," I tell her. "Will you promise not to remove the blindfold?"

Annalisa holds Bastian by both sides of his jaw, pressing her forehead to his head. "I will do anything necessary just to hear your words."

"Bastian," I say, pulling his paw. "Will you keep your word to me?"

"You have my word, Luna."

My daughter should be too young to know what love is, but it's apparent as she pulls away from Bastian. She is his, just as much as he is hers.

I pull a blanket from the bed for Bastian to cover up with and slide behind Annalisa. "Ok, you two," I say, sighing. "Here we go." I slowly wrap the bandage around my daughter's eyes. "Stay right there, child."

Grabbing the blanket, I step off the bed, gesturing for Bastian to join me. I hold it up and wait for him to shift.

Bastian nervously glances behind me. *"Luna, what do I say?"*

Moving between them, I hold the blanket up again, blocking his view. "You've been with her a while now, Bastian," I tell him, shaking the blanket. "I'm sure you'll think of something."

He shifts, and I step forward as I wrap the blanket around his waist and use his hand to hold it closed. Bastian's gaze is intense, and his jaw tightens as he pushes against me. In his human form, the pull Bastian feels is overwhelming.

I pulse small blasts of heat into his chest until he looks down at me and relaxes the pressure on my hand. His eyes soften, and he takes a deep breath.

Behind me, Annalisa shifts on the bed. "Mom?"

Bastian's eyes flick back to her.

"It's ok, baby," I tell her calmly. "We're still here. Bastian's just trying to find his words."

The young wolf stands braced against my hand, completely frozen. I imagine much of his body is telling him to crash through me and take what is his. *I'm glad he's fighting those urges.*

I curl my fingers into his chest. "Hey, sweetheart. Do you want to try this another time?"

"Please don't," Annalisa begs as she leans forward onto her hands.

"Easy, Bastian," I say as he pushes against me, trying to get closer to her. "Don't you hurt me, sweet boy." My voice seems to calm him, but his chest swells as his eyes dart between my daughter and me.

"When I was younger, Mom was gone a lot. It was just Dad and me," Annalisa starts, picking a story to tell Bastian. My daughter has learned a lot of things simply by watching me. One of these crucial skills is the art of distraction. "I remember I wanted to ride a horse when I was four. He said it was too dangerous for such a young Luna, but he'd shift and let me ride on his back when I cried."

Bastian's chest begins to move dramatically as it heaves air at the sound of her voice.

I reach one hand for his cheek, leaving the other on his chest. "Close your eyes, Bass. Just listen to her voice." He looks down at me before closing his eyes.

"I've known my grandfather my whole life," Annalisa continues. "But I heard his voice for the first time a few months ago." She pauses to sniffle. "It was beautiful."

"Don't cry."

Annalisa covers her mouth, gasping at the sound of Bastian's voice. I pulse a small amount of heat into his chest as his eyes open.

"You can't expect me not to feel when I hear beautiful things," she responds, still holding her mouth and sniffling.

Bastian blushes, looking down at the floor between us.

"Sweetheart, this won't work if she doesn't hear your voice." I hear Annalisa shift back onto her heels behind me. I know she's at her limit and about to break her promise. "Why don't you just talk to me." Bastian lifts his gaze to look into my eyes. "I've always wondered why you guys like your pads rubbed so much. What's so great about it?"

"It helps us feel connected to you," he tells me. "We spend so much time as wolves that we could lose ourselves to it without that connection." Bastian's eyes snap up as Annalisa takes a sharp breath.

"I didn't realize how important it was," I say, smiling. I clutch my chest as it tightens.

The young wolf grabs my cheek. "Luna, you need to rest."

"No, baby, this is more important," I tell him. "I'm just missing my guard."

"Do I rub your pads right?" Annalisa asks, recapturing his attention.

Bastian blushes. "Everything you do is perfect."

Annalisa giggles. "Ok. I know that's not true, but I appreciate the praise."

"Then I guess you could rub my front pads a little harder," Bastian responds, chuckling. "They get sore."

"Your laugh reminds me of my Uncle Miles," my daughter whispers. "He looked like his laugh surprised him."

I watch Bastian stare at Annalisa for a painfully long minute. "Bastian, can you pick a phrase for Annalisa to listen for?" I ask, moving around until I catch his eye. "It would be something you commonly say during a conversation."

When Bastian flashes me an apologetic smile, I try to stop him, but I'm not fast enough. "I love you," he says, looking up at Annalisa.

"Not a word, daughter," I snap as she gasps. "Bastian, you know better," I say through my teeth, narrowing my eyes at him.

"It's the only thing I commonly say," Bastian whispers, slipping his hand up my neck and pressing his forehead to mine. These simple motions are how Tarq calms me when I'm upset. This teenager has picked up more than fighting skills from my Alpha.

"Don't test me again, Bastian," I warn him. "I won't be able to stop her father."

"Yes, Luna."

After he shifts, Bastian jumps onto the bed and puts his muzzle on Annalisa's cheek. My daughter is clawing at the blindfold when I get to her. I unwrap her quickly, and she falls against her wolf, crying into his fur.

Bastian rubs his muzzle over her arm, trying to comfort her. *"Maybe I should've chosen 'please don't cry.'"*

"Probably, sweetheart," I say with a sympathetic smile and rub my chest. "The eucalyptus is starting to work. Why don't we give her a break? I think we could all use some rest."

"Thank you for that," Bastian says. *"You were right. I wouldn't have been able to resist her."* He hooks his leg over Annalisa's shoulder and pulls her down. I help him tuck her against him before lying down behind her. Bastian curls his neck over her head, laying his muzzle on my cheek. *"You need a blanket, Luna."*

Giggling, I scratch his whiskers before pulling the thick blanket over my body. "You're turning into Brock. I love you, sweet boy."

* * *

I'm unsure how long I slept, but my eyes fling open when something stabs my arm. I try to pull away, but then my eyes land on Chase.

"Easy, Dar. You'll break the needle," he says soothingly. He pulls the syringe away, holds a cloth where the needle was, and bends my arm.

Tarq's muzzle slides over my cheek. He's on my right side with the blanket draped over him. He's radiating so much heat that I can feel it in my bones.

"What are you doing?" I'm so confused that I'm not even sure who I'm asking.

Chase wraps the blanket around me and tucks it in, trapping Tarq's heat. "The kids came and got us," Chase says. "You were coughing badly, and they couldn't wake you."

"What happened?" I have so many questions, and it seems no one has answers.

"I'm not sure, Dar. I aired out the eucalyptus and gave you some steroids." He rubs my leg through the blanket. "Let's just get you warmed up for now, ok?"

I turn to Tarq, who promptly sticks his nose in my face, breathing in my breath. "Baby, what are you doing?"

"Smelling for blood. If there was blood in your lungs, I could smell it on

your breath." He leaves his nose in my face as he takes deep breaths. "*I love that your breath always smells like flowers.*"

I try to giggle but just end up coughing. "Where are the kids?" I ask.

"I'm not sure," Chase answers. "They might be hiding in the wheel-house. It's not dark yet."

"Please get them, Chase," I say. "They shouldn't be alone right now."

Chase bows before he leaves, and I roll into Tarq with a groan.

"*I know you're sick,*" Tarq grumbles. "*It's getting worse. Why are you trying to hide it?*"

Sighing, I run my fingers through his fur. The truth is complicated, and even then, we're only guessing. Not knowing will be easier for him.

"Not now, My Love," I say, tugging his fur. "The kids will be here soon. They're struggling and need to be lifted. Will you help me?" The door opens, and Bastian pushes past his uncle, followed closely by Annalisa. "Speak of the devil," I say, smiling.

Bastian steps onto the bed and sticks his nose in my face. *At least I know why they do that now.* He bumps his nose against Tarq's, and the two sneeze on me.

I reach up for his muzzle as I roll over, putting my back against Tarq. "Come here, sweetheart," I say, shaking my head. "I'm fine. Thank you for getting Chase." Bastian lies down in front of me and heats his body as I reach out for my daughter. "You too. Come here. We need to get back to work."

Annalisa relaxes against Bastian. He pokes her face with his nose, making her giggle.

"Why don't you tell Bastian a story, Annalisa?" I suggest. "He enjoys hearing about the Alphas."

We both grab a paw and begin rubbing their pads as she decides on a story. Tarq groans, rolling his head further to the side. Bastian chuckles and pokes Tarq's head with his nose. "*He probably should've told you to be firmer with the front pads long ago.*"

"*Thank you for telling us how it makes you feel,*" I say, kissing his nose when he sticks it in my face again. "*Tarq hides the things he believes may show weakness. I never knew.*"

Bastian continues to rub his muzzle over my cheek. *"The only true sign of weakness in this world is cruelty, Luna. Your love is your strength. I will let honesty be mine."*

"What a clever boy you are," I say, grinning. *"Let's pay attention to the story, though. She's chosen a good one that you haven't heard."*

The young wolf slides his nose over my forehead absentmindedly. *"I'm sad I missed everything you guys tell me about, but I'm glad I'm part of your family now."*

Snagging his muzzle, I kiss him behind his whiskers. *"We are happy to have you, sweetheart, but you're supposed to be talking to her, not me. Pay attention to the story."*

Bastian curls around Annalisa as she tells the story of the only time Tarq dared to set up a movie night on a full moon. We watched a movie about a black horse that Annalisa had chosen. Tarq stayed in human form for most of the evening and kept challenging Dax to a race. Dax finally got pissed enough and kicked his ass, breaking the TV.

"Tarq is a very different Alpha from what I grew up with," Bastian comments.

Annalisa continues, not hearing him. She giggles as she moves to his back pads and lists things her father had said to her grandfather.

"I like your laugh," Bastian says. I can almost hear him blushing. *"I hope I can make you laugh every day for the rest of our lives."* Bastian rolls upright, curling around to press his nose against Annalisa's thigh with a sigh.

"Grandpa and Daddy fight all the time," she says sadly. "You'd think they hate each other, but Daddy misses him. I can tell." She slides down to snuggle into Bastian's fur. "I bet Grandpa will love you. He respects strong wolves."

"Your grandfather hates me," Bastian says sadly. *"I'm pretty sure he thinks I'm gonna eat you."*

Annalisa giggles. "He does not," she says, swatting at his shoulder. "He's just really protective. He calls me his pride and joy, but I think that's just to poke at Daddy."

"It's nice that you grew up surrounded by so much love," Bastian tells her,

sounding quite somber. *"You have a strength within you that comes from your family."*

My daughter curls her legs, pushing Bastian's head to see his eyes as I hold my breath, trying not to laugh. "Your strength must come from your family too."

I peek quickly to see Bastian bump his nose into Annalisa's. *"We don't all grow up as you did. My strength comes from the love I feel for you."*

Annalisa rubs her nose, giggling. "You're pretty special... Wait. What did you just say? You did say something, right? Please tell me that wasn't my imagination."

Tarq stirs, disturbed by her outburst. I reach my hand under my neck and blast his muzzle with heat so he doesn't completely ruin their moment.

"I did," Bastian says, chuckling. *"I told you that I love you, and my love for you gives me the strength to protect you."* He strains to rub his muzzle against her cheek and sees my eyes open. I smile, winking at him to let him know he's not in trouble.

Annalisa sniffles as she sits up, holding him to her cheek. "I'm not allowed to love you, Bass," she whispers. I can hear that she's crying. "I'm supposed to wait for my mate, the wolf meant to be my Alpha."

"Easy, Bastian," I call out as I feel his body tensing. I hit him with a bit of heat to help him before he does anything he regrets or that Tarq will not forgive. *"She's not rejecting you, sweetheart. Don't you shut down on me. You can feel her love, can't you?"*

He closes his eyes and leans into her touch. His hum starts, and he sighs comfortably.

"There you go, baby. She's waiting for you. For now, though, she needs a guard and a friend."

Bastian nudges Annalisa until she lies back against him. She nestles into his fur, and he curls around to rest his head on her leg. *"I will love you enough for he and I until you find him."*

"Thank you, Bass," she says sleepily. "You're a good friend."

* * *

The next day, the captain pulls the boats into a shallow channel on the west side of the river. There's a large island with game to hunt and abundant trees for the crew to cut down for the engines. Everyone is excited to go to shore for the day.

"Same deal as last time, kids," I tell them as they gather on shore. "Listen to the adults, or I'll send Tarq after you."

Annalisa laughs. "Mom, you know that doesn't work on me."

I lift my eyebrow, scowling at her confidence. "It will if I send your father after Bastian for something you did."

"Ok," she pouts. "There's no need to be mean."

Bastian chuckles.

"Why are you laughing?" Annalisa whines. "I have to behave because of you."

"*You're just like your father,*" Bastian says, rubbing his muzzle on her hip.

Anthony leads the kids and Amelia into the woods. Bruce and Tarq will be helping the crew chop wood, while Chase has requested to speak with me privately.

"This island isn't named on any map I've seen," I mention to Chase as he zips my jacket up to my chin. "Why does Davis call it Bakma Island?"

Chase chuckles as he puts his arm around my shoulders to combat the December chill. "I asked him the same thing." He turns me to walk down the shore, away from the boats. "He said, 'Because a bear almost killed my ass on that island.' B-A-K-M-A."

I giggle and lean into him, trying to absorb some of his heat. "There really isn't anything normal about bayou wolves, is there?"

"Not really," Chase responds. "You'll find that out soon enough. Davis says we can steam most of the remainder of our trip."

I sigh in relief. "That's good to hear. I'm not sure the kids can take much more of being locked up on the boat."

"My nephew has come a long way." Chase looks down, sliding his hand over my cheek. "Brock seems to like him."

I smile and wrinkle my nose as he bumps it with his finger. "He does. They think a lot alike, so they make a good team."

"I know we told you not to push them, but they are well-suited," Chase says, squeezing my shoulders. "The pack will be in good hands."

We continue along in silence. Chase has something to say, but he'll tell me when he's ready. I wrap my arms around his waist and enjoy his company. The sunshine makes this a beautiful day for a stroll.

Checking on the kids, I hear Bastian tell Annalisa about how Brock shoved him in the mud. Brock is trying to defend himself, saying he had nothing to do with it, but since Annalisa can't hear him, his words are literally falling on deaf ears. When I hear Bastian chuckle and Brock whine that he didn't do it, I know their companion is getting scolded.

"Bastian, what did I tell you?" I ask.

"Yes, Luna," Bastian mumbles.

I shake my head as I hear him tell Annalisa the truth and apologize to Brock. I look up to see Chase watching me. "It's just the kids," I tell him. "Bastian is fitting right in and turning into Tarq, it would seem."

"No doubt playing the innocent Alpha," Chase says, rolling his eyes.

"Why is that so fun for them?"

"I don't know," he says, frowning. "I never got into ball either, so I might not be the right person to ask."

"You're probably right," I say, sighing.

Chase pulls me a little closer and adjusts the collar of my coat to cover more of my neck. "Dar, Ash has been helping me talk to Doc. I passed on a list of your new symptoms and updates on your numbers," he admits.

I roll my eyes and look away. Chase has always been heavily involved in our lives as our companion, but he's never willingly passed on private information. I want to be mad at him, but I know he's scared.

Chase takes a deep breath before continuing. "He wants you to go home, Dar. He thinks the trip has been too hard on your body."

My eyes narrow. "Chase, we're almost there. We're not turning around. This is too important."

Chase steps in front of me, holding my shoulders. "You know I want to make this trip. I want to see where Bristol came from." He pauses as I slide my hands over his arms. "I'm not a doctor, Dar."

I lift his hands and step into him, sliding my arms around his waist. As he collapses around me, I feel through his emotions how much this affects him. I now find fear where I would normally feel his grief from losing his mate. Chase doesn't worry about most things, but my health is scaring him.

"I want to thank you for all the care you've been giving me," I whisper. "I'm not sure this trip would be possible otherwise." Chase sniffles as he leans his cheek down onto my head. "I want to see the ocean," I tell him. "Tarq's visions are beautiful, but I want to experience them in real life." I continue sliding my hands over Chase's skin, pulling his fear in small increments. "I want to give the love of my life a winter filled with love and happiness. We can give my daughter a safe place to learn down here."

Chase slides his hand over my hair and releases a shaky breath. "You never intended to survive this trip, did you?"

"As I have told you all many times, I will not leave this world until I am ready," I tell him, sighing. "I promise I am not on this trip to die."

Chase leans back and looks down. "Tell me the truth, Dar."

I cup his cheeks and smile. "Chase, I will be here as long as I am needed. I will protect this pack and leave them with a peaceful existence. So, the truth is that I need your care and support. Can you do that?"

Chase pulls me back to his chest, resting his chin on my head. "I will help you."

22

"*I'm not sure where else to look, Luna,*" Neala tells me, frustrated. "*We've searched hundreds of miles.*"

The captain has been running the engines nearly nonstop and allowed us on deck at night, but the kids are still bored. I'm leaning against the railing, watching the boys. They've been inseparable since the hunting trip. To entertain themselves, they've started a staring contest.

"*I've held off on updating Brock,*" I respond. "*He has nothing but time on this boat. I don't want him getting stuck in his head again.*"

"*That's a good point,*" Neala agrees. "*He seemed happy the last time we talked. There's no reason to take that away from him.*"

"*How are his sisters settling in?*"

"*Good. They're in school now and asked to join the junior guard,*" Neala tells me. "*It took a while, but they've blended well with the kids.*"

Annalisa walks by Bastian, distracting him, and Brock nips his muzzle. Shaking my head, I turn away from them and look out over the water.

"*This can be a fresh start for all of them. Brock has bonded well with these two.*" I spot Chase heading my way with his stethoscope and notepad. "*Keep me posted, Neala.*"

"*Yes, Luna,*" she responds. "*Be safe.*"

Lifting my eyebrow, I smirk at Chase. "If I order the kids, they'll throw you overboard."

"Not before I tell them how sick you are," he replies.

I frown. "Touché."

"Dar, it's this, or I tell Tarq that Doc wants you to go home," he threatens. "He might not like Doc, but he'll listen to him when it comes to you." Chase slips the end of his stethoscope into my shirt.

My eyes flick over his shoulder and land on Bastian. The young wolf lies on his side while Annalisa and Amelia each rub a paw for him.

"Bastian? Explain."

The young wolf chuckles. *"She's been teaching her grandmother how to rub pads."*

Chase moves to my back, and I scan the deck for Bruce.

"I was gonna ask," Bastian explains. *"But I think she wants to do something nice for Bruce. He's gonna like it."*

When I spot Bruce by the bow, he's glaring at them.

"Alright, but Bruce doesn't look very happy about it," I tell him, grinning. *"He's new to this bonded thing. Don't press your luck."*

Bastian stretches his back legs as the ladies move to his front pads. He rolls his body up and lays his head on Annalisa's lap. *"Mm-hmm,"* is his response. That young wolf has a strong appreciation for pampering during his off time.

Chase finishes recording my numbers and follows my gaze to his nephew. "Bass seems to be enjoying himself."

"Chase, you've watched me rub Tarq's pads for years," I say, turning to him. "You've never expressed any interest in it." Since no one has mentioned this in 15 years, I need to tread lightly. I want to believe I know everything about my wolves but will occasionally say something utterly offensive to them.

"Dar, we know our place," Chase says, chuckling. "And that is not with our paws in your hands."

"I am not the only person with hands, Chase," I say with a frown. "Is that not something you would do for your mate?"

Chase considers my question before answering. "That would seem a little one-sided, wouldn't it?"

I click my tongue at him. "Are you done with me?"

"I am," Chase says, smiling.

"Good. I believe it's time to change some things around here," I say. "Go shift for me, please."

I push off the railing as Chase retreats to the ship's hold. When I approach my daughter, she's praising her grandmother's work on the sleeping wolf's pads.

"Come with me, ladies," I say, waking Bastian. "Could you please bring Bruce, Tarq, and Brock to us, Bass?"

The spoiled wolf grumbles but rolls onto his perfectly rubbed paws and jogs toward the ship's bow. I reach for Amelia's hand and pull her up, hooking our arms together.

"Amelia, you asked Annalisa to teach you something I didn't realize all wolves weren't enjoying," I tell her as I lead her to the compartment's wall. "Pad rubs are not reserved for the elite and spoiled. I thought you could help us make them commonplace within our pack."

"Luna, is everything ok?" Bruce asks, jogging around the corner.

Sitting against the wall, I raise my arm for the ladies to join me. "Bruce, while you were glaring, your wife was learning to do something for you." I hold my hand out.

"You saw that, huh?" Bruce says quietly, sliding his jaw over my hand.

"Why don't you join your wife," I say as Tarq sits beside me. His head is held high while he looks over the group as if he's ensuring my safety. "Tarq," I say, calling his attention down to me. "Love of my life… did you destroy your clothes?"

Tarq tucks his ears back. *"I had to know what that idiot was pulling my arm for."*

"Edith can't make you any more clothes out here, Tarq," I remind him. "If you run out, that's it. You'll have to stay a wolf."

"Dar," Tarq says in a tone he takes when educating me. *"Everyone appreciates my body. I'll just walk around naked."*

Bruce snaps his head in his direction and immediately begins disagreeing with him, making me giggle.

I scratch Tarq's chin. "You might be mistaken, but I still love you."

"How come I can't hear Daddy?" Annalisa pouts.

"You could if he wanted you to, daughter." I arch my eyebrow at her father. "Trust me, you don't want to hear what he's saying."

Tarq rubs his muzzle over my cheek, pushing his nose down my neck. *"I think even you shouldn't hear me sometimes."* He stays against my neck, taking deep breaths and humming.

When Chase pushes the hold door open, it's time to start. I lift my arm and wait for him to slide under it before addressing everyone. "I wanted to ask my Alpha and Annalisa's very spoiled guard to share an experience with you." I turn to Annalisa. "Since your father taught you how to do this, I assume you won't object to rubbing his pads."

"What about Bass?" she whines.

"Annalisa, I want them to experience this with their Alpha, and I will be busy with the other wolves." Bruce pricks his ears, looking confused, and Chase tucks his nose into his chest as they realize what's happening.

Tarq flops onto his side before Annalisa and sticks his paw in her face. *"Rub my pads, minion."*

Amelia holds her hand out for Bruce's paw.

"Luna?" I don't see Bruce as a human often, and I've never seen him blush, but I'm pretty sure he is right now.

"Bruce," I say, raising my eyebrow. *"Your wife just risked pissing you off by rubbing a teenager's pads to learn how to rub yours. Please lie down and let her do this for you."* I hold my hand out to Chase. He gingerly lays down, reaching his paw out. *"Can I get a little support for our companion, my Alpha?"*

Tarq groans as he repositions his body to throw his head over Chase's back while still having his pads rubbed. When Bastian reappears with Brock, I reach out to the young companion. Brock sits beside me and watches Chase flop onto his shoulder.

Tarq pokes his head a few times with his nose. *"I think you broke him."*

Brock lifts his paw for me, but his eyes nervously shift between Tarq and Bastian.

I place his paw in my lap and grab his jaw. *"Sweet boy, the Alphas and*

I want to share this with you," I say, kissing the side of his muzzle. *"You do not need to be nervous. You're safe with me."*

It's not long before Brock is laid out, just like Chase. Tarq's been standing watch, so he quickly dozes off. Annalisa takes over Chase's paws, allowing me to concentrate on Brock's. I catch Bruce gently sliding his teeth and tongue over Amelia's leg as he hums. I love giving these wolves moments of enjoyment in a world that seems determined to wipe them out.

* * *

Over the next three nights, Annalisa and I worked with the wolves to teach them how to rub pads so they could do it for others. We both cried, watching Tarq teach Bruce to rub Amelia's pads. I didn't know how to explain to Annalisa why Bastian didn't need to learn how to do it for his mate when she asked.

Relief comes the next morning when the captain announces we'll be at our destination in a day. "It'll be great to get these kids off the boat," I tell Tarq. "The boys could use a run."

Tarq pulls me to his chest. "They've handled this trip well," he reminds me. "Teaching everyone about pad rubs was ingenious."

I watch as the kids curl up with Bruce and Amelia. The four wolves curl around Annalisa. Even though Anthony has piled blankets over them, Edith is still shivering against his chest. "Why is it so cold in here?"

"It's just a cold winter day, Dar," Chase says, coming up behind me. *"We could help them, though."* He nods in the direction of Anthony and Edith.

"That's a good idea, Chase." I look up at my Alpha. "Would you shift, My Love, and help us keep them warm?" Anthony begins to protest, which makes Tarq smile. "Anthony," I say, raising my eyebrow. "I know you don't want her to be cold."

Tarq ducks out the door to shift while Chase lies down along Edith's back. He curls his neck, placing his chin on Anthony's shoulder.

"Fine, come here," Anthony grumbles, holding his arm up. "I'm changing my mind in five, four, three..."

Giggling, I jump forward and dive into the blankets with them. Edith smiles and grabs my hand as Anthony wraps his arm around me. When Tarq slides in behind me, Anthony throws the blanket over him to trap his heat.

"Will you be warm enough?" Tarq asks, poking me with his nose.

As I turn back to look at him, Tarq gently licks my cheek and gives me his muzzle for a good morning kiss. "I will be safe and warm between the two strongest men in my life," I say, snuggling back against Anthony. "Now get some rest. We have some hectic days ahead of us. Not to mention retraining everyone to sleep at night."

Anthony waits until Tarq heats up before resting his chin against my forehead. "How sick are you?" he whispers. Edith opens her eyes, squeezing my hand. "Twenty years ago, I would've danced on your grave," he says, breathing a quiet laugh. "Today, I'd rather prevent the need for one."

Edith moves to look me in the eye. "Chase stopped updating me," she whispers. "I'm starting to get worried. I've made a lot of tea for you."

When Chase's head moves, I know this is a full-on assault. They can't all see my scowl, but they'll hear it in my voice. "A daily tea might be nice, Edith, but I will choose when I leave this world," I hiss. "That is not today."

As Edith sinks back into him, Anthony kisses my forehead and whispers, "Make sure you say goodbye when that day comes."

Smiling, I cup his cheek. "I promise."

* * *

By sunset, we've reached an area of the river controlled by wolves. Davis told us we could freely move about the decks. I lean against Tarq, sipping my tea as Chase checks my lungs.

"Dar, I know Davis said it was safe, but it's still cold." Chase pulls the stethoscope from his ears, hanging it around his neck as he stares at me. When I don't move, he looks up at Tarq. "Either talk some sense into her or take her inside."

Sighing, Tarq heats his body. "When she's ready," is all he says. We watch Chase pile his equipment into a bag. He taps the underside of my teacup, urging me to drink it before leaving.

"The moon will be full soon," I say, looking at the sky. "We should prepare the kids for tomorrow. They'll need sleep to be functional around the new wolves." I turn around, placing my hands on Tarq's chest. "I don't want this to be all work, Tarq. I want them to have fun," I tell him. "They're too young to forget what that is."

"You can have the future Luna, Alpha, and their companion, or you can have kids," Tarq says. "You can't have both."

Smiling, I slide my fingers over his jaw. "Do we need a full recap of your life, My Love?"

Tarq matches my smile and cups my cheeks, pulling me to him until his lips press firmly against mine. "My fun is not appropriate for children." His tongue slides over my top lip, causing my mouth to open and accept his advance. Groaning into my mouth, Tarq grabs my thighs and wraps them around his hips as I lose myself to his kisses.

"I'm gonna kick the kids out," he says, pressing his forehead to mine.

"You are not," I say, giggling. "We have too much to do before morning."

Tarq sticks his lip out. "Ok," he pouts. "But I want to."

"I will file your grievance with the Luna council," I say, still giggling.

Tarq clicks his tongue. "Now you're just making shit up."

"Those kids are about to mingle with a lot of unknown wolves in their new roles, my sweet Alpha," I say, trying to appear sad for his benefit. "We need to talk to them."

Tarq tastes my tongue once more before releasing my legs.

"Do you want the boys or your daughter?" I ask.

Tarq wraps his arms around me as he thinks. "I'll take the boys. At least they have a job I know well."

"Why don't you take them to the wheelhouse with Chase?" I recommend. "You can lock the doors so Bastian can shift."

* * *

Annalisa spent most of her time growing up with Tarq and her grandmother, but she was raised as a Luna. She behaves appropriately and shows respect to our wolves but needs to practice hands-on techniques. Amelia and Bruce have joined us for this training. Their backgrounds offer a unique experience for her in a safe environment.

We sit together on the bed facing her grandmother and Grandpa Bruce, waiting for them to stop cuddling. "You've been handling wolves you're familiar with," I start, hoping to attract their attention. "Your Grandma has offered to help you practice before tomorrow."

I reach for Amelia's muzzle and sigh when she ignores me to continue nuzzling Bruce's cheek.

"Ok, we'll come back to Grandma," I say, annoyed. "Let's focus on Grandpa Bruce." I reach for his hand. Bruce closes his eyes and hums, leaning against Amelia's muzzle. "So this is a clear example of finding a mate and bonding at a very inappropriate time," I grumble, staring at them expectantly.

Bruce chuckles and moves Amelia's muzzle from his face. "Sorry, Luna. We're here." He moves to sit directly in front of us.

Annalisa smiles at him. "You look happy, Grandpa Bruce."

"I'll pull some of that because there's a lot of it," I say, raising my eyebrow at Bruce. "I need you to focus on your lessons, daughter, not laugh through them." Cupping Bruce's cheek, I pull enough of his emotion to stop him from overwhelming Annalisa. As I do, Amelia lays her head on his lap. "You two make an adorable couple."

Bruce grins, looking down at Amelia.

I turn back to Annalisa. "You've only been around a few humans but probably noticed they feel different."

"I feel like the wolves pull my hands toward them," she says thoughtfully.

"That is your hand wanting them," I tell her. "Your body will want to calm them. Your gift will work on anyone who is at least half-wolf."

Annalisa reaches for Bruce's hand.

"Now remember, there is a right and wrong way to do everything," I say, raising my eyebrow. "You want to calm them, not come on to them."

Bruce smiles as she pulls her hand back, wide-eyed. "You're pretty safe with me, kiddo."

"You should be more concerned with Bastian's interpretation until he learns your cues," I warn.

Annalisa frowns. "Why would he care?"

Bruce uses his finger to push her chin up. "Your guard will act first and think later. He will protect you with his life, even against a friend hugging you."

"You've spent a lot of time with him, haven't you?" Annalisa asks.

"I have," Bruce says, smiling. "He's intelligent and strong but emotional."

I hold my hand out. "You'll want to keep a flat hand when handling your wolves, not your fingertips as you do with your guard." I place my hand flat against Bruce's bare chest. "As you can see, his skin is not reacting to my touch, but I'm still able to calm him."

Annalisa mirrors my touch, grinning. "You feel happy too, Grandpa Bruce. I don't want to take that away."

"That's a nice thought, but sometimes it's necessary," I say. "Like, maybe, helping the children settle on Christmas Eve." I remove my hands from Bruce. "Ok, as we said, you're pretty safe with Grandpa Bruce. I want you to run your fingertips over his skin and watch how it reacts."

Annalisa gingerly slides her fingertips over his arm. His skin bumps up as if it's chilled, and he shivers.

"He's bonded to Grandma, so that's how his body will react to you. He knows a better feeling than your touch." I smile at Bruce before looking back at her. "Does that make sense?"

"I think so," Annalisa says, narrowing her eyes. "Their bodies call out for each other, so his body won't desire my touch, right?"

Bruce winks. "Exactly."

"But if they're not bonded? What would happen?" Annalisa whispers.

I place my hand on her shoulder and listen for Brock. When I don't hear him, I turn to Bruce. "The boys are in the wheelhouse. Can you bring them here? I need Brock in his current form."

Bruce kisses Amelia's nose, and she tries to follow him off the bed.

"We still need you, Amelia," I say apologetically. With a sigh, she moves to sit before us. *"You're like two crazy kids."*

"Yeah," she says, drawing out the word as her ears droop.

Annalisa giggles, sliding her hand under Amelia's jaw. "You two are so cute."

"Alright, quit embarrassing your grandmother," I say, smirking. "She's the perfect example to work with, though. Grandma is a wolf with a past."

"How mysterious," she says, intrigued. "What kind of past?"

Amelia pulls her head back.

"That's not your business," I tell Annalisa. "As Luna, we help them overcome their past, not make them relive it. So we offer our assistance." I reach out for Amelia's chin. "Grandma rarely closes her eyes while in hand, and I've only heard her hum a few times from my touch. More importantly, Grandma has boundaries you do not cross." Smiling, I scratch her whiskers. "It's ok, Amelia. You can react."

I slide my hand over her face and cover her eye on my way to her ear. Amelia pulls her head back, snarling, and I snatch my hand away as she snaps at it. We watch her back up and tuck her chin to her chest, ashamed of her actions.

"I love you, Amelia. Thank you for letting me do that." As she places her chin back in my hand, I turn toward Annalisa. "So we want to be careful around unknown wolves. Their bite can't hurt us, but they can do damage in other ways." I slide my fingers over Amelia's cheek with a wink. "Whether they mean to or not."

"So we should avoid their eyes," Annalisa says. "What else?" She holds her hand out and smiles when Amelia moves from my hand to hers.

"Just as your hands should stay low, so should your body," I tell her. "Walking among them is one thing, but you kneel when you address them."

The door opens, and Bruce enters, followed by everyone else. Bastian steps onto the bed and curls around Annalisa. He puts his nose to her leg and lies still. He doesn't handle the separation well. Brock looks nervous as he stands beside Tarq.

"We kneel to show our wolves the respect they deserve. There is honor in the name 'Wolf,' and we give what we expect." I step off the bed and kneel to my Alpha.

Tarq hums as he rubs his muzzle over my cheek. *"I love you."*

"You won't be humming when you find out why I've called you here," I tell him.

"Aw, Dar," Tarq whines. *"Are you gonna make me hate someone?"*

"Yes, I am," I say, laughing as I stand up. I reach out to Brock, taking his hand. "Come here, sweetheart. I want to talk to the three of you about what we're doing."

I climb back on the bed, pulling Brock with me. Amelia jumps down to give us room, and I position the teenager directly in front of Annalisa.

"Brock, everyone is here for your protection, so I want you to let your body react however it wants," I tell the wide-eyed boy. "Don't fight it."

"Luna," Brock whispers. "Why do I need so much protection?"

"Because we're about to put you in danger," I say, winking at him.

Tarq lies down behind me. The level of trust these kids have in me and each other is obvious when Brock remains seated. I reach my hand out to Bastian, and he moves to put his head between Annalisa and me.

"Beautiful, sweet guard, I will be helping you with this lesson," I tell Bastian. "We will show Annalisa what happens when she is not careful about touching her wolves."

Brock nervously glances at Bastian and shakes his head. "Luna, I'm not so sure about this."

"You are helping your Luna, Brock," I assure him. "Her guard needs to know what it feels like when she needs his help, and she needs to learn how to address her wolves properly."

"Are you sure about this, Mom?" Annalisa questions me.

"Will you kids please just do as you're told for once?" I sigh, rubbing my forehead. "Annalisa, you will use your fingertips on Brock. Brock, you will let your body react." I pull Bastian back up to me. "Bastian, you will be in your Luna's hand. You will feel her ask for your help using her grip. I will stop you before you hurt him."

Bastian pulls his head out of my hand and looks up at Annalisa. *"I don't like this. Please don't do it."*

"You know I can hear you, right?" I scowl at him. *"I'm the Luna, baby. You can't hide from me. I can hear everything my pack says."*

"Luna, please," the young wolf begs.

"Bastian, you are all perfectly safe," I assure him. "Would you like to learn this lesson in a safe environment or make horrible, untrained mistakes?"

He settles back in our hands with a sigh. *"Fine."*

"One last thing, daughter. When you've had enough, put your hand flat against Brock and pull all his emotions."

The boys look nervous, but Annalisa smiles excitedly. The tension only gets worse when Bruce moves to sit behind Brock.

"What am I about to do?" Brock whispers to Annalisa.

She smiles broadly. "I have no idea, but we're about to find out."

Tarq lays his jaw over Bastian's shoulders as Annalisa traces her fingertips up Brock's arm toward his chest. His skin rises in goosebumps, and the fine hairs stand on end. Bastian's head jerks when his companion begins to hum. Brock's eyes close, and he licks his lips. I cover Bastian's eyes as he starts to growl.

Annalisa pulls her hand away from Brock. "Mom?"

"It's ok, baby," I whisper, trying not to disturb the boys' reactions. "This will get uncomfortable, but you need to experience it."

Brock opens his eyes and fixes them on Annalisa. He moves forward, reaching for her hand. He's completely entranced with his face inches from hers and doesn't notice that she's leaning back.

He snaps when she exhales onto his face, causing a chain reaction. Annalisa pulls on Bastian's jaw as she reaches her hands out to stop Brock. Tarq latches onto Bastian's scruff, and I catch his muzzle as he lunges with a ferocious snarl at his companion. Bastian limply falls across my chest as I roll backward with him, and Brock blinks a few times, shaking his head.

"Luna, warn me next time you make me want to eat your daughter," Brock suggests.

I breathe out a laugh as Tarq releases Bastian's scruff. "You got it, sweetheart. Why don't you go shift? It'll get rid of the jitters."

He pulls one of Annalisa's hands from his chest. "We're still good, right?"

She opens her arms with a smile, and he gladly leans into them. "I think Mom was right to separate you and Rachel. There's no way she'd be able to resist you."

Rolling to cradle Bastian, I shake my head at them. "That's enough out of you two. Brock, go shift. I want your face to be the first he sees when I let him wake up."

Tarq pokes at me as I put my head on his shoulder. *You look tired, My Love.*

Smiling, I snuggle into his heat. "I am," I tell him. "It's been a long time since I've had to wrestle one of you guys, and he's a strong, emotional kid."

Annalisa pulls her fingers through Bastian's fur. "Mom, is he gonna be ok with Brock?"

"He'll be afraid of what Brock thinks of him," I inform her. "Those were all instincts, Annalisa, not choices. Bastian didn't choose to attack his friend. His instincts told him you needed his protection." I reach out my hand, urging her to lie against him. "You should rest."

Annalisa curls into Bastian's underside as Bruce opens the door, bringing Brock back. He moves about the room, throwing a blanket over me and putting more wood in the stove. Brock lays down against Annalisa and rests his nose beside Bastian's.

"I vote we never do that again, Luna."

"No, baby," I promise Brock. *"Once was enough."*

23

Tarq wraps his arm around my waist while Brock works in my hand as we travel through the forest. "You're keeping an ear on them, right?" Tarq whispers, glancing at the kids.

"Yes, My Love," I tell him, smiling. "Annalisa's talking about the Christmas night she spent with Dax." From what Bastian's saying, she's telling him about threatening to shoot her father to keep him away from the presents. *I'm not gonna remind Tarq about that.*

"I don't remember the last time my family was together on Christmas," Brock reminisces.

"Well, you're with us this year, sweetheart, so you'll be with family for the holidays," I announce, tugging Brock's jaw.

Tarq reaches across me to scratch between Brock's shoulder blades. "You're stuck with us, kid. You better get used to it."

Brock chuckles but otherwise goes back to quietly traveling in my hand. I look down at him and observe his calm, steady demeanor. *He's a lot like Chase, just less opinionated.*

"Darya, how much further?" Anthony asks. He and Edith are walking behind the kids, and he sounds nervous.

"Not far," I call out, stopping Brock. "What's up?"

Anthony lowers his voice. "Someone's following us."

I smile as I wait for them to catch up so we can all walk together. "I've told you for years to trust my wolves, Anthony. That's the pack." I point to my ear. "I might not know who I'm listening to, but they are guiding us, not trying to hurt us. We'll be there soon."

I hear a few wolves chuckle, but once we start walking again, they all begin talking at once. They moved closer when we stopped, and a few noticed Bastian. The Alpha wolves are notably larger, not in height but in thickness and build. When I first met Bastian, he easily passed as a regular wolf. Since ensuring he has ample access to food and quality training, he's filled out and caught their attention.

"You're making them nervous, Bastian," I say, looking down at him. "I want you on your best guard behavior."

"*Yes, Luna.*" Bastian lifts his head from Annalisa's hand and slides his nose down her leg. Tarq and I wear the same confused expression as he rubs his ear against her hip until she hooks his jaw and settles him.

"I used to think you were nuts for dealing with all the crazy crap Daddy did," Annalisa scoffs. She steps beside us and looks down at Brock. "Why can't they act like that?" She points at Brock, which makes him take a step back.

I stop Brock's retreat while Bastian tucks his chin. "Let's say you can change ten things about Bastian. What would they be?"

Annalisa looks down at Bastian. He silently leads her forward as she focuses on him, opening and closing her hand to rub her fingers over his muzzle. Brock tilts his head to the side to look at me.

Winking at him, I push the lesson again. "We'll make it easier. How about five things?"

Edith drags Anthony closer to watch the lesson. Bastian steers Annalisa around a root before glancing up at her. *He probably wants to hear the answer too.*

Finally, my daughter sighs. "Mom, I... How could... I don't know."

"Ok, child, we'll make this super easy," I tell her, winking. "Just name one thing. It's not the only thing you can change, just one of them."

Annalisa doesn't notice that we're all staring at her as she watches Bastian traveling quietly beside her. She frowns and sticks her lip out.

Anthony scoffs, breaking the silence. "It's a trick question, kid. She knows you wouldn't change anything about that wolf."

Edith clicks her tongue and shoves him.

"What?" he spouts. "It would've taken her half a damn day to figure that shit out. Can we just move on to the lesson, please?"

Annalisa glares at him before turning to me. "What am I supposed to be learning?"

"We love our wolves," I say, looking at Bastian and Brock. "They are fierce, protective, and intense." I look up at Tarq and slide my fingers along his jaw. "They are funny, passionate, and weird at times." Tarq leans down to kiss me. "They are a beautiful blend of everything we need, wrapped into one package."

We stop as Annalisa kneels before Bastian. "I wouldn't change anything about you. You make me laugh and feel safe at the same time. You are perfect in every way." She presses her forehead against his head and kisses the bridge of his nose before reaching for Brock. "You are steady and protective, Brock. You are the voice of reason, even in your silence. I would not change you."

Annalisa kisses his muzzle, which he's starting to take in stride. She reaches for her father. Instead of helping her up, Tarq kneels to her, showing the young wolves a form of respect for the Luna they're not accustomed to seeing.

"Daddy, you are the strongest, proudest wolf I have ever met. You have no equal, yet you've only shown me love." She cups his cheek as a tear leaks from her eye. "You taught me how to be strong and have fun. I would never want anything about you to change. I love you."

Tarq kisses her forehead and wipes the tears from her cheeks. I hear him whispering to her. It's a moment for them, and my involvement would be intrusive.

Annalisa looks up at me, smiling. "Lesson learned."

Tarq stands and backs up as Bastian steps forward to comfort his Luna. When Tarq kisses my temple, the bayou wolves begin talking again. They had assumed that Bastian was my Alpha. Chase corrects them as they all ask different questions, and their voices become overwhelming.

I step into Tarq's chest. "My Love, they've figured out who you are. They want to meet you," I whisper.

Tarq will do anything for our pack, but I will always come first. He holds me close, leaning toward my ear to whisper back. "Dar, you're not well. What if you need help?"

"If I cannot walk, Anthony will carry me," I say, cupping his cheek. "These wolves have never met my Alpha. They are nervous, My Love."

Tarq holds my chin, pressing his lips to mine. "I'll not leave you."

I slide my finger over his lower lip. "No, My Love, we'll request they come to us."

Tarq steps into the woods to shift away from his daughter and Anthony. He takes over for Brock, who happily joins his companions beside us. As we continue forward, Chase brings small groups to greet us. A few stay to travel with us for a while, but most leave right away.

"Chase, are we nearly to the village?" I ask after a while.

"*You have about 30 minutes or so. Are you feeling alright?*" He stops and lets me use his shoulders to stand after a group of bayou wolves leaves.

I frown. "*Annalisa has noticed that Bastian and Tarq are being greeted similarly.*"

"*Do you want me to tell them to stop?*"

"*That would be disrespectful,*" I remind Chase. "*I would like to give them a break.*"

"*Ok, Dar,*" Chase says, jogging away. "*I'll bring this next group, and then we'll take a break. They have a cabin for us, and I'm told it has a field behind it for ball.*"

I smile, looking toward the boys. Brock has been asking about playing for days and will be excited. I tilt my head at Bastian. "Your uncle made sure we had access to a field for tonight," I tell him. "Do you think you might want to play ball with the Alphas?" I kneel as more wolves step onto the trail ahead of us.

"*Luna, why do they keep greeting me?*" I hadn't anticipated how easily the wolves would figure out who Bastian is, and he's understandably feeling unprepared.

"*I hear we'll be at the cabin soon,*" I tell him. "*I'll try to find a way to address it there.*"

The last group of bayou wolves steps forward one at a time. Each one greets Tarq and me before stepping over to Annalisa and Bastian. They touch muzzle to cheek for the Lunas and brush whiskers with the Alphas. Every wolf addresses first the Luna and then her Alpha.

This might have been the last group for today, but it was the largest. By the time Annalisa reaches the final wolf, Bastian is fidgeting. Twala, an older wolf who had traveled quite far to meet us, allows Annalisa to draw her in so that she may rub her muzzle against the Luna's cheek. Unfortunately, that's the moment Bastian reaches his limit. He scratches his ear against Annalisa's shoulder, nearly knocking her over.

"I'm sorry, Twala," I say, mortified. *"He's young."*

Tarq tries to intervene, but I shake my head. We watch the young wolf take in Annalisa's scent before addressing Twala. Bastian steps forward and slides his muzzle over hers in an apology.

Tarq sits down. *"Our job here is done."*

* * *

The air is warmer when we reach the cabin. Chase smiles at us as we approach. He's sitting with Wyndsor, one of the southern elders I've spoken with a few times.

"We're so pleased you finally made it, Luna," Wyndsor says, reaching out to me. "I know the cabin isn't much, but Chase was adamant that there be a field for tonight."

I take her hands and cup her cheek. "We appreciate you, Wyn," I say, smiling. "It's been a long journey, and we've been sleeping during the day on the ship, so we're all pretty tired."

Wyndsor hands me a few food containers and a cloth bag as Chase opens the cabin's door for the kids. "Chase has been asking about herbs and remedies," she says. "Our healer travels quite a bit and sent this for you." She pats the bag. "It makes a lovely tea."

Their healer is a human, so I've never spoken to her. There aren't many humans who show my wolves kindness. I value those who do nearly as much as my wolves.

"We happen to like tea," I say, kissing her cheek. "Please thank your healer for us."

I watch Wyndsor walk along a fence line until I can't see her anymore. Turning back to the house, I find the front room nearly empty. Chase closes the door behind me, and I pull him toward the corner of the room.

"A tea from the healer," I hiss. My glare is clear. I understand his fear, but he has been too free with information that is not his to share.

"Dar, it's hawthorn," Chase whispers. "It has many properties, including helping your heart."

I narrow my eyes. "That is not the point."

Chase pulls me to the wall and leans against it. "Darya, I have been talking with them about herbal remedies since Bristol's death." He slides his hand over my neck and pulls me closer, kissing the top of my head. "I love you, Dar. I won't stop trying to save you. It's probably best if you just let me."

After my sacrifice, Tarq had chosen to work with Chase, but we couldn't figure out why we had such a strong connection. Jules was a wealth of information when we finally asked her to help us understand what was happening. In the past, the Luna would claim their companion through the blood bond. That was not the legacy I wanted to leave behind.

I slide my arms around his waist, soaking in his heat. "I love you too, Chase."

"I'm pretty sure the kids took over the bed before Tarq got there," he says, chuckling.

I can't help frowning. "Is there only one bedroom?"

"No," Chase says, sounding put off. "There's two. The other is... occupied."

I roll my eyes. I'd forgotten about Amelia and Bruce. They'd traveled ahead with Chase but had been silent for a while, meaning they'd shifted. I rub my eyes. "Ok, well, are you staying?"

"I'm gonna stand watch," he says. "I'll make sure everything is ready for the Alphas tonight. You should get some rest."

Kissing his cheek, I leave him to see what is happening in the remaining bedroom. The three wolves are piled up on the single mattress, with my daughter neatly tucked between her Alpha and their companion.

"Tarq, are you serious?"

"*Shh, you'll wake her and make her whine again.*" Tarq's whining makes his statement that much funnier. "*She thought the pack was being rude to Brock. I didn't know what to tell her.*"

"*So you continued to pretend that you can't talk to her,*" I finish for him as I climb onto the bed between Tarq and Bastian.

"*It was either that or telling her to ask her mother,*" Tarq says, chuckling.

I slide my arm under his neck. "*Do you have any ideas?*"

"*Dar, my only idea is to tell her that Bass is the next Alpha.*" Tarq chuckles, nuzzling my cheek. "*I don't think she'll believe he's not her mate after that.*"

"*Yeah, that's all I've got too,*" I grumble.

* * *

After a restless afternoon, I gather everyone behind the cabin for the full moon. I'd asked the local wolves to stay away from the field tonight and given the kids this time to be young and wild. Since they stepped off the boat, the teenagers have acted as their stature dictates. Watching them run around the field and play like kids again is refreshing.

Chase and Tarq sit with me as we wait for the Alphas and watch the future leaders of our pack. Tarq had hung Dax's medallion around my neck. The Alphas will focus on it so they can visit us wherever we are on the full moon evenings.

"Where are they?"

Tarq slides his muzzle along my jaw. "*They'll be here, My Love.*"

"I've been thinking," Chase says, setting aside the bag Anthony had left with him. "What would be the harm in just telling her the truth?"

"*Because I will kill him if he bonds with her.*" Tarq glares at Chase as if he's having a conversation with him.

"My Alpha," I huff. "He can't hear you. And you will not kill Bastian."

"*Well, I'll want to,*" Tarq grumbles. "*A lot.*"

"Noted."

Chase lifts his eyebrow, shifting his gaze between Tarq and me.

"Don't mind him," I say. "My hesitation would be whether she could handle Bastian staying a wolf. I fear she'd ask him to shift."

Chase lies in the grass and throws one of the balls in the air, catching it a few times. "You worried about them talking, and she's handled that just fine. I think I'd be more worried about him eating her than them bonding."

Tarq lays his chin on his crossed paws. *"There is that."*

I rub my forehead. "If we're more concerned with what Bastian will do, it doesn't make sense to keep it from her. He already knows."

"Who knows what?" There's suddenly a tremendous weight on my legs. I begin thrashing around, trying to remove the invisible force. *"Ow, Dar. What the hell are you doing?!"* Dax shouts as he appears in my lap. He jumps back as I slap him. *"Shit, Dar. You alright?"* He bumps my chest where his medallion is.

I yank it off, tossing it just before Miles appears. "That would've been useful information, Dax," I grumble. He's always been the king of partial information.

"Why do you expect me to know everything?" Dax is grumbly but still checks me for injuries. *"Where are we?"*

"Welcome to the bayou, guys. We made it here a little while ago." I hold my hand out for Dax's chin as Miles sneaks around to rub his nose on my cheek.

"Grandpa!" Annalisa jumps up and runs to her grandfather, flanked by the boys.

"Am I killing that kid?" Miles asks, eyeing the boys.

Giggling, I slide my hand over his muzzle. "Stop, Miles."

"I thought about moving the pack south a few times," Miles says. *"They had that big fire down here 30 or 40 years ago. You remember that, Dax?"*

Annalisa grabs her grandfather's jaw, dragging him off before he can answer. She sits and whispers to him while the boys lie behind her. We watch them briefly before Miles turns, shoving his nose in my face.

"What's that about?"

I click my tongue in a huff and kiss him behind his whiskers. "It's a learning process, Miles," I whisper. "We didn't realize how easily everyone would figure out who Bastian is."

"*She doesn't like him?*" he asks, confused.

"*She doesn't know,*" Tarq answers. "*We're trying to decide whether to tell her the truth or come up with another story.*"

Miles lies down and puts his paw in my lap. "*I think it's time you and I talk, Little One.*"

Taking a deep breath, I grab Miles' paw and turn to Chase. "Why don't you guys play ball?" I slide my hand over Tarq's head. "The boys could use a stretch, and, My Love, you play fair with Bastian. It's his first game." I pinch the tip of his nose.

"*In the spirit of honesty, I really hate it when you do that,*" Tarq tells me.

I raise my eyebrow at him. "Probably just as much as I hate when you lick my face." Then, as if I'd commanded it, Tarq slides his extremely wet tongue over my face before running away.

"*You want me to kill him?*" Miles asks.

"*Maybe later.*"

Miles chuckles as I pull his muzzle to me for another kiss. He lies quietly with his paw in my hand while Chase packs the ball bag. We watch him collect Annalisa and the boys and head out with the other Alphas for the game.

"What do you have for me, Miles?" I ask once we're alone.

"*Luna wanted me to pass on a message,*" he says. "*She said to tell you that the guardians didn't come for your body that night.*"

Blocking out the arguing wolves in the field, I frown down at him. "What night? Who are the guardians?"

Miles sighs. "*Listen, Dar.*" He pulls his paw from my hand and lifts his head. "*I have a great love for you. However, this is not something I feel for all Lunas.*" He gives me his other paw and rolls down onto his shoulder. "*She spoke. I listened. And then I walked my happy ass away. I did not ask questions because that would have caused her to speak again.*"

I pause, staring at Miles as he lies comfortably before me. "I miss you every day between full moons."

Miles moves just enough to lick my hand. "*I know you do, Little One.*"

"You should respect her as a Luna, though, Miles," I tell him. "It's only proper. She may not be a great person, but she's still a Luna."

"Dar, I stopped telling her to fuck off when Dax asked me to. That's respectful." Miles stretches his legs before curling around to put his head on my lap. He's never been one for pad rubs. He only asks for them when he wants me to appear occupied.

"Maybe we should change the subject." When we started this conversation, I thought it would be productive. But as Miles talks, he makes it clear that I was mistaken.

"As long as I don't have to get up."

Sighing, I look at the group in the field. Chase has Annalisa by the waist as she kicks her legs at Tarq. "Do you think I should tell her about Bastian?"

Miles fluffs his lips and works his jaw. As an immortal Alpha, Miles was an amazing strategist. I could never get ahead of him. As this wolf who bonded to me, he's an open book. He's about to tell me something he knows I won't like.

"Dar, you baby the shit out of that kid. She is not innocent. While you were off saving the world, her father raised her." Miles peeks at me, probably trying to make sure I'm not about to attack him. *"You've told her what happens when she bonds, and she's lonely while you force her to watch everyone else be in love. Give the kid a chance to grow up, Dar."*

He watches my face pull into a half-hearted scowl. Miles isn't the only one to give me this advice, but he's probably the only person I'd actually listen to. "What if she's not as together as you think? What if she convinces him to shift?" I cringe. "What if they bond?"

Miles closes his eyes. *"Then kill him."*

I click my tongue. "Miles. Please be serious."

"Ok, then I'll kill him."

As things escalate in the field, I pull Miles' head up and kiss his muzzle. "I love you, Miles."

Annalisa is still jumping around in the field, but her voice is starting to filter through the commotion. "You need to tell me!" she screams at her father. "Now Bass is lying to me! Why did they disrespect Brock?"

I climb to my feet. *"Bastian, tell her to calm down. I'm coming. It's time."* Annalisa drops to the ground, wrapping her arms around Bastian.

"It's ok. Look. Here comes Luna." Bastian says, soothing her.

Dax steps in my way before I can reach her. *"What are you doing?"*

I kneel to Dax and look toward the cabin where Amelia and Bruce are lying. I'd made them shift after they'd neglected to help with introductions. *"While I am being a mother, you will give them your blessing."* I look him in the eye, letting him know this isn't a request. *"It would also do my heart good if you would apologize to Bruce."*

Dax sits, tucking his chin toward his chest. *"Excuse me?"*

"Dax, you've moved forward in your death and bonded with a mate," I tell him. *"You should allow Amelia to be happy just as Bruce did for you all those years ago."*

Dax rolls his eyes. *"Yeah, alright."*

I kiss his muzzle before standing up. Bastian guides Annalisa the rest of the way across the field. "Come with me, daughter," I say, smiling at them. I lift my eyebrow at Bastian as I take Annalisa's arm. "I don't want to see you until you catch that ball, so you better get busy."

Chase lifts the bow out of the grass and does some kind of salute to me before yelling at everyone to set up. Annalisa clutches her chest, watching Tarq shove Bastian back toward the field.

"Come on, baby," I say, gently loosening her hand and guiding her away from the wolves. "Daddy's faster than Bastian. He'll be busy for a while, so let's talk."

Annalisa walks with me but is staring at her wolf. They don't spend much time apart, and it's nearly traumatizing for them when they do. I accept that this is my fault.

"Sometimes I don't give you enough credit," I apologize, sliding my hand down her arm. "You are your father's daughter, and prove you are every bit as amazing as he is daily."

Miles joins us as she turns to face me. *"You didn't give me a job,"* he tells me. *"I'm too damn lazy to play ball with two wolves that will always beat me."*

"Maybe you can trip Tarq when we're ready for Bastian," I suggest with a smirk.

Miles chuckles, sliding his head in my hand.

"Our wolves were not being disrespectful to Brock, my child," I say, returning my attention to the distraught teenager. "Brock is your companion. He's important to you, not them."

"He spends more time with Bastian than he does with me." Annalisa looks across the field at the wolves. They are engaging in horseplay more than playing ball.

"He does now, yes." Stopping, I attempt to find another way to approach the topic. "Chase is important to me as my companion, but do you treat him any differently than Grandpa Bruce or Neala?"

"No," she scoffs. "He's Chase. He let me ride the horses when Daddy wasn't around when I was little."

Sighing, I rub my forehead. "Well, let's not share that with Daddy."

Miles chuckles beside me.

"I thought he was Daddy's companion too," Annalisa says, confused.

"As Luna, we are in control of the pack," I explain. "Our mate is their Alpha, the second in command. He doesn't hold much power in the pack as he gets his orders from us. Our Alpha is given the highest honor we could give them besides our love." I rub my hand over her arm. "They choose our companion."

Furrowing her brow, Annalisa shakes her head. "Dad chose my companion?"

"I may have misjudged this one."

I click my tongue at Miles and let go of his jaw to hold Annalisa before me. "Baby, Daddy is not the Alpha who chose Brock."

I watch as my daughter digests what I've said. "Bass?" she whispers. Her hands tightly grab my arms, and her breath catches. When Annalisa stumbles, I lower her to the ground before she falls.

"Bastian swore two oaths to me," I whisper. "First was that he would not tell you. The second was that he would not shift in your presence."

"I'm allowed to love him?" Annalisa heaves air, holding her chest. "How is this possible when I've only known him as a wolf?"

I remember trying not to love Tarq. It was impossible. I loved when he held me for the first time, but I fell for the wolf long before I knew the man. I should've known this wouldn't work from the beginning.

"What does your heart say, my young Luna?" I ask, touching my fingers to her chest.

Annalisa takes a moment before finding her words. "Mom, I love him."

Sighing, I nod in Bastian's direction. "He's been waiting to hear you say that."

She smiles broadly and uses my shoulders to push herself to her feet. Bastian lifts his head, noticing her movement. He charges at full speed toward Annalisa. Miles slides his head under my arm as the teenagers crash into each other.

"Do you want me to help you over there?" Miles asks. He rubs his nose over my cheek and lets me lean on his shoulder.

"You were right. I think this is something they can handle on their own." I slide my fingers through his fur, soaking in his heat while we watch the kids. "Miles, can you ask Luna what she was talking about?"

"Let's compromise," Miles suggests, groaning. *"If Dax's annoying mate speaks to me, I will ask her your question."*

I look up and spot the rest of the wolves lying down, watching Annalisa and Bastian. Closing my eyes, I bury my face in Miles' fur. "I love you."

"I love you too, Little One."

24

We visited several towns and villages over the next few weeks. I'm pleased that a few are mixed with humans and wolves, but many are filled only with wolves. They want happiness and safety, the two things the militia and most humans are determined to take away from us. Over the years, I've worked closely with elders of different regions to help my wolves find peace.

We make our way slowly to the southeast and stop nightly. The weather has warmed up, and the daily teas make breathing easier. The kids have flourished in their roles. I'm confident their bond will only strengthen over time.

"Dar," Tarq says, draping his arm over my shoulders. "Why do they celebrate Christmas in a graveyard?"

"Daddy, don't be rude," Annalisa scolds.

I giggle because she'd asked me the same question a few hours ago. Having heard her voice, Bastian comes tearing up the trail on a life-saving mission to rescue his Luna. They might be handling their roles well, but they aren't any better with separation. Bastian is supposed to be running point with Bruce.

"If you don't get your ass back up there…" Tarq growls. He's had enough and is turning into Dax. *I find it quite funny.*

"Bastian, please stop pissing Tarq off," I say, grinning. "She is fine. You need to go do your job, young guard."

The smitten wolf slides in for a quick kiss behind the whiskers from my daughter and runs back ahead of us before he gets into more trouble.

"Do you know why, Luna?" Brock asks, peeking around Annalisa's hip. Chase had tried to teach him to travel silently in his Luna's hand, but that's not Brock's style.

"Yes, I do, sweetheart," I tell him, smiling. "About 30 years ago, during their celebration, the militia attacked the wolves that live here on Christmas Day. It was fast and brutal. Many victims are buried in this cemetery. It's a feast in their honor."

"Oh, I understand now," Annalisa says. "Instead of exchanging gifts, they have a meal with those they lost to honor their sacrifice."

I hook her hair behind her ear. "Exactly. They celebrate with those who no longer can."

"Now I feel like we're intruding," Brock says sadly.

"These wolves are our family, Brock," I tell him. "We may not have been in the same pack 30 years ago, but we are now. You are home, sweetheart."

"I'll miss getting my present," Tarq grumbles. He leans down to nip at my neck. My Alpha has never asked for anything that could be put under the tree. He loves our family but only requests time alone with me. I would take him into the mountains and stay in the cabin with him for three days between Christmas and the new year. I had it stocked with food, drink, and wood, so there would be no need to leave.

I slide my arm around his waist. "Your gift is spending the holiday with those you love, and, my Alpha, I heard that there will be delicious food."

Tarq twists his face in thought. "That might be acceptable."

I lean on his shoulder and whisper, "They heard you like duck."

* * *

Chase had run ahead, working out the details for our arrival. Since the first holiday, this feast has had a strict rule of no wolves in the cemetery. I have one wolf who is not allowed to shift, and my Alpha is unwilling to allow me to travel without a guard. Chase has worked out a compromise that I'm not sure everyone will agree with, but these wolves suffered a significant loss, and we will honor their traditions.

"Ok, everyone, here's the deal," I begin as we approach the cemetery. Bastian and Bruce are just ahead of us with their noses in the air. You don't have to be a wolf to smell the wonderful fragrance from the long food tables. "Guys?"

Bastian hesitates. *"Oh, Luna, that smells so good."*

I want to cry. Bastian had been conditioned to never eat unless he was given permission. The fact that he now openly desires food is a testament to Neala's ability with children. "I know, sweet boy," I tell him, sliding my hand over his muzzle as he joins us. "You'll get some. I promise."

Once Chase joins us, I kneel and explain to the group the traditions of the feast. They're allowing those in wolf form to stay along the fence line but not wander the grounds. Only one guard is allowed to accompany me. They built a shifting hut nearby and stocked it with clothing as I had at the cabin.

"Brock, I would like you to accompany me as my guard," I start before I reach for Amelia's chin. "Amelia and Bruce, I love you both equally, but I ask that only one of you shift. You know why." I lift my eyebrow, shifting my eyes from one to the other. "Amelia, I'm told there are some lovely dresses in the hut."

"I will stay with Bastian," Bruce declares.

I reach for my companion's muzzle. "Chase, will you take the ladies to change, please?"

I hear Annalisa take a sharp breath beside me. Edith left with Anthony when we reached the cabin on the full moon. They went to spend the holidays with Anthony's son, who had moved south some years earlier. This means that besides her grandmother, Annalisa is the only other lady, and I have just given her permission to dress up.

"I know you're not girlie, but if you'd like to dress for the occasion, Grandma can help you." Unable to find words, Annalisa lunges at me, wrapping her arms around my neck. I roll my eyes and point at Bastian. *"This is your fault, you know."*

Bastian chuckles, putting his nose against her back. *"You could wear a saddle blanket and still be the most beautiful girl in the cemetery,"* he tells her.

Laughing, I sit back on my heels. "You've got to love a compliment that contains the word 'cemetery.'"

Annalisa scoffs before leaning back to kiss Bastian's muzzle. She stands as Chase slides his head under her hand to lead her to the hut. Bruce and Bastian both watch the ladies leave. Bruce even leans to the side when my body blocks his view.

I shake my head and reach my hand out to Brock. "Your sisters are spending the holiday with Neala and Ash," I tell him. "Neala says she will make sure they shift to talk to you this evening."

Brock steps forward to nuzzle my cheek but tucks his chin and steps back when some bayou wolves walk behind me. Tarq sighs as I furrow my brow.

"Boys," Tarq says, snapping his fingers at Bastian to catch his attention. "Our Luna will never change. As we travel further from the lake, you'll encounter wolves that have never been in her presence." He puts his hand on my shoulder. "She will not change how she shows you love any more than she would expect you to treat her differently."

"So don't worry how others view us," I say, reaching out for Bruce as Brock returns to nuzzling me. "I am not the Alpha that they used to know. They will learn my love just as you have."

I open my arms for all three wolves, inviting them in for a hug. Bruce and Bastian each slide their chins over my shoulders while Brock curls his head under my chin.

"You better behave yourself," I hear Tarq grumble. "Show love to your wolves, not my daughter."

I giggle at Tarq's words, but both wolves' chins lift off my back as their bodies tense.

"Mom," Tarq whines. "That's my little girl."

Bastian stumbles slightly as I release him, but Bruce pushes against my shoulder when he walks forward. I grab Brock to stop myself from falling backward.

"She's a young lady, Tarq," Amelia scolds her son. "She's not a little girl anymore."

Turning, I see Amelia wearing a beautiful floral silk dress that sweeps the ground around her feet. My daughter is standing beside her, nearly unrecognizable. Amelia's done her hair, pulling it away from her face. Her cheeks are bright red as she nervously looks at Bastian.

"Do I look ok?" Annalisa asks.

Bastian shakes his head, spraying drool around us. He steps forward but still doesn't answer her. Annalisa is dressed in a simple white sun dress with tiny blue and yellow flowers. She looks stunning, but the thin straps don't conceal her second pack marking.

"I can change," she says, reaching for her chest.

"Please don't," Bastian says quietly. *"You look beautiful."*

"You do look lovely, Sweets," I tell her, slipping my shawl over her shoulders. I run my fingers down her left arm. "I wish you would stop growing up, but I know that's not in the cards."

I link my arm with hers and pull her away from Tarq, who's still pouting. Pushing her jaw with my fingers, I make her look at me instead of Bastian.

"You stay with Bastian and Grandpa Bruce," I tell her. "You don't leave their sides. We are not at home. We don't know all these people, so humans could easily enter the mix. Our second mark tells them exactly who we are. If something happens to me, our wolves will have you. If something happens to you, that's the end of the Luna line."

I pull the shawl tighter around her shoulders and smile at Chase as he approaches us.

"You look dashing," I say, reaching for him.

Chase's light skin turns bright red quickly. He's dressed in black slacks, a blue button-up shirt, and a black vest. My favorite part of his outfit choice is the loose tie around his neck. I reach for it and tighten it before kissing his cheek.

"Miles would be proud," I tell him, giggling. "Could you help Amelia gather some plates for everyone before you mingle?"

Chase smiles. "Of course, Dar."

Tarq and I guide our group into the cemetery. We're only ten feet closer to the food tables, but the smell is much more pungent once we're inside the gate. I point to our right and watch the two wolves walk along the metal fencing.

"Please, guys, do not leave this area," I beg them. Their eyes are on their mates, but their noses are taking deep breaths of the food's aroma. "They observe this tradition because the attack happened so fast that no one could shift. It would be considered disrespectful to mingle as wolves."

"*We understand, Luna,*" Bruce tells me. "*I will stay here with the kids.*"

"Bastian," Tarq growls. "That is my daughter you're staring at."

The young wolf drops his head and tips his ears back.

"Tarq, stop being mean," I say, clicking my tongue. "Bastian?" I reach for his chin. "Just don't eat her," I tell him with a wink.

His eyes brighten, and he licks my wrist. "*Yes, Luna.*"

Linking my arm with Tarq's, I slide my fingers under Brock's jaw. My young guard takes us through the clusters of people around the grave sites. We listen to some of the stories of their family member's accomplishments and contributions to the pack. Tarq grabs food from every table. I'm not brave enough to take anything from his plate as I'm quite sure he'd bite my fingers, but he feeds me some of it as we walk.

We pause at one smaller gathering. A young woman tells the story of her father, who had written a book that the Amazon would publish, but then the militia rose.

"Why would a forest publish a book?" I whisper to Tarq.

He shrugs. "They use trees to make paper. Maybe that's how it was responsible for it," he suggests, watching a little girl approach us.

"That's not fair," the girl complains. "I was told I had to shift to come to the party."

The woman telling the story jumps off her pail and runs to catch the little girl by her shoulders. "Myla," the woman hisses. "That is the Luna."

Reaching for the woman's arm, I pull her away from the little girl and cup her cheek with a smile. "This little girl is fine with us," I tell her. My touch tells me that her name is Julia. I've never met her, but she's one of my wolves. "Are you her mother?"

"I don't have one of those," Myla says, pulling on Brock's whiskers.

He playfully nips at her. "*What's up with this kid?*"

Rubbing my thumb behind Brock's whiskers, I smile at the little girl. "I'm so sorry," I say. "Myla is your name?"

"The village grandmother takes care of her," Julia tells me. "She's just over there." She points at an older woman I'd met a few days ago.

"Thank you, Julia," I say, nodding. "I can take Myla with me. She'll be fine." I watch the woman return to her pail and continue her father's story.

Myla holds her jerky out to Brock. "Is he allowed to eat?"

Kneeling before Myla, I lift Brock's muzzle to set his chin on my shoulder. "This is Brock," I tell her. "He's a Luna's guard and would trade places with you. He likes being a boy."

Myla scrunches her nose. "What does a Luna's guard do?"

"They guard me," I say, straightening out her dress. "He's an extra set of eyes that helps watch for danger."

"Why would you be in danger?" She studies Brock with her head tilted.

I frown. "It comes with the territory."

Myla gasps, backing away from me.

"*I asked permission,*" Tarq says. "*I think they were too scared to say no.*"

Knowing Tarq is probably what Myla fears, I hold my hand out for her. "Come here, sweetheart," I say quietly. "This is my Alpha, Tarq. He taught our daughter how to walk with a guard in hand. Would you like to learn?"

Myla smiles as Tarq slides his jaw over my shoulder. Apparently, the next best thing to being a wolf is hanging out with the Luna and her Alpha.

"I love you, my Alpha," I say, kissing Tarq behind his whiskers and using his shoulders to push myself back up to my feet.

Brock instantly slips his muzzle into my hand. "*Please don't let her pull my whiskers again.*" He hooks his jaw on my hip to look up at me, pleading for mercy.

I shake my head. "No, Brock," I say, giggling. "This is a job for my Alpha."

Tarq slides his head under Myla's arm until it's resting just before his ears. I pull Brock's head to my stomach to show her how I'm holding him. "You'll put your fingers under his jaw like this."

Myla regards Tarq for a moment. "He's so big," she says in awe.

"But he does have beautiful eyes," I say, rubbing his chin.

Tarq chuckles as Myla moves her fingers to his jaw.

"Ok," I say, straightening Brock out. "Now, we'll just take a short walk. Are you ready?"

Myla smiles broadly as Tarq begins pulling her forward. Brock places me beside Tarq, and I slip my fingers through my Alpha's fur, letting him know where I am.

"Is it just you and your grandmother at home?"

"She's not my grandmother," Myla says, leaving her eyes on Tarq. "Grandma Pine takes in all the orphans."

I try to hide my surprise. "Are there more children that live with you?"

Myla looks at me curiously. "There are five of us that live with her now."

"I was talking to some locals a few days ago," Tarq says. *"They said the militia has been especially active for the past few years."*

The wolves pull us to the right to avoid a group gathering around another grave site.

"You don't even have to watch where you're going!" Myla exclaims.

Sighing, I focus back on the little girl. "That's right," I tell her, smiling. "They allow me to focus on my pack and what they need." I feel only happiness when sliding the back of my fingers over her cheek.

Ending our rounds beside Grandma Pine, I listen to her stories. They are about the parents whose children she raised, including some that came after the initial attack. She has been the backbone of this group.

The kids in her care are happy and healthy. I thank her for her service and promise we will find a solution.

At the close of the day, I sit with the wolves outside the gates, waiting while the ladies change. Having heard some of the tales, no one is interested in idle chat. Tarq rests his head on my lap, occasionally sighing.

"Why don't they tell us everything?" Tarq asks, lifting his head. *"We could've been helping."*

Looking through the gate, I spot Chase talking to one of the older couples who told their daughter's story. "They aren't used to us, My Love," I say, frowning. "We might be lucky that Chase's mate was from here. They seem to have adopted him."

"Rachel could help us too," Brock offers.

When I see Chase turn around, I smile. He's holding a large serving platter covered with an oversized white cloth. Approaching us, he places it beside me and kisses my cheek.

"Merry Christmas, Dar," Chase whispers.

"Merry Christmas, Chase," I whisper back. When I turn to the wolves, Tarq is leaning over my lap, trying to smell the platter. "I have arranged for some presents for my guards. We can't carry anything extra on our trip, so I have arranged a special meal for each of you."

I pull back part of the cloth to reveal some prepared raw meat. At home, my Alpha is always served first at a feast. I'm unsure if Lunas previously observed this tradition, but we do now. Tarq sits up, licking his lips, knowing he'll get his present first.

Picking up the duck carcass, I turn to face him. My favorite thing that Tarq does as a wolf is an excited dance he can't contain when he's about to eat duck. His front legs dance around while he drools. At 41, my Alpha resembles a puppy when a duck carcass is nearby.

"I love you, Tarq," I say, placing the duck before his dancing paws. "Merry Christmas."

Tarq licks his lips to catch the drool and gently slips the tip of his tongue over my cheek. *"Best present ever. Merry Christmas. I love you too."*

Next is the rabbit for Bastian. I lean forward to place it before him and kiss his nose. *"Merry Christmas, my beautiful boy. I love you very much."*

Bastian stands and steps over the rabbit to slide into my arms. He silently rests his jaw on my back. As I hold his neck, Tarq moves behind me to rub his muzzle against Bastian's. I meant this to be a simple gift-giving, but I hadn't thought about how much this might mean to the young Alpha. This teenage boy probably hadn't received a present in years.

"I love you, Luna," Bastian says quietly.

"We love having you as part of our family, sweetheart." I slide my hands over his legs.

Bastian steps back, nuzzling my cheek before lying down with his rabbit. Although Tarq starts eating his duck immediately, Bastian rubs whiskers with Brock, indicating that he'll be waiting for his companion.

"Next, we have Brock," I say. "Merry Christmas, young wolf. You are proving to be a wonderful companion with a bright future." I pull back the cloth to reveal a turtle whose bottom shell has been cut to allow easy access.

"How did you know?" Brock sounds shocked.

"You are my wolf. Stop trying to hide things from me," I say, raising my eyebrow. "When I say you're stuck with me for Christmas, I mean it."

Brock stands to nuzzle my cheek. *"Merry Christmas, Luna."*

"Merry Christmas, sweetheart."

Bastian leans to the side to look around me. I turn to see Annalisa approaching with her grandmother in hand.

"Good," I say as Amelia lies down beside Bruce. "The hardest wolves to figure out happen to be the oldest in our group. They spent so long denying the truth that I had to dig into their pasts and discover who they were before they met. I'm unsure when you last had this, but history says you have the same favorite meal."

I remove the rest of the cloth to reveal two slabs of gator tail.

"We love you, Mom and Dad," I say, smiling. "Merry Christmas."

They step forward and slide their jaws over my shoulders for a group hug. They rub their noses together along my back. Tarq steps forward to nuzzle them both, making me somehow feel left out.

"*Thank you,*" Bruce says.

"*You're welcome,*" I tell him.

Giving the wolves time to enjoy their meals, I lead my daughter to a patch of grass across from the changing huts. Our guards can still see us, but we can talk privately.

"You seem to be doing well with Bastian," I say as we sit. "How is that going?"

Annalisa sighs. "He doesn't talk about himself," she says, studying her wolf. "He wants me to tell him stories all the time, but when I ask him things, he shuts down."

I hold my hand out for hers. "Bastian had a very different childhood from the one you experienced. It may take a while before he's ready to talk about it."

"He'll be ok, though, right?"

I pull her to me and hold her against my shoulder. "Bastian has overcome a lot," I tell her. "He's fierce in everything he does. He'll protect you with the full extent of his strength. That boy will love you with a ferocity that will take your breath away, and when he's ready, he'll tell you why."

Annalisa blushes. "You make him sound perfect."

"Did you think I would bring you a boy who wasn't?" I ask, scoffing.

As my daughter leans on my shoulder, Chase brings us some rags. He bumps my nose with his finger and bows before ducking into the changing hut.

"Mom, I don't think I could ever do what you do," Annalisa sighs. "You take on so much by yourself. I'll never be that strong."

"I've made mistakes, child," I tell her, sliding my fingers through her hair. "Your father is a pain in the ass goofball, but he is so smart. He says it's not our mistakes but how we fix them that counts. Look at all that I've missed trying to do everything myself."

Annalisa pulls away to look into my eyes. "What are you doing to fix it?"

"First, Neala and Ash will be checking in on all the children within a three-day run of the lake," I tell her, twisting my face in thought.

"I like that plan," she says, smiling.

"We'll expand the guard," I continue. "They'll have small patrols that will travel and check on those that live further out." I narrow my gaze upon the last bayou wolves filtering from the cemetery. "We need to look into something like a liaison with them. These wolves are so far away that they've been left to fend for themselves."

Annalisa sighs. "They seem to struggle, but all I feel from them is happiness."

"Odd combination, isn't it?" I smirk at her. Turning my eyes to the wolves, I see that Tarq and Bastian have finished and are rubbing their muzzles over their paws. I hold a rag out to Annalisa. "Are you ready for Bass?"

She smiles, and I nod to the boys to tell them they can come to us. Both of their muzzles are covered in mashed meat. I hold up my rag, and Tarq slides his muzzle into it.

"Before we bonded, you would rub my muzzle for hours under the ruse of cleaning it." Tarq hums with his eyes closed, just as he would back in those days.

"I remember," I say, smiling. "You would sit still with your eyes closed and let me look at how beautiful you were."

"It felt like that was your way of telling me you loved me. I wanted so badly to hear you say the words."

"I have always loved you, Tarq," I whisper. "I was made to stand beside you, and you were made to hold my heart."

Tarq pulls his muzzle from the rag and slides it across my cheek before resting his jaw on my shoulder. *"I love you, Dar."*

"I love you too, my Alpha."

Annalisa sighs. "I want that."

Bastian pulls his muzzle out of his rag and stares into Annalisa's eyes. He chuckles as he steps forward and pushes her over with his chest. The young wolf lies down on her, sticking his nose in her face. *"You will just have to wait your turn, my Luna.*" He then slides his tongue over her face, leaving a trail of slobber before jumping away from her.

"Bastian! Gross!" Annalisa yells, wiping her face.

Laughing, I help her sit up. "Don't think I don't have that too. Where do you think Bass learned it from?"

Beside me, Tarq shakes his head as if he is not the teacher of these wayward ways.

"My Alpha," I say sharply, taking his chin in my hand. "You are not innocent, so please stop the disapproving head shake."

Tarq steps to me just as Bastian had done. He knocks me onto my back and stands over me, rubbing his whiskers over my face.

"Don't you dare ruin my Christmas," I warn him.

Tarq tucks his nose beside my neck, nuzzling my ear and taking a deep breath. When he pulls back, I notice that he's swung his hips, moving his back claws away from me.

"Tarq?" I say, frowning.

"I do love you, Dar," he says before he slides his extremely wet tongue over my face and jumps away. *"That's how you do it, kid!"*

I swat uselessly at him as the two wolves dart away from us. They tumble and rough-house across the grass. They probably look like they're fighting, but a few seconds of listening to them talk to each other would cure that.

"Does it ever stop?" Annalisa asks.

Laughing, I wipe my face. "Would you want it to?"

As she watches Bastian play with her father, Annalisa sighs and smiles. "No."

"You're growing up so fast," I say, tugging the tips of her hair. "You two complement each other very well."

"I'm not growing up, Mom," she says, bumping her shoulder into mine. "I'm learning, and I have a pretty great teacher."

<h1 style="text-align:center">25</h1>

Chase assures me we'll reach the beach tomorrow when we stop beside a narrow tributary on the eve of the full moon. The gators won't travel here, but plenty of fish swim through. Tarq was excited to challenge Bastian to a fishing contest.

"How are you holding up, Brock?" I ask, looking down at the resting wolf.

The teenager's eyes open. *"I'm tired, Luna,"* he says. *"I didn't realize how lazy I was."* He gives me his paw when I request it. *"Don't tell Annalisa, but I think you're better at this."*

"I've had a lot more practice, silly boy," I say, giggling. *"Besides, she's distracted."* I glance at my daughter.

Brock follows my gaze. *"She seems distracted a lot."*

Annalisa's zoned out, staring at Bastian.

"This is new to her," I remind him. *"Bastian's shift mutes it for him but not her. Can you imagine how confusing that must be?"*

Brock watches her for a minute. *"So it's like a bird and a fish?"*

"Exactly," I tell him. *"She knows he's a boy, but she only gets the wolf. It's not easy."*

"I can't help her, can I?"

"Not with this, sweetheart," I say, frowning. *"She'll have to find a way to be satisfied with what she has. She'll get there."*

Both Alphas continue throwing fish onto the grass until Chase yells at them. He'd already thrown half of them back, as there was plenty to feed all of us tonight.

"Who caught the most?" Tarq asks.

I look up, ready to ask how I would know, but he's not looking at me. Both stare at Chase as he prepares the fish beside the fire.

"You can tell him, Uncle Chase," Bastian says. *"He should get used to defeat."*

"What are you two doing?" I ask, baffled. "He can't hear you."

"I'm not sure our pack will survive without you, Luna," Brock says, turning his head toward the Alphas.

I'm never sure if Brock is joking or serious with his dry humor, but that was perfectly timed. "Then you'll go down laughing, won't you?"

Brock lays his head down and gives me his other front paw. *"Well, there is that, I guess."*

"Ok, that is never gonna be normal," Tarq says sadly.

"Leave him alone," I tell Tarq, laughing. "He has to put up with your crap all the time. The least he should get is a pad rub."

"My pads are sore and need attention," Tarq whines, holding up his paw as if injured.

"But this poor teenager needs love too," I gush, leaning over Brock. Grabbing his muzzle, I give him several noisy kisses as Tarq stares at me, unimpressed.

Brock sighs. *"You're gonna get me killed one of these days."*

Laughing, I give him one more kiss behind the whiskers. "Today is not that day. Go on, though. I'm sure Annalisa would love to finish your rub."

Annalisa jumps slightly. "Huh?" She hadn't heard anything I said.

"Is she ok?" Tarq asks, sliding into Brock's vacated space. He holds his paw up while watching her.

Bastian slips behind her and braces her back with his shoulder. Annalisa sighs as she relaxes into his warmth.

"I don't know," I answer Tarq. *"I might have her work with Miles."*

* * *

Chase fills the water bottles in his pack the following day, saying we won't find drinkable water as we get closer to the ocean. He's right, but they've made his bag heavy. Tarq runs point for us while Chase takes Brock into the woods to teach him how to flank us. It's not long before Bastian's had enough of listening to my labored breathing.

"Dar, come down here, please," Chase requests as he approaches after Bastian asks him to check on me.

I kneel to him, placing the pack on the ground. Chase steps around my outstretched arms and pushes his head against me until his ear reaches my chest.

"Tarq, one of us needs to shift to carry the water," Chase says without my permission.

I scowl at him.

"I got it," Tarq responds, bounding down the trail toward us. He slides to a stop and sticks his nose in my face to smell my breath. *"Grab me some clothes, Dar."* He waits patiently while I pull some from the pack before disappearing into the woods.

Chase sits in front of me. *"Please stop pushing yourself,"* he begs. *"Why are you being so stubborn?"*

I wave my hand slightly to indicate my daughter. *"Chase, look at them. Annalisa needs her mother and a teacher. Bastian needs support. Brock needs a loving parent. Amelia and Bruce need encouragement. And then there's you, Chase. We've been through everything together."* I slide my fingers through his fur, pulling his anxiety. *"What would you do without me to lean on when you need help? And do you really want to see Tarq frown all the time?"*

With a sigh, Chase turns away from the kids and leans his muzzle against my cheek. *"This is a lot for me to carry on my own, Dar."*

"I know, and I'm sorry to ask that of you, but we're so close, Chase." At this point, I know I'm begging, but I'm afraid Chase is on the verge of telling everyone we need to go home. *"Let's get to the beach and give them that experience."*

Emerging from the woods, Tarq kneels beside us. "What aren't you telling me?"

Chase turns to me, placing his nose against mine. *"You're on your own."* He spins around and darts up the trail to take Tarq's place.

Tarq watches him leave before turning back to me. "He obviously isn't going to tell me."

"My Love, this has been a very long trip," I say, cupping his cheek. "I'm just tired."

Tarq stands, lifting the pack and offering me his hand. "We're not far from the beach," he informs me with a smile. "We can stay there for a while. Chase was told there was a farm nearby owned by a wolf that has horses I can train for you."

"That sounds wonderful," I say, smiling.

* * *

It takes us a few more hours to reach the beach. Tarq stops at the tree line and watches our daughter as she looks around in awe. I step forward to link our arms and kiss her head.

"Did you know it was this beautiful?" Annalisa whispers.

I lean my cheek against her head, sighing. "I thought it might be."

"Luna, I really want to throw her in that."

Wiping a tear from my cheek, I look down at Bastian. *"I know, baby. I'm sorry, but maybe her Daddy can help you."*

With perfect timing, Tarq grabs Annalisa, pulling her from my arms. He spins around to walk backward toward the water with our daughter thrown over his shoulder. "You coming, Bass?"

Bastian jumps up and barrels after him. I sink into the sand to watch them.

"You know your wolf can swim, right?" Tarq yells at Annalisa. He laughs as she tries to escape them by swimming away.

"Did you ever figure out why he always wants to throw you in the water?" Chase asks, plopping down beside me.

I watch Amelia and Bruce walk past us, holding hands. "No," I say, happily sighing. "It's probably an Alpha thing because Bastian likes to do it too." I scowl as Chase pulls out the stethoscope.

I lean back on my hands to let him examine me, and we watch Brock sprawl out in the sand, soaking up the sun. He rolls a few times before stretching his neck and sighing with his eyes closed. Brock loves lying in the sun. He doesn't mind the water and will wash the sand out of his coat when he wakes up, but he prefers a dry location in the sunshine.

"He reminds me of Miles," I say, giggling.

"He's a good kid," Chase murmurs, still listening to my lungs. "He asks about you a few times a day."

I sigh. "I know. I hear him." Chase lied to Brock, telling him I'm getting better. I disagree with lying, but I understand why he does it.

"Brock's just a kid, Dar," Chase says, lifting the back of my shirt and urging me to lean forward. "It's not his job to worry about you. He needs to learn how to support his companions."

I follow his eyes to the water and watch Bastian trying to bite Tarq's arm to keep him away from Annalisa. "I wish I could give Bastian more of a childhood," I whisper, leaning against Chase. "He missed out on so much having his stolen from him."

Chase hooks the stethoscope around his neck. "His past will always affect him, but you've shown him so much love in this short time, Dar." He kisses my temple. "You've left your mark."

"Have I done enough, though? I've missed so many things."

Chase points to the water. "Look at your family. Does it look like you've let them down?"

Annalisa is in the water with her father. She's trying to escape him, and he's pretending she has a chance. Bastian is rolling in the shallow waves while Brock is passed out in the sun. Amelia and Bruce are sitting together down the beach from us. Bruce sits behind Amelia with his arms wrapped around her while she laughs at something he's said.

I slide my hand over Chase's cheek. "Thank you."

He lies back with his head on the bag of supplies. "You're welcome. Now come here." He holds his arm out. "You need to rest, and I should nap before the Alphas get here."

I roll down onto his shoulder and stretch out in the sun.

"Bristol said there's a whole city out there underneath the water," Chase whispers, leaning his chin against my forehead. "They called it New Orleans."

"Rosalee mentioned a jazz party she went to a few times there." My great-aunt enjoyed discussing it, but I didn't think it was true. "There was some kind of parade."

"What's a parade?" Chase asks.

"She said people would walk down the street and throw beads."

Chase bursts out laughing. "Dar, that doesn't sound right." He pulls my head, making me look up at him. "Why would anyone want to get hit with beads?"

"I don't know. I'm just telling you what she said." I join in his laughter.

He kisses my forehead and puts his arm behind his head. "We'll ask Dax tonight."

I relax into Chase with a sigh, watching my family play.

* * *

Annalisa approaches me as I set the medallion out in the sand that night. "Mom, can you shoot tonight?" She holds the bow out to me and walks away as soon as it touches my hand.

"What's up, kiddo?" I ask her, jogging after her with Chase in tow. "You've been out of sorts."

Tears stream from her eyes as she turns and latches onto me.

"Hey, talk to me. What's wrong?" I see Tarq and Bastian stand up, watching us. *"This is a girl thing, guys. Send Miles to me when he gets here, please."*

Tarq lowers his head, but Bastian stays at attention with his eyes focused on his Luna. I nod to Chase, and he pulls the bow from my shoulder.

"Do you want to sit down?" I ask my daughter.

She collapses onto the sand, dragging me with her. I cradle her in a heap, tucking her under my chin. She continues to sob as I rock her in my arms.

"It's ok, sweetheart," I whisper. "Let it all out." As I continue rocking her, I run my fingers through her hair until she's breathing evenly.

"There's so much pain and sadness in the world," Annalisa sputters. "How do you do this?"

"You have one more fundamental lesson to learn," I say. "You've been spending time with Brock. With his parents still missing, he's overwhelming you. I'm sure he appreciates you, but you need to help without feeling the emotions." I wipe the tears from her cheeks as she pulls away from me.

Annalisa sighs, leaning her forehead against mine.

"You can release all of this on Bastian, and then I'll let you practice on Uncle Miles."

My daughter clicks her tongue. "Uncle Miles doesn't care about anything, Mom," she scoffs.

"Miles is perfect for what you need to learn, you'll see," I say, winking at her. *"Bastian, come here, baby. Your Luna needs a heat release."*

Bastian jumps up, charging at us as if leading troops into battle.

"Well, he's an over-reactor, isn't he?" I grumble.

Annalisa giggles. "Did you see him when I tripped? I thought he would tear down the tree for daring to have a root." She pushes her hands into Bastian's fur as he slides to a stop and nuzzles her cheek. The young wolf hums loudly as his legs begin to buckle under him.

"I love hearing your hum, sweetheart," I tell Bastian, pulling his chin over her shoulder. "It took us a long time to find that."

Bastian sticks his tongue out to gently lick my fingers as his hips collapse. I help Annalisa roll with him and lay him down in the sand. The young wolf licks his lips before his eyes roll closed.

I smile when the Alphas appear on the beach. "Now that you're running on empty, it's time to introduce you to the real Uncle Miles."

She follows my eyes and watches Miles jog toward us. He wants to run to me, and the tension causes a spring in his step. Miles slides into my arms and relaxes as his jaw rests on my back.

"I told you that you need to learn your wolves," I say quietly to Annalisa. "This one was one of my toughest wolves to crack. I almost didn't." I turn my face into Miles' fur and tightly hug his neck. This might be a teaching moment, but I've still missed him. He heats up against my chest, and I turn back to my daughter. "What do you see when you look at Uncle Miles?"

"A really lazy wolf," Annalisa says, frowning.

Clicking my tongue, I rub the side of my face against Miles' neck. "Maybe you could look a little deeper to see past what Miles is trying to show you. Do you notice anything about what's happening right now?"

Her eyes wander over Miles first and then me. They settle on my hands, sliding over his legs to indicate I'm done with the hug, but Miles isn't moving. She tilts her head and looks at his face behind my back. Miles has a very low hum, but I can feel it, so his eyes are probably closed.

"Ok, I see it now." She smiles as she realizes what he's trying to hide. *"There's nothing to see here. Move along,"* Miles grumbles.

I giggle as I push him back. "Miles is built differently," I continue with Annalisa's lesson, ignoring Miles' pouting. "It's probably because he's so lazy. He's tall, thin, and lanky, so he balls perfectly against me."

I push against Miles' chest until he rolls over his hip and crashes onto his shoulder. I land beside him, smiling. His neck curls so his head rests under my chin while my thighs hold his hips, forming a ball with his body. His back claws are tucked behind his front legs to protect me, and he cuddles up like a puppy. I rub Miles' jaw for a minute while he relaxes into me.

Sliding my arm under my head, I look up at Annalisa. "Much like your mate, Miles didn't grow up in a nurturing, loving environment. He loved his mate but couldn't show it. He didn't know how." I slide my fingers through his fur, and his hum starts up again, and this time, Annalisa is close enough to hear it. "What's worse is that Miles didn't know how to accept love. I worked with Miles, just as I worked with Bastian."

Annalisa scoots near Miles' back and runs her fingers through his fur. Her eyes open wide. "Oh, wow," she hisses at me as if he can't hear her.

"In general, Miles loves love," I say, smiling. "He's not the best at showing it in the traditional ways, but he enjoys feeling our love. His emotions are stronger because he accidentally bonded to me, which is why I stress being careful with your blood."

I let Annalisa pull some of his emotions. This is Miles' favorite thing to do. He's nearly cuddled up like a baby and feels the same things as Tarq does when he touches me. She will never be able to fully drain him in his happy place. She lies down against his back and pulls the fur on his neck.

"Now, I want you to focus on what is coming from him. You'll take a deep breath and release it, letting those emotions leave with the exhale." I wave my hand as I breathe out for emphasis. "It's not hard work, but rather a relaxation exercise."

Annalisa tries a few deep breaths but raises her eyebrow at me. "Why can't I hold onto the good emotions?"

I chuckle at her. "Because if you don't get rid of it, you'll probably end up licking Miles."

"Mom, that's just gross," she says, wrinkling her nose.

"You're gonna think it's gross when you do it and can't stop yourself," I say, laughing.

Annalisa scrunches her face in disgust as Miles shifts around to cuddle closer to me.

"I'm not gonna lie, Dar. I'm really going to enjoy it when you die." Miles groans a bit as he settles into his snuggle.

I push my hand back through his limbs and find his jaw again. *"I might find that offensive if I didn't know you just want access to me all the time."*

Miles wiggles his shoulders to push more of his neck against my chest and heats his body. *"How's she doing?"*

I watch Annalisa close her eyes and breathe out slowly. *"She seems to be trying. Did you talk to Luna about her message?"*

"You remember I told you if she spoke to me, I'd ask?"

I roll my eyes. *"She didn't talk to you."*

"It was a perfect month free of bitching and whining," Miles says whimsically. *"Why would I screw that up?"*

"She wouldn't have said it if it wasn't important, Miles," I scold. *"Please, can you do this for me?"*

Miles sighs, licking his lips. *"Yeah, alright."* Which I've realized is the standard grumbly wolf answer to everything.

Allowing Miles to enjoy his cuddles, I turn to Annalisa. "How are you doing?"

She takes a deep breath and sighs before opening her eyes. "Do you remember when I got sick a few years ago and couldn't stop throwing up?"

"Um, ok," I say, furrowing my brow. "I'll bite. Yes, I do."

"Taking deep breaths and letting them out slowly helped my stomach." She breathes deeply again. "This is a lot like that."

"So," I start, drawing out the word. "You're figuring it out?"

Annalisa lifts her eyebrow. "Well, I haven't licked Uncle Miles yet."

"That is true," Miles says calmly. *"I have yet to be licked."*

I stare at Miles for a moment. "Miles, I actually didn't need you to confirm that," I say, shaking my head slowly. "But I appreciate that. Thank you."

Miles licks his lips and adjusts his legs. *"My pleasure, Dar. I'm here for you."*

Annalisa tugs his ear, and he playfully nips at her.

"Kid, don't ever interrupt an Alpha during a cuddle."

I shake as I laugh at Miles, rocking his body with mine. "Miles, that might be the least masculine thing you've ever said!"

Miles groans as he straightens his back and stretches his legs over my hip. He lays his head back on the sand and looks up at me. *"And yet I could kill any of those fools for interrupting my cuddles."* Miles lets out a gaping mouth yawn. *"I love you, Dar."*

I scoop my arms around his neck. "I love you too, you ole softy." I probably cuddle with him for too long because when I open my eyes, the other wolves have snuck down the beach and are staring at me. "What's up, guys?"

"We got worried," Bastian tells me, poking at his Luna.

"He got worried," Tarq announces. *"I got jealous."* He pokes his nose at Miles, who snaps at him.

"*I don't care,*" Dax says, flopping in the sand. "*I just didn't want to be the only one on that side of the beach.*"

Miles nuzzles my neck. "*See? You're better off with me.*"

"It's becoming clear to me why there is only ever one Alpha." I kiss Miles behind the whiskers and look over the group. Winking, I reach for Annalisa. "Come on, kid. It's time to practice your new skill on Brock."

The young wolf's ears droop, making me giggle.

"It's not like last time, baby," I say, rubbing his jaw. "We didn't do this to Miles. This is all him."

"*She's lying,*" Miles grumbles. "*She does this to me every time, so everyone thinks it's normal.*"

"Miles, stop," I say, clicking my tongue. I send the kids off to sit by the fire. "*Bass, try to get Brock to tell you about his parents,*" I say as he follows. He looks back to nod.

With the air turning chilly, I lie in the sand with my head against Tarq while Miles and Dax line my legs. I don't often get time alone with all the Alphas, with Annalisa pulling Dax away constantly to complain or Tarq starting shit with him. I'm reminded of simpler times when it was just us.

"*That kid's come a long way since we first met him,*" Dax remarks.

"*He's a good kid, Dad,*" Tarq brags. "*He works hard and guards Annalisa well.*"

"I'm proud of him," I say, smiling. I follow Dax's eyes and see he's watching Bruce and Amelia. They are lying side-by-side, and Amelia has curled her muzzle into Bruce's chest. He's twisted so his jaw lies over her neck, and he can watch over the kids while she sleeps. "Dax, what exactly did you say to them?"

He turns his head toward me and lays it on Tarq's leg. "*I don't know, Dar. Something like I'm dead, so they might as well be together.*"

My entire body participates in an aggravated sigh.

"*Darya, I was their Alpha for over a century,*" he grumbles. "*I don't apologize for shit.*"

"Can you try to ignore them until we go home?" I ask. "At least there, they can avoid the full moon gatherings."

Dax turns back to them, narrowing his eyes.

"Dax, stop staring at them!" I don't raise my voice at the Alphas. They earned the respect I give them, but this is not the first time I've had this conversation with Dax. I'm desperate for it to be the last.

The grumpy Alpha rolls his back against me to face the other direction. "*Fine. Quit your yelling. You're getting bossy in your old age.*"

"*Dad, she's happy, and he's good to her,*" Tarq says, lying his chin over his father's shoulders. "*It would mean a lot if you could find a way to be happy for them.*"

"*You know what works for me, Dax?*" Miles says, and I know we're about to hear some weird Miles logic. "*I don't give a shit about people. It seems to do the trick.*" I look down at Miles. He's pushed his way under my shirt to lick my hip with the tip of his tongue. *Doesn't give a shit, my ass.*

I turn my attention to Dax and slide my fingers through his fur, feeling exactly what he's going through. The grumpy Alpha still loves Amelia. I slide my hands over his face and muzzle, pulling all his negative feelings until he relaxes. The kids have fallen asleep by the fire, and there's finally silence other than the Alphas' hums. I use the time to review everything that has happened and some things Neala and Ash have passed on.

"Dax?" I say, looking at the calm black wolf. "Do you remember Darius?"

"*Vaguely,*" is his response.

"He's missing," I tell him. "Any ideas?"

My Alpha lifts his head and spots Miles' nose in my shirt. "*Miles,*" Tarq growls. "*My wife better still taste like flowers down there.*"

"*Baby Alpha, one of us will eventually get to the center of this Luna-pop.*"

Shaking my head, I pull Miles off my hip. He crawls to lay his jaw on my shoulder and pushes his nose into my neck. Tarq and I allow these little behaviors because we know how hard it is to fight a bond. I only let Miles do these things when Tarq is nearby, so there is no confusion. I love him, but my mind, body, and soul only want Tarq.

"Darius's parents kept bees up in the eastern hills," Dax says, distracting us. *"Any chance he'd be trying to start that again?"*

"It's been a while since we've had a honey supplier," I think out loud. *"Bruce? You stand the eastern watch. Have you seen anything?"*

"I have seen him up there, Luna," he replies without moving from his tangle with Amelia.

Tarq and Dax begin trying to pinpoint where the hives are. *"I'll have Nate send some guards in that direction,"* Tarq says. *"We pulled them out of there after the meeting with Tynan."*

I lean against Miles. He never entirely checks out like Tarq. *"Miles, I can't see Darius anymore,"* I admit. *"Do you have any idea why?"*

"I'm gonna need more details, Dar."

"I see Brock's parents as if they were standing before me," I say slowly. I close my eyes to see them without the background. *"But when I think of Darius, I can't see his face."*

Miles is quiet for a moment. *"Dar, what do you see when you think of that historian? The one that blessed your union."*

When I try to see her, I can clearly make out her braids, but her face is blurred. *"Almost the same."*

"Dar, I think we have to consider the possibility," Miles says sadly.

Jules died a few years after my sacrifice. She was a fountain of wisdom, and I loved visiting her as often as possible. Thinking of her is hard enough. Realizing that Darius is dead by using her as an example has me at my limit. I roll into Miles before I lose him to the sun. *"I love you, Miles,"* I whisper, burying my face in his fur.

26

With the warm weather, we decided to spend a few days on the beach before heading toward the ranch. The kids begin to relax and play as they would at home, involving Bastian as if he'd grown up with them. Chase has been studying herbs, which he seems to enjoy. The kids are laughing, and Amelia and Bruce are whispering to each other instead of arguing. Seeing my family smile has made this trip worthwhile.

On the fourth day, Tarq and I lie on the beach watching Bastian teach Brock how to fish while Chase restrings the bow with Annalisa. "Can we talk shop while everyone's busy?" Tarq asks, rubbing his fingers over my arm.

I smile at him. "Of course, My Love."

"Nate found the hives in the eastern hills," he tells me. "No one has worked them in a while."

Pushing Tarq onto his back, I rest my ear against his chest. "I want them out of there," I say, relaxing to his heartbeat. I feel him tense and know he's about to protest. "Tarq, Darius is dead. I will not lose any more of my wolves. The Blood Pack's compound is to the east. You will pull them out of there."

Tarq slides his fingers over my face. "So, I have a little more bad news," he says.

"Bring it on," I tell him. "I doubt I could screw this up any worse."

"The wolf that owns the ranch is older," Tarq says, sighing. "His grandson used to shift and chase the horses from the field. I'm going to have to start from scratch with them."

My eyes drift to the kids. Bastian and Brock have returned to shore with a few fish for Chase to prepare. They are messing with Annalisa as she tries to sharpen some of her arrows. "Bastian hasn't had any luck getting Brock to talk about his parents. Could you nudge him?"

"Sure," Tarq says, rolling toward me. "We'll have time."

* * *

We leave for the ranch the next day. Walking there takes a full day, and Tarq urges Brock to talk about his parents. With Bastian's help, he finally starts to open up and talk about some things he noticed. After a while, Bastian starts asking strange, pointed questions. I raise my eyebrow when he asks about the moonshine and the scents from the sheds holding the stills, but he just shakes his head at me.

The sun is sinking when we reach the ranch. Chase leads us to a large barn. "I thought you'd prefer the privacy over the comfort of the old guy's small house, Dar," he tells me. Taking my hand, Chase escorts me up the stairs to the hay loft. He drops the bags and ushers me to some wooden crates. "While they're looking at the horses, let me listen to you."

Sighing, I pull my coat off. Chase hands me my tea vial, but I wait for him to finish listening to my lungs before I drink it.

"Let me have your arm." Chase reaches out, turning his head as claws tap on the stairs.

My eyes land on Bastian. "Hey, sweetheart," I say, smiling.

The young wolf stops beside the bags and shifts. "We need to talk," Bastian says, pulling out some pants.

"Where is Annalisa?" I hiss.

"She's out in the field, Luna," he tells me. "It's probably my fault, but she hears everything I say. I'll let you decide if she should know this." He looks at the vial Chase is holding. "What's that?"

Chase draws the dosage before handing the vial to Bastian. "It's just steroids," he explains. "Her heart and lungs have a lot of damage from the poison. The steroids reduce the inflammation around them so they can handle the work."

"Why does Brock think she's getting better?" Bastian buttons the pants and sits on a crate beside me.

Chase rolls his eyes. "I might have told him she was. He has enough to worry about."

Bastian watches him inject the medicine into my arm and returns the vial. "I appreciate that." He takes a deep breath and relaxes against the haystack behind us.

I've remained quiet through this exchange. Bastian's comfort in his semi-commanding role makes me smile. He easily asked questions, expecting an answer, and even thanked Chase for his decision. I turn toward him as Chase indicates he's ready to listen to the back of my lungs and hold my arms out to the young wolf.

Bastian smiles. "I've missed your hugs."

"You have grown into such a strong wolf, you beautiful boy," I say as tears stream down my face. "I could probably hang onto you for hours, but my daughter will miss you."

Bastian chuckles. "That's true. This ache sucks." He stretches his chest.

I push some small bursts of heat to help him before sliding my hands over his ribs. "Ask Tarq to help you with that," I tell him, pushing on his muscles the way Neala taught me. "Chase, this feels a little thick to me. Can you check him?"

"Luna, Brock's been telling us about his parents," Bastian says, lifting his arm for his uncle. "He said that they would say something about a rooster crowing."

"Mm-hmm." Admittedly, I'm barely paying attention. My eyes are on Chase's hands as he slides them across Bastian's ribs, following them to his spine. It's been months since I've had my hands on him, and we don't have much time before my daughter misses him. "Check his hips too, Chase."

"Luna!" Bastian grabs my cheeks, pushing my jaw with his thumbs. "This is important."

"Bastian," I say, sighing. "Sweetheart, as a wolf, you have nearly doubled in size in just a few months. Because I have allowed you around my daughter, we rarely get the chance to check you when your muscles are this thin. Please, child. This is important too."

"She's right, Bass," Chase says. "If you lie down for me, I'll check your joints, and you two can talk."

Bastian moves to lie on the floor while holding my hand so he can pull me down with him. "Luna, the Blood Pack's bar is owned by a wolf named Rooster. Last time I was... there, Tynan was drinking blueberry moonshine."

Now he's got my attention. I understand why he was asking about smells and timelines. My mind wanders over all the facts. *Brock's parents were flavoring their liquor. I would have never thought I needed to forbid my wolves from dealing with the Blood Pack.*

"Why would they kidnap their moonshine dealers?" I ask.

These two wolves in front of me understand the Blood Pack better than anyone else. But instead of having an answer, they both shrug.

I watch Chase bend Bastian's legs, feeling his hips and knees. I narrow my eyes. "Neala said Gaine wasn't gone long, but Darius is dead. Brock's parents are alive. I can still see them."

"None of this makes sense, Luna," Bastian says.

"I agree," I tell him as Chase helps him sit up. "You were right not to share this. There's no sense in worrying them. Let the guard handle this for now."

I wrap my arms back around the teenager. He's thicker than he was, but he's still the kid who spent hours in my arms learning how to feel safe. I don't miss how broken he was, but I miss showing him love. "I am so proud of you, sweetheart," I whisper to Bastian. "I love you."

"Luna, none of this would be possible without you or Neala," he whispers. "I will always be grateful for you both." He pulls back and lets me cup his cheeks as he grabs his chest. "I need to shift, though. I'm thinking about doing something that would make you mad."

Giggling, I kiss his cheek. "Probably, sweetheart."

* * *

A week later, nothing new was reported from the lake. There is still no sign of the missing wolves. The kids work beside Tarq with the horses daily, but the nights are long and quiet. Taking turns, we tell bedtime stories to keep them entertained. Tarq begins helping Bastian, teaching him different techniques to relieve the pressure in his chest.

"How's their companion doing?" Tarq whispers as I settle into the mound of hay I'd molded perfectly to my body.

"He's struggling," I whisper back, watching Brock sleep between Bastian and Annalisa. "He doesn't seem worried about his parents but repeatedly asks if I've heard from Neala about his sisters."

Tarq lays his head in my lap and throws one of the rubber balls in the air. "He seems to have a better relationship with them."

"How's it going with the horses?" I normally sit underneath a tree at the edge of the field with Chase. He's taken to fussing over me while Tarq takes the kids to—*well, I don't know what they're doing.*

"We're close," Tarq says, sighing. "They quit running from us."

"What are you doing out there then?"

Tarq rolls over and wraps his arms around my waist, nuzzling his face into my stomach. "We're waiting for some of them to approach us. Those are the horses we can train."

I stifle a giggle and slide my hand through his hair. "So, to be clear, you've been lying around the field for a week doing absolutely nothing?"

Tarq rubs his face against me and yawns. "Dar, you steal them; I train them," he whispers, opening his eyes. "As Dax would say, stay in your lane." After I stare at him without responding, he flashes a grin. "It's a process, Dar." He tightens his arms around my waist. "If our presence at the lake drastically improved anything, I would rush, but it won't. You will enjoy the warmth, and the boys will learn how to train the horses correctly."

Frowning, I tug on his hair. "Maybe we could go for a walk to-morrow," I suggest. "Even if it's just for an hour."

"I like that idea, My Love," Tarq says with a sleepy smile. He nips at my hip and crawls up my body. "Come on, Dar. The kids are asleep.

Mom and Bruce are on watch, and I have no idea what Chase is doing. Let's get some sleep."

Tarq pushes his arm under my neck and rolls over me. He uses my hay cradle to trap his heat around me. I rub my face against his chest and accept another day of standing still as he lulls me to sleep.

* * *

Just after sunrise, I sit on the fence watching Tarq work with the kids. Chase is grumbling as he usually does after listening to my lungs. Even his dismay can't steal my smile. I like watching Tarq interact with the kids. I imagine this closely resembles how it was for him and Dax. His daughter pouts and questions everything while the boys play around. Tarq will get upset at least once daily and pick Annalisa up, threatening to throw her at one of them.

He's been looking forward to some time alone, so it's not long before he's scooping me off the fence. We walk along the edge of the field, hidden by the trees but still able to watch over the kids.

"So, tell me again, Gaine said she went to spend time with a friend?" Tarq has my arm linked with his as we catch up on some of what Neala has told me.

"Just as her sister said, she's not telling us who she was with," I say, nodding. "But she was gone for just over two weeks."

Tarq arches his eyebrow. "The sister said it was a boy."

We approach the stream that runs through the field, supplying the horses with water. I sit in the lush grass beside it and pull Tarq with me. "She did, but Gaine hasn't mentioned a boy."

Grabbing my waist, Tarq pulls me onto his lap. "It's always about a boy." His hands slide over my legs before finding their way up my shirt. He spreads his fingers, touching as much of me as he can. My Alpha is easy to resist when he's wearing fur or surrounded by kids, but it's impossible right now. "I've missed you," he whispers.

I surrender to my nerves, allowing them to call to Tarq and beg for his attention. We make the most of our time alone by enjoying our bodies and reacquainting them with each other. When my Alpha joins me in release, I know he hasn't had enough, but he can hear how hard my chest is working to supply my body with oxygen. He will always put me ahead of himself.

Tarq relaxes, twisting to the side to avoid putting pressure on my chest. He smiles down at me and teases my jawline with his fingertips. "I know we haven't always done the best job, but I have loved my life with you."

"You made my life worth living, my Alpha," I whisper, closing my eyes to enjoy his touch. "You kept me coming back when giving up would've been much easier."

Tarq rolls us onto our sides and studies my face. "Dar, what are we gonna do about Tynan? I've never seen a wolf act with so little honor."

I've been thinking about this for months. The Blood Pack's Alpha seems more human than wolf. My wolves would never act as he has. "Byron said his research showed abuse to be commonplace back in the old days of the Luna," I say, slowly piecing different bits of information together. "All the kids we have that struggled or suffered abuse—it was always from humans. Miles said he had to squash him a few times but never said what he was doing."

"We're missing something."

I can't disagree with him. Nothing about Tynan's behavior has made sense. Bastian still shuts down whenever I try to talk to him about that horrible man, and Miles is too distracting for me to remember to ask him.

"Luna? Can you tell Tarq the black horse is ready?" the beautiful boy himself calls out. *"Annalisa keeps calling it Bones."*

Sighing, I rub my eyes. *"Yes, sweetheart. Thank you."*

Tarq is lying with his eyes closed. I trace his jaw with my finger, admiring his beauty. The stubble on his chin is as soft as velvet. His grin is sweet and playful. This strong wolf is larger than life and needs only to snarl to strike fear into any living creature, but he chooses compassion and kindness to gain the respect he is shown. If only everyone had his strength.

My Alpha opens his eyes to find me still staring at him.

"Bastian says the black horse is ready," I tell him, rubbing the fuzz under his lower lip. I can't blame Annalisa for liking it. It truly is very soft.

Taking a deep breath, Tarq moves my fingers to his lips and kisses them. He rolls away from me and begins collecting our clothes.

"Do you think he has them?" I ask, watching my Alpha comfortably walk around in his skin. "Brock's parents?"

Tarq slides his shorts up his legs with a mixed groan and sigh. "Dar, I'm nearly positive he does."

"What could he possibly want with them? They didn't work with us." I roll onto my back and rub my hands over my face, wanting something to make sense. "We didn't even know they were gone." Putting my fists to my forehead, I cringe and turn to Tarq. "Doesn't that highlight my Luna greatness?"

Tarq breathes out a chuckle but then narrows his eyes. "Maybe that was the point. He took them because he knew they wouldn't be missed."

I tap my lips before reaching out for the shirt he's holding. "I don't understand evil. I can't figure out this game he's playing."

* * *

Tarq goes back to working with the horses. He teaches both boys how to train them to follow wolves and some of the different commands he uses to control them. Unfortunately, that was the easy part. The horses have never been ridden, so they need to be broken to ride.

I watch them work on the black horse my daughter had reused Bones' name on from under my tree while I talk to Ash. *Did Nate make it back from the sweep?*

"Yes, Luna," Ash answers. *"The eastern hills are cleared. We did it quietly, so no one has questioned us."*

I narrow my eyes in thought, focusing on my daughter attempting to mount the black horse. Ash has taken over the daily reports now that it's snowed, and Neala has her hands full. When the weather turns, she calls the junior guards to the bunkhouse. Food can be an issue for families with teenagers as they need a lot to maintain their muscle tone, and we stock the guards' storage all summer to keep them strong throughout the winter.

"I appreciate everything you've done," I tell him. *"I'm sure you've been busy."*

"The kids have been harder to settle without you or Annalisa home," Ash admits.

"Why don't you bring them to my house for a movie night," I suggest. *"It'll entertain them, and our scent will surround them."*

"That's not a bad idea," Ash says.

"I do have my moments," I reply. *"Tell Neala I'll talk to her later. I miss her breakfasts."* My attention returns to the field, and I watch the horse Annalisa calls Bones take off with her. Smiling, I arch an eyebrow. "Going well?"

Tarq scowls. "Go get them, Bastian."

The young wolf darts after the wayward horse who stole his mate.

"There's been snow at the lake," I tell Tarq as he kneels before me under the tree. "Neala brought the junior guards in for the winter."

Tarq smiles. "She loves having that bunkhouse full." He checks for the teenagers in the field. "Have you heard they call her Mama Bear?"

I smile. "I've heard the name but didn't know they were referring to her. It suits her. She does a great job of protecting them."

Tarq sighs. "Here they come." He nods toward the far side of the field, where Bastian leads the rogue horse in our direction. "Let me get back to work."

* * *

Two weeks later, Tarq has a sorrel gelding trained for Annalisa. He's resigned to letting me ride the black horse as long as Bastian stays nearby because it's still unpredictable. We put the kids to bed in the straw for the final time. The boys have taken to touching their noses to my cheek before they fall asleep. Annalisa shakes her head, but I love giving them the motherly experience they were missing.

The bayou wolves had offered to stand watch so we could all rest tonight. I lean against Tarq and watch Bruce curl around Amelia across the loft. Chase is stretched out along my front with his ear against my chest. He fell asleep listening to my heart.

"Have you decided on a route?" I ask, sliding my fingers through our companion's fur.

"Sort of," Tarq murmurs. He's relaxing in my perfectly molded straw cradle. He doesn't fit in my bed but has enjoyed stealing it so that I'll sprawl over the top of him.

"The weather has gotten worse," I say, lost in thought. "February is always the coldest."

Tarq kisses my temple. "Just take your medicine and be honest with me, and I'll get you there, Dar."

* * *

We've fallen into a comfortable rhythm after a few days on the trail. Brock's sisters were excited to hear that their brother was coming home and told him about the fresh snow that had fallen. As we travel together through the woods, he carries on about snowball fights and forts.

"*You'll love it, Bass,*" Brock says. "*It's so much fun. My sisters say the lake is nearly frozen, so it should be ready when we get home.*"

Bastian silently jogs in front of my horse, listening to Brock describe how to make the perfect snowball and where the best hiding spots are.

"*Annalisa used to play with us, but she got hurt a few years ago,*" Brock says sadly. "*She had some tea, so she was fine. Tarq said he'd break us in half if we ever threw a snowball at her again, though.*"

Bastian looks up at Annalisa. "*I'll sit with her while you play,*" he tells Brock. "*I wouldn't be able to join in anyway.*"

Swinging down from my saddle, I step in front of the horse. "Bastian, come here."

As he approaches, Annalisa dismounts and joins us.

"Tarq likes to be a wolf," I tell him. "Sometimes, I think he prefers it. The entire month before Annalisa was born, he stayed a wolf. When I asked him why, he said —"

"*I said I wanted to be strong enough to kill anyone who would harm the body containing everything I ever wanted."* Tarq steps out of the woods beside us.

"So, you see, Bastian, your mentor knows how to do almost anything as a wolf," I say, smiling as I kneel to my Alpha. "You have the opportunity to learn from the best."

"It's true," Brock chimes. *"He normally pummels us with snow before we even know he's there."*

Tarq chuckles. *"Y'all don't even play fair with each other, so get over it."*

"That is also true," Brock says, laying his jaw over his crossed paws.

Giggling, I tug Brock's fur.

"There's a town ahead," Tarq says, nuzzling my cheek. *"We'll stop soon for the night and scout the best way around it."* He slips under my hair and licks my neck before darting up the trail to find a good place to camp.

"He leaves you like he doesn't care about your safety, but I know that's not true," Bastian says, confused. We've worked hard training him on his role in guarding the Luna but haven't spent much time teaching him what other guard members do.

I hold my hand out, and Bastian places his jaw on it. "I'm never alone, sweetheart," I tell him. "I haven't been alone in over 15 years." I point to my left, and Chase steps out of the brush. I lean forward to see around Annalisa and look to the right as Bruce appears between two trees.

My guards bow their heads and shrink back into their hidden areas.

"My Alpha never leaves me unguarded. He always knows where I am."

"Not always," Annalisa says, frowning. "There was that one time."

"We don't talk about that," I remind her.

"It was that bad?" Bastian asks.

I rub my hand over his jaw. "Tarq is a proud wolf. Although it is a great learning story, he doesn't like me to tell it." I kiss Bastian's muzzle. "I love him very much, so I honor his request."

"I hope we have a love like that," Bastian says shyly.

Annalisa pulls his muzzle to her lips, and he nuzzles her cheek. "We do, my Alpha."

With a sigh, I push myself to my feet. "Come on, young people. Let's get going."

* * *

The town we're outside of is called Stark. Amelia reported seeing wagons and transports in the center of town. She thought there might be an event.

"It's fine, Tarq," I tell him as we relax beside the small fire. "We're going around. They can do whatever they want."

Tarq hasn't relaxed for a moment of this trip. He's left Chase to keep me warm at night while he stands watch. Chase throws another log on the fire and settles in, hoping Tarq will stay with me. The kids are exhausted and quickly fall asleep after they eat.

"Will you stay with me tonight?" I ask Tarq. "Let others watch over our camp for one night."

Tarq smiles and reaches his arm out to me. I snuggle into his chest with a happy sigh as he wraps me in his arms. "I don't like the duck pond story," he whispers. "That was the scariest day of my life."

"I know, My Love. That's why I don't tell it."

"I love you, Dar." Tarq kisses my forehead and heats his body.

* * *

We strike out to the west side of town in the morning. Bruce and Amelia are behind us, ensuring we're not followed, and Tarq is running point. Chase takes Brock to our left and works with him on the guard positioning. Bastian hasn't left Annalisa's side. She's telling him a story about some of her friends, so he's not paying attention until the sorrel gelding begins jumping around.

"What's wrong with this horse?" Annalisa whines.

I can't see anything obvious. "Maybe it's the saddle," I suggest.

She begins to dismount as someone shoots a shotgun close by. The two horses crouch in fear. I quickly settle the black horse, but Annalisa is only halfway on, and her horse takes off. Bastian darts after it, and I kick my horse.

"MOM!" Annalisa yells.

We stay with her as the horse cuts through the trees and narrow openings, nearly knocking her off several times.

"*Luna, you need to stop,*" Bastian shouts. "*We're headed right into that town!*"

"Bastian, I will not leave her!" I snap. I kick my horse until it's nearly beside the sorrel. "Come here, baby girl!" I shout to Annalisa as we reach the well-traveled roads of the town. "Grab onto me!"

Annalisa dives toward me, latching onto my waist and trying to pull herself onto my horse. More shots begin to ring out around us. Bastian's scream is unmistakable when it hits my ears.

"BASS!" Annalisa shouts.

She lets go of me as a bullet plunges through the black horse's neck. It stumbles and falls to the ground, throwing me over its shoulder. I stick my arms out, but the force is too great, and my head still smacks the hard road, producing stars in my vision.

As I try to look around to find my daughter, I'm covered with a sharp-smelling, peppery powder. "What the fuck?" I shout, coughing.

My head is wrenched around by someone grabbing my hair. My eyes widen as they fall on General Kerst.

"What the fuck, indeed, bitch." His fist slams into the side of my head.

27

My head feels like someone is inside my skull with a hammer when I wake. There's a blindfold tightly wrapped over my eyes and a tug against my throat when I lean forward. *Of course, there's a noose. How is that man still alive?*

The General had a deep gash down his face and across his eye, rendering it useless. The guys probably thought they'd handled him. I try to put my thoughts together, but a scent distracts me. *What the hell is that spicy smell?*

It's silent in my head for the first time since I became the Luna. I can't hear a single wolf. There's only a steady thumping, and I'm sure my seat is rocking.

"Hello?" I whisper.

"Luna?"

I sigh in relief at the sound of Bastian's voice. His scream will have no equal. When I smile, my face sears. *"Hi, sweetheart,"* I say, wincing. *"Are you ok?"*

"I'm ok," he answers. *"Annalisa is here. She's not talking, but we're alone."*

"I'm right here, baby girl," I hiss loudly over the thumping. "I'll get you out of here. I promise." In the silence, I fear the horrible things that could've been done to her. "Bastian says we're alone. You can talk to me."

"Help him, Mom," Annalisa sobs. "He's been shot."

"Ok," I say, trying to sound calm. "We'll figure that out. Bass, where are we?"

"Some kind of container, but it's moving," he answers.

My hands are tied above my head while something holds my feet down. *"How badly are you hurt, sweetheart?"* I ask. *"Can you untie me?"*

Bastian groans. *"It's in my back, Luna. I can't feel my back legs."*

"Ok, baby," I say, faking confidence. *"I have tea. You're getting out of here too."*

I'm not used to the silence in my head, but I do my best to concentrate. *Bastian said we're in a container that's moving. It's rocking, and there's that thumping.* There's a screech, and our container jolts a few times before stopping. *Hang on. This was in one of Tarq's movies.* A loud whistle blows in the distance. "We're on a train!" I accidentally shout.

Something bangs, and metal begins to scrape. This is followed by a door sliding over rollers.

"Kade," Bastian snarls. *"I should've known."*

"Bass, who's Kade? What's going on?" The ropes rip my skin when I pull against them.

Quiet footsteps begin moving around. Bastian's growl is weak, but his message is clear. Kade is not a friend. The footsteps move away from me.

"Don't you touch her," I snarl between my teeth.

The footsteps stop. "Shh, Luna," a voice whispers. "I'm here to help."

My head is muddled up. *Bastian's snarl tells me he's my enemy. Blood Pack, probably... They cleaned the field. They must be the reason that asshole is still alive.*

My body freezes as a hand touches my arm. "Get your hands off me," I snap.

"Is that Bastian?" Kade asks, ignoring my demand. "Shit, he's huge."

My jaw slacks at his casualness. "Forgive me, Kade," I say, disgusted. "I'm not interested in exchanging pleasantries with you. Now get your hands off me."

He releases my arms, and something creaks beside me. "Ok. I'll just sit here and wait for you to untie yourself," Kade says. "You don't have anything to drink, do you? I'm parched."

Bastian chuckles, and I lean my head back. *Yeah, I deserved that.*

The train jolts again.

"They're gonna come check on you," Kade hisses. "You need to act unconscious. I'll be back."

The door slides, followed by a scuffling above us. *Kade must be on the roof.*

"Bastian, who was that?" Annalisa whispers.

"You know when you were playing at the lake, and there was that kid no one went near?" Bastian asks. I would tell him to stop, but I want to know who Kade is too. *"The one you wouldn't dare splash or get sand on because he'd probably skin you alive? That's Kade. He's Tynan's enforcer. When Alpha wanted something done, Kade made it happen."*

I hold my breath, hoping my daughter doesn't realize —

"How do you know that?" Annalisa's whisper is barely audible.

The lock begins to slide again. I'm thankful the blindfold hides my tears. *There are a million acceptable ways Annalisa could learn where Bastian came from. Not one of them would be in captivity.*

The footsteps that enter this time are different. They clunk as if their owner has no grace—clearly, not a wolf.

"This guy's been here a few times," Bastian says. *"You won't like this, but follow Kade's advice, and he'll leave."*

Moments later, my face receives a backhanded slap. *At least that explains why my cheek hurts.*

"There you go," Bastian says soothingly. *"He's coming to you next, Annalisa. It'll hurt, but you'll be ok. I promise."*

The footsteps move across the floor. I hold my breath, bracing for the slap that will hurt my daughter's face, but when it doesn't come, Bastian snarls. The feet stomp across the floor, and Bastian yelps. The owner of the clumsy footfalls mutters, and then the door slides shut again.

"Bastian?" I'm whispering my thoughts.

The shuffling overhead returns. I don't want that wolf coming back in here without eyes on him, but Bastian isn't responding. I catch the creak of the door just before the container bangs, and the wheels under us screech loudly, drowning out any noise the door would make.

"Luna?" Kade's voice is right beside me.

I'm not getting free without help, so I swallow my pride. "Kade, if you're really here to help, untie me." I can't be sure he's still there until I feel his hands on me again. I jerk away from the sudden contact.

"Easy, Luna," Kade whispers into my ear. "You're bleeding. Let me take this blindfold off." He unties its knot, stepping back as it falls.

Focusing my eyes, I find my daughter tied like I am across the container. She's still wearing her jacket, so they probably don't know who she is. She's sobbing but otherwise seems unharmed. Bastian lies between us, tethered to the wall by a thick metal collar and chain.

My eyes shift to the man before me. He's unlike any Blood Pack member I've encountered. His skin is flawless, and his clothes and hair are clean. The leather jacket looks like it was made to fit him. For lack of a better word, Kade is beautiful. "Who are you?" I ask, studying him.

Kade lifts an eyebrow. "You know who I am," he states. "You've been calling me by my name. Which means this must be Bastian." He crouches over the young wolf, cringing. "That looks bad, Luna. There's no bouncing back from that. You want me to put him out of his misery?"

"Please don't hurt him!" Annalisa sobs.

Kade scoffs. "I didn't hurt him, sweetheart. I'm just offering to end his suffering." He drops to his knee, reaching for Bastian's head.

"Don't you dare," I sneer. "I will break every pack law to protect those I love."

He scans the wolf before turning toward me. "I think we should start over, Luna."

With his hands up in surrender, he stands and slowly closes the gap between us. I watch as he carefully reaches for the noose around my neck.

"My name is Kade," he starts. "I'm the Blood Pack's enforcer. I was sent to help the militia capture you." His face remains expressionless as he reveals his horrible identity. "I broke their lights so they could only travel during the day. I kept them off the river. I even sent them to an event in a town." Kade winces as he tightens the noose before slipping the leather through the buckle, freeing me. "I didn't expect you to run right at them. What was that about?"

Kade leans toward me, reaching for the ropes binding my wrists. I notice his body stiffen and look up to watch his throat as he swallows hard.

"Shit, Luna," Kade says, abandoning the ropes. "What is that smell?"

"Easy, Kade," I say softly as his eyes roll closed. "You don't want to do that."

Kade opens his eyes and stares at the blood running from under the ropes. Taking another deep breath, he licks his lips. "No, Luna, I'm pretty sure I do."

"You're not bonded, are you?" I ask. I've been careful over the years, but I remember this hunger in Miles' eyes.

"You won't be my first if that's what you're asking." Kade's voice is silky smooth. I imagine it's hard for women to say no to him once he decides he wants them. "Just a little taste, Luna. You smell delicious."

"I'm the Luna, Kade," I say quickly, stopping him. "My scent is enticing by design. It comes from my heart and is carried by my blood. If you do that, you won't be able to return to your pack."

Kade mashes his lips and rolls his eyes upward in thought. "I'm ok with that." He advances on my arm again.

"You'll belong to me," I spout. "You'll never be able to bond to your mate."

He stares at my arm, chewing on his lower lip. "You're sure about that?"

"Yes, Kade, I'm sure," I say, lifting my eyebrow at the strange wolf. "I'd even let you if you were bonded."

"Damn Gaine," Kade scowls, reaching for the ropes. "Alright, let's get you down from here." He unties the ropes and carefully peels them out of my wounds.

I look across the container as Kade works on my ankles. The light coming through the door is fading. "How are you doing over there, little girl?"

"I'm fine," she says. "Is Bastian ok?"

Kade tries to help me stand, but my shaky limbs aren't interested in holding me.

"I'll check on him while Kade unties you," I tell her. I grab Kade's wrist and pull his ear close to my lips. "If you hurt her, you will beg for death," I sneer.

Kade puts his hands up. "I get it. Precious cargo."

I crawl to Bastian while watching Kade. Bastian doesn't react to my touch. His ribs are moving, but his limbs are limp. "Where's my pack, Kade?"

Annalisa pulls away from Kade as soon as she's untied and crawls behind Bastian, crying into his fur.

"I have no idea," he responds, watching my daughter curiously. "That Alpha of yours just about got himself killed trying to get to you." He kneels beside me.

"I can't hear them."

"Ah, yeah, there is that," he says, digging in his pockets. He pulls out a flashlight and slaps it a few times to make it turn on. He shines the light around, showing me the symbols on the ceiling, walls, and floor. "Nothing gets in or out. I used to sneak in here for some peace. Now I have to shift to take a break from that moron continuously screaming, 'Bring me that bitch.'"

I look out the door at the slow-moving foliage. "I thought trains were fast."

"They are," Kade says. "I told you I broke their light. They were stopping at night, but now that they have the Luna, they've got men walking out front. There's crap all over these tracks." Kade chuckles and takes a deep breath. "I might have added some shit."

I narrow my eyes. "Why are you helping me?"

Kade clicks the flashlight off, sticking it back in his pocket. "Gaine," he mumbles. "That damn woman. I was happy. I was an asshole, and no one fucked with me. Then Gaine showed up in the basin." Kade reaches forward, yanking a clip holding the collar on Bastian. It clangs to the floor. "You women make us soft. She's got me doing good shit like I actually want to."

I study Kade closely. He's just like Miles. "Do you have a knife?" I ask.

Kade looks depressed as he pulls several knives from his pockets and hands them to me.

"Can we use your light?"

Kade is the oddest wolf I've encountered. I feel I should hate him, but he is somehow utterly likable. He pulls the flashlight back out and bangs it until it lights up.

Leaning forward, I tap Annalisa's hand and point to Bastian's muzzle, indicating that she should use her heat to subdue him. I tuck Bastian's legs against his body and roll him onto his stomach so I can dig out the bullet. Bastian flinches a few times, but Annalisa keeps him calm.

"You're who Gaine was with?"

Kade huffs. "She's refusing me. I didn't even know that was a thing," he whines. "Can you order her to bond with me?"

Dumbfounded, I turn to him. "Kade," I say slowly. "I don't even know where to start."

"How about 'Gaine, go bond with Kade?'" The quirky wolf smiles broadly.

I rub my forearm over my brow. "That's not how it works, sweetheart," I tell him, watching his face fall. "It's her choice."

"Well, fuck," Kade grumbles. "I'm never gonna be good enough for the virgin queen."

I've hit my limit with Kade and burst out laughing. "Not if you call her that." Shaking my head, I turn to Bastian's back and dig for the bullet. "Gaine asked you to help us?" I ask the pouting wolf.

"She said if I ever wanted to see her again, I'd better stop them from catching you. I hope she'll forgive me if I get you out of this situation." Kade cringes, watching me pry the bullet from Bastian's spine. "Why are you even bothering with that? We need to leave. The Bass I knew would've left you long ago."

"Can you please look for something to cover him?" I ask Kade as the bullet falls to the floor.

Kade shrugs and stands to search through the crate in the corner.

I lean over Bastian, kissing the side of his muzzle. "Hey there, baby," I whisper. "I have tea for you, but you'll have to shift. I love you very much, sweetheart, and I need you to save my daughter. Don't you give up on me now."

As I sit up, Kade approaches us with a canvas-type tarp. I throw it over Bastian and tuck it down between the teenagers.

I raise my eyebrow at Annalisa. "Little girl, this wolf is about to become a naked boy. You behave yourself, or I'll tell your parents." She tucks her face into Bastian's neck.

Bastian's breathing speeds up as he grows more nervous about shifting. I push my fingers against his fur, giving him a full burst of heat.

"Why don't I tell you the story about the first time my Alpha lost track of me?" I suggest. I smile at Bastian as he bumps my leg with his paw. "I had to visit some wolves who lived far away. We were gone almost two weeks when my companion fell asleep on watch."

"Wasn't your companion a Blood wolf too?" Kade asks. "You seem to have a type."

Shaking my head, I continue. "The point is, Kade, that when my companion fell asleep, my Alpha couldn't reach either of us. You've heard about my Alpha, haven't you? How strong he is? Well, that intensifies when he believes his Luna is in danger."

Kade shifts uncomfortably, understanding that this story is meant to be a warning.

"Someone we both love very much wanted to keep ducks as pets, so we had a flock at the lake. My Alpha's story goes like this: the ducks jumped into his mouth, begging to be eaten." I smile at Bastian, sliding my hand over his head before holding his paw. "In his panic, he could only think about killing anything in his way. He shredded the ducks. He didn't eat them." I turn to look at Kade. "That was six hours. How long have we been here?"

"Five days." Kade's eyes are a shade of blue that appears nearly silver. They shine even in the darkness as he lifts them to my face.

Bastian's paw shifts into a hand, grabbing tightly onto my fingers. I jump to my knees and pull the tea from my pocket. Bastian groans as I push the vial into the corner of his mouth.

I lean to whisper to both teenagers. "I have allowed you to break your vow this one time so that you can save her life after I save yours."

Annalisa peeks at me from behind Bastian.

"You keep that heat on him," I tell her. "He's in a lot of pain. You better not make me regret saving him for you."

She tucks her face behind his neck, tightening her grip on him. Bastian squeezes my hand before releasing it to thread his fingers with hers.

I slide the vial back into my pocket and feel Dax's medallion. "Kade, what day is it?"

"How should I know?" Kade's focused on Bastian. "Is that stuff healing him?"

"Kade!" I clap my hands loudly in his face, making him jump. "When is the full moon?"

"Well, that's a little more specific, isn't it?" Kade flashes a smile that only infuriates me.

I press my clenched fists to my forehead and bite my lower lip, trying not to freak out on our only help.

"My, my, Luna," Kade says, clicking his tongue. "You do have quite the temper. You should do something about that."

I'm ready to scream at him when weight presses on my hip. I pull out the necklace and throw it across the container. Miles appears halfway between me and where the medallion fell.

The Alpha sidesteps to put himself between the kids and me while facing the unknown wolf. Lowering his head, Miles snarls. *"Dar... highlights."*

I slide my hand over his hips, relieved. "Do you remember Miles, Kade?"

My smirk disappears as Miles quiets and Kade laughs. "Nice!" He holds his fist out, and Miles bumps it with his nose. "The original grumpy wolf got his shift back. Good for you!"

I stare at them. Even in the low light, it's easy to see them relax.

"This kid stole cookies from the pantry to pay for his lessons," Miles says, chuckling. *"You should see him throw a knife."*

"Miles, can you please focus?" I beg.

"Yeah, sorry. Where are we?" Miles bumps my cheek before looking around.

"In a train," I tell him.

Miles lifts his head. *"No shit,"* he says in awe. *"They got one of them running?"*

Frowning, I slump to the floor, exhausted and out of breath. My chest has had enough of this excitement.

"Ok, so this isn't by choice?"

I open my arms to Miles. He seems to trust Kade, and it's cold. A little warmth would be comforting. *"Miles, did you talk to Luna?"*

He slides his jaw down my back. *"She said Dax told you the wolves came for you the night you died, but that wasn't true."* He curls his body, putting more of it against me. *"She called them Guardians. They are the keepers of the first laws. They came for the wolf who killed the Luna."*

"They were there for Tarq." I raise my head, realizing what she is trying to tell me.

"Ask the kid where this train is going. What are we facing?"

Luna's message has me so distracted that I nearly missed Miles' request. "Kade, where are we going?"

Kade's returned to staring at Bastian. "That Kerst guy is taking you to Tynan." He leans forward to get a closer look. "That stuff is healing him, isn't it?"

"Give me a few more minutes, Kade," Bastian snarls. "No tea could bring you back from where I'll send you."

Kade puts his hands up. "Look, man, I'm here to help. Bygones."

Holding my wrists out for Miles to close, my eyes dart between Kade and Bastian. "What is this about?"

Kade groans, running his hand through his hair. "I may have taken the kid to Tynan when his parents died."

"May have?" Bastian growls.

Kade cringes slightly before muttering, "And burned down their house."

Bastian's growl deepens, vibrating the walls.

"Listen, we don't have time for this," Kade says, frowning. "They'll be back to check on you at dawn, and then we'll be going too fast to jump."

I turn toward Bastian and see Annalisa's hand resting on his chest. "Bastian, will you accept a judgment passed down by pack law?"

The young wolf quiets, turning to me. "I will accept your decision, Luna."

"Kade," I say, rising to my feet. "You will be marked for everything I do not have time to name right now and for causing this boy years of pain and torment."

"Marked?" Kade backs up with wide eyes. "Look, Luna. I said I was sorry." Kade's eyes shift to each of us as we stare at him until his gaze fixes on Bastian. "You know, I'm the one that paid the witch to get you out of there."

"Remove your shirt," I order.

Kade slowly removes his coat and shirt before nervously standing before me.

"From this day forward, you will wear the mark of shame for all to see," I tell him. "You have brought dishonor to the name Wolf. Your heart will be covered and your wolf altered. Do you accept this punishment for your crimes?"

Kade looks down at Miles and sighs when the Alpha nods. "I do."

I've never done this before, but Jules had advised me how to create this mark. I press my hand over Kade's heart, firing it. His eyes widen, and his teeth clench as he resists the urge to scream. I watch as my hand burns his skin until it suddenly turns silver, freezing my handprint to his skin. As I lower my hand, Kade gasps, seeing the mark left behind.

I cup Kade's cheek as he releases a shaky breath. "You have paid for your past. I hope your future will be honorable because the price will be far worse next time." I step away from Kade and kneel beside the teenagers and Miles. "Have you healed, Bastian?"

"I'm healed enough, Luna," Bastian tells me. "Kade's right. We should use the cover of night to get as far away as possible."

I freeze, suddenly noticing someone is missing. "Miles? Where the hell is Dax?"

Miles' lips fluff. *"He didn't want to watch the lovebirds. He went to the lake."*

My jaw clenches. "I don't have time for this selfish bullshit right now," I say through my teeth. "You two have five minutes, and then we're leaving."

I point to the kids and signal Miles to watch them. Grabbing Kade's arm, I pull him toward the doorway. When I look back at the kids, he opens his coat for me, noticing my shivering. "Show that mark to Gaine," I tell him, stepping closer. "Tell her that her sister will know what it means. Now, you owe me for that forgiveness." I look up as I whisper. "She will fight you, but you get her out of here. You protect my little girl with everything you have because you owe us."

Kade ducks into his coat, shaking his head. "That wasn't the deal. She told me to save you, not some kid."

"Kade, that kid is the future Luna, and that boy you helped break is her Alpha. You will get them out of here."

Kade squints his eyes and clenches his jaw. "Yeah, alright."

Annalisa lies with her ear over Bastian's heart when I turn to the rest of the group. The young wolf is watching me as he slips his fingers through her hair. I kneel to Miles, keeping my eyes on them. *"Get them out of here, Miles. I know underneath all that asshole is the sweetest wolf I have ever met. You do this for me."*

Miles steps into me, sliding his jaw down my back because there are no words for this moment. I wipe away my tears as he steps back.

"Come on, girl," I say, reaching for Annalisa. I pull her away from Bastian and drag her to the door. Grabbing her cheeks, I turn her to me. "Look at me. No naked boys for your young eyes, my daughter." I pick up Dax's medallion and fasten it around her neck. "You wear this now. It looks good on you. You're so strong, sweetheart. You've got this."

Annalisa watches Kade jump from the train. Miles follows him, keeping his eyes on me.

"Go ahead, baby girl," I say, kissing my daughter's cheek. "We'll be right behind you. I love you very much."

Annalisa smiles. "I love you too, Mom." With one more glance at Bastian, she sits in the doorway and hops down to join the men walking beside the train.

When I turn around, Bastian is standing behind me. "You're not coming, are you?"

Pushing him away from the doorway, I latch onto him and let my tears flow. "I have loved every minute of my life with my family. They are yours now, Bastian. I need you to protect them."

Bastian's body begins to shake as his grip threatens to break me. His tears drip down my shoulder. "Luna, please come with us," he begs. "We can't do this without you."

"Yes, you can, baby," I whisper. "I taught you how. You have everything you need, and you have each other."

Bastian pulls back and grabs my face. I reach for his cheeks, wiping his tears.

"You don't tell Tarq where I am," I say, shaking my head slightly.

"Yes, Luna," he answers between heaving breaths.

"You don't tell him where they're taking me," I add.

"Yes, Luna." Bastian is hard to understand, but he's nodding.

I smile through my tears. "I love you so much. You are perfect in every way, beautiful boy."

Bastian lets out a shaky breath, pulling me back into his arms. "I love you too, Luna," he whispers. "Thank you for giving me this life. I will protect her. I promise."

I squeeze him tightly and push him back. "Ok, sweetheart, it's time to go. Kade will take care of Annalisa. You and Miles protect them."

I kiss his cheek, and he kisses my forehead before stepping back to shift.

"I love you, Luna."

"I love you too, sweet boy," I say, nodding. "Go protect our family."

We walk to the door together, and I slide my hand over his head before he jumps down. I look down at my daughter and watch her smile at Bastian when he slides his muzzle into her hand.

Annalisa looks up and frowns. "Mom, come on. We need to go."

"I love you, little girl," I call to her. "Take good care of our pack. Tell Daddy I love him very much." I wipe my tears.

"Mom! NO!" she screams.

Nodding to Kade, I grab the door. He latches onto her waist from behind and covers her mouth. She fights him but is no match.

"Everything is going to be ok," I mumble, sliding the door closed as Annalisa tries to fight harder against Kade.

Once the latch clicks, I fall to the floor.

28

After a few minutes, I couldn't hear Annalisa calling for me anymore. Kade said no one would come to check on me until morning, so I allowed myself the night to feel this loss. When I've drained myself of energy, my head is pounding, and I find comfort in the fact that there were no shots or yells.

I've made the right decision. My captors won't waste time looking for random kids that happened to be with me. They have their target. Tynan wanted Annalisa or me. I would never give him my daughter. Miles gave me the information I needed to protect my family.

I haven't had my medicine for nearly a week, so my chest aches from the full extent of my illness. I close my eyes and see Tarq's playful smile and soft gaze. I fall asleep, smiling back at him.

* * *

Shouting wakes me in the morning. I claw across the floor to lean against the wall I'd been tied to. I'm too weak to get on the seat. Trying to erase evidence of my pain, I quickly wipe away my tears. I manage a few deep breaths before the door slides open.

"Where the fuck are my prisoners?!" General Kerst screams. He jumps into the container and sees me untied in the dark corner. "You stupid bitch," he snarls. "Where are they?"

Another man looks into the container. The General turns to the door and kicks the man's head before slamming the door closed. He storms over to me.

"You have ruined my goddamn life, bitch," he screams in my face, hauling me off the floor by my throat. "I'm indebted to a fucking psychopath because of you, and now you've freed my prisoners!" He drops me on the seat and leans to put his face in mine. "I was gonna use them to make you behave. Now I'm just gonna have to beat the shit out of you instead." The General slams my head against the wall as he straightens up, causing me to miss his fist aimed at my temple.

I look at the hateful man through the stars as he tightens the collar around my throat. "Which bothers you more?" I start, letting a smile spread across my lips. "Is it that you couldn't kill me the first time or that you're not allowed to kill me this time?"

The General pulls my head to the side by my hair and leans down to whisper in my ear. "You'll wish I could kill you this time." One more punch to the temple is all it takes to knock me back out.

* * *

The blindfold is back when I wake. It's just as well. It would probably be worse if I could see the punches coming. It also protects my eyes from that horrible-smelling powder they keep throwing at me. Once they realized how sick I was, the General had me moved so the cold air and snow would blast me nonstop when they opened the side doors.

I escape my torment by returning to the flower fields in my mind. I play with Annalisa and giggle as Tarq pretends she has a chance to hide from him.

When they catch me sleeping, they raise my bindings so that I can't sit. I only need to stay alive until I get to Tynan. My pack needs me to make it to the right killer.

* * *

"What the fuck is wrong with you, asshole!"

I never thought I'd be happy to hear Tynan's voice, but when his shout pulls me out of unconsciousness, I nearly smile with relief. This will finally be over soon.

"Get her down," Tynan shouts.

A gun goes off so close to my face that I immediately smell the gunpowder. My ears ring so loudly that I can't make out any other sounds.

I'm taken down from the wall and collapse to the floor. Someone tries to set me on my feet, but I'm thrown over a shoulder and carried when I fall again. One might take this as an act of kindness if they didn't throw me on the ground upon reaching our destination.

When Tynan pulls my blindfold off, I instantly recognize where he's chaining me. I saw this cellar through Bastian's eyes. Tynan stinks of moonshine, making me cringe as he finishes with the shackles.

I try to find Tarq's voice, but it's silent.

Tynan points at the ceiling with his mouth moving, but I can't hear anything. I look up to see the same symbols from the train container. *Maybe he's not as stupid as I'd hoped.* He waves his arms erratically and climbs the stairs, leaving me alone.

I remember how happy Bastian was when he shifted into our pack. He'd never come back to this room. His sweet smile and easy laugh brightened my world. Annalisa will experience that for the rest of her life.

Tynan rejoins me, and his mouth is moving again. *He has got to be completely dense.* "Hey, thick one," I shout. "I can't hear you!"

That's probably not my best plan since he backhands me so hard that blood flies from my mouth. But when I look up, he's talking again. I look around to see if anyone else is in the room with us. There's no one here.

I just shouted that I couldn't hear him. *So why the hell is he still talking?* The fact that he's crazy would explain a lot about this asshole. *Now I kinda want to hear what he's saying. Perhaps he'll listen if I don't shout.*

I concentrate on speaking softly. "Tynan, you shot a gun in my face. I cannot hear you."

Nope. Here comes his fist.

* * *

I dream of my wedding day. Tarq was beyond beautiful. His eyes were filled with so much love as Dax stopped him from running to me.

Each of the Alphas turns me around the dancing area, showing me off to all of my wolves while Nate sings. I let them spin me until I throw up, waking myself to return to my nightmare.

I lift my eyes to rest them on none other than Jaxson. He's holding a cup out to me with his finger to his lips. His greasy brown hair is shoulder-length. A deep scar across his cheek healed long ago. His jacket has a few tears, and the lining is falling out.

"Damn, Jaxson," I say, *or maybe shout—I don't know.* "You look like shit. I mean, it's a vast improvement from the stupid you usually resemble."

When his mouth moves, I squint at his lips. I'd heard of lipreading. Apparently, it's a skill I don't possess. He holds the cup up again. My thirst gets the best of me, and I lick my lips. I'm thankful to recognize the tea that has kept me going for months.

Jaxson lowers the cup and resumes talking. Clearly, the years haven't made him any smarter. He messes with the shackle holding my wrist, and I hiss through my teeth as he touches the open wound. "Sorry. I didn't mean to hurt you," I finally hear Jaxson say.

"Holy hell," I whisper. "I could never live deaf. Those people are bloody saints."

"Um, ok," Jaxson whispers, confused. "So, can you get a ride?" I can hear him but don't know what he's talking about. "Why are you just staring at me?"

"That idiot shot a gun in my face," I tell him. "I haven't heard a thing since I got here."

Jaxson frowns. "He didn't need Kerst anymore. People are a bit expendable around here."

"And yet, he lets you live," I sneer. "Why is that?"

"Darya, your throne doesn't work here," Jaxson says, sighing. "We do what we're told or end up like Kerst." Jaxson seems genuine and might have some useful information.

"I'm missing some wolves, Jaxson. Do you know anything about that?"

The witch cringes. He rechecks my wound to find it healed. "There are a few of them here," he tells me. "He killed one, but I convinced him the other two are helping."

"What are they helping with?" I take a sharp breath.

Jaxson narrows his eyes when he hears me wheeze. "What's wrong with you?"

"I'm pretty sure my question came first." My health is none of his business, and I'm not interested in changing the subject. "What are they helping Tynan with?"

Jaxson jumps as a pair of heavy boots clunk across the floor. I remember Bastian waking up and cowering in the corner when we heard footsteps in the hall. I assumed it was because someone was coming, but now I realize the footfalls were what scared him.

"He's coming," Jaxson hisses. "Pretend I didn't give you tea."

"I told you to give her water," Tynan snarls. "Don't pet my dog! Get out of here, witch!"

After Jaxson scurries up the stairs, Tynan clicks his tongue at me, shaking his head. He ambles over and grabs my chin. "All you had to do was bring me your daughter," he tells me. "I don't want you. You're used. Shit, you look half dead." He drops my chin and turns to the shelves on my left. "You know, I like you better when you're quiet."

Tynan walks along the shelves, poking at things. They seem to be trinkets he's collected.

"My mother used to tell me I couldn't shift because I was too young," he scoffs. "Can you imagine that? Lying to her own son." He takes a jar off the shelf and shakes it. "That's the last of her."

As he puts it back, I watch the thick liquid slide along the glass and realize I'm looking at blood. Next, he pulls a severed head from the shelf. He doesn't need to speak for this one. My eyes widen as I gasp.

"Well, don't be rude," Tynan sneers. "Dad was actually a good-looking guy." He holds the head up so its face is beside his. "Can't you see the family resemblance? Nah, you're right. I take after my mother."

He throws the head on the ground, and I watch it roll toward me.

"So, like I was saying, it took a while to track him down," Tynan continues. "Apparently, rapists don't like to be found. Who knew, right?"

This seems to be some weird version of therapy for Tynan. I can't help hoping Bastian didn't have to hear this crap.

"Turns out my mother was barely a wolf," Tynan says, making me look at him. "Her blood was useless because she didn't have enough wolf genes." He idles toward me, tapping his lips with his finger. "Those two from your pack, though... Universal donors. The witch says they are making me more wolf."

Tynan leans against the post beside me and runs his eyes over my body a few times, making this much more awkward.

"But I need to claim your daughter if I want to take control," he tells me. "Don't worry. I'll find her. She won't be missing for long." He slides his thumb over my cheek, making my stomach lurch. "We can celebrate her birthday together on my wedding day." Tynan's face twitches as he stares at me. Then, with a snort, he turns and walks up the stairs.

Everything makes sense as I listen to his boots clunking across the floor above me. Beyond a shadow of a doubt, I know I've made the right decision. Tynan isn't enough wolf for me to help, but he is at least some because he can hear them. I can't kill him, but he will be held accountable like any other wolf.

The lamp runs out of oil after the light from the doorway fades. It's the end of another day. I can understand why Bastian gave up. Standing in the dark, in pain and cold while chained to this wall sucks as an adult. For a child, it must have been unimaginable torture.

It's been hours, and my mind goes into overdrive. I begin imagining horrible scenarios. The trouble with not being able to hear my wolves is that I don't know where they are. They could be just beyond this psychopath's reach, about to be caught. *I need help. I can't do this alone.*

After what feels like years, light begins to filter in from upstairs. A bird chirps, or maybe I imagine it, but I don't care. It still makes me smile, remembering Tarq standing in the balcony doorway of Edith's guest cottage. He is perfect and beautiful. The birds seemed to sing to him. I sniffle as tears drip down my cheeks.

The boots that cross the floor above me aren't clunky like Tynan's.

He walks with absolutely no grace. I sniffle and try to wipe my cheeks on my shoulders, but the pain from moving proves too much.

"Shit, Darya. Hang on," Jaxson hisses. He grabs a stool hidden by a board under the shelf. "Here, I'm gonna put this under you. Tynan's the only one with the cuffs' keys, but you can at least rest your legs."

He sets the stool behind me. My hips and legs burn as he helps me slowly slip onto it. My whole body tenses as I whimper and bite my lips. I close my eyes and work to slow my breathing. Everyone wishes they would be strong in a situation like this, but a body can only take so much before breaking would just be easier.

"It's not much, but it's probably been a while since anyone let you eat."

I open my eyes to see Jaxson's holding up a soup container, and my tongue slides over my lips. He cleans off my face and feeds me some.

"How long? What day?" My thoughts are in complete sentences, but my words aren't. I try again. "Where?" *What the hell?* I look at Jaxson, confused.

"It won't help right away," he tells me. "I think you're dehydrated." He opens a canteen and holds it to my lips. "Easy. Not too fast. You'll make yourself sick."

I need the answers to my questions. I let Jaxson feed me more soup before trying again. "When was full moon?" I say my words slowly, so most of them come out.

"About two weeks ago," Jaxson answers. "Why?"

They've had me for about three weeks. Tarq must be going out of his mind. "What day? Today?"

Jaxson holds the canteen to my lips for a few more gulps. "The thirteenth, I think." He shakes his head, confused. "Darya, what's this about?"

March 13th. Tomorrow is her birthday. Tarq will figure this out. I need to keep him away, or he'll kill Tynan. That's inexcusable. Forbidden. I'd have to banish him, or worse. He can't be allowed near Tynan.

"Help. Pack. Away." *This is infuriating!* My eyes dart around, looking for help, and land on the canteen. "Water?" I feel weak and pitiful, but it's been weeks since I've had anything substantial to drink. Besides the snow blowing in my face and the buckets of water thrown on me on the train, I've had two cups of liquid to drink. *I have no idea how I've survived.*

Jaxson holds the canteen to my lips as I drain it completely. My stomach is not excited about all that water, but I take a few deep breaths as Annalisa said had helped her. "Edith made boundary," I manage to say.

Nodding, Jaxson jams the canteen into his pocket. "Yeah, the ward around her house."

"Keep pack away." Tears begin streaming down my face. I need his help and can't get these damn words out. "Mate. Save my mate." I yank against the chains as my chest begins aching. Now that my body has had a chance to rest, it wants my Alpha. "Please, Jax. Ward."

Jaxson looks about to cry, watching me beg for help. We both look up as boots clunk across the floor upstairs.

"Please," I whisper desperately.

He scoops me off the stool and runs across the cellar to quickly stash the soup container and jam the seat back in its hiding spot. He kicks the dirt around to remove the divots from the stool before the boots descend the stairs.

"Didn't I tell you to fix her?" Tynan barks. "Why does she still look like an overridden workhorse?" His eyes scan me as if he's considering a purchase at the stockyards. "She can't attend her daughter's wedding like this."

"I just got here, Alpha," Jaxson murmurs. "I have it right here." He digs into a different pocket, producing a small flask. He stands so that his body blocks Tynan's view of me. "It's tea," he whispers. He lets me take a few sips and then nods as he pulls it away. "I'll help."

I sigh in relief. Jaxson gives me the rest of the tea and bows his head at me before leaving. I face Tynan, feeling more confident than I have in weeks. With Jaxson's help, I'll beat this asshole at his own game.

Tynan unlocks my shackles and drags me up the stairs. My legs barely work, so I fall to my knees several times. Tynan scoffs at me every time as if it's by choice.

"Will I get both those pack markings like you when I'm named Alpha?" he asks. "What kind of suit should I wear?" The man rambles like a lunatic as I stare at the back of his head. "Here, I got you a dress. Well, I stole it, but she won't notice. Dead people don't wear clothes, do they?"

There is no way this man is being serious. People aren't really this crazy, are they?

"What are you doing?" Tynan yells in my face. "Put the shit on!"

At this point, normally, I'd be laughing, but I've never dealt with this brand of psycho. That might not be a good idea. The tea begins to work, and my mouth and tongue feel functional. I move them around to test their mobility before trying to use them.

"Do you need help?" Tynan snarls.

"No," I snap.

He hands me a thin, lacy white dress and watches as I change. He wraps a chain twice around my neck before fastening it. I recognize the gem hanging from it as a magical ward. It'll stop me from talking to my wolves.

"It's too cold to be outside in this," I scoff. "You said I had until my daughter's birthday. That's not today."

"It is pretty cold out there," Tynan remarks, nodding as he ties my hands behind my back. He drags me out the door and marches me into a field, muttering the entire time.

I try to focus on what he's rambling about. It's just a matter of pissing him off now. The sooner Tynan kills me, the sooner my wolves will be rid of him. We approach a single tree in the field when I hear him mention my dress. "What's wrong with my dress?" I ask. "Didn't you pick it out?"

Tynan frowns. "It's the color. The color's off. I don't think whores are supposed to wear white." He's talking like he makes sense, and the rest of the world be damned.

My brow furrows. "Why the hell do you think I'm a whore?"

Tynan suddenly realizes this conversation is happening out loud and turns around, surprised that I expect an answer from him.

"Shut up," he screams. "Nobody asked you to speak."

Some of his pack stand at the field's edge as he backhands me, sending me to the ground. Hands cover gasping faces, and some women tuck into the chests of the tense men beside them. The clenched fists I see are not for me but for their Alpha. They are his prisoners, not wolves in his pack.

Tynan yanks me off the ground and slams me against the tree. The wolves watch but don't approach us.

"Touch her, and you'll take her place," he screams, echoing across the field.

Tynan ties my neck, hands, and ankles to the tree. I'll hang myself if I fall, and the Guardians won't come for him. After he storms off, I realize I'm facing west, toward my pack. I'm bait for my Alpha.

It's a long day with a bitter cold breeze that feels sharp enough to cut my skin. No one approaches me, but they all stare—some cry. One woman touches her chest before reaching out. I don't know what it means, but it appears to be a sign of love or honor as others follow suit while crying.

I let my tears out once the sun goes down and I'm no longer visible. I thought this pack supported Tynan. I was terribly mistaken. These wolves need to be freed, just like Bastian.

It's warmer than on the train, but it's still cold. My bones ache as my body shakes from the chill. I close my eyes and lean on the ropes, hoping for relief.

"Hey Luna, you ready to come with me yet?"

My chest tightens, and tears pour from my eyes at the sound of Kade's voice. A warm blanket wraps around me. He tucks it over my shoulders and steps in close.

"The kids," I sputter. "Are the kids safe?"

Kade heats his body, holding my head to his chest. "They made it back with your Alpha," he tells me. "I'm sure they'd like you to join them."

I breathe a sigh of relief. "I can't do that, Kade. These wolves need to be free of that man."

"How is your death going to free anyone?" Kade growls. "You Lunar wolves are crazy."

I want to cup his cheeks and help him to feel my love, but I'm tied to this stupid tree. "Let me explain so that you will help me protect my family," I tell him, nuzzling into his warmth. "Killing a wolf is against pack law. If any wolf were to kill Tynan, it would be punishable by exile."

Kade pulls back, looking down at me. "Luna, he's not even a full wolf."

"From what he's rambled, he's a quarter wolf," I explain. "Enough that we can't kill him, but not enough for me to help." I rest my forehead against Kade's chin. "Killing a Luna breaks a First Law. These are the laws of the first wolves and are enforced by the Guardians. Killing a Luna only has one penalty. Death."

Sighing, Kade rubs his hands over my arms. "Can't I talk you out of this? What if I just untie you and throw you over my shoulder?"

Smiling, I push against the ropes to put my cheek against his. "You secured the future for my wolves. You can be one of us now, and we'd be happy to have you."

"At least let me untie you."

"Kade, which one of these wolves should pay for that?" I ask.

He closes the gap between our legs to heat my entire body. "Well, at least they stopped throwing cloves on you," Kade mumbles. "That shit burned my eyes."

"Was that the horrible-smelling stuff?"

"Yeah," Kade says, sighing. "It was to mask your scent so your Alpha couldn't track you. This has been hard on him. He loves you."

"I know he does," I whisper as my tears flow again. "I love him very much." I look up to see the sun is starting to rise. "Kade, try talking to Chase. You were both raised under Miles. He could help you find a new use for your talents."

Kade wraps his arms around me as best as possible with the tree in the way. "Luna, please stop trying to take care of everyone else. Just come with me."

"I gave you a fresh start, Kade. Take it," I urge him. "Love Gaine with everything you have, just as I have Tarq. Have an epic love."

Kade scoffs as his chin trembles slightly. "You women are making me soft." He kisses my forehead. "I love you, Luna."

"I love you too, Kade. Thank you for saving my family."

Kade bows and removes the blanket before backing away. As I watch him leave, I feel something cold on my chest. I look down and find a large red pendant hanging from a thin wire around my neck. I spend too long staring at it because when I look up, Kade's gone, and I can't ask what it is.

It probably doesn't matter. Tynan will be here soon anyway.

* * *

"Where the hell is your daughter?!" Tynan's been pacing for hours.

"I told you she's not coming," I say, exasperated. This is the twelfth time I've had to say the words. "No one would ever marry you, Tynan. You are unbalanced at best."

He storms over and grabs my throat. "I have perfect balance, you stupid bitch."

Years of banter with Tarq have prepared me for this moment. "Yes, Tynan. I see a tightrope in your future."

"What's this shit?" He grabs the red pendant, yanking it off my neck.

I feel the trickle of blood down my back, and suddenly, voices flood into my head for the first time in weeks. Edith was always a better witch than her brother.

I search through the voices, looking for one. When I find him, he's begging me not to do this. I can't stop my tears. *"You are the beauty in my world, my reason for being, and everything in between,"* I tell him. *"I love you. I always will."*

"*Please don't leave me, Dar,*" Tarq begs. "*Let me in so I can save you. I can't do this without you.*"

He must be close enough to see me if he knows he can't get to me. I look around, trying to find him.

"A new pack member brought me," Tarq says sadly. *"He said you women made him soft and that I should be able to say goodbye. Dar, I don't want to say goodbye."*

Then I see the silver wolf. Kade's coat shimmers in the sunlight. He will never hide again—his shame for all to see. Tarq stands beside him, just as beautiful as he was the first time I touched him.

"I will always be with you, My Love," I vow. *"I will never leave you. I will love you until the end of time."*

My eyes are blurry from tears, but they follow Tynan as his pacing becomes more erratic.

"I am yours, and you are mine," Tarq says, trying anything that might make me change my mind.

I look up at the trees where they're standing and see Anthony step into view. He taps his temple and points to Tarq, telling me he'll look after him. I nod, taking a shaky breath.

"What the fuck are you crying about?!" Tynan screams. "Shut up!"

As he marches toward me, I leave my eyes on Tarq. *"I love you, my Alpha. Forever yours."*

Tynan pulls a knife from his coat and stabs it into my neck. Hot blood pours down my chest.

I hear a howl in the distance and recognize it as Tarq's beautiful voice. He calls out to me one more time before I slip away.

"I love you, Dar."

29

I died on my birthday 15 and a half years ago. Today, I died on my daughter's birthday. Happy birthday, right? I bled to death, staring at the most beautiful wolf I had ever seen. Leaving him hurt worse than that knife ever could.

I was their Luna, and I was dying. When Kerst and his men found me, they showed me how hard things would've been. In the end, I would've been a burden to my pack. Miles gave me the information to help those who needed me.

Miles. Sweet Miles. Where is that man? I look around this incessant black pit of hell. *Why am I here? I need to learn how to fix this.*

"Easy, Baby Luna," a voice I'm not really in the mood to hear says. "You're only here so that we can talk."

I sigh, aggravated. "Luna, I know I named my child after you, but I'm not in the mood for you right now."

Luna frowns, looking genuinely sad.

Now I feel obligated to comfort her. "Damn you, Luna." I reach out, pulling her into my arms.

She stays tense for a moment but then wraps her arms around me. "Dax has started calling me Aylee," Luna tells me. "He says he can't call me by his granddaughter's name when we're having sex."

Although Luna lived for another seven years after bonding with her mate, she obviously stopped maturing.

I push her back by her shoulders to look into her eyes. "Luna, Aylee...

I will call you the Queen of Bees, if you will, please, never talk to me about your sex life with Dax."

Luna pouts. "He didn't want me to tell you about the Guardians. He's mad at me."

"How is that my problem? Go talk to him. I need to see Miles," I say as I look around. "Where is he?"

Luna... Aylee... whoever she wants to be, starts crying.

Great. Like I need this shit right now.

"You know I can hear your thoughts, right?" Luna says sadly.

"Just... Fuck, Luna," I sputter. "I need to talk to Miles. Can we do your drama later?"

She pouts. "I thought it would be nice having another girl here to talk to, but I guess not."

I've reached my limit with her. "Luna, I am 40 years old. I am not a girl anymore. I'm a mother and a wife, and I left them behind to save their lives. I will play with you later, but right now, I need Miles! Where is he?"

My forgiveness and 15 years of having a new mate have not changed Luna. She backs away from me with a look of pure hate. "Fine," she barks before disappearing.

I need to figure out how to change my surroundings. Luna made it seem so easy. I blink my eyes a few times, but that doesn't do anything. I try picturing the last place I saw Tarq. The trees at the edge of the field and Anthony's expression come to mind, but my view doesn't change. I finally give up and fold my legs to sit down as my surroundings change.

"Hey, Little One," I hear Miles say. "Let's take a walk."

Through no fault of Miles, I crash onto the dirt road that appeared underneath me and begin crying in relief. I needed him. Miles' love only has one equal, and after weeks of pain and hate, it's all I want to feel.

"No, sweetheart. Come here." Miles reaches out, and I latch onto him as he pulls me back to my feet. "Ok, Little One. It's ok." He strokes his hand over my hair. "I've got you." He cradles my head against his chest as I mumble and mutter, trying to make words out of my thoughts. "Easy now," Miles whispers. "We can stay here for as long as you'd like."

That would be great. Easily breathing while hanging onto his warm body in the sun's heat is heavenly. But somewhere in the real world, Tarq is falling apart, probably killing everyone around him. He needs my help.

"Miles, can you take me back to Tarq?" I ask. "I need to help him. I have to try." In my mind, I'm pulling away from Miles' chest to look up into his eyes, but my body doesn't move. With all my pain gone, all I feel is Miles' love and warmth.

"He'll be fine, Dar," Miles tells me soothingly. "Time isn't moving right now. He can't get into trouble without us."

His words don't make sense, but I don't care right now. I just died after weeks of torment. I've earned a moment of selfishness. My arms tighten around Miles' waist. His heart thumps calmly under my ear, and his hands tenderly rub my body. Miles has always had a natural woodsy and leather scent, but its comforting effect on me is overwhelming now. His hum is like a beautiful song.

Sighing, I allow myself to completely relax into him. "I made the right decision, didn't I, Miles?"

Miles squeezes me before taking a deep breath and running his hand over my hair. "You made the only decision you could, sweetheart," he says, kissing my head. "You did an amazing job with those kids. They did so well."

"Kade said they made it back to Tarq," I whisper.

"They did," he tells me. "Aylee watched them for the rest of the trip after I returned. That young Alpha has a good head for the job. Your little Luna, she loves you so much. That was hard on her, but her Alpha helped her to understand. They are safe and will protect the pack using the skills you taught them."

Whether Miles is saying these things just to calm me down or not, they are working. My arms have loosened their grip on him in my relaxation. My tears have stopped, and I'm only listening to his words and heartbeat.

I reach up and cup his cheeks. "Thank you, Miles."

He grabs my face and pulls my forehead to his lips. Closing his eyes, Miles takes a deep breath. "Come on, sweetheart. Let's take that walk. I promise time isn't moving right now. I'll get you back there to help him."

Miles turns, slipping his arm around my waist to guide me up the trail. His fingers lightly pull at my hip bone. He seems to need to work through his thoughts before talking about them.

"When I was a boy, my father walked me down this trail to tell me he was leaving." Miles' eyes narrow in thought as he stares ahead. "I was six or seven years old at the time. I loved my father. He visited me, but I couldn't walk this trail again. It became the trail of bad news, you know?" Miles looks down and gives me a weak smile. "You have shown me more love than I felt in 183 years. You brought honor to the name Wolf."

Miles threads his fingers with mine as I slide my hand across his back to rest it on his hip.

"Did you know only four Lunas were murdered before you?" he asks. "Not many wolves have tested the first laws."

I tuck under his arm, placing my head on his shoulder and my hand on his chest. His touch is so comforting that I'm having trouble focusing on anything else. "Do you know why they were killed?"

"No, Dar," Miles says, sighing. "Probably no damn reason, just like you. Just some psycho with a little dick trying to rule the world."

I frown. "I wasn't very good at my job. I kept letting them down. I didn't even know until it was too late."

"Dar, that kid is gonna get his parents back because of you," Miles reminds me. "The southern wolves will get the help they need."

"It's not enough."

Miles pulls me around and holds my face so that I'm looking up at him. "Stop this, Dar," he orders. "You died for them. You stood up to the most horrific treatment just to bleed for them. You do not look down."

My mind wanders to Tarq and Annalisa. My tears start again as I recall Anthony trying to reassure me.

"Come on, Little One," Miles says, smiling gently. "I cashed in a favor, but you won't have much time. You showed me so much love. Let me give something back to you."

Miles takes me to the edge of the field where I'd been tied. I cover my mouth, barely able to breathe. My eyes stay fixed on my beautiful Alpha as he stands between the silver wolf and Anthony. All three are frozen in time, looking defeated.

Grabbing me from behind, Miles catches me as my knees buckle. He wraps his arms around me, holding me to his chest. "I told you time isn't moving. You've just died. They have not moved from this spot."

My chest heaves as I process his words. Nothing terrible has happened yet. Tarq has not condemned himself. "Will they be ok?" My hands slide over Miles' arms, and he lifts his fingers to thread them with mine.

"I can't see the future, Little One," Miles answers, turning me around. "I can just give you one final gift. When you touch each one, they will wake up." Holding me by my face, Miles slides his thumbs over my cheeks to wipe away my tears. "Time is limited now that we're here, Dar. I recommend leaving your Alpha for last. That's gonna be a hard one."

I turn back around to look at Tarq. "Miles, what do I say?"

I crumble before him, clutching my chest, and Miles falls to his knees as he catches me. He holds onto me tightly as I lose control of my emotions. Miles moves me to his lap, and our tears mix as he leans forward over my shoulder to put his cheek against mine.

"Miles, I love him so much," I sob. "How do I say goodbye?"

Miles rocks my body as he cries with me. He takes a few deep breaths and wipes my face. "I don't have that answer, Dar," he whispers.

A howl sounds in the distance. The world may be standing still, but the Guardians are not.

"Clock's ticking, sweetheart," Miles says, nodding toward the trio. He helps me stand up and supports me as I walk forward.

My eyes stay on Tarq as Miles guides me toward Anthony. He holds my hand out, and Anthony comes to life when I touch him.

"Darya?" he shouts, surprised.

My tears instantly spring back into action as I jump into his arms. "I told you I would say goodbye," I sputter between sobs. "I had to say goodbye."

Anthony sniffles, and I feel him reach toward Miles. He whispers a thank you to the Alpha. "Darya, how do I help him? This is gonna break him."

I hang onto Anthony, wiping my face as I turn to rest my head against his shoulder. I look down at my beautiful Alpha. He looks tired—as if he hasn't slept in weeks. I pull back and smile at Anthony. "Miles, do we have a little time to talk?"

Miles rests his hand on my shoulder. "Sure, Dar," he tells me. "We have a few minutes."

I sit in the grass, pulling Anthony with me. I hold both of his hands as he sits before me. "You made my life a living hell," I say, laughing a bit. "You hunted and found me anywhere I went. My one true joy in life was making you bleed."

Anthony laughs weakly. "Don't I know it. I'm still carrying around the scars."

"And then Nate beat the shit out of you, and you suddenly became so much more. You lift me, Anthony, and I love you." I reach up to wipe a tear from his cheek.

"I don't know how many times I told you that you ruined my life, but I lied," he sobs. "Every time. They were all lies."

"I know, Anthony," I say with a little grin, trying to channel my inner Luna to dial back my emotions. "I think I made your life more exciting."

Anthony breathes a small laugh. "No one needs this much excitement, sweetheart."

I look behind me at my body still tied to the tree. Blood has run down, soaking through the front of the white dress. "I'm still dead, though," I say, turning back to Anthony. "This really is goodbye this time."

"I know." Anthony presses his forehead to mine. "I'm just a little less ready for it than I thought."

"Me too," I admit. "But Miles tells me I can only talk to you one at a time, and I need to say goodbye to Tarq."

Anthony nods, knowing this is important and Tarq needs it.

Miles puts his hand on my shoulder. "When you touch Tarq, Anthony will freeze. I'm told that he will shift. I'm requesting that you picture him in clothes, please."

I smile at Anthony. "He sounds like you now."

Anthony scoffs. "Darya, I'm quite sure I've seen your man naked more than you have."

"I might doubt that if I didn't know my Alpha so well," I say, laughing.

Anthony catches my fingers when I reach out for his hand. He kisses my knuckles. "It has been a pleasure to have dealt with you all these years, Darya. You will be missed."

I lean forward onto my knees and wrap my arms around his neck. "You watch over my family for me, Anthony. I love you."

Standing, Anthony lifts me to my feet. "I love you too, kiddo. Give your wolf a proper goodbye. It might help him."

We kiss each other's cheeks, and he lets go of me, gesturing toward Tarq. I look down at my beautiful wolf and reach my hand back for Miles. Anthony watches as I step before Tarq.

"So, I just touch him and picture him in clothes?" I ask, feeling my chest tighten. "He'll just shift right into those clothes?"

Miles snorts. "That's what I'm told. Worse case, I'll be forced to see him naked." He shrugs. "For you, Little One, I'll endure." His hand slips over my cheek before he reaches out to Anthony. The two shake hands and seem to have a profound exchange in their silence.

They both turn to me, signaling it's time to wake Tarq. I nod to Anthony and reach my hands out to my wolf. I take a few slow, deep breaths and shake my head.

"Go on, Darya," Anthony says. "It's not gonna get any easier." He nods with a small smile.

Exhaling, I slide my hands along the sides of my wolf's face, and Tarq shifts right into my arms. He instantly latches onto me, trembling. I dig my fingers into his back as we both sob uncontrollably.

"Please tell me you're coming back," Tarq begs between breaths. "I can't be without you."

I'm not ready for words. I've felt nothing but cruelty for nearly a month and wanted nothing more than to feel his touch. Tarq falls to his knees, taking me with him. His face stays buried in my neck, and his tears run over my shoulder.

"I love you," I whisper. "I didn't know what love was until I met you. You have been in my heart since the moment you first touched me. You made me so happy. I laughed every day because you were perfect."

"I failed you," Tarq sobs. "I couldn't protect you. I couldn't find you."

I take a few more deep breaths, pushing my fingers through his hair. I'm a Luna, and, as Tarq said, a Luna's job is never done. "Sweet man, you could not have stopped this."

Tarq pulls away from my neck, grabbing my face. "I could've hunted and killed him," he declares. "I could've killed them all."

Cupping his cheeks, I pull his lips to mine for a tear-soaked kiss. "My Love, that would've cost me you." I look into Tarq's beautiful eyes. "That man is crazy and not enough of a wolf for me to help." I slide my thumb over his cheek to wipe away a tear. "Our daughter and pack needed this. You and I are strong enough to carry this pain for them. You are so strong." I'm whispering by the time I finish. I believe my words, but they are so hard to say.

Tarq shakes his head, lowering his eyes. "Dar, I'm only strong because of you. Without you, who am I? I'm just the wolf who lost the woman he loves."

I pull his chin until he looks into my eyes. "You are so much more than that," I tell him sharply. "You are a father to a strong young lady and a role model to her mate. You are the Alpha. You are the man who taught many generations of wolves that it's ok to feel love and to be fierce about it. You taught Bastian that not all men cause pain. You taught that boy how to feel love so that he could love our little girl."

"What am I going to tell them?" Tarq stares at me, nearly frozen. His only movement is his thumb sliding just below my lower lip.

Although I could never answer that question, it caused many new thoughts to come crashing in. I take a deep breath and let it out slowly. "Miles says we don't have much time," I tell Tarq. "I need to tell you some things, and I need you to hear me, My Love." My fingers grip the sides of his neck.

Tarq licks his lips and lets out a deep sigh. "Ok, I'm here."

"Do you remember when I first woke up, and all those voices came flooding in at once?" I ask, searching his eyes. "Remember how scary that was for me?"

Tarq frowns. "That was horrible. I couldn't help you."

Shaking my head, I smile. "No, My Love, you helped much more than you think. Do you remember singing to me?"

"Are you talking about that nursery rhyme?" Tarq asks, confused. "I don't even remember what it was."

"It was Twinkle, Twinkle Little Star, but that's not important," I say. "You sang it over and over quietly right into my ear until I fell asleep."

"Dar, why are we talking about a nursery rhyme?" Tarq's exhausted and highly emotional. Any conversation would be difficult for him right now.

I slide my hand over his cheek, trying to soothe him, but my hand won't fire. *That must only be a gift for the living.* "My Love, I just died," I remind him. "Our daughter is the Luna now. She is going from hearing one wolf to all of them."

Tarq leans back. He closes his eyes with a sigh. "And she's alone with only that wolf to help her."

I pull him back to me. "The world is on pause right now, My Love," I say, sweeping my hand around to point to the frozen people at the edge of the field. "She isn't hearing it yet but will once I leave."

Tarq's expression lightens. "So I can tell Bass how to help her."

"Exactly," I say with a smile. "He can help her until she learns to filter them out or until you get home."

The wolves howl again, this time much closer.

"I'm not leaving without you," Tarq declares.

"You'll be able to soon, my Alpha." I slide my hands over his face, holding his hair from his eyes. "The Guardians came for you that night, not me. Those wolves are here for Tynan."

Tarq frowns. "This was your plan all along."

I rub my thumbs over his cheeks. "My sweet man, I was dying," I finally admit. "It wouldn't be long before I became a burden, and I would still leave you. My death means something this way, and I've freed all these people from that horrible man. Bastian and Annalisa are free to be happy together."

The wolves' howl is so close this time that I turn to see them stepping out of the woods. There are four of them.

"I think we're running out of time," I whisper to Tarq, watching the Guardians.

The wolves circle my body and then bow to it. They lie down with their noses pointed toward my feet. My blood is pooled on the ground as if running out of my body this whole time. The wolves don't touch it.

Miles kneels beside us.

"Are they waiting for me to finish?" I ask him.

Miles blows a shaky breath, putting a hand on each of us. "No, Dar. They're waiting for me."

I shake my head, confused. "Why are they waiting for you, Miles?" My chest starts heaving air as I realize what he's been trying to tell me this whole time. "Miles, what did you do?"

A tear drops from Miles' eye as he slides his hand over my cheek. "Her Alpha avenges a fallen Luna."

I look from Miles to Tarq and back again. My lungs can only pull tiny bursts of air, and tears won't fall in my panic.

"I couldn't let him take your daughter's mother and father. You deserve nothing short of endless love, sweetheart."

I close my eyes. *Four Lunas, Four Guardians. I sacrificed myself for my family and my pack. Miles sacrificed himself for me.* I pull him to me, and Tarq holds both of us.

"You knew, didn't you?" I whisper. "When you told me what she meant. You knew."

"I'm sorry, Dar," Miles whispers back. "If you knew, you would've broken the law, and we both would've lost you. As an Alpha who's bonded to you, I have the unique ability to give you this gift. This is how I can repay you for showing me true love. I will forever avenge our future Lunas who are lost to wolves."

Miles pulls back and grabs the back of Tarq's neck, giving it a shake.

"Your father's pain in the ass Luna had a message for you too," he says with a pained smile. "She said you only need to say when you are ready."

Miles pauses, looking into Tarq's eyes. He's upset and only half listening. My Alpha is losing the love of his life and his uncle at the same time.

"Like Dax, your place is eternally beside your Luna," Miles continues when he sees Tarq take a breath. "You still won't age, but when you're ready, you may join your Luna."

"Will he come back?" I ask, thinking about how much Annalisa enjoys spending time with her grandfather. "As you guys have? Will he be able to visit his granddaughter?"

"Yes. It's supposed to be a curse, but I loved returning to you." Miles hooks his fingers around my jaw and pulls me to him. "I have to go," he tells me before turning to Tarq. "I'm going to kiss your Luna, Baby Alpha. You have until she disappears. You just love each other with all you have while you can, ok?"

Tarq nods as we both start to cry.

Miles turns to me and shakes his head slightly. "Don't cry, sweetheart," he whispers. "I knew a love that I didn't deserve because of you. You truly were a gift to us, and I love you."

He pulls me to him. I press my tear-soaked lips to his until he pulls away.

"I love you, Miles."

"I know, sweetheart," he says, wiping my face. "That's what kept me coming back."

Miles stands up and steps back. He nods to the wolves before blowing me a kiss. "I love you, Little One." Miles takes another step back and seamlessly shifts into the black-and-white peppered wolf I've often cuddled with.

Tarq pulls me to him and twists as he holds me so I can watch Miles run across the field to my body. "Dar, what's gonna happen?"

I pull on his ribs with my fingers and close my eyes, listening to his heart beating calmly. "I don't know, My Love," I tell him. "I'll be here for as long as possible, though."

I open my eyes to watch the wolves in the field. They step back as Miles joins them. He approaches my body with his head bowed. He curls one leg under his chest, lowering his body into a full bow. Miles dips the sides of his muzzle in the blood pooled at my feet and bows again before backing away.

"Oh, Miles," I whisper sadly. I can feel my tears soaking through Tarq's shirt. His hand tightens around my head as Miles joins the other wolves. They begin to circle Tynan. Their heads are low, and their growls vibrate everything around us. I didn't know how I would handle having them both in the afterworld, but losing one was never considered.

"You'll have to leave soon." Luna's voice makes me jump and tighten my grip on Tarq. "I'll give you as much time as possible, but I've used up nearly all the magic I have left."

I look around to see Luna standing a short distance away, watching the Guardians. Tarq hasn't responded at all.

"He can't see or hear me," Luna explains without me needing to ask. "Miles said I owed you after what I did to you all those years ago."

I pull at Tarq, remembering that loss. This will hurt much more. I straighten up and pull him to my lips. "I don't have much longer," I tell him. "I need you to know that I love you. Luna will teach me how to visit. I will never leave you. You are mine, and I am yours."

Tarq crashes into my lips. I part them for him, inviting him to taste my tongue one more time before I pull back.

In the field, the wolves stop circling and face Tynan, ready to pounce.

"You're out of time, Baby Luna," Luna says sadly. "Say goodbye."

"I love you," I whisper one final time, leaning against Tarq's cheek before the world around us starts to move again.

As Tarq shifts back to a wolf, the four wolves in the field snarl ferociously, and Miles leaps at Tynan. Anthony nearly falls on top of Tarq, trying to wrap his arms around his neck. Tarq slides his jaw down the man's back in a sorrowful hug as his eyes stay fixed on the field.

Miles latches onto Tynan's head, ripping it from his neck. He turns to Tarq and bows.

I slide my hand over Tarq's muzzle and feel him lean into my touch. His hum nearly breaks my heart, but then the field fades away.

"I'm sorry," Luna says. "It's time."

30

My name is Annalisa. My mother, the Luna, was the most beautiful woman I knew. She taught me how to be strong and gentle at the same time. She showed me that love is the most powerful weapon in the world. My mother died on my 15th birthday. A week later, my father brought her back down from the mountains.

We burned her body tonight, which is the custom for Lunas' bodies. I haven't looked away from the flames. "She's really gone, isn't she?" I want the answer to change this time.

"*I'm sorry, Little Luna,*" Grandpa says. "*She's not coming back this time.*"

"She's with you, though?" I ask.

"*She is. She visits your father often and is with him every night.*" Grandpa's always been the silent, supportive type. We waited for the full moon for this because I needed him to be here. Edith said that Mom's body would keep because it was drained of blood.

Dad's struggling. I don't know how to help him. "I hear him crying at night."

"*She does too,*" Grandpa says, placing his chin on my knee. "*They had a love like no other. Maybe one day you'll feel as they did.*" He looks to my left at Bastian. My Alpha is exhausted and flopped on his side, staring at the fire. He and my mother were very close. Neither of us sleeps well these days. "*When you're ready,*" Grandpa adds.

Grandpa told me about Uncle Miles taking my father's place among the Guardians. He said they both took that very hard. Miles was bonded to my mother, so I didn't spend much time with him. I still strangely feel his absence within my heart. I wish I could thank him for allowing me to keep my father. That might be the most selfless act I have ever heard of or experienced.

"I'm going to sit with your father," Grandpa says, sitting up. *"You stick close to your guard and watch over your father for me, ok, kiddo?"*

"I love you, Grandpa," I say, frowning.

He taps his nose to my cheek, and I kiss him behind his whiskers before he leaves to join my father closer to the fire. I watch them lie together for a little while. My father is broken. He says he doesn't remember how to live without Mom.

"Maybe with Luna laid to rest, you can sleep tonight," Bastian says.

I love Bastian. He's felt this loss just as much as I have. He told me what that man did to him and that my mother had taken him to the cabin, saving him from giving up on life. I remember being so mad at Mom for leaving me with Dad when she was there with Bass.

"I wish I could hug her one more time," I whisper, sliding my fingers through his fur. "I'd thank her for saving you and bringing you to me."

"She knows. She always knew," Bastian says. *"She had this way of knowing things long before any of us did."*

I smile at him, opening my arms. "Come here. I need some of that inner strength."

Bastian sits up and leans his shoulder toward me. I snuggle into his fur as we watch the flames until the sun begins to rise. Grandpa stands and nods at me as he disappears.

I watch Daddy as he continues to lie still, watching the flames. "Do you think he'll be ok?"

"One day," Bastian answers.

We wait for Daddy to be ready to leave, but he refuses, so Bastian convinces him to lie with us beside the altar and try to sleep. As they both heat up, I swear a hand brushes over my cheek, and right after, my father mumbles in his sleep, *"I love you too, Dar."*

I sleep for the first time in over a month without waking up, screaming for my mother.